MINE

A REVERSE AGE GAP ROMANCE

CLIO EVANS

Copyright © 2025 Clio Evans

Cover Designed by Emily Wittig

Editing: Emily in the Archives @emilyinthearchives

Art of Salt with mask: Vamorii @vamorii__

Art of Salt and Pepper: Rey Vest @rey_vest

clioevansauthor.com

CONTENT WARNING

•Religious trauma
  •Discussions of purity culture and leaving the church
  •Ex-husband drama
  •Discussions of cheating
  •Parental abuse
  •Discussions of mental health
  •Discussions of alcoholism
  •Parental death from alcoholism (not on page)
  •Body insecurities
  •*Detailed* sex scenes with: BDSM Dom/sub dynamics, power exchange, degradation, praise, humiliation, CNC, spanking, biting, ball-gags, exhibitionism, voyeurism, forced orgasms, Shibari, impact play with bruising, use of pillory, butt plugs, oral sex, squirting, throat fucking, a scene without aftercare, rimming, sensation deprivation, sexting, sex toys, and boot play.

If you have any questions regarding content warnings, please reach out to me clioe-vansauthor@gmail.com

To anyone who got a praise kink from their religious trauma

ONE
PEPPER

THE BEST ADVICE I ever received was to never go into business with someone you loved.

It was damn good advice, but I didn't take it.

Rosethorn Records was *my* company. As the founder and CEO, it was my vision that came to life, and my taste in music which led to our rise in success. Over the last fifteen years, I'd become one of the most successful women in the music industry. I was *really* good at two things—finding unique talent and making a shit ton of money with them.

Rosethorn was mine.

But it was also *his*, too.

If I could go back in time to my younger, bright-eyed twenty-two-year-old self—I would have told her many things.

Don't marry Jeff. Don't let him be your business partner. Don't make him the president of your company, because then you'll have to see how fucking happy he is without you—

My ex-husband lifted up his two-year-old daughter and perched her on his lap, his eyes full of stars.

Ellen shot me a grim look before shutting the door to the

massive meeting room. Glass walls surrounded us, and Nashville stretched out below, the morning sun flooding the windows. The four other members of the board sat around the oval table, steam curling from clutched coffee mugs. Tommy was our vice president and director of artists and repertoire, or A&R as the music industry called it. Kendra, our director of marketing. Lee, our director of promotions. Scott, our director of legal.

All of their eyes were on Jeff and Paisleigh.

She wore baby pink today with an oversized glitter bow, her cheeks rosy, blue eyes piercing and bright and full of so much happiness that it made my chest ache.

What kind of name was Paisleigh? Seriously. I would have never—

And you never did, because you never had kids with him, and he traded you in for the sexy intern who's now happily married to him, with a daughter and baby number two on the way.

"Hope you don't mind, Pepper," Jeff said as Paisleigh giggled, grabbing hold of one of his pens to scribble all over his meeting notepad. "Ally had a doctor's appointment and the nanny was sick with the flu."

All attention shifted to me. It was times like this when I hated that we all were on a first name basis. I hated hearing him say my name. I hated knowing they all pitied me.

Actually, Jeff, I do fucking mind because two years ago you would have fucking lost it if someone else brought their kid to work, but here you are? "No worries. We'll get started." *Deep breath, deep breath, deep breath.* "Rosethorn Records has had a strong start to the year. Our projections are right on track, and even trending slightly above what we predicted. What today's meeting is about is who we are at our core and what we're doing to further the company."

Years of practice at being the boss sank their teeth in, and I relaxed fully. I'd come a long way from the small-town girl who could barely speak above a polite whisper.

"We need something new and fresh. I know we have a roster of artists we've been keeping an eye on, but we *need* someone who will make waves in the industry. We've done it twice already, I know we can do it again. What have we got? I know—"

"I have an idea," Jeff interrupted.

My temper flared, but I smothered it as best as I could.

"I think we should bring on someone who will appeal to the apps. Like, whatever it's called. Instagram. Tiktok. That stuff." Paisleigh leaned forward, attempting to grab his coffee cup. He successfully steered her away from it, making her giggle again.

Kendra's expression flickered with annoyance. She glanced up at me, clearly biting her tongue.

"Obviously we're going to bring someone on who appeals from a marketing perspective, Jeff," I said patiently. Fifteen years of being married to the idiot had given me that skill. "I'm talking about sound. Music. The heart of—"

Paisleigh knocked over his cup of coffee. Chaos unfolded as Jeff jumped up, rescuing her from getting any spilled on her dress. But it splashed everywhere across the table, across his notes, the papers sprawled at the center. Everyone jumped up to help him.

I stood up, every muscle rigid as I pressed the intercom button. "Ellen, please bring some paper towels, there's been a coffee spill."

Deep breath, deep breath, deep breath.

Paisleigh started to cry.

This was how I knew I'd never be a good mother. There was a tug in my chest—but it wasn't maternal.

Nope. It was annoyance.

This is why he'd left me, right? Because I didn't want kids. I didn't want the white-picket-fence life he'd suddenly decided was right for him. It wasn't like it was too late for me... *that's a lie.* I was thirty-seven and unless a hot, intelligent man plopped on my high-rise apartment doorstep, children were out of the picture.

Ellen hurried back into the room quickly with supplies. It took fifteen minutes and a collective effort to get Paisleigh's tears dried, coffee cleaned up, and everyone resettled.

"Pepper," Scott said, leaning over. "I have another meeting soon with the lawyers. The Jenna Hart situation..."

Deep breath, deep breath. That was a media nightmare we were trying to smooth over. "Okay. You can go, we'll send an email recap. I want updates on that situation, Scott. Make sure she's protected."

Scott nodded and jumped up, giving everyone a wave. "I will. Sorry, everyone, legal duties and all that jazz."

He left swiftly and Tommy held up his hand. I raised a brow at him. Aside from Jeff, he'd also helped found our company. We'd been friends since I was nineteen. He knew better than to raise his hand like a preschooler.

"What?" I asked him.

Tommy cleared his throat. "We have a list of artists we've been keeping an eye on. There's one in particular who's gathering a lot of attention, especially online. He has a great social media presence. People are feral for him."

Lee snorted. "Is this the one I think it is? Masked guy?"

"Yep, that's the one."

"What's his name?" I asked.

"He goes by Salt. He writes his own songs, plays guitar, and has a damn good voice," Tommy said.

"We don't need another singer-songwriter," I quipped. "We already have some of the best songwriters in the world."

Kendra shook her head, a smirk spreading across her face as if she knew a secret. "No, he's not just that. He has an appealing stage presence and a band now, too. The sound is like... hmm."

"It's indie rock with R&B, blues, and synthwave undertones. His songs are very *intimate*," Tommy explained, adjusting in his seat.

Lee nodded seriously. "Yeah, my wife sends videos to me all the time. She's definitely a fan, although I don't know if it's his music or appearance."

Kendra laughed. "Well, he's very attractive."

"Agreed," Tommy said with a sly smile. He refocused on me. "His band is playing tomorrow night at a bar downtown if we want to scout them out. You could come with me. I think it would be a good idea."

"Pepper in a bar on a Friday night?" Jeff made a face. "Unlikely."

"Jeff," Lee scolded, giving him a dirty look. "Really?"

"What?" He looked up from Paisleigh, his brows shooting up. "Was that offensive? It's the truth. You hate going to bars."

"I don't hate going to bars. I used to go to all of them," I argued.

That was how Rosethorn started. Me, Jeff, and Tommy going to bars and finding songwriters and musicians with potential. I'd always had a knack for finding the next big thing, and we'd been lucky. Music was one of the reasons I was still alive, and getting good music into the hands of other people was what led me to imagine a record label like Rosethorn. One that was fair to its artists with a broad reach, too.

"Well that was back when you were a fun person," Jeff said lightly. The silence in the room thickened and he looked up from his daughter. "I'm joking, I'm joking."

"Right," I said, biting the inside of my mouth so hard I

tasted blood. The pain soothed me, kept me grounded. "Well, let's dive into it. I'll keep this short."

Our group spent the next forty minutes going over our current artists, what we had coming down the pipeline for the rest of the quarter, and then circled back around to who we were currently scouting.

"I want new material," I said. "Find me *someone*. That's your job and why you still work here, why we still have a record label, and why I pay all of you. Got it?"

Everyone nodded curtly.

Paisleigh was smiling again, apple cheeks rosy. *Fuck, I'm gonna lose my mind.* Every day, I thought I was going to lose it.

Jeff was *happy*.

"Great. We're all wrapped up."

I stayed seated as everyone but Tommy shuffled out of the room. He waited until Jeff was out of earshot before leaning back in his chair with a heavy sigh. "What the fuck was that?"

"Don't even start with me right now," I muttered, massaging my temples.

"Why don't you just fire him?"

I swallowed hard. "It's complicated—"

"Just treat it like business, Pepper."

"You know it's not *just* business with him."

Tommy pressed his lips into a thin line. "I know. We've been friends for almost two decades, and I just hate seeing you this way."

I hated it too. "He's your friend, too."

Tommy shook his head. "He's not the same person he was, Pep."

My stomach twisted. I sank back in my chair, studying him. "Do you really think that one artist is worth scouting? The one who's playing tomorrow."

Tommy always had a good eye for artists. In the early days,

we'd been the ones surfing bars, meeting musicians, finding new sounds and new drugs and having *fun*. Jeff had the cash though, which was how our label eventually came together. Without the seed money, we probably wouldn't be sitting here. But without our insight, Jeff would just be another trust fund baby searching for a passion project.

He nodded. "He's young. Hot. Has a grunge look going for him. He wears a mask on stage and it creates a sexy mysterious persona. His songs are very erotic. Dan loves him."

Tommy was happily married to our friend Dan, a producer who had more than a handful of Grammys under his belt.

I wrinkled my nose, not completely sold. "What happened to good old-fashioned love songs?"

Tommy rolled his eyes. "Sex sells, Pepper. Especially songs about kinky, hot sex."

Oh god. "I don't care about anything but the music itself. But I guess if you're saying it's that good, it has to be decent, right?"

His hand flattened over his heart in feigned offense, but then he grinned. "*Wow.* You're damn cold sometimes. But that's why you're the boss, *right?*"

I gave him a flat look. "Don't you know you don't need to kiss my ass?"

"Well, you do sign my checks," he teased.

"Oh, fuck off," I muttered, leaning forward. I planted my forehead against the table and sighed. "I don't know what I'm doing."

"I do. You're coming out with me and Dan tomorrow night," Tommy insisted. "It's been too long. We'll have some drinks and hear some fresh music. It'll be good for you. Maybe you'll meet someone."

"I doubt it," I muttered, sitting back up.

His smile softened into a boyish grin. Flecks of silver

glinted in his sandy brown hair. Had I ever noticed those before?

"You're getting old," I noted.

Tommy feigned a gasp. "My god, you are in a bad mood today. Come on, now. You're not too old to go out."

"That's absolutely not true."

"We're not even forty yet. We still have at least half our lives left." He leaned back in his chair and studied me. "It's been a couple years since the divorce, but it's like…"

I gave him a sharp look. "I don't want to talk about it. And it hasn't been a couple years. It's been a year and a half."

"Are you seeing a therapist?" he asked gently. "Have you actually thought about firing him?"

I think about watching him choke on burnt broccoli. "Of course," I whispered. I felt like I was swallowing glass. "But he's as much of a part of Rosethorn as I am. I can't escape him, can I?"

"It's your company. You're the CEO for a reason, babe. And I'm not the only one who has these feelings."

"Everyone thinks of Jeff when they think of Rosethorn, not just me. If he left, it would be a media hellstorm. I don't want that for the company or our artists."

"It would blow over," Tommy said. "You know it would. People would pick it apart for a couple days and then move on to the next best thing."

"Well, Jeff is good at his job when he's not being a babysitter. He's been good at it for years."

"Pepper—"

"I'll go out with you and Dan tomorrow," I interrupted, willing to do anything to move on from the conversation about Jeff. I stood abruptly, needing a break. "I'm going to pop over to the coffee shop around the corner to stretch my legs. I'll be back after lunch."

"Okay," he sighed. "Take care of yourself, darling."

I gathered my notes, slid my phone into my pocket, and left the meeting room. I darted across the floor to my office, ignoring everyone.

We'd been in this building for five years, and I was thankful I'd had the foresight to give my office walls, instead of all windows. A designer I met at a venue years ago designed every inch perfectly, making it truly feel like a truly luxurious home for music. Bea also had the wisdom to give me an office that veered from the open-concept flow, allowing me privacy. Which meant I could spiral without being watched.

The moment I closed my office door, I bit the inside of my mouth so hard that more blood bloomed, the heavy taste of metal thick on my tongue.

Fuck. What was *wrong* with me?

I made money. I made filthy, *filthy* amounts of money. I had everything I could possibly want. I was one of the most successful businesswomen in the music industry. I'd even made *Forty Under 40* last year.

Rosethorn Records was an icon. Everyone kissed the floor I walked on. Musicians and artists across the world wanted to be part of our label, but I was picky. I only chose the best of the best, the ones who fit my vision.

Something was *missing*. It was a nagging feeling that started out as a seed a few years ago but had grown into a vine that was strangling me to death. I couldn't blame Jeff for divorcing me, because he was right. I wasn't fun anymore. I didn't have a life outside of Rosethorn.

Rosethorn *was* my life.

A soft knock at the door forced me to compose myself. I crossed the room to my desk and threw my notes down. "Come in."

Ellen poked her head in.

I waved my hand. She was my assistant, but more than that, she was my best friend. The reason I hadn't murdered Jeff at this point was probably thanks to her keeping me caffeinated and fed.

She shut the door behind her and made a face. "What the hell was that?"

"I'm going to get coffee," I said lightly. "I need a little air."

"You need to tell Jeff he can't come in with his child," Ellen scolded. "You have to put your foot down. That meeting was a waste of everyone's time."

"It wasn't," I argued. "They had a lead. We talked through everything we needed to cover."

"But you caved for him."

That stung. I shot her a dirty look, but she waved it off before sweeping her midnight-blue curls into a claw clip. She'd put on a new highlighter this morning, and it looked gorgeous against her brown skin.

"Which highlighter is that?" I asked her. "You look beautiful today."

Ellen returned my dirty look and then shook her head. "I'll send you the link. And nice try. You're not redirecting me. You know what I'm saying about Jeff is the truth."

"It's... complicated."

"It's been two years," she hissed.

"It hasn't been," I snapped. "Why is everyone on my ass about this today?"

Ally got pregnant with Paisleigh while Jeff and I were still together. She was four months along when he finally told me he wanted a divorce.

Of course, I didn't know that part until after we signed the papers.

Everyone else knew, though. Oh, yes. That part stung the most. Well, maybe not the *most*, but it hurt. I was smart and insightful—but I didn't know his intern was pregnant with my husband's child.

Ellen hadn't known because I hired her after the divorce. I'd met her in a spin class over a year ago and we hit it off. One bottle of wine, a basket of breadsticks, and life stories exchanged later—we became friends. She was the better version of me. She had her life together, knew exactly what she wanted, and was perfectly content with being 'thirty-seven with all the money, all the prospects, not a burden to her parents, unfrightened, and friends with her sex toys.'

"Remember, I don't give two shits about anyone else here but you," she said. "Except for Tommy and Kendra. And Lee. They've all grown on me. Scott is annoying, though."

"Well that's because he's a lawyer," I snorted. "It's his job to be annoying." I slid on my camel Dior coat, tightened the belt around my waist, and pulled my purse from the bottom drawer of my desk. "I'll be back after lunch. I need to breathe and then get back, send out emails, and—"

"Rub one out?"

"Oh god," I laughed. "*Ellen!*"

She shrugged. "Don't be a prude. I'm just saying, it might do you good."

"Thanks. I'll keep your advice under consideration."

She rolled her eyes and reached for the door, opening it for me. "Go get your caffeine fix. I'll hold down the fort."

Happy toddler squeals echoed from Jeff's office on the other side of the floor. I slid on my sunglasses and steeled myself before heading to the elevators. I kept my head high, my shoulders squared, my strides long. It was times like this that having a stone-cold resting bitch face came in handy, because no one dared to bother me.

Rosethorn Records resided on floor fifteen and sixteen of a high-rise at the center of downtown Nashville. My condo was only a few blocks away, which made my life easy. When Jeff and I divorced, he took the house in Green Hills, per my request. It'd made sense then to have him take the house since it was perfect for raising a family and by that point, Ally was already pregnant.

It'd been a quiet divorce. *Cold.* Easy. *Painful.* Relieving. *Humiliating.*

I took the elevator down to the bottom floor, my heels clicking on the smooth marble floors. I sailed out the front doors and onto the sidewalk, autopilot kicking in as I made my way to my coffee shop.

Valentine's Day was coming up. There was no way to escape it, either. Every storefront along the way bursted with red and pink hearts. I ignored all of them, pretending they didn't exist, my thoughts spinning like a broken record until I made it to Adagio.

Adagio was better than any lover I could ever have. Consistent, always available, sweet and savory. The moment I stepped through the heavy wooden door, I inhaled the scent of fresh-ground coffee beans. The blend of chatter and indie grunge music instantly eased the pressure at the back of my head. Red brick peeked through the signed band posters on the walls, a sagging leather couch sat in the back corner, and patrons held onto their mugs like they were lifelines. I resonated with that a little too much. In fact, I definitely drank too much caffeine, but it was either mild forms of self-destruction or a full blown breakdown.

So, I opted for coffee.

My therapist was going to have a fucking field day with me next week.

My phone buzzed as I joined the line for the barista. I sighed and pulled it out. *Jeff.* Why was he calling me? Could I not escape him for five fucking minutes?

More deep breaths. Some days I was tired of breathing. I answered my phone. "Jeff. I just stepped out for coffee."

"Hey, Pepper. Sorry to interrupt."

"I'll be back after lunch," I said stiffly.

The back of my neck prickled as I heard someone step up behind me. I almost turned back to look, but that would have been rude.

Jeff didn't skip a beat. "Well, I just wanted to run something by you real quick. The Guild of Music Supervisors Awards are coming up, and I know it was going to just be you and me going, but I was thinking Ally could come. It would be good for her to do something not mommy-related, you know? I think I'll take Paisleigh to Mimi."

Mimi, also known as Matilda, the mother-in-law straight from hell. At least I'd escaped that witch since our divorce. She never liked me, and I could now admit I never liked her either.

"Also, you may want to schedule an appointment with your doctor. Maybe get a little forehead touchup? You were definitely scowling a lot in the meeting earlier. Anyways, Ally will—"

"I don't think that's a good idea," I interrupted.

The looming presence behind me inched closer. This time I glanced back, but only briefly, enough to spot a tattoo on the top of his hand. A flower with an eye at the center. *Weird.*

I swallowed hard, my ears burning. He wasn't touching me. He wasn't more in my space than any other person in this small, packed coffee shop. But I felt him. I felt him under my skin, wrapping around me like a vine, a poison, an *infection.*

Ba-bump, ba-bump, ba-bump. My heart hammered faster and faster.

Maybe Ellen was right. Maybe I needed a date with my vibrator.

Jeff continued on. "Why not? I mean it's not like you'd have to sit next to her—"

For fuck's sake. I was tired of Jeff never listening. "The awards have assigned seating, Jeff. You know that."

"We could add her. You know *that*. They'll add someone if *you* ask."

"I said no." My voice strained.

"*Hang up.*"

Two words. They were soft, so soft only I could hear him. A whisper, even. The stranger's voice sent a shiver up my spine. It was deep and delicious, with a graveled edge that made my chest lurch.

But the command in his tone, the unwavering command...

I swallowed hard.

I didn't like being told what to do.

But...

Jeff never shut up on the line, not even noticing that I wasn't talking. What was he even saying? He was going on and on about how this would be good for Ally. How going to LA would be a break for her. They needed to go on a date and get away from the pressure of being parents. It was a lot of pressure, a lot of work. I wouldn't know though, of course. I wasn't the mother of his child. I was being cold by saying no. Didn't I have feelings?

"*Hang. Up.*"

I swallowed hard. Did I turn around and see who was talking to me? Did I yell at him for speaking to me that way? I was a CEO. I was the one who always told others what to do. I was always the one in control, always the one to lead.

The woman in front of me finished her coffee order and stepped away.

"Do it."

Jeff's grating words were clipped as I hung up on him. *I can't believe I just did that.*

"*Good girl.*"

That short-circuited my brain. What the fuck? What was wrong with me? I swallowed hard. I should have turned around to kick him—

"Order your coffee."

I was under a trance. I stepped forward, meeting the barista's expectant gaze. "I'll have a flat white with an extra shot."

They nodded, their gaze constantly flicking past me. "Um, name?"

"Pepper."

The presence behind me only grew more potent. Above the scent of coffee, there was something more masculine, more delicious. Smokey and tempting.

My *mouth* watered.

I paid quickly and stepped to the side, keeping my gaze forward. I didn't even want to see the stranger's face. I didn't want him to think he'd affected me. My cheeks flamed as I waited patiently, choosing a brick on the wall to examine. The grooves and flecks of orange and brown and—

The presence was behind me again. Waiting.

"Pepper. Flat white," the barista called.

I lunged forward and snatched my to-go cup off the counter. I beelined it out of Adagio.

Good girl.

I scoffed as I raised my coffee cup to eye level, seeing my name scrawled in black.

"Bastard," I whispered, thinking of the stranger.

Who says something like that? What a freak.

My phone buzzed and buzzed in my pocket, but I ignored

it. I wasn't going back to work today. Jeff was probably already waiting in my office, and I just...

I just couldn't do it.

I was going home.

My cheeks burned as I rushed across the street, speed-walking the four blocks to my condo. Cold wind blew through my wool coat as I used my keycard to go through the front doors. The building faced the river, every loft leased by other music industry professionals. For the most part, everyone left each other alone. It was an unspoken rule, and one I was grateful for as I took the elevator to the penthouse.

I finally took a sip of my coffee and closed my eyes, leaning against the wall.

Good girl. Everyone thought I was good.

But I didn't want to be good anymore.

TWO
SALT

I NEEDED to be locked up.

There'd been *something* about the woman at the coffee shop. I couldn't remember the last time someone had sparked the feral side of me.

Dark brown hair with silver strands framing her heart-shaped face. Hips I wanted to trace with my calloused fingers. An ass I wanted to bite.

Of course, I hadn't really seen her ass, given she was wearing a coat.

But every ass was biteable. Spankable.

She didn't see how the room moved for her. It was frustrating. Her phone held to her ear, shoulders beyond tense. I'd heard snippets of whatever the fucker on the other side of the call said, and it'd infuriated me. I couldn't believe she'd let anyone speak to her that way.

My head tipped back as I stroked my cock faster. Soft whimpers echoed through my bathroom. Hot water streaked down my back muscles, heating my skin and scalding me with the same burn my thoughts carried.

She wouldn't even look at me.

I'd called her a good girl.

It had slipped out before I could stop myself.

Like I said, I needed to be locked up. I couldn't just go around dominating people in coffee shops on random Thursday mornings. Not only was that probably against the ethics of practicing good and safe kink, it was fucking weird.

Most people would have looked back, but not her. Why wouldn't she fucking look at me? Why couldn't she have yelled at me? Scoffed at me?

A growl left me as I stroked faster, my calloused palm gliding over every inch. *So close, so close, so close—*

My thoughts became dirtier. They were wrong. But that wrongness seeped down to my bones, and I knew the only thing that would make me come was imagining *Pepper* getting on her knees for me. That'd been her name, right? Pepper.

Salt and Pepper.

I wondered if Pepper was her real name. Salt *was* my real name, but it wasn't my first, it was my last.

Had her parents really named her Pepper?

Her coat had been so fucking expensive. A five-thousand-dollar coat. She reeked of the kind of wealth I would never see. I imagined coming on her face and watching her pink tongue dart out to lap up every drop, even watching it drip down to her luxurious coat, staining the fine wool.

"Fuck," I grunted, giving one final pump.

Cum burst from my cock, the endorphins swallowing me up in their waves of pleasure. The thoughts of the stranger faded with the orgasm, my moans melting along with the rest of my body.

I breathed out, basking in the momentary relief.

Just a few seconds of bliss.

My mind didn't allow me to feel content for long. Instead, all my problems came flooding back in once my cock stopped throbbing. I stood still for a moment and then reached for my soap, washing down quickly.

The numbness set back in, colors leached away. I flipped off the water and dragged the shower curtain back, snatching my towel from the bar on the wall.

I hated this bathroom. I hated this house. The last time I was here was seven years ago, the night I'd run away from my father for good. It'd been the last time I saw him alive, too.

I dried off quickly, stepped out of the shower, and opened the door to let steam swirl out. While I knew my father was dead, every single muscle tensed in my body as I thought about all the times I'd been scared to leave the bathroom. All the times I'd been yelled at or hit.

The mirror reflected my misery. I sucked in a breath, trying to pull it together.

It'd been six months since I'd gotten the call that he died. After years of alcoholism, his body had finally given out.

That part didn't shock me.

What did was the fact that he'd left the house to me, along with all the money he had in the bank. Not that it'd been a lot, but it was enough to help me bury him properly.

I'd let the house sit empty for three months. I couldn't bring myself to walk through the front door at first, but then my apartment lease was up, and I'd needed more space for the band to practice. Doing that in a house instead of an apartment made a lot more sense, and I wanted us to be as perfect as possible.

So, I'd moved in. And I was looking forward to the day I could move out.

About a year ago, I started posting videos online of songs I'd written. I never dreamed it would go anywhere. Music was just an outlet for me, a way to pour all of my dark parts into something healthy. In fact, my therapist was the one who'd recommended I do that.

But then people liked it. They liked it a lot. And I started having fun with it, bringing all the stuff I enjoyed most to my songs. Sex. Fucking. Kink.

And people really, *really* liked that.

Now, I had a band and was playing Nashville. I wasn't sure how long I'd be able to make it in this house, but for now, I had to stay.

One day, I'd sell it for good. I'd have enough money to finally leave the ghosts who haunted these broken and bruised walls. I'd be able to get rid of the guitar my asshole father gave me years ago, and buy something shiny and new.

It was fucked up that the one thing he'd given me, aside from multiple broken bones and a sadistic streak, was a love for music.

Music kept me alive years ago, and it kept me alive now.

I stepped out into the hall and stood still for a moment, listening for the creak of footsteps, as if his ghost lingered. I'd seen his body put in the ground, but the fear I harbored while living here stained the walls like cigarette smoke—permeating the floorboards, the ceilings, the windows.

I wasn't sure how he'd managed to keep the house. I thought about that as I padded down the hall to my bedroom, picked up my guitar, and sprawled out on my bed, fingering the neck while the fan made lazy, squeaky laps.

My eyes closed as I played, my fingers moving on autopilot. I needed to text the band. Jack was my bass player, Tyler was my drummer, and Eric was my pianist—and making sure they were ready for the show tomorrow was a priority. I needed to plan some thirst traps for my social media accounts. I also needed to put together a fresh setlist, something that had a mix of original work and familiar songs to keep the crowd engaged.

Being a songwriter in Nashville was the equivalent of being a shiny penny in a fountain. We were all used up wishes waiting to be picked up and dried off, or forever forgotten.

Regardless, I still wrote my songs. And enough people liked them now that maybe, just maybe, I'd be able to grow into something substantial.

Wearing a mask and being shirtless on stage helped.

That reminded me, I needed to finish making the leather harness I'd started a few days ago. I sighed, trying to wade through the clouds of stress. Normally, I didn't feel this way, but being in this house made me feel like I was suffocating.

Music was technically my secondary job. My primary source of income was creating custom leather goods and sex furniture. I'd been doing it for a few years now, and enjoyed everything about it. I liked working with my hands. I liked making client's erotic fantasies some true.

Anytime I told someone what I built, they always got a glazed look of surprise on their face. Jack, Tyler, and Eric liked to give me shit about it, though they were certainly jealous.

I'd always been good with my hands. I'd always been creative, too. Working with hard wood, the kind that came from trees, was second nature to me.

It was how I ended up joining the kink community to begin with.

My mentor was a fifty-seven-year-old lesbian Dominatrix named Nancy. She'd been in the BDSM community for over two decades and had shown me immense kindness. Truly, I wouldn't have been who I was today without her and her wife, Beth.

Seven years ago, I met her outside a sex club, and she'd kept me from doing something stupid with a stranger. At the time, I had no money. I'd run from my father the year before but never found a place to live. Somehow, I made it work, working odd jobs here and there. A man offered me a hundred bucks to let him fuck me, and that had seemed like a lot of money then. It would have been enough to keep me fed for the month if I was smart with it.

I'd been lucky, though.

Nancy intervened, and it'd been a whirlwind from there. I ended up going home with her and sleeping in her guest bedroom for two days straight. She and Beth kept me fed without asking any questions.

It was the first time I'd ever slept under a roof and felt safe.

Beth was a professional woodworker. Nancy was a professional Dominatrix. They'd given me a home, a job, and sent me to therapy. They'd been patient with me while I figured out how to navigate being an adult.

If Nancy ever found out I'd called a random woman a *good girl* in the middle of a coffee shop, she'd disown me.

Well, she probably wouldn't—but she'd give me an icy stare down that would make me piss myself.

I sighed and put my guitar down.

Maybe this weekend I'd finish gutting the house of my father's belongings. His bedroom and office were all that was left, but even touching the doorknob made my heart feel like it was going to burst out of my chest.

Really, I just wanted to light everything on fire and watch it all burn to ash.

Despite the desire to rot in bed, I reached for my phone and opened up Instagram. One of my videos went viral last week, and the comments never failed to make me laugh.

Men, in general, were an insecure bunch of fuckwads. Most of the comments were positive, until it landed on the wrong side of the algorithm. Then videos of me playing my songs were flooded with comments from right-wing idiots trying to hurl insults at me.

They weren't good at it, though. I wasn't really sure what the goal was, but the last thing that would actually fuck me up was a comment from someone who couldn't tell the difference between *their*, *there*, and *they're*.

Also, they were just helping my videos get to more people. That was the kicker of it all.

I scrolled for a bit, thinking about what I'd post next. I had a song I was working on, but the riff wasn't exactly where I wanted it yet. It was torturing me.

A text message flashed across the top of the screen from Beth and I sighed.

> We have two St. Andrew's crosses to build today and a spanking bench. Stop playing with your little band and get your ass to the workshop.

I snorted.

> Yes, ma'am

> Pick me up some of that bubble tea too. The one with the balls. And don't tell Nancy. I'm supposed to be off sugar

I rolled my eyes.

> I'm not supposed to encourage you being a brat

> Respect your elders

I barked out a laugh and sat up. Beth was right, unfortunately.

I had sex furniture to build, songs to write, and money to make. Wallowing in my dead father's house didn't fit into that picture.

Neither did fantasizing about a stranger in a coffee shop.

THREE
PEPPER

BODIES PRESSED against mine as people danced, voices muted by the music that thrummed so loud it reverberated in my bones. I searched for Tommy, my stomach twisting with nerves at being in a crowd. Venues like this used to appeal to me, but now I was so completely out of place, I just wanted to evaporate into thin air.

It had been too long since I'd gone out into the world on a Friday night. My skin prickled as I felt eyes on me, on the short black dress and heels I wore.

The entire outfit practically screamed that I was fun, right?

Then again, maybe I was overdressed. And that maybe made me *not* fun? Who the fuck was I even dressing for, aside from myself? It wasn't like I was going to meet someone, even though Tommy would have loved to see that happen.

Beaumont's was a well-known live music venue I used to frequent a few times a week back in the day. Back then, it hadn't been more than a seedy dive bar, but over the years it had grown into something more chic and high end. They still had the old neon beer signs on the wall behind the counter, dim blue lights, and the random dollar bills pinned to the ceiling, though.

While I had a special place in my heart for Beaumont's, it wasn't my scene anymore. It hadn't been for over a decade. Now I listened to music in my office, and it was through the lens of—could this make us money? Could Rosethorn benefit from having an artist like this on our roster?

"*Pepper!*"

Dan's voice boomed across the bar and I turned, spotting him standing at a small round table in a roped-off area with a good view of the stage. I waved and wove my way over to him. One of Beaumont's bouncers opened the rope for me and I stepped into the section.

"Since when does Beaumont's have a VIP area?" I asked.

"Since I graced them with my presence," Dan teased.

I grinned and leaned up to kiss his cheek. "Hey, handsome."

Silver glitter shimmered beneath the blue lights on his dark brown skin, his simple black T-shirt showing off broad shoulders and abundance of corded muscles. I'd known Tommy for over a decade, and I cared deeply for him—but Dan was my favorite. He was everything good in the world, and had a deep love for music that gave him the ability to make magic in the studio.

He also knew when I was struggling with just one look at me. He was far too intuitive for his own good. And just like that, he narrowed his gaze on me. "What's going on with you? You can't even come over for dinner because you're *so busy?* You never text. You never call. I'm sick of it."

I wrinkled my nose at him as he shoved a beer into my hands. "Well, any time you invite me over, Jeff is also usually invited, so..."

Dan shook his head. "We don't invite him over anymore."

"Really?" I scowled in surprise. When Jeff and I divorced, most of our friends gravitated towards him. Only Tommy and Dan kept up with me, but last I heard, they still grabbed the occasional lunch with him. "Since when?"

He made a face. "Mm, no. Not getting involved with any of that. You better talk to my husband."

Damn it, Tommy. What aren't you telling me? "Speaking of, where is he?" I asked, glancing around us.

"Getting us real drinks and stools so our feet don't ache. I'm too old to be standing here until three a.m."

I relaxed a fraction. "Thank god. I'd be leaving early if that were the case."

"So would I. But, I want to hear this guy. Tommy has been thirsting over his videos online. He has a little crush, I think. Which is good. Keeps things spicy after nine years."

I took a sip of my beer and shifted to be across the table from Dan. There were other standing tables too, each crowded with people clinking glasses and chatting. This area had more breathing room than the rest of the bar, which was completely packed. I looked up at the stage and spotted a single electric guitar waiting for the next set. "Well, we'll see what happens. He dragged me here for this too, so he must think this guy is someone special. Found him on Instagram or something."

"Oh, yeah. Hasn't shut up since. The comments are all either women or Tommy lusting over the guy."

Ha. "Hope it's a burner account. Also, I'm sorry I've been..."

"MIA?" he asked flatly.

"A bad friend." *There*, that was progress, right? Showing my feelings. Admitting I'd been staying away from anyone and everyone who reminded me of the absolute humiliation Jeff had caused.

Dan sighed and took a long sip of his beer. "Maybe a little

bit. I can't blame you for putting your head down and just working for a while. Honestly, I hate Jeff. I never liked him. I told you that years ago when we first met, but you and Tommy didn't listen to me."

I remembered that. All the times he'd made a passing criticism of Jeff that I'd laughed off when I shouldn't have. "I wish I would have listened to you."

"Well, hindsight is twenty-twenty. But it's been two years—"

"A year and a half," I corrected. *A long eighteen months.* "He cheated on me and got the intern pregnant before our divorce, remember? And they kept it a secret. And I found out after everyone else knew."

Now it was his turn to wrinkle his nose. "I genuinely thought you knew."

"You thought I knew? And was just fine with it?" I hissed. "Really, Dan?"

He threw up his hands. "I don't know what your kink is, honey. Cuckolding is a thing."

"Oh my *god.*" Irritation bubbled up as I clunked my beer on the table.

"Let's forget about the bastard for tonight. Oh, look who it is, just in time," Dan said lightly as Tommy approached us.

He'd been victorious. A couple of waitresses helped him bring over three cracked red leather barstools and three dirty martinis. Within a few minutes, the three of us were situated around the tiny table, chatting about anything but work. Dan showed me pictures of the new fur baby they'd just adopted, an older gray cat with a forever-grumpy expression on his cute little face. They'd named him Prince Albert.

"Why Prince Albert?" I asked as I popped an olive in my mouth.

Dan choked on his martini and Tommy burst out laughing. "Well, you know."

I stared at them blankly.

Tommy put his arm around me and kissed my cheek. "I forget how innocent you are. Prudish Pepper is alive and well. "

"I'm not innocent," I protested.

"A Prince Albert is a type of cock piercing," Dan said, giving his husband an all too knowing look.

"*Oh.*" My cheeks flamed and the two of them burst into laughter again. I couldn't help but join them. "Why would you —why would you name your cat after a... *piercing?*"

"A *cock* piercing?" Dan teased.

"Oh my god!" I exclaimed, bursting into a fit of giggles. I'd seen porn with men who had piercings before, but I didn't know they had names. I didn't say that though, already wanting to sink into the beer-stained floor.

We had tears in our eyes. Tommy threw his arm around me and kissed the top of my head. "Just like old times, remember? You're still fun. You're a vibrant star waiting to be snatched up by one lucky wisher."

"I'm gonna feel like absolute shit in the morning," I said. "And wake up alone, and childless, and..."

"Rich," Dan finished. "Talented. Smart. Powerful. And much better off without *Jeff.* Fuck that guy."

"Damn," I said.

He was right, though. It felt good to be out on a Friday night, despite my reservations. I released a long breath, more tension melting away. Maybe it was the alcohol, or the music, or the people—but I felt better than I had in a long time.

A ripple of energy rolled through the crowd as a shadow emerged on stage. The music playing overhead faded as a man walked up to the guitar, tall and muscled and commanding attention in a way that made my heart skip a beat.

I wasn't the only one enchanted. The hush that followed as he picked up the guitar was soon replaced by cheers and a few whistles.

Tommy turned to look at me and smiled. "I'm gonna be saying *I told you so* when we're rolling in more money."

"Let's hear him first," I said.

Dan winked and then we refocused on *him*.

"Where's his band? I thought you said there was a band," I asked.

"Shush," Tommy hissed.

The man wore black jeans with leather boots, a studded belt, and a black leather mask. It covered the lower half of his face, with space for part of his mouth to still be seen. Enough space to not fuck with the mic while singing.

Then tension curling through Beaumont's was unreal. Even as jaded as I was, I could see what Tommy was talking about. His presence was ethereal. It was devilish. It was very much out of place in a city like Nashville, where everyone sang country music, Americana, and bluegrass.

"It's just him and a guitar," I said to Tommy. "And a bar full of people who want to party. This is silly."

"They don't want to party, Pepper. They want to kiss that guy's boot. Be patient," he said without looking back.

"Good evening, everyone." His voice was deep, an orgasmic ripple of excitement rolling through me. It was familiar, too. *What is wrong with me?* "Thank you to Beaumont's for having me tonight. My name is Salt."

A few shouts and hollers echoed through the venue.

His nimble fingers moved over the strings as he started playing his guitar riff, and despite not wanting to look away, I closed my eyes. Because humans were chameleons. Anyone could be masked and buff and primed and primped, but not just anyone could create music that *moved*.

His music moved.

It was an original song, which was typically a terrible way to open a set on a Friday night. Especially without a band. It shouldn't have worked. Everyone at the bar should have shifted attention back to their conversations, but that didn't happen. Like an incubus, he sucked up the energy of the room, funneling it into blues-inspired hooks.

And then he opened his mouth again.

His voice reverberated through the room. *I swear I know his voice.* I couldn't place it. I didn't have a spare thought to even consider where I'd heard it before, completely consumed with the sound of him. He knew how to play and was clearly talented, but it wasn't as smooth as some of the seasoned musicians I was used to hearing. But that edge worked in his favor.

The music was sexual, thirsty, *hungry* for touch. For *something* deep and carnal and dirty. The lyrics were full of pain. He was drowning, dying, begging to be rescued. By me. By the listener. He was begging to be saved. To be seen.

I knew that feeling all too well.

My eyes snapped open, and even from across the room, I swore he was looking right at me.

Tommy stiffened and then glanced back, raising a brow. *I fucking told you,* he mouthed.

I ignored Tommy and swallowed hard, my gaze locked on Salt. Was he looking at me? He wasn't. It had to be a trick of the light.

Every nerve in my body was alive. Yearning.

A bass note dropped and I realized there *was* a band. They'd come on stage some time during the first verse.

The beat dropped for the chorus, followed by shouts and whistles, people grinding together. Heat crept through me as I watched the floor come alive—a cult of Dionysus, and he was our god. His performance was good alone, but with the rest of the band, it created something irresistible.

"God *damn*," Dan said. "Baby, I want to dance."

Tommy nodded and held out his hand. "We'll be back, Pepper."

"I'll be here." *With his music.*

Tommy tugged Dan close, the two of them getting lost in a kiss before slipping out of the VIP area and onto the dance floor. I watched them for a moment, then turned my focus back to him.

Salt.

What kind of a name was Salt?

Ironic, coming from me. Regardless, every part of me knew exactly what I wanted.

I want his music to be mine.

FOUR
SALT

I SAW HER.

From the stage, behind the throng of strangers grinding and swaying and cheering.

It was her. Finally looking at me.

I knew it was her because I hadn't been able to purge that woman from my mind over the last twenty-four hours.

Singing to strangers never made me nervous. But now, I was singing straight to her. My voice crooned, my callused fingers gliding over my guitar with ease born from years of practice. My gaze never left her. I couldn't look away.

Her eyes never left mine, either. My heart stuttered in my chest, the song possessing me as I gave it everything I had.

I came to the end, using my pedal to suspend the final chord. I glanced over at Jack and he nodded, hitting a bass note that rolled smoothly into the next song, one everyone knew. Claps and cheers and whistles filled the venue, but I tuned it out, focusing on my guitar. On my voice. On the song.

Music was burned into the cells of my toxic, cursed blood. The buzz of it hummed through me as I sang. It was an addiction burning through me, *ruining* me and everyone who heard it.

But I had a corruption kink. And this was where I felt most at home—turning a crowd of strangers into heathens and feeding off the energy like it was my lifeline. I liked their attention. I liked imagining that one day, we'd play a massive, sold-out venue. That I'd sing about fucking the person of my dreams and the entire world would be listening.

The rest of the set flew by. By the time it ended, my body was drenched in sweat from the stage lights. I thanked the crowd and unplugged my guitar.

Jack clapped my shoulder. "That was great, man," he called.

"You did great." I smiled at him, Tyler, and Eric.

A couple of screams startled us and I started to turn back, but Jack gave me a shove. "Get off stage man, they're feral for you."

I glanced back and realized I was being filmed by a few women in the front. Their boyfriends glowered at me, and I winked at them before heading off stage.

I needed water and food, especially since I never ate before a show. Even though I loved it, I sometimes felt sick from nerves.

Adam, the booking manager at Beaumont's, waited in the back. I ducked my head to avoid the doorframe and took the three short steps down into the pit. The band playing after me was made up of three guys and a woman dressed in cowgirl boots and a glittery dress.

"That was hot," she said as she passed by, her gaze sweeping over me. "You busy after the show?"

I smirked. Normally I'd say no, but I wasn't interested in anyone but the coffee shop woman. "Yeah, I'm busy," I said.

"Your loss."

I watched her step on stage, offering nods to the band as they followed her out to set up.

Adam held out his hand as I walked up to him. "That was great, man."

"Thanks," I said. I shook his hand and reached for my guitar case, quickly packing away my prized possession. I was eager to leave now. "As always, loved playing here."

Adam nodded as I rose back up, standing my guitar case on end and leaning against it.

He raised both brows. "You got people watching you. The kind of people who change lives. I think you're going places, Salt. I'm glad you got a fucking band. They're doing good."

I was paying them well, so I hoped so. "Good. Thanks for that suggestion. Bigger venues are starting to reach out."

"I bet. Always remember Beaumont's though," he chuckled. "Where you got your big break."

"I haven't broken anything yet."

Adam laughed, and then winced when mic feedback reverberated through the venue. We both leaned back to glance at the stage.

"Dammit," he muttered.

I smiled. "That's why I liked playing alone. Now, I have to worry about that shit too."

He rolled his eyes and then clapped my shoulder. "Good problems. I'll see you next Friday. Now, go say hi to Daniel Park and his husband, Tommy. I also spotted the Rosethorn CEO, although I can't remember her name to save my life. Something weird. They were all in the VIP area."

"I've met Tommy," I said.

He was a nice guy and I knew he was big in the industry. He'd been on me to set up a meeting with his record label, but I wasn't sure it was what I wanted. That felt like such a large step, and I'd only been playing with my band for a couple months now.

"I gotta go," Adam sighed as another mic screech split our ears. "They're having sound problems. I'll pay you out when the bar closes, you made a shit ton of tips and drink sales for us. It'll be a good one."

"Thanks man, have a good night." I watched as he darted up the steps. Jack, Eric, and Tyler emerged and joined me. "You did great," I said. "He'll pay me out once the show is over, and I'll pay you guys too. You don't need to hang around if you want to pack up." I needed them out of my hair so I could find the dream girl.

"Thanks," Eric said. "That was a solid set."

"You were a little laggy," Jack quipped.

Eric glowered. "I couldn't hear you for a minute there."

"We all settled into it," Tyler said, giving me a tired smile. He was a large, bearish man who radiated kindness. "Shoot me a text when you know the next practice time."

I nodded, and the three of them split to gather their instruments and pack up. I rolled my shoulders and wove through what was basically a storage room—cluttered with chairs, tables, and random equipment.

Once I stepped into the dark hallway, I paused and leaned against the wall, exhaling slowly. It was the only semi-quiet spot in Beaumont's—a kind of purgatory, tucked between the stage and the rest of the bar, where no one usually wandered.

Movement in the corner of my eye had my head snapping up.

It's her.

My body was moving before my thoughts had time to catch up. Her back was to me, heels giving her a little more height than when I saw her the first time. She stood at the end of the hall, one shoulder leaning against the grungy brick, her attention fixed elsewhere.

I slowed as I came up behind her. My fingertips grazed her arm and she stiffened. I lowered my voice. "Are you stalking me?"

"I *knew* it was you," she said. "I should ask you the same."

The neon lights glowed midnight blue, casting an iridescent sheen on the silver strands that framed the side of her face. She still continued to look away from me, but I couldn't help myself. I stepped closer, the tension between us unbearable. From here, I could see the dance floor, but the energy wasn't the same as it'd been earlier.

What the fuck am I doing?

"Are you going to look at me?" I whispered. I just wanted to see her face up close. "I know you were watching me across the bar. I saw you."

"Everyone was watching you," she said. "I recognized your voice. I was listening to you sing, and then you said something that made it click. *That's* the guy from Adagio. It took a minute, but your voice is not an easy one to forget."

I wasn't sure if that was a compliment. The way she said it was beyond cold. Clinical, almost.

I closed the distance between us. It was a risk. It was stupid, it was wrong, but *something* pulled me closer. She was a magnet.

"I should yell for someone," she said.

"Do it," I urged. "Or you could scream out my name."

She cursed under her breath, her head turning slightly. I drank in the curves of her cheeks, her cute nose, the softness of her red lips. Smoky shadow darkened her eyes, her lashes long. "I don't know your real name."

I was breaking all the rules. I didn't just grab people, I

didn't cage women against walls in small bar hallways. It was fucking predatory. It was wrong, and yet—

"Do you want to know it?" I asked, planting my hand on the wall next to her face.

She pushed back against me with her ass. My eyes shuttered closed and I thought about hiking up her skirt and fucking her right here and now.

Both of us froze.

"What the fuck is wrong with me?" she whispered.

"Whatever it is, it's wrong with me too."

Her breath slipped out in a frustrated huff. "Do you just go around calling strangers a good girl?"

"Not typically," I admitted.

"Tell me your name."

"Ask me nicely."

"*Tell me* your name." Her tone was nicer, but it still wasn't a question.

Her disobedience stoked the fires of dominance within me. Despite my best judgement, I shoved her against the wall, my cock now fully hard and nestling between her perfect ass cheeks. *God*, this dress. I wanted to rip it off. "I told you to fucking ask me. You don't take directions well, do you?"

"Not at all."

"Pepper? Where'd you go?"

A familiar voice echoed close by and I stepped away, turning to adjust my raging cock so it wouldn't be blatantly obvious. I spun right as Tommy rounded the corner, the guy who had been headhunting me from the label. He was like a bloodhound.

Tommy grinned when he saw us. "Oh, hey. You guys met."

"He was just about to introduce himself officially," Pepper said.

She changed her demeanor so quickly, like flipping a

switch. Her cheeks were flushed red, but her gaze was ice. Completely different from the woman I'd just been grinding my cock against.

"Oh. Okay, well. This is Simon. Otherwise, known as—"

"Salt," I said, holding out my hand. "You can call me Salt. Nice to meet you, *Pepper*."

The corner of her mouth tugged as she held out her hand. I shook it, noting the way her gaze dropped to the tattoos winding up my arm. My right hand had a flower with an eye at the center, more blooms climbing upward. I liked flowers—my favorite tattoo artist did too—so we'd gotten a little carried away with the ink.

I didn't like the way she looked at them, though. Her gaze moved back to my face. To my mask. "Do you always wear that?" she asked.

I smiled and reached up, unclasping it and pulling it away. Her eyes widened slightly.

"See," Tommy said excitedly. "I told you, Pepper. I fucking told you."

"You did," she said, sounding unimpressed.

"Pepper is the CEO of Rosethorn Records."

Oh. *Oh shit.*

Welp, there went any sort of career I might have had with that label.

I'd just been grinding my cock against the woman who could have been my boss.

But also, of course *she* was a suit. Of course the stranger who had stained my existence for the last twenty-four hours was someone I shouldn't want.

She had that look about her, too. Like she was the boss, used to being the one in control.

Except when she was between a wall and my body.

Pepper offered a dry smile. "Tommy is right, that *is* who I am."

Rosethorn. I'd heard about Rosethorn. It was one of the most coveted labels in the industry. It was small but powerful, having represented some of the largest artists who had hit the scene in the last decade.

"Didn't Rosethorn start with your husband?" I asked casually.

Her smile turned sharp, her eyes narrowing. Tommy interjected before she could speak.

"It actually started with the three of us," he said. "Jeff is her ex-husband."

Pepper threw up her hands. "Do we now lay out my personal life for everyone, Tommy?"

He winced. "I was just—"

"It was rude of me to ask," I said quickly, trying to smooth things over just enough to keep Tommy out of trouble. "I was just curious. I've heard about Rosethorn."

"Everyone has," she said sweetly.

I had to fight a laugh. She was *not* happy with me. "Well, it's a pleasure to meet you, Pepper."

"I'm glad you two met in a more casual environment. Pepper is known to be a little scary in the office," Tommy laughed nervously.

Her expression turned unreadable and I frowned. I didn't like the walls that went up.

Tommy didn't seem to notice. And if he did, he acted like he didn't. "Come on, Dan is getting us more drinks. I'll buy us all a round."

Pepper shook her head. "I'm done for the night, Tommy."

"What? You just got here," he complained. "You've only been here for an hour. There's so much more you could get into tonight. Like, you know, have some fun with someone..."

"I heard the one you wanted me to hear," she said tightly. "That's all I came for."

The one he wanted her to hear. Like I was a product. Like I hadn't wrapped her in my words, in my music, pulling her across the room, down the hall, into my nasty, obsessive grip.

"Come on," Tommy pleaded. "When was the last time you stayed out late? It's been too long since you've just enjoyed music the way you used to. Come have a drink and sit with us."

Pepper gave him a harsh look that would have withered the balls on any other man alive. I could see why she was the boss.

But, I couldn't help wondering why it had been so long since she had enjoyed music. Why hadn't she been out in so long? The ease between her and Tommy felt like more than just coworkers—they were friends. Even if he was clearly trying to push her to do something she wasn't going to do.

I couldn't believe coffee girl was the fucking CEO of Rosethorn Records.

I was unlucky. Truly.

"I don't want to impose," I said. "Besides, I don't drink."

"Nonsense," Tommy said easily. "You don't want a beer or something?"

"I don't drink," I said again firmly. "But if there's food involved, I'm open."

He nodded eagerly, giving Pepper a pleading look. "Come on, Pep. We can always go to a restaurant and grab some dinner. Get to know Mr. Salt. He's hungry."

I *was* hungry.

I was hungry for her. I was hungry for whatever just happened, whatever was happening.

I wasn't sure I'd make it through an entire dinner with her though. Not while wondering about the part of her that had pushed her ass against me.

Pepper shook her head. "I'm sorry. We'll talk on Monday, Tommy. I don't want to go to dinner."

"I can walk you to your car," I offered.

"I only live a few blocks from here," she said. "I'll walk."

Tommy shook his head. "You can't just walk home. Don't make me go get Dan."

That made her laugh, her expression loosening for a split second. She bumped Tommy's shoulder with her own, and both of them seemed to relax significantly.

"I do it all the time and I'm fine," she insisted.

He grabbed hold of her face with a familiarity that made an ugly emotion rear its head. *Jealousy?* From the sounds of it, Tommy was happily married to Dan. And yet... Fuck. Yeah, that's what it was. Jealousy. Over someone I didn't even know. I had absolutely no right to feel jealous.

"You're killing me," he said. "Are you sure you don't want to get dinner?"

Her laughter rang over the terrible crowing of the band on stage. "I'm sure. We'll do this again though."

He sighed dramatically and gave me a determined look. "Walk her home. Get her contact information. We'll set up a meeting next week."

Pepper slapped his chest. "You can't just do that."

"I can," he said.

"I don't mind," I said. "I could stretch my legs."

"He's hungry," she argued like I wasn't there.

"I am," I said, staring directly at her. "But I'll eat after I walk you home."

Her cheeks reddened.

Tommy grinned, clearly feeling victorious. "Wonderful. In that case, I'm going to leave business to you, my dearly beloved boss."

"Tommy, my darling, *fuck off*," she seethed.

His grin didn't falter. He held out his hand and I shook it. "See you next week, Salt. I'm gonna go play with my husband."

"Have fun," I chuckled.

He left us alone in the hall. The moment he was out of earshot, Pepper huffed, shooting me a dark glare. "You don't need to walk me home."

"You have all the money in the world," I said. "Why won't you just take an Uber?"

"Because I like the walk." She shrugged her shoulders. "Like I said, I don't need an escort. I'm almost forty, for god's sake."

My brows shot up. She didn't look like she was almost forty. And really, I didn't care if she was.

If anything, it only made me want to fuck her more.

"How old are you actually?"

If looks could kill, I'd be dead. "Thirty-seven."

I rolled my eyes at her, and she scoffed.

"Did you just roll your eyes at me?"

"Yeah, I did."

Her glare intensified. "What are you, twenty?"

"Twenty-five." I enjoyed the way her expression twisted with shock.

"You don't look twenty-five," she muttered.

"Well, look at us. Two peas in a pod already," I said easily. "And I don't really care if you don't want me to, I will be walking you home."

Her pretty lips pulled into a thin line. "Fine."

"Good girl."

Her mouth dropped, and I expected her to slap me. Instead, she shook her head, her eyes full of fire as she turned on her heels and stormed down the hallway.

I grabbed my guitar case and followed after her.

It felt like a lamb being led to slaughter, but I wasn't sure who held the knife. Was it her? Was it me? It was probably bad for any sort of PR, but I ignored anyone who tried to stop me to talk, anyone who tried to intercept. My attention belonged to her. We wove through the crowd until she made it out the door and into the cool city night.

She turned around, and I watched it dawn on her that I hadn't let her escape. Annoyance flickered over her pretty face. "You don't need to do this."

"I want to," I said.

"Maybe I don't want you to see where I live."

"Maybe I want to come home with you."

I was pushing it. I knew I was, but I wanted her. I couldn't remember the last time I'd wanted to be with someone like this, and I'd already ruined any chance of being signed by humping her in the hallway.

So.

Might as well go for it, right?

Pepper sucked in a breath, clearly thrown off. "I don't... I don't do that. With strangers. Especially not strangers twelve years younger than me."

"I'm hardly a stranger," I quipped. "I've called you a good girl twice."

People on the sidewalks moved around us, but I still took a step closer. She looked to the side. I could see her thinking. Weighing my words.

"Take me home with you," I whispered. "I want you. I promise it'll be good."

"You just want me for what I could do for you."

"I could say the same thing about you."

She scoffed, but didn't push me away. She didn't back up. Instead, she tipped her head back, looking up at me in a way that made me imagine her on her knees. That's how she'd look from that angle. *Fuck.* I *needed* her.

"You can always change your mind," I whispered. "At any point. I don't care at what point."

I leaned in, my lips pressing against her ear.

"I want you," I said. "Take me home with you."

"This is wrong. You're too young. You're not my type. God, everyone is staring at you. Go home with one of them."

She gestured toward whoever was watching us, but I didn't look up. "I don't care about them."

I didn't. I knew I was being reckless. That was one of my flaws. Once I set my sights on something, I couldn't let it go. Right now, that was Pepper. The entire world faded away and I was consumed by her black cherry scent and the inch between our bodies. We weren't touching, but I still felt the burn of her.

"I need to hear you say it," I said. "I need you to ask me to come home with you."

"I..."

"I want you. I want to see whatever *this* is. But, I need to hear the words, Pepper."

She stood still, clearly weighing the pros and cons.

"I'll call you a cab," I said, starting to break away.

"Wait." She grabbed hold of my jacket, keeping me in place. "Salt. Stop."

I raised a brow. "Then ask me."

She stared at me, her posture tensing. She didn't like being told what to do, and yet I knew she craved the release of it. Of not having to make decisions.

Pepper crossed her arms, giving me a hard stare that made the hair stand up on the back of my neck. I could see why she was the CEO, why she ran her own company, and why the entire world moved around her like she was a boulder lodged in a stream. "Come home with me."

Hah. "I said *ask* me."

Frustration flashed, hazel eyes burning holes into me. "*Salt, will you come home with me?*"

I smirked. "I thought you'd never ask."

Pepper scoffed as I reached for her hand. She shook her head and pulled away before we touched, glancing around us.

I may have thought she was paranoid, but people *were* watching us. I glanced around too, but I didn't recognize anyone. And I knew Tommy was still inside the bar dancing the night away with his husband.

Pepper exhaled sharply. "People know who I am. I don't want any rumors starting about me going home with someone half my age."

"Half your age is a pretty big leap." A really big leap, actually. "Besides, we're two consenting adults. Age is just a number."

She didn't say anything else as she started down the street. It didn't take much to keep up with her, though. Between my long legs and the fact that she was in heels, we settled into an easy walk down the block.

Silence wrapped around us, giving me time to think. I sucked in the freezing night air, turning my attention to our surroundings. The blinding lights that flashed at open bars, the countless people going in and out, the echo of music from within. Country, bluegrass, rock, Americana, and even some punk and blues. All blending into an orchestra of comfort that settled deep in my chest.

I knew these streets well. The building where I'd met Nancy years ago was a few blocks over. It used to be a club, but it was now closed down, and for good reason. I craned my head back as we passed a high-rise, the bars spacing out as we made our way to a part of the city I didn't belong in.

The part where she lived.

I studied her without shame this time. The silver strands

that framed her face were tucked behind her ears, her expression cool and unyielding.

There was something about her. The twelve years between us didn't matter to me. It might to a lot of people, but not to me. If anything, it only made me wonder why someone else wasn't with her.

Who was Pepper? Who was the woman that moved through life like a shark, but was otherwise in desperate need of a net?

She glanced up at me, dark brows furrowing before focusing her gaze back on the sidewalk.

"Stop staring," she snapped.

"Never. I think you're beautiful."

"I bet you say that to everyone who throws themself at you." She didn't like being told no. "You're just a flirt."

Well, I was a flirt. "I am flirting, but you're also beautiful. Both can be true."

A long sigh. "Maybe I'll change my mind. I shouldn't do this."

"That's fine," I said nonchalantly, but decided to add, "I wouldn't be mad if you did. Because I'm not going to fuck you unless you're begging me to, Pepper."

FIVE
PEPPER

I'D LOST IT. Truly, I'd lost it. What was I doing?

I'd been unable to keep from going to him. After his set ended, I blinked and was waiting in the hall. Then torturing myself over standing there like some idiot.

But I remembered his voice.

The stranger that brazenly called me a *good girl* in broad fucking daylight. The words had awakened something in me.

I slowed as we approached my building. I wasn't sure exactly what I was doing yet.

Salt seemed to pick up on that as I stopped in front of the doors, turning to face him. He loomed in front of me, his guitar case in one hand, his other tucked in his leather jacket. Dark eyes, dark hair, a face that belonged to a god, not a mortal man. Especially not a man who wanted me.

"What do you want?" he asked gently.

"I don't know," I said. "I don't know. I've never done anything like this. I've never—"

"Gone home with someone?"

"You're too young," I snapped, my thoughts racing.

I was panicking. I was going back and forth between logic and the desire that had overcome me. Maybe Jeff saying I wasn't fun anymore was going to my head. Maybe I just needed to do something for myself.

I should send him home. That was the answer. Drive him away and forget about tonight. "You're way too young for me. How old did you say you were?"

A smirk tugged at his lips. He cocked his head. "Twenty-five."

God, this was crazy. What had gotten into me? I couldn't remember the last time I'd been with someone new in the bedroom. *Years.* I didn't just go home with strangers, especially a stranger who was over a decade younger than me and a potential client for Rosethorn.

"Your brain has barely finished growing. What on earth could you possibly know about—"

Salt pinned me against the wall, his knee spreading my thighs. My eyes widened, my body responding to him in a way that had my thoughts short-circuiting. Every complaint vanished as my gaze locked with his, the lust burning hot in his eyes.

He leaned in, lips almost touching mine. "Aren't you tired?" he whispered. "Tired of fighting? You know you want me. Why are you fighting what you want? You're a CEO, a woman who gets everything she wants all the time without so much as a blink. Are you worried about what people might think—someone who looks like you, walking home with someone who looks like me? Is it the tattoos, Pepper? The clothes I wear?"

My chest rose and fell with uneven breaths, my eyes never leaving his. Darkness emanated from him in waves, but it was the kind of darkness I wanted to get lost in. The kind of darkness that held the same wonder of lying in a field and staring up at a starry sky. Like a pot of ink, waiting to be spun into words.

It was the kind of darkness I couldn't turn away from, because I had that darkness, too.

A depravity that yearned for something more.

Jeff had smothered it when we were married. It was wrong to be wanted like that, wasn't it? All the years spent being raised in a small town by religious zealots told me it was wrong.

But every part of me screamed for more. Begged for it. Whatever this was, it made me act foolishly.

But really, was it wrong to be wanted?

To *want* to be wanted?

"This is wrong," I murmured.

A slight smile tugged at the corner of his mouth. "I don't think it's wrong at all."

His presence leached my ability to turn away. I wanted him. His age didn't matter. The fact that he could be a part of my business one day didn't matter, even though it was breaking the rules.

I didn't date our artists.

And he *would* be ours.

He would be mine. After hearing his music tonight, I knew Tommy was right. He'd struck gold. He'd found someone who made the kind of music that led me to run away from the life my mother so eagerly wanted for me.

Salt had the voice of the devil.

And I really wanted to be a good little sinner.

For years, I'd been perfect. I had a reputation for being smart, steady, and calculated. I always made good choices. It was ingrained into me from the start.

But I wasn't happy. That was what I'd come to terms with earlier this week. Jeff leaving me had only ripped the first bandaid off, and there were plenty more to go.

I was tired of being perfect.

I wanted to be ruined. There were so many things I'd missed out on sexually, I was certain of it. Maybe Salt could show me things I hadn't experienced. I wanted to find out, even though it was a bad idea.

The temptation was too great.

But, I still tried to put up a fight. "You're potentially signing with my label. You're nothing like me."

"I don't want you to sign me," he bit back. "You didn't like my music—"

"That's not true," I gasped. It wasn't true at all. His music had made me lose my fucking mind. "Your music was good, Salt. I'm not just saying that. Otherwise, I wouldn't have told Tommy to set a meeting with you next week."

He shook his head at me. "No. You didn't get it."

My temper reared its ugly head and I grabbed his jaw, noting the way his nostrils flared at my sudden touch. "You're a goddamn incubus," I growled. "Your *music* made me want to come in front of god and everyone. It made me want to lose everything. It was *dangerous*."

He braced his forearm above me against the wall, his very presence swallowing me whole. "You wouldn't survive my appetite."

I glowered. "Why wouldn't I? I'm older than you. More experienced, right?"

His laugh was brutal and abrupt. "Do you know what an incubus feeds off of?"

My breath caught.

"Say it," he whispered. "Say the word. It must feel so dirty on those perfect lips."

"Sex," I snapped. "*Sex* isn't a dirty word. I'm not a prude."

Another teasing smile pricked like a thorn. "Then why did every muscle in your body tense? *Sex*. Is that what you want,

Pepper? Do you want sex? Do you want to be fucked? Does your pussy crave a cock that'll make her weep?"

I stared at him. I was lost. I was so lost in him. Who was this stranger? This singer? This *demon?*

"Answer me."

What am I doing? "My..." I trailed off, swallowing down the burn in my throat. "My ex-husband never enjoyed sex with me. I thought there was something wrong with me. I just want to know if there's something wrong with me? Maybe I'm bad at this—"

His eyes immediately softened. Fuck, I hated that look. Everyone always looked at me like that when they found out Jeff left me, or in this case, that our long marriage wasn't satisfying in the way it should have been. I shook my head, shoving him away hard enough that he took a step back.

"Don't pity me. Don't look at me like that. This was stupid, this was—"

"Pepper. *Stop.*"

Another command. One that made me freeze in place, unable to look at him. The doors to my building were only a few feet away. I could go in, go upstairs, and never see him again.

I could end this before it even started.

"Look at me."

I didn't want to. I didn't want to be seen. If he looked at me right now, I'd shatter. I'd break. And I couldn't break. I wasn't breakable, I wasn't—

"Look at me, Pepper. Right now."

I shivered, then finally looked at him. He stood so close again, his entire presence sucking me in.

"I haven't wanted to fuck someone this badly in my entire life," he whispered. "So you're not doing anything wrong. I want you. I want your submission."

I frowned. "I'm not—"

"I mean in the bedroom," he corrected. "Outside the bedroom, I doubt anyone could truly tell you what to do. But behind closed doors, in my arms, vulnerable. *Needy.*"

My knees felt like jelly. He was speaking the desires I'd locked away long ago, dragging them out into the open—and it was both jarring and freeing.

"Do you crave giving in?"

All I could do was nod. "All the time."

"Then give in to me for tonight. You don't owe me anything else. Nothing to do with your company or my music. I don't care if you want a meeting this week or not. I think I let that go when I realized who I dry humped in the hall at Beaumont's. What I do care about tonight is you. I haven't been able to get you off my mind since I saw you in the coffee shop."

"Do you normally hit on strangers?" I asked.

"Yes," he said earnestly. "All the time. But I don't ask to go home with them. In fact, I don't do shit like this at all. I also don't cage women against walls in clubs or call them a good girl without their consent."

"But you did with me."

"I did," he whispered.

I pressed my lips together, looking around us. It was the middle of the night and I couldn't remember the last time I'd been out this late.

His body language softened and he offered me a more genuine smile. One with dimples. I couldn't help but stare before my gaze followed the trail of tattoos that licked up his neck the way I wanted to.

My resistance crumbled. "Only tonight," I said.

He nodded. "If that's all you want."

It had to be. "I should make you sign a NDA."

"I will, if you want me to."

My muscles stiffened. Was that silly?

"You have trust issues," he said.

"I have to have trust issues," I snapped. I reached into my purse, pulling out my keys. "You can't tell anyone about this, Salt. No one. Not a single fucking soul, or I'll make sure your career never happens."

The smile disappeared and he cocked his head thoughtfully. "Is this your attempt to put me in my place?"

"Fuck off," I hissed. "Fuck. Why am I doing this?"

His hand darted out, circling my wrist with an ease that made my thighs squeeze tighter. Inked fingers plucked the keys from my hand, and then he was guiding me to the doors.

"I won't tell anyone," he said. "I'll sign an NDA if it makes you feel better. I have no interest in what you can do to me or my career, Pepper. I just want to know what *this* is."

I wasn't sure I should believe him. This was stupid, careless, reckless.

Heat tugged at my core as he held me close, possessive. Lust boiled in my blood as we crossed the empty lobby to the elevator, not a soul in sight but us. The silver doors slid open and we stepped inside. Salt set his guitar case down as I pressed the button quickly.

Then I found myself against the wall again.

I arched against him this time. I was going to give in. The resistance was unraveling, slipping further and further out of reach.

He gripped my hair and pulled my head back, swiping his tongue along my neck. His lips hovered over my pulse, teeth grazing my skin. "Do you know what a safe word is?"

My head spun. "Yes. I've read a lot about it. But, I've never done anything... kinky."

"I see. Your safe word is red. Promise me that if you ever

need things to slow down, you'll tell me. That you'll speak up for yourself."

I scoffed. "I speak up for myself."

"Can you, when it has nothing to do with work?"

My cheeks burned. It was a little too on the nose. "I don't like you."

The elevator slowed, the doors opening for us. Once again, he was controlling me. Like a puppet with a master they'd willingly handed their strings to.

"Is there anything you know you like?" he asked as we made it to my door. "Spanking? Sensations? Is there anything that might actually cause you harm or you know you don't want? Or do you just want sex?"

"I don't know." I unlocked my door and we went in. I kicked off my heels and sighed, wrinkling my nose as I thought about it. Salt glanced around, a hum leaving him as he took in my penthouse.

"Do you live alone?" he asked.

"Yes," I said.

"Good. No one will hear you scream, then."

I raised a brow, and despite everything, the moment we looked at each other, we laughed.

"Sorry," he chuckled. "That sounded creepy. I didn't mean it that way."

"I know," I said, locking the front door. "Besides, my best friend has my phone location turned on. So if you do anything, you'll get caught. And Tommy knows you walked me home."

"I won't do anything you don't consent to," he said.

He was still standing there, looming and out of place in my home. I craned my neck to look up at him.

Desire was like a drug. It hit my system with the same urgency, the same potency. My resistance crumbled and everything shifted. The tension in the air, the stiffness of my muscles. I relaxed, the knots in my shoulders easing ever so slightly.

Behind closed doors, I didn't have to be Pepper anymore. I didn't have to be the CEO. I didn't have to be the one who had all the answers.

No one could see us.

No one could see me but him.

Salt stepped closer to me. "Do you want to know what I want?"

"Yes," I decided.

"I want you to kneel down on the floor and unlace my boots."

My breath hitched. I looked down at his black boots and the midnight blue laces that crossed each other until they knotted at the top.

He was patient. He didn't say anything else, waiting for me to make the choice.

Was I going to get on my knees for him?

Was I going to submit to him?

Yes.

It was awkward, but I slowly lowered my knees to the hardwoods, kneeling before him. God, what if my knees cracked? My hands trembled as I reached out, tugging on the knot on his left boot.

His palm settled on top of my head, gently petting me. Stroking me. I closed my eyes for a moment, basking in his touch before hurrying to unlace both boots.

Once I finished, I helped pull them off and set them next to my heels. Even seeing them side by side felt absurd. Louboutin red-soled pumps next to his beat up Dr. Martens with tattered blue laces, dirt streaking the sides.

I looked up at him. Rough calluses cradled my chin.

"Good girl," he whispered. "What's your safe word?"

"Red," I answered.

"Good."

His praise washed over me, awakening something deep and feral in my bones.

"What do you want me to do to you?"

"Anything," I rasped.

He shook his head. "No. Not anything. Tell me what you like. What do you want to try?"

Anything? Everything? It'd been a long time since I'd been in a situation where I didn't know exactly what to do. "I can't think straight. I've never done this before. I've never…"

"Okay. We'll test the waters. Close your eyes."

I closed them. All of the other sensations around me intensified. The scent of his cologne, the way he held my chin, the pounding in my chest.

A reckless heart with a taste for destruction. I was finally indulging a part of me I had always ignored.

I was pretty sure Salt looked exactly like the kind of man my mother imagined would cast a spell on me and whisk me off to hell.

"Take a deep breath," he instructed.

I did as he asked. I filled my lungs, holding my breath for a few moments before exhaling slowly. My nerves relaxed.

"What do you imagine me doing to you?"

My throat constricted. I imagined him forcing me to take his cock. I couldn't say that aloud though, could I? That would be zero to sixty, and I wasn't sure—

"Pepper," he whispered. I heard him lean over, his hand sliding to my throat.

My pussy responded, weeping for him. Desperate for him. I couldn't remember the last time I'd felt this kind of want. It wasn't something Jeff had ever sparked.

Salt didn't squeeze my neck, instead just letting his grip rest there, a necklace of comfort.

"Answer me, baby girl."

Tears prickled. "I want you to force me to take you. I want to fight you. I want you to make me. I want to scream *no* over and over while every other part of me screams *yes*. There's something wrong with me. I don't know why I'm like this. You probably think I'm terrible."

"There's nothing wrong with you," he said gently. "That's called CNC. Consensual-non-consent. Have you heard of it?"

I shook my head, my cheeks flaming. For as long as I could remember, I'd had fantasies like that. And for the first time, I'd spoken them aloud, and instead of being shamed the way I expected, I was embraced.

His thumb brushed back and forth along my neck. "Open your eyes."

I did, but everything was blurry for a moment. I blinked tears away, seeing him.

Only Salt.

"Keep telling me," he urged.

"I imagine being tied up," I said. "I imagine being blind-folded. Spanked. Bruised. It's all I think about when I touch myself."

"How often do you touch yourself?"

"Every night. Every morning. Too much, probably. It was a problem when I was married."

He nodded, understanding shining in his face. "When you were married, did you ever tell him these things?"

"I tried."

Jeff had every right not to do something that made him uncomfortable, but the way he'd shut any sort of sexual explo-ration down with me still stung. That was part of why him cheating shocked the hell out of me. I thought he just didn't enjoy sex.

But really, he just didn't enjoy it with me.

"He said it was weird. That I needed god, but I don't believe in god. I stopped a long time ago. It was always a problem in our relationship."

"He didn't deserve you."

"Yeah." My voice was small. "Well, he never made me come, anyway. He'd fuck me and finish and then I'd go touch myself in the shower after and think about…"

"Being fucked the way you want."

I nodded slowly. "I want to hurt. But I want to feel good."

"I can give you both."

His promise made my heart skip a beat.

"I want it," I whispered. "I want it so badly. I want you. I want whatever you want to do to me. I know my safe word. I know you'll stop if I need you to."

"We'll try to go slow tonight. You'll need aftercare."

"I'll be fine."

"No," he said. "It's non-negotiable, Pepper. If you don't want aftercare, then we don't play. I know this is all new to you, but I've engaged in kinks like this for years. It's not something to be flippant about. I was mentored by someone who would literally disown me if I didn't do this the right way. After we finish, you'll need something. If you don't know what it is yet, that's fine, we'll figure it out. But I can't leave you right afterwards, unless you plan to call someone else."

He was serious about it. I mulled over his words, and then agreed. "Then stay the night. I couldn't tell you what kind of aftercare I might need. I don't even really get why it's needed."

"When you do things like this, you can have an endorphin drop," he said. "It can be really intense emotionally. It can bring up a lot."

"I'll be fine," I snorted. "But okay. So long as you leave before the sun rises."

"Okay." His nostrils flared and he released my throat, pulling me back to my feet. Before I could protest, he lifted me with an ease that made me yelp, my body now draped over his broad shoulder.

"Where's your bedroom in this money maze?"

"Down the hall on the right."

This was crazy. That's all I could think as he carried me through my apartment, humming as he looked at the walls full of framed records.

He slapped my ass, drawing out a sharp gasp. "I'm no mind reader, but I can feel how fucking tense you get when you're spiraling."

"I'm just losing my mind."

Salt stepped into my bedroom and took me to my bed, tossing me down on the center of the mattress. "You and me both."

SIX

SALT

PEPPER'S DRESS slid up her thighs, giving me a peek at her panties before she reached down to adjust it. I swatted her hand away with a *tsk*. "No," I said. "You won't hide yourself from me."

Her brown eyes widened, cheeks flaming cherry red.

For many reasons, I agreed with her. We'd lost our minds, this *was* a bad idea, and we weren't right for each other.

But the chemistry between us was corrosive—eating us alive with every second that passed. I *needed* her.

"Lift your skirt up," I demanded.

"No," she quipped.

"Then I'll leave." I started to turn, but she quickly sat up, grabbing my hand.

"Stop, stop," she said quickly. "Don't go. I'm not used to being told what to do."

I spun around and lunged onto the bed, enjoying her scream as I pinned her beneath me. My face hovered above hers, her body going still. "We don't have time for you to be a brat tonight," I said. "If you want to do this again, then we'll find another time for you to try and disobey. Understood?"

"Yes," she rasped.

I guided her arms above her head, holding her wrists together with one hand while I looked down over her body. She didn't like to be looked at this way. It made her uncomfortable. And I enjoyed watching her squirm.

It infuriated me that she didn't see herself the way I did. She didn't see how beautiful she was. Clearly, her ex-husband had done a number on her. It only made me want to show her that this type of hunger—this type of *carnal* desperation— wasn't *wrong*. In fact, it was normal.

I could safely say that kink, just like music, changed my life. Because of BDSM, I was able to engage and do things to other people in a way that didn't actually harm them.

Just like Pepper had always been masochistic, I'd always been sadistic.

I straddled her hips, studying every inch of her. The way her dark hair splayed out over the sheets, save for the silver highlights that framed her face. The countless freckles, like stars I wanted to taste. She shivered and I placed my hand on her chest, feeling her heart beat wildly, like a bird attempting to flee its cage. That's what she was—a caged bird, frantic to be free.

I liked knowing that only I held the key.

She swallowed audibly. "You're so hard."

I looked down at myself. My cock strained against my pants. I'd been hard for a while now, but my focus was on her.

And the way her pretty brown eyes glazed over with pure lust.

She craved corruption.

I craved corrupting her. Ruining her. Fucking her until she begged and cried and came over and over.

"Are you going to behave?" I asked her.

"I'll certainly try."

I kept my expression serious, but amusement flared. She kept making me laugh. It was a problem, because I liked people who could make me laugh.

She bucked her hips impatiently beneath me. "Cold feet? Scared of me?"

"No," I snorted.

I needed days with her, not one night. It wouldn't be enough.

I swooped down and bit her bottom lip. She squealed, shock eclipsing her bratty expression as I slid off her and then off the bed. I circled back to the foot, overlooking her like a king.

"Lift your fucking dress," I demanded. "Now."

Her pink tongue darted over the bite mark, lips swollen now. She reached down and grabbed the hem, pulling it up with clear discomfort.

"I didn't expect someone to come home with me," she whispered.

I ignored the self-depreciation. "The panties are coming off anyway," I said. "Why do you think wearing something comfortable would stop me from fucking you senseless? Take them off."

Her brows pulled together as she reached down, pulling them off quickly and tossing them to the floor. Her thighs immediately clamped shut, an attempt to hide herself from me.

"Spread them," I commanded.

"Spread..."

"Spread your legs."

She swallowed hard. "I don't like being looked at like this."

"Pepper," I said sharply. "I don't care. If you don't show me your pussy right now, then I'll force you to."

When she didn't immediately spread her fucking thighs, a laugh bubbled up from me. I was going to have to make her, I realized.

"What's your safe word?" I asked her.

"Red."

I grabbed my belt buckle and undid it quickly, pulling the strip of leather free. She gasped as I jumped back onto the bed and grabbed her hips, forcing her to roll over. She kicked back at me and missed, her yelp echoing through her room as she struggled against me.

My cock raged. Her fighting me was only turning me on more. I shoved her face into the blankets and hauled her ass over my lap, pulling her to the edge of the bed so I could balance her over my knee. Despite her squirming, she was no match for my strength.

She fought hard. I grunted as her nails raked down my arm, her cries growing louder as I slapped her ass with my belt.

A shriek pierced my ears, her body freezing.

I spanked her again, the leather snapping against her ass. She bucked, a series of curses tumbling from her lips.

"Is this what you want?" I growled, bringing the belt down again. Pepper screamed, still struggling. Fighting. Making my cock throb in a way that was going to be the death of me. "Being punished like a little brat, spanked and forced into submission. Fucking *answer* me. Now."

"Yes," she sobbed, reaching back to try and block the next spanking. I shoved her hand away, bringing the belt down. "*Fuck!* Fuck you!"

I pushed two fingers against her pussy. A haughty laugh escaped me. I knew she was turned on, but it was beyond satisfying to feel how wet her cunt was. I slid my fingers to her clit, using her wetness to tease her. "You're fucking soaked. This pretty little cunt is dripping for me."

I was trying to be a good Dom. I was trying to take this slow. I didn't want to drop her into the middle of a situation that would scare her or harm her.

But she was making the most delicious sounds.

Another sob loosened in her chest. I paused, but I didn't stop. I had to trust that she would use her safe word.

She'd made a promise.

I'd made a promise, too.

I spread my hand and spanked each asscheek repeatedly until her skin blossomed bright red, the blood coming to the surface along with heat. Angry streaks were left from the belt, but I wanted more.

She'd gone still, her body draping over me in acceptance. *Submission.*

"Fuck," I whispered to myself.

I savored it for a moment. Just a second. Long enough to recenter myself internally. I brought the belt strap down again, her cries ringing over and over with each spanking, until I felt her trembling and her ass was thoroughly marked. I dropped the belt, running my fingertips over her soaked slit.

"God, you're a slut," I whispered.

She sucked in a breath as I pulled my hand away. "*No.*"

"No?"

Her hips moved, begging for more.

"Use your words," I growled.

"I want you to touch me... there."

"Where?"

"*There.*"

I waited for her to actually say it. Because this was silly. We were adults, consenting adults, and I wanted her to use adult language. Finally, she looked over her shoulder and glared daggers.

"I want you to touch my pussy."

"Good girl," I praised, rubbing her ass gently. "Was that so hard?"

Every muscle tensed. "Yes."

I swept her hair out of her face and slid her off my lap to her knees. She looked up at me, mascara streaking down her cheeks. *Fuck.* My cock pulsed in response.

My imagination was running wild. The things I wanted to do with her. *To* her.

"Fuck," I mumbled, wiping her face gently. "Are you okay?"

"I didn't use my word, did I?" she asked, grabbing my hand. I paused, letting her guide it until she brought my fingers to her mouth.

"That's not the point of this type of power exchange," I whispered, my voice gravelly. "If you say your safe word, then everything stops. Because it's for your safety. So you don't get hurt. I don't want to harm you."

"You're not harming me."

She swiped her tongue over the same fingers that'd just been touching her pussy.

"I want you," she said. "I brought you home with me, remember?"

My cock jumped as she sucked my fingers. It was a pleasant surprise. I cradled the back of her head with my free hand, holding her in place as I shoved my fingers deeper. She moaned, her eyes rolling back as I pushed them to the back of her throat, but she wasn't gagging yet.

I felt her muscles seize and drew my fingers back, hooking her cheek.

"You are too fucking sexy," I said.

Her breaths were rapid. "I want more."

"I know." *Me too.* "Take off all your clothes."

She tucked her hair behind her ear and then lifted her

dress, pulling it free. All that was left now was her bra. I drank in every inch of her from her soft thighs to her stomach and hips to her full breasts as she got rid of the bra too. She sat naked in front of me, kneeling on the floor, her pussy wet and needy, her gaze raking me over coals of lust.

"What about you?" she asked curiously.

"You don't worry about me. For once, you don't need to worry about anyone else."

Her shoulders finally relaxed as she let my words soak in. I closed the distance between us, crushing her mouth against mine. She moaned softly as she took our kiss deeper, her tongue fighting against mine until she truly gave up control.

It was taking every ounce of restraint not to undo my fly, put her on the bed, and fuck her. My cock raged, all my blood flowing directly toward it. I wanted to fuck her endlessly, but I wanted to take my time. I didn't know if there would be another moment like this with her, and so I wasn't going to rush it.

Her arms wound around my neck. I grunted and lifted her, pulling her legs around my waist. The heat of her pussy rested against my straining cock, her hips rocking as she held onto me, grinding against me.

Fuck.

Maybe I couldn't be patient. Fuck, maybe I wasn't as well-behaved as I'd believed. I wrapped my arms around her, covering her mouth as I drew us to the center of the bed. "I can't take this anymore," I growled.

"What are you—"

I flipped her around, her ass pressing against my cock, still muffling her with one hand while the other slid over her pussy.

Pepper whimpered, pushing her ass back against me as I slid two fingers against her clit. Her muscles strained, her voice lost as I pinned her leg with mine, trapping her while I rubbed her clit in quick circles.

"You're going to come for me."

"*No.*"

"Yes," I snarled.

Her whimpers vibrated against me as I pressed my lips to her ear. "You're mine," I rasped. "Mine to fuck and mine to play with. Mine to make come over and over again until you're my perfect little mess."

She bucked, fighting the pleasure. Fuck, she was fighting it, her whimpers and moans growing louder. I strained to keep her under control, my muscles rippling as I held her down.

"Your pleasure is my *gift* to you," I growled. "You're going to come for me even if you don't want to. I don't care what you want. Only what *I* want, and that's for you to come on my fingers."

I kept circling her clit and then dipped two fingers inside of her, holding tight as she stiffened against me, a longer moan drawn out as I started to fuck her with them. Even with how wet she was, she was still tight, milking my fingers with her silky cunt. I added a third, the wet vulgar noises echoing through her bedroom.

I brought my hand at her mouth to her throat, her shout making my ears ring as I wrestled her, driving her further and further to the edge.

"No," she sobbed. "I feel like I'm going to pee—"

"I'm not stopping," I growled.

"No, no, no—"

I kept going. Was she going to squirt? I wanted her to. I wanted that to happen more than anything else.

"No! I don't want to! I don't want to," she cried. "*Fuck!*"

Her body arched like a bow, her strangled gasp lost as I

forced her to come. Hot liquid gushed over my hand, and fuck—

Blinding light followed as I came in my pants, unable to stop myself after making her squirt. I cursed, shaking against her as my cum wet my jeans, my cock bursting at the seams.

"Fuck," I rasped. "*Pepper.*"

She melted against me, both of us panting. I couldn't think straight. I closed my eyes, my head spinning.

"Oh my god," she squeaked. "Did I just—"

"That wasn't piss, baby. You squirted," I said, tightening my arms around her before she could roll away. "*Stay.*"

It was a command. Pepper went still, her body stiff for a few seconds before she seemed to accept that I wasn't letting her go.

"Did you come just now?" she whispered.

"Yes. Making you squirt made me come in my pants," I gritted out.

"Oh."

I hadn't seen that coming. Maybe I should have, given how hard I'd been for so long, but it was *her* that sent me over the edge. I thought about her begging, and then frowned.

CNC was something I thoroughly enjoyed, but without fail, there was always a rush of concern that came after. Did I hurt her? Did I actually harm her? Did I do anything wrong? What if—

"Are you okay?" I asked, my eyes flying open.

"Yes," she said. "I'm more than okay."

My worries eased a fraction. "Good. You said no a lot."

"I thought that was part of CNC?"

"Well, it is. That doesn't mean I don't feel worried."

"Oh. That makes sense. I've never... squirted before."

I closed my eyes and pressed my face against her hair. Her scent was smokey and addicting, making my mouth water.

"Well, I've never come in my pants from making someone squirt before."

Her soft laugh made me smile.

"Salt."

"Yes?"

She turned slightly, looking over her shoulder at me. "I want to see your tattoos. Please. I'll be good for you."

My cock perked up at that promise.

"I'm just curious about how many you have."

Amused, I nodded and rolled over onto my back, watching her through slanted eyes as she sat up, and then looked down at herself.

Her cheeks were flushed, her hair mussed. "I made a mess. I should clean up."

"We'll clean up after I fuck you a few times."

Pink brightened her face. "Oh. Okay."

"Take off my clothes, Pepper."

She hesitated for a moment, but then her head tilted. Her fingers grazed over my jeans until they met the button. She unzipped me and then unbuttoned them. I lifted my hips so she could pull them down, taking my boxers too. Her mouth dropped as my cock sprang free, slick with cum.

"Fuck," she whispered, her tongue darting over her bottom lip.

"You can taste me if you want," I whispered.

Her hand hovered over my cock for a moment, but then she slid her fingers around me gently. Tentative. I sucked in a breath from her touch, my heart pounding.

"This would kill me," she mumbled, giving me a stroke.

"Pepper," I gritted out. "Suck my fucking cock."

"Yes, Sir."

Fuck. Fuck me. I propped myself up and watched as she lowered her lips to the head, that sweet tongue brushing the tip.

I shivered, fighting every instinct that told me to grab a fistful of her hair and face fuck her.

Not yet. I liked watching her explore me. I liked seeing the light of discovery on her face as she did things she'd never done before.

This was one of my favorite things about sex and kink. The release of societal expectations, the giving in to pure desire. The trust that would bind us together.

Her eyes lifted to mine as she slowly took me into her mouth.

Fuck. She looked at me like I was the center of the universe. I was trapped in her brown eyes, my cock jerking against her tongue as she took me deeper.

I ground my teeth together, my fingers gripping the blankets. She started to suck me, her eyes watering as she tried to take me deep. *Patience. Patience. Fucking patience.* That word kept drilling in my head as I made myself still, allowing her to find her rhythm.

"Good girl," I praised. "Fuck. You feel so good."

She pulled off for a moment. "Am I bad at this?"

"No," I growled. "Keep sucking me, Pepper, before I fuck your throat without mercy."

SEVEN
PEPPER

I KEPT VOLLEYING between the fear that I was terrible at this and the raw pleasure corrupting me.

Salt's words hummed through me.

Keep sucking me, Pepper, before I fuck your throat without mercy.

The thing was, I wanted him to face fuck me.

I wanted him to be rough. I wanted to be used without mercy.

Something was happening to me, a dark yearning brought to the surface, eager to get a taste of what was happening between us.

My gaze trailed up his hard stomach to where his eyes feasted on me. Pleasure raptured his beautiful face, all the harsh lines of his jaw and cheekbones cast golden by the bedroom lights. I took his cock deeper, the salty taste of his cum sitting on my tongue. He grunted, his hips flexing, pushing his cock further.

Serving him felt *right.*

I loved the taste of him. I wanted to do this for hours. I

could stay on my knees here, licking and teasing and sucking as long as he demanded.

I just wanted to make him come again.

A whimper escaped between sucking motions, my eyes watering as he hit the back of my throat. Salt released a low hiss, his hips bucking again.

"Fuck," he grunted, his fingers flexing. Inked thorns and roses climbed up his forearms, veins bulging as he gripped the blankets. His body was a museum, intricate designs blending with simple ones. The word *mine* was inked on the inside of his wrist. Possessive and demanding, just like him. "Fuck. You feel so good, Pepper. Are you wet, baby? Touch yourself."

His words spun around me, wrapping me in their silky filth. I slid two fingers down to my pussy as I kept sucking, moaning. I pulled off just for a moment. "I'm so turned on," I rasped. "I've never felt like this with someone before."

"Me neither, baby." I wasn't sure if I believed him, even though he sounded genuinely tortured. His graveled voice became raspy as he reached for me. "Come here."

The way he manhandled me sent a wave of shock through my entire body. I squeaked as he pulled me over him, turning me so my knees pressed into the blankets above his shoulders. "Wait," I protested. "What are you doing?"

"Sit on my face while you choke on my cock," he demanded.

"I don't want to hurt you—"

He slapped my ass hard enough I gasped.

"You won't hurt me," he said. His fingertips dug into my hips and he brought my pussy down on his face, shock rolling through me as his tongue brushed my clit.

Fuck. I went still, my brain short circuiting. Jeff had always refused to go down on me because he said it was gross, but Salt was *demanding* it. His breath was hot against my pussy, his fingers kneading me as his tongue circled my clit, drawing involuntary moans from me.

No one had ever touched me like this before. Without hesitation, without making some backhanded comment about my body. I'd always imagined someone wanting me like this, but I'd never experienced it. I was unnerved by his touch.

Was I too much? What if he didn't like the taste of me? What if hurt him?

He suddenly slapped my ass again, shattering all of my self-doubt. His tongue drew back. "Pepper, I swear to fucking god if you don't suck my cock right now, I'm going to force you to."

That only made the pulsing between my thighs more intense.

He could tell. A low growl left him as he pushed a finger inside of me, rubbing a spot inside me that made me yelp.

"Fuck," I groaned "What are you doing to me?"

"Pleasing you."

A shiver rolled down my spine as I looked down at his beautiful cock, thick with veins bulging along the shaft. I circled the base and guided him to my mouth as he lapped at my clit.

I could barely think straight as I started to suck. My eyes closed as I focused on the sensation of him gliding in and out of my mouth, the weight of his cock on my tongue. He held me firmly in place, even as I tried to keep my weight lifted off him.

Teeth sank into my ass cheek and I cried out.

"Sit on my face. *Now.*"

His hand slid up my side to the back of my head. He shoved me down, and I choked around his cock as he pulled my pussy on his face, forcing my full weight on him, forcing me to stay put. I struggled against him, but he didn't let up.

Fuck. My entire body buzzed with electricity, pleasure pumping through me. I whimpered, tears streaming down my cheeks as he lessened the pressure on the back of my head for just a moment before pushing it back down, creating a choppy rhythm, fucking my throat as he sucked my clit.

The sensations flooded every part of me, overwhelming me until I was nothing but a wet, shaking fuck toy. The mere thought of being his to use dragged me close to the edge again, another orgasm threatening to overtake me.

He didn't let up. My toes curled as I choked around him, coming right on his face, his tongue driving in and out of me and catching every drop of my pleasure. He released his hold on my head, allowing me to come up for full gasps of air, my nails digging into his thighs as I arched back.

"Good girl," he panted against my pussy. His tongue darted out, licking me again. He moaned, getting lost in the taste of me.

The bliss lasted for a few moments, but then something ugly and unwanted raised its head. Panic? Fear? What in the hell was I doing? What was I thinking?

I immediately rolled off him and the bed, only for his hand to snatch my wrist and drag me back against him.

"No," he said. "You're not running."

"*Stop*," I gasped. "This was a mistake. This was..."

"Pepper," he said gently, grabbing hold of my cheeks.

He forced me to look at him, so I closed my eyes.

"What just happened?" he murmured.

"I don't know. I feel like I'm losing my mind." I was shaking. I wanted more. I wanted so much more, but I didn't know how to ask for it. For the first time in fifteen years, I found myself needing more from someone than they needed from me.

He stroked my face gently with his thumbs—patient. Too patient.

"Stop looking at me," I muttered, squeezing my eyes shut

even tighter. I could *feel* him, just like I did in the coffee shop. His presence suffocated me. It freed me.

"No."

"I hate this."

"I don't."

My eyes flew open to glare. "Fuck you."

His skin glistened from my pussy, and he licked his lips. "You're more than welcome to again if you want."

I shoved at his chest, but he caught hold of my hands.

"What's your safe word?" he asked.

My breath caught in my throat.

"We can stop. At any time. Any moment. I told you that earlier, and I meant it." His dark brows pulled together in concern. "I can't tell what is happening right now because you're not telling me. Do you want me to actually stop?"

I didn't want it to end. I didn't want any of this to end. "No," I whispered.

His shoulders relaxed a fraction. "Then use your words."

Heat flamed in my cheeks. I was embarrassed. "I've never been with anyone like this. And I don't know what to do with myself. I feel like I'm doing everything wrong. I came but then I felt humiliated. I've never squirted before, and then you made me come again, but... I've never had sex with someone who actually made me orgasm."

Something hot glinted in his eyes. "That's a tragedy, honestly. You don't like it when you're not the one in control, do you? It's unfamiliar."

I nodded. "I hate it. But there's relief in it? And now I'm naked in front of a stranger ten years younger than me, having a breakdown. If anyone knew about this—"

"Pepper. Stop." He dragged me close, his arms wrapping around me. I wasn't sure what he was going to do to me, but then he just...

He just hugged me.

Salt was hugging me.

Tears burned as I slowly pressed my face against his chest.

"You need someone who will make you forget about all of that," he murmured. "Someone with a firm hand, hmm? Someone who won't judge you for whatever you want to try."

I nodded. "Yes."

His fingers massaged the back of my head, working magic. A shiver rolled through me and I leaned into him. My spiral was winding down, but then a wave of guilt followed for ruining the night.

"I'm sorry," I whispered. "I ruined this."

"No, you didn't. Do you feel like you're falling off a ledge and have no idea if you'll survive hitting the bottom?"

"Yes," I croaked.

"That's called sub drop. Which is why I wanted to make sure I was ready with some sort of aftercare."

"Oh."

"It's normal, Pepper."

Normal. For some reason, that helped. Maybe it was knowing that I wasn't completely flawed or broken. He kept massaging my head, drawing out a groan from me. "You know a lot about this stuff," I mumbled.

"I do. Which is why I think we should get some water and relax."

I frowned and looked up at him. "But don't you want more?"

"Of course I do," he snorted. "But for now, we're going to take a shower and I'm going to massage your shoulders."

My lips formed a pout. I wanted him to fuck me. "I don't want this to end, though."

"It doesn't have to," he whispered. "But we do need to take a break for now."

A flash of disappointment came first, followed by a flood of emotions, all of them tied up in the hidden, ugly insecurities I kept from the rest of the world. But he saw them. And that horrified me.

Protect yourself. Protect. The cool, intellectual part of me took over, smothering everything else. "This is just a one night stand," I said.

He *laughed.* "Yeah." His hands slid down my body, cupping my ass. "We'll see."

I yelped as I was suddenly lifted, his muscles hard against me as he held me like a bride.

"Oh my god," I hissed. "You're insane."

"I can be. Where's the shower?"

I shook my head at him, but pointed at a doorway on the other side of my bedroom. He carried me across the room, flipped on the light, and let out a low whistle.

"Music industry pays well."

I couldn't remember the last time I saw my bathroom through new eyes. I was used to the luxuries I'd afforded myself. This bathroom was literally the reason why I'd wanted this apartment in the first place. Jeff could keep the house in Green Hills—it didn't have the deep soaking tub or the gorgeous shower or the pristine counters or countless mirrors. Black-and-gray marbled tiles swept up from the floors and climbed the walls, a rack holding my silk robe and a stack of fluffy towels.

"I've been lucky," I said. "I didn't have anything like this growing up."

"No? Where did you grow up?" His gaze was still sweeping over everything, taking it all in. For a moment, he looked even younger.

Fuck. I hesitated. Why did I even mention anything? I

didn't talk about the past or my childhood for a multitude of reasons. "Small town. Where did you grow up?"

He tensed, his expression tightening. "A little outside North Nashville. Let's forget about any of that."

I nodded, eager to leave it behind, too. He took me to the shower and opened the door, setting me down gently.

Salt scowled. "How the fuck does this shower work?"

I snorted as I touched a button on the wall, the screen lighting up. The water temperature was already set to how I liked it, and with one more press, the water streamed from overhead.

"Magic," I said.

My stomach flipped as he stepped closer, slowly backing me against the shower wall. Hot water rolled down his back, licking his thorny vines and rose tattoos as the door shut and steam began to fill the space.

"Are you... are you sure you don't want more?" I asked.

"I do want more," he said. "But I also want to take care of you right now."

"Why? You don't have any reason to," I said.

Salt's eyes danced with a hint of amusement. He didn't say anything though, instead dragging me to the center, water rinsing down my body. The heat felt good, all of my muscles relaxing. I shut my eyes and tipped my head back, my awareness of him only growing more acute. But the discomfort was slowly fading. It had been a long time since I'd showered with someone else, and while I was painfully aware of the fact that we were standing completely naked together, it didn't feel as foreign as it had minutes before.

His fingers grazed up my side, cupping my breasts. I whimpered, eyes flying open. The look on his face was one of pure reverence, undoing me completely. I swayed against him, leaning up on my tiptoes to kiss him.

He took control, his tongue sweeping against mine. I wound my arms around his neck, finding myself lifted, legs winding around his waist. He moaned, kissing me harder, his hunger making me wet in other ways.

"Damn it," he muttered between kisses. "*Pepper.*"

I didn't care. I rocked my hips, grinding against him. "I want you," I whined. "I want to know what you feel like inside me. Only for tonight."

He hissed between clenched teeth. "I don't want to do anything you might regret."

"Would you regret it?"

Salt frowned. "No."

"Then I won't either."

His gaze searched my face, his brows drawing together. "Do you always get what you want?"

"*Always.*"

"Do you want to know how to get me to do what you want?"

"How?" I asked.

"*Beg,*" Salt demanded. "I told you earlier I'm not fucking you until you beg for it, Pepper. Beg me for this cock. Beg me to breed your needy little cunt. *Beg* me to fuck you until you forget who you are."

EIGHT

PEPPER

I KNEW HOW TO BEG.

It'd been a really, really long time since I had to. All that I'd begged for in the past were things I never should have needed to beg for to begin with. The unadulterated desperation was for something I should have never lost.

Everything I'd begged for in my life came roaring back.

A mother who loved me.

A father who loved me.

A husband who loved me.

A *god* who loved me.

Begging never gave me what I wanted. My mother, father, husband, god—none of them loved me. None of them ever saw me, heard me, cared for me.

But begging Salt to fuck me? He heard me. He saw me. I knew he would follow through. He would hear my prayers and grant my dirty wishes. He'd give me exactly what I so desperately wanted—I was willing to do *anything* for a taste. A touch.

"*Please*," I whispered. "Please."

Steam danced between our lips. I was drowning in his presence. Suddenly, he put me down, releasing me.

"*Salt.*"

He turned, reaching for the shower door.

"Salt, please," I said, my voice growing needier. "I want to feel you inside of me. I want..."

The door started to open. *No, no, no.* My chance was slipping away.

"Salt," I yelled, my knees buckling.

I went to the floor. The tiles were cool against my flesh, the drops of water hot. They streamed down my face as my heart hammered. "Please," I gasped. "Please. Please fuck me with your cock."

He didn't move a muscle.

"I want you to breed my needy little cunt." I couldn't believe I'd just said that, but the words were out and I meant every desperate one of them. "Please, Salt. Please. I need to feel you. I need to be fucked. It's been too long. No one has ever made me come during sex before you. No one has ever made me feel this way."

"Feel what way?"

"Desperate," I rasped. "Needy. Please. *Please, please.*"

He turned slightly, his dark hair much longer when wet. It curled down the back of his neck and his face. He pushed it out of his eyes, finally looking at me.

Even his gaze landing on me made me feel desperate.

"Please fuck me," I whispered. "I need it. I need it more than anything else."

"You need my cock more than anything else?"

"Yes." My lips buzzed with the admission. "More than anything else. I need it to live."

The corner of his mouth tugged. "You need my *cock* to live?"

"Yes. Please. *Please.*"

When he turned around, I sucked in a breath. Fuck, he was hard. He was beautiful. The door shut behind him as he stepped closer, his cock right in front of my face.

"Earn it," he said.

How? I wasn't sure how. My tongue dragged over my lip as I looked at him, drinking in the length and girth of him. It was rude to think about my ex-husband's dick while on my knees for another man, but I couldn't help but think—

I'd been missing out.

"I don't know how," I said.

"You're a smart girl. You'll figure it out."

I bit my bottom lip.

Earn it. I ran my hands up his thighs and gently cupped his balls. His cock twitched, pre-cum dripping from the tip. I opened my mouth wide and showed him my tongue, noticing the way his breath huffed out.

I licked the tip. Just a gentle lick.

His hands settled at his sides, flexing. I wound my fingers around the base of his cock, stroking him as I sucked the head, taking him deeper. All while maintaining eye contact and praying he'd fuck me.

It was all I wanted.

"Please," I rasped between sucks. "Please take me with this cock."

"Take you?" he questioned. "Such a romantic word. *Taking.*"

"Please fuck me with this cock."

"Better."

His praise encouraged me to keep going.

"Please breed my pussy with this cock." *Oh god.* Had I really just said that?

Salt smiled. "Good. I like that."

Before I had a chance to respond, he gripped my hair, sliding his cock in my mouth until he hit the back of my throat. My eyes rolled back, my pussy pulsing.

Maybe I was a cock slut.

Maybe this was what I'd been waiting for my entire life.

I sank into him, letting him use me, giving myself to him. I choked around him and he drew back, groaning.

"Stand up."

I got to my feet and he pressed the button on the wall, turning off the shower. He dragged me into a kiss as he backed me out of the shower, water dripping from our naked bodies as we made our way back to the bed.

Suddenly I was falling back. I gasped as I landed on the bed, pushing myself back as he followed me, kneeling between my legs.

"Do you have lube?" he asked.

I shook my head. "No. I haven't needed it."

His expression flashed with surprise. "Not even for toys?"

"I... I don't have any."

"Seriously?" he grumbled. "How the fuck have you been masturbating? Just with your fingers? You need to treat this pussy better."

I swallowed hard. "We shouldn't need any, though. I'm really wet—"

"Oh, I know you are," he said. "But lube is still important. We'll make it work. Spread your legs further apart."

I felt a jolt deep in my stomach as I spread them further for him. The way he looked at me made me want to swoon, scream, and hide all at the same time.

Salt stroked himself. Water droplets clung to his smooth skin, from his broad shoulders to the V-line of his hips.

"Touch yourself. Show me how wet you are for my cock."

I reached down and touched my clit first. A bolt of need

rocked through me from my fingertips, cool to the touch as I slid them inside myself.

My pussy was weeping for him.

Begging. Begging for his cock.

"I'm so wet," I gasped.

"Good." He moved closer, planting a hand next to my head.

We both watched as he lowered the head of his cock to my entrance. He was slow, gentle. I moaned as Salt pushed his cock inside of me, taking his sweet time as he gave me the first couple of inches. My pussy stretched around him, a sharp breath trapped in my throat.

"*Fuck*," he moaned. "You're squeezing me."

"Sorry," I gasped.

"Don't do that. Don't apologize."

All I could do was nod as I adjusted to the size of him. I clenched around his cock, my pussy reshaping for him. I whimpered and bucked my hips, taking more of him.

"Patience," he demanded.

It was hard to be patient, though. It'd been so long since I'd been with someone, and now that he was inside me, all I wanted was more. I wanted the rest of his cock slamming into me relentlessly while I screamed his name until my voice was hoarse.

"Please," I moaned. "Please. I want you to use me. I can take you."

Salt leaned down, his lips brushing mine. I arched against him right as he drove the last few inches in, taking me completely. He swallowed my gasp, our kiss all consuming.

I clenched around him, moaning as he dragged back and thrusted again.

"This poor pussy has been neglected," he growled against my lips.

"It has," I cried. "It has. It's needed you."

"I know." He thrusted harder, slowly building up the rhythm, giving me time to adjust to him.

"Fuck," I moaned. "Fuck. It feels so good."

He kissed me again, biting my bottom lip hard. The pain shot through me, coupled with the pleasure of him pumping in and out, his cock filling me with each stroke.

"You feel so good."

I kissed down his jaw, lost in the feel of him. I sucked the side of his neck, biting hard enough that he groaned and drew back, eyes blazing.

"You bit me." He sounded surprised.

It felt like I'd made a mistake in doing so for a moment, but then he started to fuck me harder. All worries disappeared, everything melting away.

I had no thoughts in my head as he fucked me with the same passion as when he played guitar, his body creating a melodic slapping rhythm with mine. I chanted his name over and over, my arms wound around his neck, pleasure bombarding my system in wave after wave.

"Harder," I gasped. "*Please*. Use me however you need to."

Salt groaned. "*Fuck*, Pepper."

Something snapped inside him. His control, his restraint. Every touch and movement turned harsher. My screams echoed through the bedroom as he fucked me without mercy, pinning me down into the blankets. His hand closed around my throat, my arms falling back above my head as he held me in place, his brows pulling together as he stared down at me.

In that moment, he was my savior. He was my god. A sense of subservient reverence washed over me as his fingers squeezed the sides of my neck, my breath lost as his cock speared me.

I'd give him anything. Anything he wanted. Any part of me.

My lips parted on a hoarse cry, my body bowing as an orgasm twisted around me, my cunt squeezing him. He cursed but didn't slow, instead doubling down on the rhythm he created until I released a sob as my orgasm ebbed.

"I hope you're on birth control."

What? The alarm bells rang through me, my eyes flying open as he gave one final thrust. Heat filled me as he came hard, his head tipping back.

I stared in awe, savoring him. His expression, his body, the way his cock pumped me full of his seed. He sighed, relaxing slightly, looking at me once more. I leaned up, capturing his mouth against mine, our lips meeting again in a fevered kiss. His cock pulsed inside me, reminding me that the fullness was from him.

His kisses softened until he pressed his forehead to mine. "Sorry," he whispered. "I didn't ask."

"I told you to use me," I whispered back. My throat constricted and I averted my gaze. "I can't have kids, so don't worry."

He turned my face, forcing me to look at him. "Do you want them?"

I thought about Paisleigh and her screaming. Then I thought about my mother, and her screaming. The older I got, the more I understood why my mother slowly lost her mind.

"No," I finally said. "I don't think I'd be a good mom."

"I don't think I'd be a good dad."

For some reason, that comforted me.

He kissed my forehead gently. "Doesn't mean I don't have a breeding kink, though."

A laugh bubbled up. I grinned as he leaned back and

grabbed hold of my legs, pushing them far apart as he focused on my pussy. "Mmm. You're such a mess."

"I guess we have to take a shower again," I said shyly.

He snorted and shook his head. He pulled out quickly and then made me squeal as he folded me in half, nestling his face between my thighs.

"*Salt*," I gasped.

I couldn't twist away. His grip on me tightened, his tongue spreading me and lapping up his cum.

"Fuck," I gasped. "Oh my god."

"What? I like the taste of us together. I want to remember it all weekend."

I didn't have a chance to respond. I moaned, my head flopped back as he licked me, thorough with his cleanup. He didn't stop until I was shaking again.

"I can't," I moaned. "I can't come again."

I felt raw and exposed. He'd used my pussy for hours and I'd lost track of how many orgasms he'd given me.

"Too bad," he huffed.

"Salt," I whimpered, curling my fingers in his dark hair.

But he didn't let up, his tongue working my clit as he slid two fingers inside me, coaxing my pleasure to the surface again, forcing me back to the edge.

"I can't."

"I'm not really giving you a choice," he said.

I gripped the blankets, bucking against him as he kept teasing me. Every muscle coiled as he patiently played with me, not letting up until I was a panting, wet mess.

He knew I was close. I thought I didn't have anything left in me, but I was wrong. His fingers slid in and out faster, his tongue circling my clit relentlessly until finally—I came for him again, a euphoric rush burning me up.

"Good girl," he praised as I came down from the high.

I couldn't think, couldn't move. I melted into the bed, my eyes closing slowly as he settled down next to me. His arm slid around my waist and he turned me on my side, pulling me against him.

"Did I do well?" I whispered.

"Yes." His answer came without hesitation. "Did I?"

I was taken aback by the vulnerability. Maybe I wasn't the only one experiencing new things tonight. "Yes," I said. "Thank you."

He hummed. "Sleep."

I didn't want to.

"When you wake up, I'll be gone," he said softly.

And that was the problem.

I didn't want him to go.

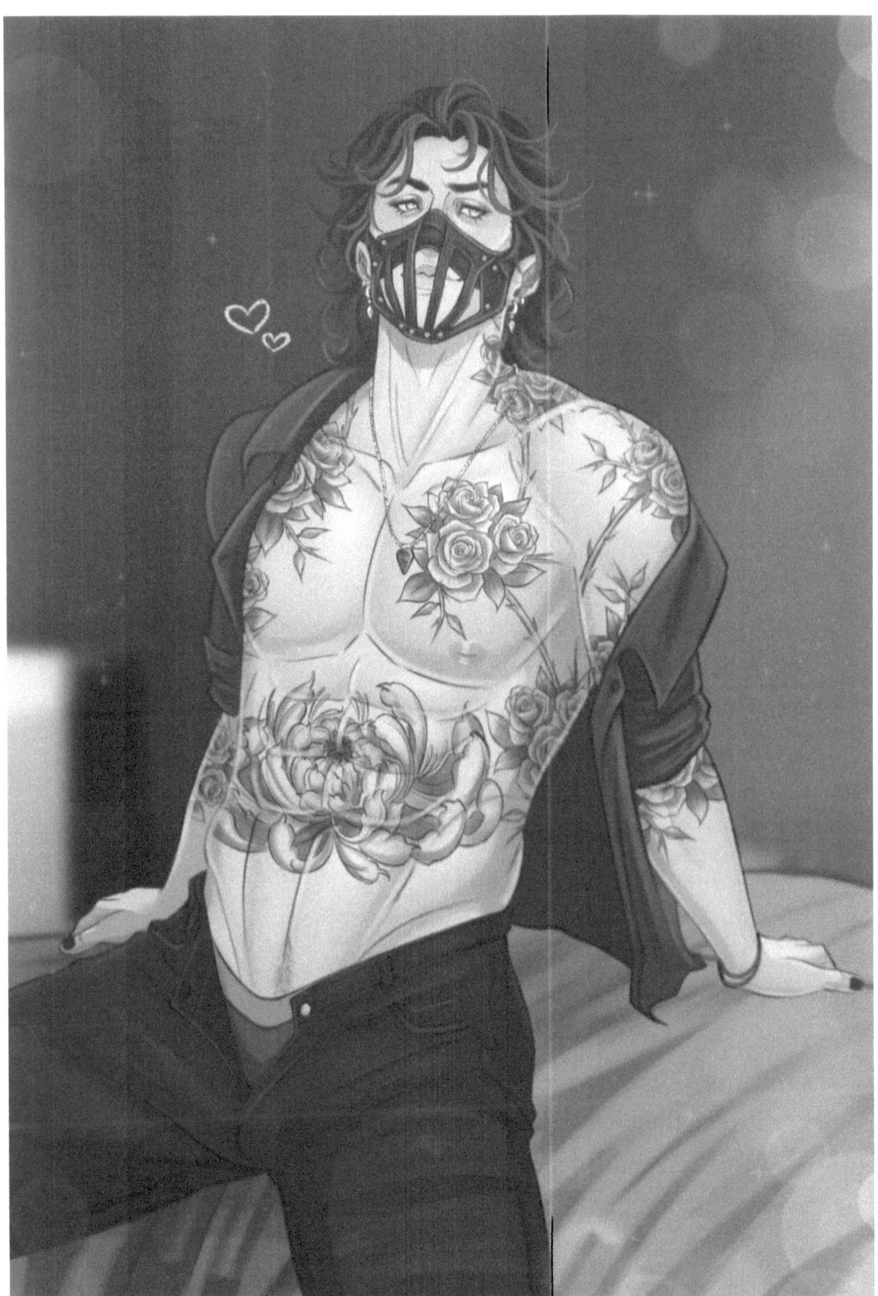

NINE
SALT

I LEFT before the sun rose, just like we agreed.

My entire body resisted each step I took away from Pepper, but I needed to leave before we did anything else stupid. I managed to make it to the nearest bus stop, guitar in hand, and begin the long ride home. It'd take about thirty minutes, which was plenty of time to think about what the fuck had happened last night.

I'd left her a note, at least, with my phone number and a few words.

I want more. If you want more, text me.

Her choice.

Last night was something I'd never forget. The scent of her still clung to me, and my eyes shuttered closed as I leaned back in the seat, the bus jostling over the narrow downtown streets.

I'd been with countless people over the years. Men, women, nonbinary people. I'd been in group scenes, in one-on-one scenes, and participated in orgies that lasted for days. I loved sex. I loved fucking. I loved kink and BDSM, the give and take of being a Dom. I knew how to do it all, too. I knew how to spank, flog, whip, use sensations like heat or cold, do wax play, and more.

I loved dominating others in the bedroom, turning them on, and making them beg for more.

But last night with Pepper?

Something about her had altered everything I knew about BDSM.

I *wanted* her. Just *her*. Her submission and exploration were stray sparks that kindled the dry waste of my soul into a roaring flame.

It turned me on knowing that she was older. She had a career she built from the ground up. She was a powerful woman who was always in control, always making decisions. I'd seen snippets of that part of her in how she spoke to me at the club when other people were around. It was evident in the way she spoke and carried herself.

But she'd knelt for me. She'd obeyed me. She'd opened up a door to submission, and seeing the way she melted right into it made me want to do other things with her.

She's been so adamant that I was too young. That what we'd done was crazy. But she'd also opened up about her desires, finally giving into them. Giving them a chance.

How many more kinks were there under that tough exterior? Just waiting for someone to come along and coax them out?

The thing about me was that I didn't care what other people would think of us together. Then again, I didn't have a reputation to protect the way she did.

Any music career I might have had was probably fucked now, though. One, I doubted she'd text me. Two, I also doubted I'd ever hear from Rosethorn again.

I sighed. I thought that being with her would satiate the craving, but I'd been wrong. Selfishly, I just wanted more, more, more. More of her riding my cock, more leaving marks on her, more claiming her as mine.

The sadistic part of me screamed for her submission.

My phone buzzed in my pocket. My heart jumped to my throat as I pulled it out. Would it be her?

Hey Salt, it's Tommy! Hope it's okay I grabbed your contact info from Adam. Do you have time to schedule a meeting next week?

"What the fuck?" I whispered.

He was really persistent. I had to give him that.

But did that mean Pepper had already reached out to him? I'd left her sleeping in her bed, sheets tangled around her, dark hair splayed out. Her expression while sleeping was so damn peaceful.

Fuck. I bit my bottom lip hard enough for the pain to snap me out of thinking about her again, but only for a split second.

This was one of my problems. The moment someone showed even the slightest genuine interest in me, I attached myself to them like a damn vampire. And it didn't help that the chemistry between us was unlike anything I'd ever experienced before. It also didn't help that she was so new to exploring her kinks.

I liked teaching.

I liked corrupting.

I blinked, staring at Tommy's text. I didn't know what to think. What was I supposed to do?

I'd been playing guitar since I was a kid, and it was one of the only things my father would ever do with me. In moments of rare parental attention, he'd teach me how to play a few chords. Probably out of guilt for beating the shit out of me other times. But those moments still sat with me, shiny pennies gleaming on a muddy street.

Playing music made me enough money to survive until Nancy and Beth adopted me into their lives. It had been a lifeline over the years.

I wasn't sure any of the songs I'd written were actually good, but people seemed to like them. And being on stage was maybe the closest to paradise I'd ever be.

I needed to think about my career, and if this was something I really wanted. Did I want my music to become a product they could sell?

Was I going to let other people in my home?

Having a band was a start. I loved the sound we created together, even if I didn't necessarily like working with other people. Jack, Eric, and Tyler had made a difference in live shows though. A good difference.

I wanted to be on the stage.

I wanted to be seen by the whole damn world.

If my father were still alive, I'd show him what I'd done. What I'd built. I wasn't worthless and cursed, I was good and talented. *Right?*

All of my emotions piled together into a big, ugly, erratic ball—but then there was last night. There was Pepper. And all I could think about was that setting up a meeting with Tommy would give me another reason to see her.

My fingers moved rapidly and I typed out a message, pressing send before I second guessed myself.

Hey! I have time early next Friday

His reply was almost immediate.

> Yep, I'll make that work. 10 a.m.? Send me an email address, and I'll send an official invite with everything

I didn't even have an official email for my music. I mean, I had the one I used to sign up for all my social media accounts, but it was a personal one.

"Damn it," I muttered.

It didn't matter, right?

> saltybitch01110 @ gmail.com

Nice

The pressure at the back of my head eased. I exhaled and relaxed into my seat, looking out the window. I watched Nashville pass by, and tried not to get my hopes up.

This was just a meeting. It didn't actually mean anything— I knew how the music industry was.

Pepper was just another shark. And I was throwing myself into the deep end while bathed in blood.

I liked that type of power exchange. It made her submission last night that much sweeter.

I scrolled away from Tommy's text and hummed to myself, checking my other messages. Jack texted me a couple times about setlist notes. I'd forgotten to pay all of them out last night, so I did that quickly before opening up Instagram. I instantly regretted it—too many notifications, not enough coffee. Still, I started scrolling anyway.

Before the show, I'd posted a video of a riff from one of my songs. I'd gotten pretty good at lighting and creating a mood in my videos, and it was finally paying off. I chuckled as I read the comments, smirking at the thirsty ones and rolling my eyes at the nastier ones. I posted a couple of pictures I'd taken backstage before the show last night and then closed the app again.

I needed a hot shower. I needed to purge Pepper from my rotten soul, and head over to Nancy and Beth's to finish building a couple pieces of furniture.

And decide if I was actually going to show up for that meeting with Rosethorn.

TEN
SALT

THE WORKSHOP DOOR was wide open, letting in a draft of cool air. I crossed the threshold and wasn't surprised to see Beth tied down to one of the sex benches we'd built on Thursday. Nancy stood to the side with a very evil grin on her face, one that made me chuckle.

"Do I need to come back later?" I asked.

Nancy shook her head. "No. Just making sure the product is well-built."

"Uh-huh," I said as I hung my backpack on the hook.

The workshop was a massive three-car garage with everything we'd ever need for furniture construction. A grid wall held every tool imaginable, lumber was neatly stacked, and cans of wood finishes sat on the floor.

Then there was the wall on the opposite side that held every *kink* tool imaginable. That was Nancy's side of the garage, where she stored her floggers, whips, riding crops, and whatever else she'd gathered over two decades of putting people on their knees.

Beth's bright blue eyes were full of smiles as I approached

and crossed my arms. She was wearing gray sweats and a black sweater with a rooster—*a cock*—on it. She was about a foot shorter than me with curves for days, and a neon pink mohawk that was hard to miss.

Nancy, on the other hand, was willowy, tall, and wore her hair in a silver bob. A lot of people looked at her and assumed she was more passive, but that wasn't true at all.

It was weird to other people maybe, but I really did think of the two of them as my adoptive moms. But in a way that was like—kink-godmothers? Was that even a thing? It was for us. I'd drive them to doctor appointments, do a load of their laundry, but would pretend to gag if they kissed in a romantic way. I'd seen both of them naked at one of the BDSM clubs downtown countless times, but was still completely scandalized from the one time I accidentally walked in on them having sex. That was like three years ago, and my eyes still hadn't recovered.

A big misunderstanding about the kink community was that everything was sexual. Seeing Beth tied down on a sex bench in the middle of the day was just another work day for us.

"Well, well, well," Beth drawled, yanking at the restraints around her wrists. "Look who decided to show up well past noon."

"It's Saturday," I protested. "I had a show last night."

Nancy raised a brow. She was wearing black slacks and a nice blouse with a diamond necklace one of her clients gave her a couple years ago. "How'd it go, Mr. Rockstar?"

I fought the urge to roll my eyes. "Good."

It was a vague answer, and we all knew it. Both of them narrowed their eyes on me.

"Good, huh?" Beth asked. "What's that on your neck?"

I slapped my hand over the spot Pepper bit me at some point last night. "Nothing."

"*Uh-huh.*" Nancy shook her head, her silver bob swinging. "Well, Beth made some tortilla soup if you want something before you get to work. This bench has been Beth-verified."

I grinned. "Oh, good—and thanks. I don't think I've eaten since yesterday."

Nancy pointed a crimson nail at me. "What are we going to do with you? Why wouldn't you eat breakfast? Especially after whatever nonsense you were up to last night that got you that mark. Get the fuck inside and feed yourself."

I fought a smile. "Hey, I am not your sub."

Beth shook her head. "He's disrespectful."

"He is," Nancy said. "Such a fucking brat. I think having all those little followers online is going to his head."

"Probably," Beth said.

"Okay," I chuckled. I was hungry, so I wasn't going to wait another minute. Especially when it was something Beth cooked. "I'll eat real quick and then get to work on the cross." I glanced over at the piece I'd started Thursday. It was built, but needed a coat of stain and a few other customizations that'd been requested.

I wondered how tall Pepper was... exactly.

I snapped out of my reverie and realized they were both staring at me. Nancy made a face. "Are you high?"

"No," I sighed. "Just thinking."

"About?" Nancy pressed.

"None of your business."

"Alright," Beth said. "Let me loose, pretty please?"

Nancy smirked. I covered my ears before she said anything and left the garage quickly, a lingering cackle following me down the path to their house.

They lived in a nice, quiet neighborhood outside of Nash-ville, and had a few acres of land. There was even a barn, which was really just used for storing the van we used to deliver furniture. Or when Nancy had a kidnapping CNC scene to play out.

The back door was unlocked. I slipped inside, kicked off my shoes, and went through the sunroom to the kitchen. A pot simmered on the stove and I inhaled the delicious scent of soup, my stomach grumbling in response.

My heart leaped into my throat at the feeling of my phone rattling against my thigh. I pulled it out immediately.

Not Pepper.

I sighed. It was just an email notification from Tommy. I opened it, quickly looking over the contents. On Friday at ten a.m. I was meeting with him and some guy named Jeff. My brows shot up when I saw that his email was *VP@rosethorn-records.com*.

Did that mean I was meeting with the vice president, too? What the fuck was happening? Wasn't that skipping a whole lot of other steps?

I ignored the other notifications on my phone and put it back in my pocket. A few minutes later, I settled at the kitchen bar with a heaping bowl of soup and tortilla chips.

I was getting a little obsessed, wasn't I?

It wasn't healthy, probably.

Beth came through the kitchen doorway. "Coffee?"

"Yes, please," I said between bites. "The soup is great."

"Ya know what else is great?"

Oh god. "I'm afraid to ask."

"An invite to your show."

My mouth opened and then closed. I hadn't expected that. "It's downtown."

"And?"

"It's loud."

"And?"

"I just didn't think either of you would want to go out on a Friday night."

"And why not?" Beth asked as she started the coffee maker. "We go out on Fridays all the time. We may be older, but we're not dead. I think we have more of a social life than you do."

"Probably."

She came to the counter and leaned against it. "Something's up with you. I've known you long enough, Simon. And my kids may be long grown, but it doesn't mean I don't know what *that* look is."

Oh right, the other kids. I always forgot about them. I shouldn't have, given that I saw them during the holidays when Nancy guilted me to participate. Beth had a daughter named Jessica who was a few years older than me, a clay artist who lived in Maine and visited at Christmas. Then there was Zach. He was around my age, and more of a mystery than even I was. I knew he worked with computers, and that was really it.

"How are the *kids*?" I asked.

"Oh my god," she sighed. "You're as bad as Nancy when you're being stubborn."

"I got an invite to meet with a record label on Friday," I said.

Her eyes lit up. "What?! That's what you're being weird about?"

Nope. It was Pepper. It was knowing that I'd fucked the CEO for hours last night and wanted more. Like some feral, unchained beast, I thirsted for her in a way that was uprooting all the little dark parts of me I worked hard to actively lock away. It wasn't just a one night stand. It was a night I wanted to repeat over and over.

"I just don't want to get my hopes up," I said.

"Well, if you'd unblock us on social media, maybe we could support you more."

I groaned. "My god. I just don't want you to see all the comments. People get weird."

"Can't be any weirder than seeing you put a cock cage on a senator last year."

My laugh came from my very full belly. I sighed, the tension and anxiety melting. There'd been a sex party I'd gone to last year, and I'd ended up playing with a couple who needed a *firm* hand. I didn't have intercourse with them, because *almost* all of the time I didn't mix that with kink. But I had put a cock cage on him. Then made his wife rim him while I flogged him. *Good times.*

Apparently he was a senator. I didn't really care. But Beth had been giggling about it on and off for months now.

"You're so shy about your music with us," she chuckled.

I scoffed. "I'm not shy."

"Yeah, you are. Still just a little boy sometimes."

"Okay, I'm definitely not that," I argued. "You should have seen the crowd last night. A den of Dionysus. *Revelry.*" I didn't tell her that was the name of one of my songs.

She just smiled. "I've heard you sing and play, Simon. You're special. I told Nancy that years ago. I can't wait for you to bring me bubble tea on Friday and tell me all about the meeting."

"*Bubble tea?*"

"Darn it," Beth sighed as Nancy joined us.

"Are you conspiring with Beth?" Nancy asked. "You know she's off sugar right now."

I held up my hands. "I have no idea what you're talking about. But I will say they have no-sugar options."

"Simon has a meeting with a record label on Friday," Beth said with a knowing smirk. I was now certain they'd played me in order to squeeze some more information out of me, but I also knew it was done out of love.

Nancy's brows raised. "*That's* why you're being shady. Nervous?"

"Yeah," I admitted. "I don't know if it's what I want. I mean, I still have to deal with the house, and I don't know."

"You could renovate the house," Nancy said. "Turn it into—"

"No," I said firmly. "That place will never be a home to me."

She pressed her lips, but nodded. "Understood."

"Let us help you purge the place," Beth said. "We can have a 'get rid of everything' party. I know there are still a couple more spaces that need work."

I hesitated. It was one thing to hold band practice in the garage. Jack, Tyler, and Eric liked the space, and it made our lives easier. But they were just co-workers.

I wasn't sure I even wanted people I loved to step foot in there. It was a house of broken bones and pain. *My* broken bones and pain.

"Just think on it," Nancy said lightly.

"Okay," I agreed. "I will."

ELEVEN

PEPPER

I SPENT the entire weekend reading about BDSM.

Bondage and discipline. Domination and submission. Sadism and masochism.

By the time Monday morning rolled around, I was torturing myself over texting Salt. I knew I shouldn't. I'd spent all of Sunday reading about Doms, subs, and kinks—and thinking he'd awakened something in me that I couldn't explore by myself.

But texting him would be wrong. Tommy told me he set up a meeting, which meant from here on out, I had to be a professional. I couldn't risk a repeat of Friday night with Salt. If I did, it would be my responsibility to inform members of our board that I was engaging in a relationship with him. And that would jeopardize so much.

I want him.

It was such a pesky thought. It didn't help that I'd even dreamed about him.

Once I discovered something I enjoyed, I threw myself at it

entirely. I'd spent my entire marriage thinking I hated sex, but that wasn't true at all.

For the first time in what felt like forever, I didn't feel a single shred of sadness, guilt, or jealousy when Jeff walked into my office.

"Morning," he chirped.

I offered him a bland smile, angling my computer screen out of his view before he could see I was reading an article about the best sex toys for women—my online cart was already up to five hundred dollars.

"What do you need?" I asked.

Jeff blew out a breath and dragged a chair against the wall over to my desk. "Well, you never answered me about Ally attending the awards show."

"Yes, I did," I said. "I told you no."

His posture adjusted slightly. I knew that motion all too well. The way he stiffened when he wasn't getting his way.

"It's just... I think it would be really good for us."

"Jeff, I do not care. The only suggestion I have is that if you'd like her to go, find a babysitter for her during the awards show. We're not asking them to make room for someone who's not in the industry. That's the most I'm compromising on this."

His eyes widened. He started to say something, but for once words seemed to fail him.

I held his gaze, unwavering. We could have heard a pin drop in the silence between us.

"Are you feeling jealous or something?" he blurted out.

I blinked. Slowly. Was this gonna be the day I killed my ex-husband? Was this going to be it? "Jeff," I said, leaning forward. "I have a confession."

He leaned forward slightly in anticipation.

"I have nothing to be jealous of."

Jeff sat back as if I'd slapped him. "Oh."

I smiled. "Did you need something else? Or should you be getting to your actual job?"

He blew out a long breath and stood up. "You don't have to be a bitch about it."

"That wasn't me being a bitch. Do you want me to be a bitch? Is that what it takes to get you to stop behaving like an idiot? Bringing your child to work every other day? Slacking off on getting your paperwork done? Everyone has been picking up the slack for you, and I'm done. I'm not going to baby you, I'm not going to protect you."

Jeff's ears were red, his mouth dropping. "What the hell is wrong with you? You can't just speak to me this way."

"I can and will because you don't listen to me otherwise. Never have."

He scoffed. "Oh, come on. Don't bring our marriage into this."

"Jeff," I warned, standing up. I could feel eyes on us as people passed the doorway, spectators starving for something juicy to talk about. "It is Monday morning. We have a busy month ahead of us. Go do the job that I sign your checks for, or resign."

His eyes bugged out of his head. He stood up and shook his head, muttering under his breath on his way out. I caught just a couple words, 'bitch' and 'psycho', and picked up my stapler to hurl—but then Ellen stepped into the doorway, her eyes bright with forced professionalism.

"Good morning," she said quickly. "I have your coffee and a blueberry muffin with a crumble top."

"Shut the door," I growled.

She kicked it shut behind her and whispered, "What the fuck?"

"I'm sick of him," I hissed, plopping down in my chair. "I've had enough. I can't keep dealing with his incompetence. Why the fuck did I start a company with him?"

Maybe Tommy was right about firing Jeff. The idea of doing so stoked a lot of fear, especially since a lot of the industry thought of Jeff as the face of Rosethorn.

Ellen's brows shot up as she put my coffee down along with my muffin with one hand, leaning forward enough that she saw my computer screen.

"Oh?!" she exclaimed.

My cheeks flamed as I started to close the tab, but she swatted my hand.

"Nope, I don't think so. Unhand that mouse."

I gave her a flat look, but swiveled my computer screen. She grinned. "Okay," she said. "Let's see what you've got in your cart. My god, I'm so proud right now. I've been trying to get you to buy toys for years... What made you change your mind?"

"Well..."

She slowly turned to look at me then gasped. "Oh my god."

I covered my face, sinking further back into my chair.

"You got *laid*," she said. "You broke the streak. You had sex. Who? When? Where? How?"

I giggled nervously spread my fingers to peek at her. "I can't tell you."

"*What* do you mean?" She lowered her voice to a whisper. "You're gonna tell me everything. Every. Single. Detail."

I hissed through my teeth and leaned forward. "You can't tell a soul."

"Who am I gonna tell? Scott from legal? Oh hey Scott, happy Monday morning, your boss got railed over the weekend?" she growled. "I work for *you*, not Rosethorn. Remember? Also, I'm *your* friend. The only reason I work for you is because it works for us."

I nodded. "Okay. So, you know how I went out with Tommy and Dan on Friday night?"

"Oh my god, did you sleep with them—"

"God, no," I laughed. "They're gay. And married. *Ellen.*"

She threw up her hands and settled down in the chair. "I don't know. People are flexible."

I shook my head. "They're both very gay and very happy together. It's hard to see sometimes."

She pressed her lips in understanding. "Okay... so?"

I chewed my bottom lip. I wasn't going to tell her the whole truth. I knew I wasn't going to be able to keep everything from her, though. "I ran into someone young and hot. He ended up going home with me."

She hummed, studying me. "And how was it?"

"I think he broke me," I whispered.

Her cackle rang through the office. "Okay. I want all the details."

I didn't tell her *everything*. I skipped over the parts where I begged for Salt to fuck me. I also skipped over the part where the young, hot stranger was a potential artist Rosethorn was signing. And that he was going to be here on Friday.

By the time I finished explaining—very awkwardly—my previous Friday night, Ellen's jaw had nearly unhinged.

"Damn," she said.

I reached for my coffee and took a long sip. God, I couldn't even think about coffee without thinking about him now. The tension I'd felt in the coffee shop last Thursday was a drop in the bucket compared to the tension that burned us alive Friday night. I didn't think that sort of connection could exist in real life.

"You went from nothing to all," she said.

"Well, you know me," I sighed. "I don't half-ass anything."

She nodded and reached for my muffin, splitting it for us.

Our rule was that any baked goods we had were always fair game.

"So. When do you see him again?"

I blew out a breath. "Never."

Her eyes widened. "You didn't get his number?"

"I did, but I can't see him again."

"What? Why not? You have his number. Just text him."

"I can't," I said.

I wanted to. I wanted every night of the rest of my life to be like Friday night. And now that I'd read up on BDSM, I was eager to try more things.

But it couldn't be with Salt.

"If you're not gonna text him, then give me his number," she said. "I want whatever that is."

"*Ellen.*" I laughed, but then an ugly streak of jealousy bloomed in my chest. What if he was with someone else? Why wouldn't he be? Why did I hate that idea so much? "Just go out with Tommy and Dan. I'm sure you'll meet someone."

She smirked. "I don't know. We should go out together."

"We should," I said, surprising both of us enough that I stared at her, and she stared at me.

"Damn," she said, shaking her head as she stood. "He must have been something else. You're buying an arsenal of sex toys and are willing to get out of your apartment."

"I told you," I said, fighting a smile. "I think he broke me."

"Mm-hmm. Well, enjoy your coffee. I'll go keep an eye on Jeff. Also, you have about fifty emails to get through and a meeting at noon with Kendra and Lee. Sounds like they cracked the case on Jenna Hart, but need your approval. And I think you have an afternoon meeting for financial overviews."

"Thanks."

Ellen winked and left the office, leaving the door open. I finished my coffee as I bought all the toys in my cart, including some I wouldn't be able to use alone. Like a flogger. And bondage tape. And anything else that sounded interesting.

What the hell am I doing? I wasn't sure.

My heart pounded as I opened up a new browser and logged into Instagram. It didn't take long to find Salt's account.

"Damn," I muttered.

He had a lot of followers. I clicked on his most recent post and just stared. Dark, tousled hair and an arrogant, shit-eating grin that peeked through the leather mask he wore. I swallowed hard as I scrolled to the next post, this one a video of him playing. Shirtless. Red lighting highlighted his muscles and tattoos, and I got another good look at what I'd explored on Friday night. The countless flowers that inked his skin, the roses and thorns around his neck.

He was beautiful.

But I was an idiot. Friday night was probably just another experience for him. All of the comments on his posts of people throwing themselves at him...

He could choose anyone he wanted.

I knew how artists like this were. They had charisma. They walked into a room, and everyone wanted to get on their knees for them. Sexuality oozed off of them in irresistible waves.

Salt was exactly like that.

There was a reason I was a CEO and not a musician.

Despite my best efforts, my attention slowly slid to my phone.

Texting him was out of the question. Even though I'd already saved his number to my phone...

The scent of caramel and coffee wrapped around me as I stared at it, weighing the pros and cons. Maybe he could recommend someone else?

Would that be crazy to ask him?

He wasn't a Rosethorn artist. *Yet.*

I groaned and reached for my phone. I opened the messaging app, and hesitated.

It was a bad idea.

A terrible one.

I made good decisions. Always. Careful, calculated ones—never the kind that could lead to self-sabotage like this had the potential to.

Deep breath.

Hey Salt, it's Pepper… I have a question. Do you know of any BDSM clubs you can recommend?

TWELVE
SALT

"ARE YOU FUCKING KIDDING ME?" I whispered.

I clutched my guitar against my body and stared at my phone like it was radioactive.

Pepper's text gleamed on the screen. *Do you know of any BDSM clubs you can recommend?*

The very thought of her going to one without me sent a wave of jealousy through me that made me nauseous. I stood up from the stool I was perched on, the strap tethering my guitar to me.

I was using my acoustic this morning, a sleek, black dreadnought that always tore up my fingertips after a few hours of practice. I liked the pain, though. It made the music sweeter.

My fingers moved over the strings out of habit. I tipped my head back, staring at the ceiling as I thought about Pepper on her knees for another Dom. Begging them the way she'd begged me.

I'd fucking lose it.

I waited all weekend for her text. All fucking weekend.

Then I'd convinced myself that it'd been some sort of wild dream and I'd never see her again.

But here she was. Texting me on a Monday morning, asking me for sex club recommendations.

"Everything alright, man?" Eric asked.

"Yeah," I said quickly.

I'd forgotten about them the moment her text came through. Jack was fucking around on his bass, the deep notes bouncing through the garage. We were still waiting on Tyler to get here, which would probably be another thirty minutes. He was usually late on Mondays.

"Did anything ever come from those suits at Beaumont's last Friday?" Jack asked.

Fuck. I needed to stop thinking about her. I turned to look at them, putting my phone in my back pocket. "Well, I have a meeting this Friday with Rosethorn."

"Hell yeah," Eric beamed. "That's great. I've heard good things about them."

"Mostly good things," Jack snorted. "They treat their artists well but they're notoriously hard to get signed with. Their CEO is a bitch."

My nostrils flared. "I met the CEO, and she was nice."

His brows shot up. "Really? I've met her before in passing. I was a replacement for one of their artists. Their bass player was sick so I got a call for the gig. She was cold."

That was the thing. Pepper *was* cold.

Except not with me.

"She made one of the sound guys cry." He laughed. "A big burly dude too. I don't know. She's a bitch. The whole industry knows that."

"Is she a bitch or is she just good at her job?" I snapped.

Jack held up his hands. "Look, man. I don't know. I'm just telling you what I've heard. I'm a feminist."

Damn. Maybe I needed a new bass player.

He continued before I said anything else. "But maybe you'll have good luck."

"Maybe," I muttered.

I needed to get the fuck out of the garage before I blew up on him.

I throttled the chord I was playing and lifted my guitar, setting it down on the stand. "I'm going to go get some water and something to eat. Do either of you want anything?"

"I'll take a water," Eric said.

"I'm good. I'm going to fuck around for a bit," Jack said, his attention returning to his bass.

I darted through the door that led into the house. The moment I shut it behind me, I pulled my phone from my pocket and texted Pepper back.

> No hi? How are you, Salt? Good morning???

Bubbles appeared and then disappeared. I narrowed my eyes as I waited, growing impatient.

> Why do you want to go to a BDSM club?

> I'm looking for a Dom.

I blinked. Slowly. My heart quickened as I shook my head.

> You already have a Dom.

> You know it can't be you, Salt.

I'd given this a lot of thought, between my delusional visions of us having a future together.

> 1. I'm not a signed artist with your label.

> 2. It's not against the law for us to see each other even if I am. I looked it up.

> 3. I won't recommend a club or Dom for you. Not sorry. I won't share you.

1. You have a meeting with my label Friday.

2. No, but it IS unprofessional.

3. It was just a one night stand. I don't belong to you.

I laughed. She was still fighting. Fighting *everything* so hard.

I reread her messages, then decided—fuck it. If she wanted something from me, she was going to have to earn it.

> I do have club recommendations, but any worth going to, you have to be vetted for. I can get you in, for a price.

Name your price, then.

> I have a show tomorrow night at 9PM at Russo's. You will be there, you will wear a red dress, no panties, but with sheer black tights. Heels. Make sure it's cheap so I can cut it off while you take my cock.

The bubbles appeared and disappeared a few times. She was probably going to block me. Probably tell Tommy to never talk to me again. And really, that would be best for both of us. To end this before it caught fire and burned us up.

I'll see you tomorrow. I expect you to get me into the best sex club there is in all of Nashville.

> Wouldn't dream of taking you anywhere else.

The brat responded with a fucking thumbs up. *A thumbs up.* I glowered at it and sat back.

I'd see her tomorrow. I inhaled slowly and then exhaled. I went to my fridge, grabbed a couple of waters, and uncapped one. I stared at the wall as I downed it, thinking about Pepper.

Beautiful, infuriating, addicting Pepper.

I hummed a melody, thinking about everything I wanted to do to her. I needed to focus on band practice right now. The guys were over, and here I was in my kitchen thinking about fucking her. Imagining putting her in spreader bars, tying a vibrator to her pretty little cunt, and making her weep from the constant barrage of orgasms I would give her.

What would she look like straining against them, fighting every stroke of pleasure? My cock sliding in and out of her mouth, letting her head fall back so she could take me even deeper.

Fuck. I needed her.

I couldn't get her out of my system. I tried. Because truth be told, she was right. The two of us were so different. Different worlds, different ages, different *everything*.

But the idea of even attempting to satiate my lust with someone else made me recoil.

I wasn't sure I was patient enough to wait until tomorrow night. I picked up my phone again and sent another text.

Video call me when you get off work tonight.
It'll be fun.

You've lost your mind

You're too young for me

Twelve years is nothing

Twelve years is A LOT

> How about I give you an orgasm for every year between us

Salt, for fuck's sake. Your frontal lobe hasn't fully developed.

> Maybe, but my cock has. Want to see it?

My god. This is exactly what I'm talking about. Why would sending me a dick pic be something I want?

I laughed again. I knew better than to send one, but it was still entertaining to see her flustered response.

She was really hung up on our age gap. Twelve years wasn't *that* much. It'd be different if she were thirty and I was eighteen.

I knew what I wanted. I knew what I liked. And I'd been on my own for years, aside from when Nancy and Beth stepped in. Not only did I technically run my own business, I was building up my music career. Even if the meeting on Friday was a complete failure, I'd been building an audience. I wasn't sure if they just liked seeing my mask and tattoos or if they actually liked my music, but still.

Besides, I'd be twenty-six soon. My birthday was in just a couple weeks. Less than, actually. I should probably have told her that, but I hated my birthday. It was always the worst day of the year.

I looked at her text message again, and decided to be a little reckless. I pressed the voice recording button.

"Pepper, I want to see your face tonight," I said, keeping my voice low and seductive. *"I want to hear about your work day. I want you to touch yourself at my command and help relieve any stress you have from working so hard. Is that such a bad thing?"*

I ended the message and hit send.

And strangled a laugh when a voice memo appeared in response. I pressed play.

"*You're a little shit,*" she snapped. "*You can't send me things like that while I'm at work. You can't talk to me that way while I'm in the office. What if someone heard me?*"

I pressed the record button. "*You mean what if you got caught? What if? What if you got caught talking to the twenty-five year old who fucked you all night this past weekend and wants to do it again?*"

I was no psychic, but I could feel her sexual frustration warring with her business brain all the way from here.

She didn't respond this time. Maybe I'd pushed her too far.

I didn't regret it, though.

My phone chirped. Another message.

I'm **off** at 5.

THIRTEEN
PEPPER

IT WAS WELL past six when I actually walked through my front door, dropped my purse to the floor, and headed straight to my kitchen for a glass of wine.

Fuck Jeff. Really, he was the root of all of my problems some days. The meetings had flown by, but then Jeff, being the entitled fucking twat he was, had gotten into it with Kendra. Kendra had then come to me about Jeff's behavior, and I had to talk to Jeff.

Everyone was growing tired of his antics. Especially me.

I opened my fridge and pulled out a bottle of red wine. I was a heathen and liked my cabernets cold. A perk of living alone, I didn't have a dumbass husband to judge me for twisting the top off and drinking it straight from the bottle. It didn't matter how much money I had, I still liked a cheap red in the middle of a work week.

My eyes closed as the tannins hit my tongue and I sighed, trying to release whatever tension I could. I still needed to schedule a massage, a facial appointment, and a dress fitting for the awards show.

I needed to *not* be thinking about that damn voice message Salt sent me earlier.

"Fuck," I mumbled, remembering I'd told him we'd call.

Why had I done that? Why couldn't I tell him no? A firm, direct no? I wasn't a stranger to telling men no, or even bossing them around, and yet...

The pulse between my thighs and the rush of heat across my skin told me I couldn't just tell him no, because I wanted him. It didn't matter that I'd just ordered every sex toy I could find that looked interesting, or had spent hours devouring articles about kink over the weekend, I wanted him.

"Twelve years," I whispered to myself.

He was twelve years younger than me. I shouldn't have anything to do with a twenty-five year old man, no matter how amazing he was in bed.

But I'd been missing out.

Married to Jeff for fifteen years, and he'd never made me come the way Salt had. It didn't help that I'd been raised in a conservative Christian cult who taught me everything sexual was sinful. I'd gone into that marriage without ever having slept with anyone before. I'd never been able to explore that part of me. And when Jeff and I were married, every time I tried to try something new, I was shut down.

The shame I felt around my desire made my insides freeze. It made me feel like there was something wrong with me. It made me think about all the times my mother had chided me if I wasn't dressed perfectly or if I asked too many questions.

I'd done so much work around trying to heal from my childhood, but I'd never be perfect.

Fuck, it was so stupid. It was so, so stupid. A hard, bitter shell formed around my memories of my childhood, and every day I was glad I left. But I also wished that I could have saved my relationship with my parents. With my mom.

I glanced at the calendar on my fridge and took another swig of wine.

Her death day was coming up.

I needed to cancel any plans that came up the day before or after it. It'd been years since she died, but the guilt and pain and sadness that swallowed me whole during those days meant I wouldn't get out of bed for anything but to visit her grave and grab food orders from my doorstep.

Jeff used to give me such a hard time about it. He didn't at first, of course. But over the years, her death was something that *annoyed* him.

My *grief* was annoying.

Why did I ever allow myself to be with someone who treated me that way?

And why wouldn't I pursue the type of sex I'd experienced on Friday night? With someone who wanted me for *whatever* reason?

As if I'd summoned him, my phone chimed on the counter. I stared for a moment and then reached forward. He was video calling.

"Shit," I whispered.

My finger pressed the button before I let my logic get in the way.

Salt's unbearably handsome face appeared on my phone. His dark hair was tousled and he was clearly shirtless. Just like in his damn videos online. Inked vines crawled up his throat, disappearing around his neck.

"Are you in bed?" I blurted out.

He grinned. "Yeah. And you're in your kitchen."

I decided to take another sip from my wine bottle, my body tensing as I expected him to chide me. Instead his smile grew broader.

"Next time I'm over, I'll lick that off your body."

I choked and dropped the phone on the counter before I spit all over it. His soft laugh followed as I coughed over my sink, cursing him. "God damn it," I grunted.

Well, I'd failed at being sexy. My ego was dead to the entire world.

"*Baby, come back,*" he sang. "*You can blame it all on me...*"

I put the wine back in the fridge, done with it after that, and picked up my phone again. "You're a nuisance. Also, that song is almost fifty years old. I'm shocked you even know it."

"Well, I do have good taste in music," he said. "At least, that's what I've been told."

"Hmm." I smiled as I carried the phone to my bedroom. "I don't know why you wanted to see me. You can have anyone you want. All the women who were at the bar on Friday would have thrown themselves at your feet."

"I don't want just anyone. I want you."

"You're like a puppy," I muttered.

"Mm, yes. Keep insulting me, I'll keep it in mind tomorrow when you're on your knees for me again."

My breath hitched as I looked at him. There was that charisma again. Why was I being so stupid? All artists were like this. They had to be. Having that sort of charm helped their careers—it kept listeners addicted to them. Even the fantasy that Salt might look their way and want them was enough to keep them crawling back for more.

They were hungry for scraps.

I wasn't any different, was I? And I wasn't just hungry, I was starving.

A video call had been a bad idea.

"Tell me about your day," he said.

I breathed out slowly. "Why? It was boring..."

"Do you usually drink wine immediately after *boring?*"

I snorted and winced, looking around. I wanted to get in bed, but I needed to change.

Did I tease him?

Was I even brave enough to do that? *What am I doing? Why can't I just stop this madness?*

I had a hang-up when it came to my body. I loved watching other people who were comfortable in their own skin. But it was hard for me at times, especially in sexual situations. I always found ten different reasons as to why I was doing something wrong, and then my mind attached to that and spiraled.

"What are you scowling about?" he asked gently.

"I was going to change," I said. "Then I thought about teasing you. But…"

He sat up, frowning as he studied me, his acute attention making my skin prickle. "But what?"

"I don't know," I sighed. "I always feel like I'm bad at this stuff. It's stupid that someone my age would even feel like this. Like I'm not new to sex, but…"

"You're overthinking it," he said.

"Probably. That's what Ellen would say."

"Who's Ellen?"

"My best friend and assistant."

His lips tugged. "Ellen would be right. Do you want my help, Pepper?"

"How?" I bit out. "You're on the other side of Nashville."

"I could tell you what to do. With your consent, of course."

"*Dominate* me? That's what you are when you're not signing, right? A Dom?" I asked, thinking about all the terms I'd learned.

Salt lifted a brow. "Someone's been reading, hmm?"

I nodded. And I'd be a damn liar if I didn't admit I liked the sound of praise in his tone. It stroked something deep inside me. "I read a lot over the weekend."

"How very voracious of you."

I couldn't fight my stupid smile this time. This was flirting wasn't it? The light banter, the teasing. I was rusty at it, but I liked how it made me feel.

Did I want Salt to dominate me again?

Yes. The thought was immediate and resounding.

"To answer your question, yes," he said. "I am a Dom. And I'm not just saying that. I've been in the kink community for the last five years, and I've learned from the best. When I'm not playing music, I'm building sex furniture."

"*Sex* furniture?" I echoed, bewildered.

"Yes. With my..." he trailed off and hummed. "She's sort of my adoptive mom. That's the best way to describe her. But it's not weird that we build sex furniture together."

"Interesting," I chuckled. "Well, she sounds fun."

"She is," he said, his tone softening. "I just want you to know that I'm not just some twenty-year-old telling you I know how to be a Dom. I have the classes and experience to back it up."

I studied him, and he seemed to mean it. I'd gotten pretty good at spotting bullshit over the years, and his words were genuine. "Do you have other submissives?" I asked.

"No," he said. "Not currently. I do occasionally play with others if I'm in the mood for it, but typically in public settings. I also don't usually mix penetrative sex and kink."

"Really?" I asked curiously. "Why?"

"Most of the time, my focus is on my submissive's pleasure. I like making people come. I like giving them orgasms. It satisfies me." He smiled. "I think you made me realize that it's fun to mix the two, though."

I couldn't help it, I bit my bottom lip. "I think you ruined me. I bought a lot of sex toys online today."

His eyes brightened. "Really?"

"Yes," I sighed.

"If you need recommendations, let me know," he said lightly.

"I will..." I trailed off and then took a deep breath, releasing it slowly. *This is a bad idea. Bad, bad idea. But—* "Salt?"

"Yes?"

"Will you dominate me?"

"Yes," he answered. "I'd be honored to. I've been thinking about you non-stop since Saturday morning."

"I've been thinking about you too," I admitted.

"Did you learn more about safe words?"

I nodded. "Yes. Red means stop. Yellow means slow. Green is go."

"Good girl," he praised, his deliciously deep voice making me shiver. "Find a place to set your phone down so I can still see you."

"Okay." I took my phone to my dresser and balanced it on top, using a bottle of perfume to help prop it up. Now, I didn't know what to do with my hands. I grimaced, folding them together in front of me.

"Are you nervous?"

"Yes." I bit the inside of my mouth hard, my nerves rattling.

"Pepper. Look at me."

I did look at him.

"Good." Even through the phone, his gaze was unnerving. "I want you to undo the tie on your pants. The big ribbon."

"Okay," I mumbled.

I was wearing high waisted pants with a fabric sash I'd tied into a bow. I undid the knot and gave it a tug.

"Good. Turn around."

My mouth was dry. I needed more wine.

"Focus on me. On my voice. On my commands."

I closed my eyes, my heart thumping as I turned around, my cheeks hotter than irons.

"Very good. Now slowly pull your dress pants down."

Oh my god, I can't believe I'm doing this. Why was I trusting him? Why was I doing this? Despite my thoughts, I slowly eased my pants down, bending over and becoming painfully aware of the panties I wore. They were black and high waisted, good for working out or being at the office—not for stripping in front of a hot Dom.

My hot Dom.

"Good." His praise eased my worries. "God, you're fucking gorgeous. If I were there right now, I'd bury my face between your sweet thighs. Stand up and turn to face me."

My entire body was on fire. I turned around slowly and faced him, knowing I was going too far, but craving this connection more than anything.

"Very good." Salt cocked his head. "Take off your shirt."

I held his gaze as I reached for the hem, tugging it over head. Now, I was just wearing a bra and panties for him.

"How do you feel?" he asked gently.

"Vulnerable," I whispered. "Embarrassed."

"Do you want to know how you make me feel?"

I nodded, my throat constricting.

"Just seeing you standing there has made me so fucking hard, I feel like I could come at any moment. You're beautiful. Absolutely fucking gorgeous. I want you to take off your bra and panties."

"Do I have to?" I asked.

"You don't have to do anything."

I narrowed my eyes on him. That felt like a trap. Salt gave me a slow, teasing smile.

"You want to, though. Don't you? You want to please me. And you want to be admired, even if you're feeling unsure."

He was right, damn it.

I reached around and unclasped my bra, throwing it to the floor like I was ripping a bandaid off. I expected him to laugh or *something*, but he just watched me. My heart raced faster as I stripped out of my panties too, now fully naked in front of him.

"Good job, Pepper," he praised. "Move your hands away from your breasts. Put them behind your back. Come closer."

I hadn't even realized I was covering them. I clasped my hands behind my back and stepped closer to my phone. Cool air caressed my body, my skin prickling.

Salt let out a soft grunt. "Fuck. Look at you. I like it when you're this obedient for me."

"You could do this with anyone," I said quietly. "Anyone you wanted. Someone closer to your age."

"I don't want anyone else. I want *you*. I want to see you naked in front of me, taking my cock. Coming undone like my perfect little slut. I want *you*, Pepper. Take the phone to your bed and kneel in the center, knees wide. Prop your phone against a pillow so I can see you."

"Okay." I picked up the phone, wrinkling my nose at him. "I don't understand you."

"What about me?" he teased.

"Nothing," I muttered, climbing onto my bed.

I messed with my abundance of pillows, blushing as I realized I was just letting everything hang out. Completely naked, on all fours, trying to set up a phone so he could *watch* me.

My body was my body, I reminded myself. If I were on the other end of this phone call, wouldn't I be admiring the person in front of me? I knew I would be, and yet I couldn't find a shred of confidence at being the one naked. *Why am I like this?*

"Pepper," Salt said softly. "What's going on in that pretty head of yours?"

"I'm just thinking that you could put me in front of a boardroom of men who hate me, and I wouldn't feel this way," I said, finally getting the phone to stay put. "I've given countless talks over the years. I've met with high-profile celebrities and people in the industry who have far more experience than I do, but it's never mattered. I've always excelled under pressure. I change lives with a single signature on paper. I've found artists who were poor, with nothing but their talent, and helped them grow a career. I've done things that infuriate other people in the industry, like giving my artists health insurance, and making sure they have stable income during the process of recording. And yet, I feel stupid right now. I feel so silly."

"What is silly about this?"

"I don't know," I whispered. "I was married for a long time, you know."

"You've mentioned," he said seriously. "But he never appreciated you the way you should have been appreciated."

"He never made me orgasm."

"*Ever?*"

"Ever," I whispered. "I really thought I was doing something wrong. I'd read a romance book and wonder why I wasn't having the same mind-blowing orgasms that the characters were having. Or I'd watch porn and think they had to just be acting right? That couldn't be real."

"I promise you it can be. What about touching yourself?" Salt asked.

"I mean, I have..."

"And have you made yourself orgasm?"

"Yes," I said. "Of course. I'm not completely incompetent."

"This isn't about being incompetent," he said. "Nothing about this is something you can be a boss about, Pepper. You can't be the CEO of orgasms. Well, maybe you could..."

Despite the raw ineptitude I felt, I laughed. "I'll add it to my list of life goals."

He smirked. "Add having a hot Dom who wants to fuck you every day to that list too. Since you always get what you want."

I narrowed my eyes on him. "You don't take 'no' for an answer, either."

"It depends." He relaxed against his bed, holding his phone above so I could see his chest and abs. "Pepper?"

"Yes?"

"I want you to sit back with your knees spread and touch yourself. Show me how wet you are. Right now."

PRE-CUM DRIPPED from my cock onto my lower stomach as I watched Pepper obey. She was stiff, fighting every step of the way, but I was starting to understand why.

Her bedroom lights made her body glow against her cream blankets, her dark hair tumbling over her shoulders. I drank in the sight of her, from her breasts to her thighs to her pussy. Her nails gleamed as she moved her hand down tentatively to touch herself.

"Close your eyes," I murmured. Her lashes fluttered and I felt a stroke of satisfaction. "Good. Forget about everything else around you. Focus on my voice."

"I like your voice," she whispered.

God, this woman. I needed her in my bed. I needed to fuck her for hours and show her everything she'd been missing out on in her marriage. I wanted to spank her, fuck her, make her beg for me to breed her. And the list was only growing with every moment.

Knowing that she read about BDSM over the weekend

pleased me. It also made me wonder—what sort of kinks lay under the surface? What could I help her discover?

"You're doing very well for me," I praised, watching the way she preened under my compliment.

She definitely had a praise kink. It made sense, given that I doubted anyone regularly told her just how amazing she was. It didn't matter how competent someone was, sometimes hearing it was more important than anything else.

"I want you to slide your fingers inside yourself... Very good..." My mouth watered as two fingers disappeared inside her.

"I'm so wet," she gasped in surprise. "I didn't realize how wet I was."

"Is it because you felt humiliated?"

She scowled, but didn't immediately respond. I knew she was thinking about it.

"Maybe? Is that bad?"

"Not at all," I said. "It's just something we can explore more at another time. Degradation can be fun, well—fun for *me*. But we'd need to talk through it more."

She nodded, her eyes still firmly closed. "I like it when you say nice things to me, too."

"Oh, I know. I enjoy praising you."

"I can't believe I'm doing this..."

There were those pesky self-doubts again. "Pepper. Focus on me. On obeying *me*. Nothing else. Whatever little voice inside your head is telling you things, don't listen to it. Its opinion doesn't fucking matter, because I am here. You obey *me* and me alone. Understood?"

"Yes." Her shoulders softened.

"Yes *what*?"

"Sir?"

"Good. I like it when you call me Sir." Fuck, my cock was

killing me. I closed my eyes for a moment and then opened them, refocusing on her. "Show me how you touch yourself. I want to watch you make yourself come. Do whatever you normally do in order to get there."

Her eyes started to open.

"Do *not* open your eyes," I commanded.

"Yes... Sir."

"Someone's a quick learner."

Once again, she relaxed. Her fingers moved to her clit, alternating between moving in slow circles and sliding inside herself. Her other hand moved up to her breasts, teasing her nipples.

I couldn't help myself now. I held my phone in one hand and gripped my cock with the other, huffing out as I watched her.

"I'm going to get off on watching you," I whispered.

Her blush deepened. "I like that."

I groaned as I stroked myself. I'd been unbearably hard since she started to strip and was in need of relief.

"Fuck," she whimpered.

Something snapped. I wasn't sure what it was, but I saw the moment in real time. The second her body gave in to her hunger for an orgasm, the moment that voice in her head fell silent.

"Good girl," I praised. "You make me so hard, baby girl. I'm dripping all over myself watching you touch your needy cunt. How long has it been since you orgasmed?"

"Yesterday," she panted, her movements becoming hurried.

"Aww, poor thing," I purred, stroking my cock faster. "You deserve one after working so hard today. Don't you?"

"*Yes, Sir,*" she cried, her expression melting as she got closer and closer.

"I'm so close," I groaned. "You're the reason I'm about to

come. Seeing you touch yourself and become my slut is going to make me come."

"Yes," she gasped. "Fuck. *Fuck.*"

"Keep going," I urged. "Keep pleasing that pussy for me. Keep going. Good girl. You're such a good girl for me. I can't wait to watch you come for me. Because you like pleasing me, don't you?"

"Yes, yes, yes," she chanted.

Pepper touching herself without any reservations was the most beautiful thing I'd seen in my entire life.

"Come," I growled. "I need you to come for me. *Now.*"

Her voice pitched, her head tossing back as she orgasmed, her fingers working her clit relentlessly through it. I grunted as cum spurted from my cock and I jerked myself, my whole attention on everything *Pepper.*

"Oh my god," she rasped, sinking back.

"Open your eyes," I demanded. "Take the phone and show me your pussy."

"But... I haven't shaved, I haven't—"

"Pepper. I do not give a fuck. It's your body, and regardless of if you've shaved or not, I'm going to worship you just the same. Do as I say and show me your pussy."

Her breaths steadied as she grabbed the phone, but then she hesitated. "I don't know how to do this."

"That's what I'm here for. Lay it flat between your thighs," I instructed.

"Yes, Sir." She did exactly that.

"Good. Show me how wet you are."

She spread her labia, her essence glistening against the deep pink of her pussy. Even though I'd just come, my cock remained hard in my grip.

"Like this?" she whispered.

"Yes. Exactly like that. Fuck." I stroked my cock again,

moaning unapologetically as I jerked off to the sight of her. "I can't wait to fuck you tomorrow."

"You shouldn't," she said.

"*Yes*, I should."

"Are you going to come just from seeing me?"

She sounded so shocked. I grunted, making a mental note to remind her tomorrow *in person* just how much she turned me on. "I already fucking came once, Pepper," I growled, stroking myself faster. "And I'm about to come again thinking about being inside you tomorrow."

The sound of her breath catching was what sent me over the edge. I groaned as I came again, cum splashing over my body. The euphoric rush of my orgasm made me moan, but I never closed my eyes. I was focused solely on her.

Fuck. "Show me your face."

The phone lifted and she held it up, looking at me with wide hazel eyes. I angled mine down, showing her the mess. "Look at what you did to me."

She *licked her lips.* "That's a lot."

"It is." My muscles melted into my bed. I gave her a satisfied smile. "Thank you."

Pepper grinned and fell to the side, sprawling over her bed. "Thank *you*. That was unlike anything I've ever experienced. Which seems to be something you excel at."

I chuckled and leaned over, grabbing a tissue from the box on my side table and cleaning myself off. I rolled over and tossed it into the trash, settling on my stomach.

Pepper had pulled a blanket around herself. "What are we doing?" she asked.

"Breaking all your rules," I said, settling on my side as well. With a dash of delusion, I could imagine us laying next to each other like this. "I like you."

She wrinkled her nose. "We can't date."

"Why not?" I asked. "I could take you on a real date, you know. I know a good brunch spot with mimosas."

She sighed. "You have a meeting with Tommy on Friday. Salt, I'm going to be honest, we want you. I want to own your music."

And I want to own your heart.

"I don't even know if I want that," I said. "I haven't decided. I'm going to hear him out, and that's it."

She frowned. "Regardless, we can't keep doing this."

"We could keep it a secret," I said. "No one has to know. I'll sign a NDA if that's what it takes for you to trust me."

"It's not just that. I'm obligated to inform my company that I'm seeing a client if... If we continue. I have to tell them. Why don't you go out with someone else?"

I groaned dramatically. "Who do you think I am?"

"Well—"

"Truly," I said. "What do you imagine I do every day?"

"Post selfies, play music, and brood."

"*Brood?*" I scoffed. Although she wasn't wrong.

"You're ridiculously handsome," she said. "You're talented. And you apparently build sex furniture. Why aren't you in a serious relationship?"

Because I'm damaged and any one who gets close to me discovers that and leaves.

"Maybe I'm a lone wolf," I said lightly.

She laughed. "No one chooses to be a *lone wolf*. Ask me how I know."

"How do you know?"

Pepper rolled her eyes. "I'm too old for that kind of ploy. You can't distract me when I want to know something. It's your turn to feel uncomfortable," she teased.

I gave her a dirty look, but she had a point. "I'll tell you one thing, and you can tell me one thing."

"Fine. Go on."

"I've dated," I said. "Most of my relationships are casual hookups. I've attempted to date people more seriously over the years. But, usually, we would hit the three-month point and things would implode."

"Why?" she asked.

"Usually my fault," I said. "I'd get too serious too fast. Or my sexual appetite was too much."

"I doubt that."

I raised a brow. "Sex every single day? Sometimes a few times a day?"

"Sounds like heaven to me."

"And yet you've been resisting me *sooo* hard."

"Okay, *well*, I have reasons for that. Reasons that make a whole lot of sense given the context."

"You're not wrong, but I still stand by what I said earlier. Which is that we can make this work."

She sighed. "You've known me for a few days."

"And?"

"This is wild, Salt. It's wild."

I shrugged. "I've done wilder, I'm sure." Which wasn't a lie. Although, the way Pepper made me feel was definitely borderline crazy. The obsession was rooting deep, which meant it had the potential to become unhealthy.

But I wanted her. It was that, plain and simple. I wanted her to be mine.

"Well, I haven't."

"Always the good girl, hmm?" I asked.

That struck a nerve. Her expression pinched into a glare and she rolled over onto her back, her hair sprawling across the pillow. "I don't like it, but it's true."

"Tell me," I said. "Since I told you something about me."

"You already know so much about me," she said. "Way

more than I know about you. But, fine. It was how I was raised. I grew up in a very small, conservative town outside of Nashville. My parents got married young, had me young, and I was expected to turn into something I wasn't. Music is what saved me."

My heart skipped a beat. "You too, huh?"

She paused, but then hummed. "Yeah," she whispered. "Me too."

"It's the only reason I'm still here," I said. "It means everything to me. I don't even know if I'm good at it."

"You are. You can't doubt yourself like that. And even if you weren't, you just said that it saved you. Why would you ever doubt its place in your life?"

My chest tightened and I stared at her for a moment. "Is this how you talk artists down?"

She gave a ruthless smile. "Yes. But I mean it. If I didn't mean it, I wouldn't be so concerned about dating you, because I wouldn't feel like you belonged to Rosethorn. Which is a massive conflict of interest."

I pressed my lips together. It made sense logically, although I still had a hard time accepting that I was good at music. I wasn't sure that doubt would ever truly go away.

But, she was right, of course.

Music had saved me. I loved it. Regardless, I belonged to the mysterious internal melody that not only bound me to music, but to Pepper in a way, too.

"One day, I'll write you a song," I decided.

She shook her head and stifled a laugh. "About what? A bitter woman who's missed out on everything?'

"No," I said. "That's not how I see you."

"How do you see me?"

I raked my fingers through my hair. "You'll have to wait and see."

"I suppose," she said. "Although who knows. Maybe one day you'll write a song about how I ruined your life. And how you wish you never would've met me."

"I don't think so," I said. "I think, if anything, it could be the other way around. That you'll hate me."

I would never regret what happened between us over the last few days. Even if it had been a whirlwind, and my obsession was already spiraling out of control, I would cherish the moments we had together.

But, I knew what I was. I knew why my relationships always failed, and why everyone in my life always disappeared. Nancy and Beth were the only exceptions, although there was a very small voice inside my head that told me they would eventually leave one day, too.

Was that the curse my father had given me? The one I never seemed to be able to break? To just be nothing more than a cursed beast, bound to music and sex? To always hurt the ones I loved the most?

"I don't know," she sighed. "I don't know if I could ever hate you."

Just give me time, that little voice said.

FIFTEEN

PEPPER

I DID EXACTLY as Salt told me to on Tuesday evening.

I wore a red dress, black heels, and black pantyhose.

And that was all.

The work day had flown by and I was all too aware of the fact that he was meeting with Tommy on Friday morning. If their meeting went well, I'd be receiving an email by the end of the week with information about the man I'd had phone sex with last night, asking for my approval.

Rosethorn would be lucky to have him. I knew that. And as I told him, that's what made all of this *wrong*.

I tugged my skirt down my thighs, hyper aware that if I spread them, anyone would be able to see my pussy. The Uber driver occasionally glanced back at me, but didn't say anything to me on the drive, which was a relief.

My phone vibrated against my palm. I turned it over, seeing Ellen's text across the screen.

Want to get dinner tonight?

Not tonight! Later this week, please

Okay, just figured you needed to get out of
the apartment…

If she only knew where I was headed.

I texted her back a flimsy excuse about just wanting to enjoy a movie and a bubble bath to relax and forget about everything to do with my company. She bought it, because why would I have a reason to lie?

Going out in the middle of a work week to a club to hear a twenty-five-year-old play music was so out of character, no one would ever guess that was exactly what I was doing.

With no panties on.

I had no reason to follow through on this, even after our conversation last night. I knew he was using my desire to go to a BDSM club against me, but I liked that. It was a little ruthless, and that turned me on.

Did I really want to try this sort of stuff with anyone aside from Salt? That was the biggest question.

I knew the answer and hated it. I hated that I was feeling things I'd never felt before, because emotions like that got in the way of making good decisions. That's why I always put emotions on the back burner.

He was corrupting me, but I was reveling in that corruption. I was clinging to the fringe of something I'd never had before—sex with someone who wanted me in a way that was captivating. The desires he'd dug up were shackling me to him and all of the bad decisions we were making.

Going to him tonight meant he'd introduce me to a club, which meant I could find another Dom, and put this all behind me. That was the professional thing to do.

Not that showing up to see a client without underwear was

professional in any way, but I was doing my best. *You're playing with fire.*

The car came to a stop, and I got out, giving the driver a wave before heading towards the front door of Russo's. There was a line, but Salt told me to give them my name, and that they would let me in. I avoided eye contact with the people waiting as I approached the bouncer, holding my head high even as a cool breeze brushed my skin through my pantyhose.

The man raised a brow as I approached. "Hi," I said. "Salt told me to come to the front door. My name is Pepper."

The man snorted. "Oh, yeah. Is that like a kink thing or something?"

Heat immediately rushed to my cheeks. "What?"

"Your names? Salt and Pepper?"

"Oh. No, it's not," I said, completely taken aback.

"Okay, then. Alright, well, go in. Show starts in thirty and your boy has a fucking crowd."

I glanced back at the line. Every single person waiting was beyond gorgeous. Women in beautiful dresses and outfits who exuded sexual energy. *Why the hell is he interested in me?*

The man stepped to the side to let me go by. "Have fun."

My pulse raced as I slipped past him and stepped into the venue. It'd been a long time since I'd been at Russo's, and it looked like they'd made some updates for the better. A bar ran the length of the entire wall to the right, and different levels of seating all faced the stage at the back corner.

Some of the house lights were still on. I checked my watch and raised a brow, wondering if they were having set up issues. I went up three steps and looked over a balcony, searching for Salt.

When I saw him, every muscle in my body froze. I swallowed hard, even more aware of what I'd worn for him, and that coming here was putting us in jeopardy. Russo's wasn't the best bar to hear music, but it was still frequented by a lot of people in the industry. This was Nashville, after all.

Salt stood on the stage talking to a man I vaguely recognized. Other musicians bustled around the two of them, setting up quickly. I recognized the three band members who were at the last show. More than likely, Salt was opening for whoever their headliner was.

He turned his head and I sucked in a breath as his gaze met mine.

This was the first time I'd seen him in person since Friday night.

He held up his hand and crooked a finger. A potent mix of frustration and tension seeped into my muscles. I scowled as I went down the stairs and made my way to the stage.

"*This* is your guest?" the guy said, his eyes widening.

"Yep," Salt said without missing a beat.

He startled me by jumping off the stage, landing in front of me with a kind of ease that reminded me my knees were not like they were a decade ago. *When I was his age. What the fuck am I doing?*

Salt held out his hand and I shook it, pulling away before he could kiss my knuckles. Amusement glimmered in his dark gaze as he turned to look up at the man. "This is Pepper."

"Oh, I know her," he snorted, his tone not disguising his disdain.

Great. My expression hardened and I slipped on my business mask, everything turning to stone. "Do you?"

"Yeah. You're the reason my sister never got signed to a record label."

"I'm certain I had nothing to do with that," I answered coolly.

"Well, it's your label, isn't it?"

I fought a smile. "What was your sister's name?"

"Amelia," he sneered. "Great voice. Talented songwriter. Ended up with another label, better than yours."

I knew exactly who he was talking about. I remembered her, her grating voice, and the sense of entitlement she had. And really, the nail in the coffin was that she was a bitch to Tommy. The only reason she got picked up by another label was because of a friend of their family. Last I'd heard, they dropped her for making homophobic statements online. *Good fucking riddance.*

"Amelia, Amelia, hmm..." I trailed off, and then shrugged. "Oh, I remember. Is that the Amelia who got dropped last month by her label for being homophobic online?"

The man's ears turned red, his face dropping. "That was a misunderstanding."

"I doubt it," I said pleasantly, fluttering my lashes.

Salt looked away, hiding a laugh from the guy on stage. I felt more eyes on us and glanced up. The bass player was watching us closely. It made me feel anxious. Salt found a shred of composure, raked his fingers through his hair, and turned to face the dipshit. "Um, well. She's my guest regardless, so can she have a badge, Dale?"

Dale fumed, but shrugged his shoulders, mimicking me. "Fine. I'll get her one. You better be fucking worth it."

Salt bristled. "I could leave instead, and let everyone waiting outside know that you changed your mind at the last minute, if you'd like."

He held up his hands. "No need for that, man. I'll go grab the badge."

Salt didn't say anything else, giving Dale a glare as he scampered to the back.

I shook my head. "This was a mistake. I shouldn't be here. I showed up like you asked—"

"Are you just wearing pantyhose?"

My brain short circuited. "Yes," I hissed. "Fuck. This is—"

He stepped closer and dipped down, his lips brushing my ear. "I'm proud of you for doing as I asked."

Ba-bump, ba-bump, ba-bump. My heart beat thrummed through every part of my body, including my pussy.

"You're going to watch me play and then when I'm finished, I'm going to come backstage and fuck you until you're singing my name."

"Salt," I hissed, giving him a light shove. I turned around, spotting Dale scrutinizing us as he approached. He wasn't the only one. "There are people here. *Behave.*"

Salt smiled as if nothing had happened. "Thanks, Dale."

"Sure," he muttered. "You know your way around a stage, I'm assuming?"

I fought the urge to roll my eyes at him. But, to be fair, it had been awhile since I was backstage. "Of course. Who else is playing tonight?"

"An indie rock band out of Chicago," Salt said. "They're good."

One of the techs on stage yelled for Dale and he grumbled as he walked away. I crossed my arms over my chest, taking it all in.

"How many songs are you playing?" I asked.

"Six," he said. "Nothing too big. The guys are almost set up. Eric and Tyler have to go as soon as we finish, and Jack will go off on his own and enjoy the rest of the night."

"So..."

He smiled. "So what I'm saying is you'll have me alone once we finish performing."

"Have you thought about adding another guitarist?" I asked.

"Yes," he said. "But I don't know if I want to."

I frowned, glancing up at him. "Why?"

"I don't know," he sighed.

"It seems you're reluctant to all of this. Why? And don't tell me it's your artist ego."

The corner of his mouth tugged. "You go into CEO mode so quickly. Don't worry about my music, Pepper, it's not yours. Yet."

Yet. I gave him a dirty look and stepped away before he could touch me, the back of my neck prickling beneath Salt's gaze. His very presence felt like a brand on my soul, and I couldn't help but feel as though he were staking his claim. I glanced up at the bass player who watched us, but he looked away quickly.

"Show me how to get backstage," I said.

The house lights in the venue went out, replaced by the swamp green stage lights they'd chosen. I didn't love the green —in fact, I hated it—but didn't have time to stew about it as Salt gripped my elbow gently and steered me towards a door. We went down a short dark hall, and into a room buzzing with people and equipment.

I jerked my elbow out of his grip before anyone stared at us. A young woman sat on an amp while talking to a couple of guys. She had bright purple hair that was pulled into a french braid, golden brown skin, and wore a black leather bustier with matching leather pants and boots. Absolutely gorgeous, with that magnetism I could spot by now. She was definitely a performer who drew crowds. The two guys talking to her gave her a nod and went on their way, taking whatever directions she'd given them to heart.

No one had to tell me she was the lead singer—it was beyond clear.

"Look who it is," she called, grinning at Salt. Her eyes darted to me and she offered a genuine smile too, but remained seated.

I liked her.

Salt chuckled and led me over to her. "Hey, Tara. This is Pepper."

Her eyes lit up and she beamed at me, charisma oozing off her in waves. I felt myself relax—this was one of my favorite parts of my job.

"Hi Tara," I said. "Nice to meet you."

"It's a pleasure to meet you. I'm assuming you're here to scout Mr. Mysterious." She winked at Salt, and I felt yucky jealousy claw at my chest.

"She's a friend," Salt said. "I'll be back. I need to put on my mask and tune my guitar. And check in with the guys. Pepper, do you need anything?"

"She's safe with me, handsome," Tara purred, giving him an appreciative once over.

Salt gave my shoulder a gentle squeeze and then left us. It took every shred of strength I possessed not to follow after him like some lost puppy.

What is wrong with me? I forced a smile and focused on Tara. "I'm excited to hear you play tonight."

"Thanks," she said, sliding off the amp. "I'm excited to be here."

I nodded. "You're from Chicago?"

"Yes," she said. "There's four of us in the band. My brother and I started it five years ago, and I don't know. It kind of went from there."

"Do you write your own music?" I asked.

"We do," she said. "Well, my brother, Tanner, mostly writes the lyrics. I write the melodies. And then our friends, Mario and Al, have been essential to creating our sound. We make a good team."

I glanced up, spotting the two who were probably Mario and Al. Another man, who was definitely her brother, gave us a wave but went back to unraveling an abundance of chords. The drummer and keyboard player from Salt's band came down the steps into the room, their groups forming a circle as they clearly worked through whatever issues they were having.

"Fuck," she sighed. "I don't love this venue. It's not what we were told it would be. I should probably double check a few things while Salt plays."

"Do you need help with anything?" I asked.

She raised a brow. "Aren't you a label executive?"

"Yes," I laughed. "And?"

"I just figured you're here to listen. And definitely not work."

"Well, I *am* here to listen," I said. "But I know how to run a sound system, among other things. Like lighting. It's been awhile since I've been backstage, but I can help. Put me to work."

I needed to do *something* that wasn't fawning over Salt.

She chewed on her bottom lip and hummed. "Actually... You know how to run lights?"

"Yep."

"Okay... Obviously you can say no, but I think I would rather you run lights than the asshole they have doing it."

I grimaced. "The green is hideous."

She nodded in agreement. "Oh my god, it's horrible. Okay, yeah, let's go kick him out. I can pay you—"

"Don't be silly," I said.

Tara hesitated, but then looked over at the rest of her band. Salt's bass player joined the fray and it made me wonder how many men it really took to fix whatever issue they were having. "Are you sure?"

"Yep."

"Okay. You'll have a great view of the stage, too. And won't have to deal with all the stage smoke or the drunks."

"Perfect. Show me where the lighting booth is," I said.

I glanced over at Salt and smiled to myself. He was sinking into his stage presence. His mask was on, his shirt off, and every part of me wanted to get back on my knees in front of him and suck him off while he sang me a song.

And now, more than ever, I remembered poignantly that I was not wearing underwear.

I smoothed my hands down my dress and followed Tara back out into the main part of the venue, skirting around the edge as people flowed in. The bar was already hopping, chatter blending with the warble of music.

We went through a door that had seen better days, up a dimly lit set of stairs to another door. She knocked on it impatiently and it swung open.

"Hi," she chirped. "Drew, right?"

The boy on the other side had to be in college. He barely looked old enough to drink. "Yes," he said. "Something wrong?"

"Nothing is wrong, but Pepper here is going to take over lighting tonight. She's a professional."

We both expected resistance, but instead, Drew breathed out a sigh of relief. "Thank god. I told Dale I don't know how to run this lighting system. It's crazy outdated. And I was supposed to be doing sound downstairs."

He stepped aside and we filed into the small room. It was a massive lighting console facing a window that overlooked the entire club. On one hand, it was completely overkill for the size of this venue, on the other—at least it was a professional piece of equipment.

"Ugh," Tara groaned. "We're so fucked."

"It'll be fine," I said, looking around. "I know how to run this. It looks like a lot, but it's not. Where did you set the green lights?"

Drew pointed to the left side of the board. I moved in closer, squinting at the labels with sharpie scrawled on them. The good news was it looked like each of the color lights were labeled correctly.

It'd been awhile since I'd done this, but I certainly hadn't forgotten. Some of the first bands Rosethorn ended up taking on were people I'd run sound and lighting for early in my career. That being a decade ago worked in my favor because he was right, this board was outdated.

"What the hell is going on?"

Our heads whipped up as Dale filled the doorframe. He was barely taller than me, but his broad shoulders and the way he carried himself felt threatening. Even though I knew he wasn't, and I also knew he'd back off the moment someone snapped back at him.

"She's running our lights," Tara said, her voice hardening.

I knew too well what that felt like. Having to adjust how you spoke to someone because otherwise they wouldn't listen. If you were too polite, you'd get walked all over. If you were too blunt, you were a bitch.

Long ago, I decided I'd rather be called a bitch.

"She's not—"

"Dale, you lied to us about the size of this venue and I'm certain you overcharged us for playing."

"He charged *you*?" I scoffed. "Did he charge Salt?"

"Yeah," she said quickly. "I mean, we should make it back with ticket sales, but—"

"That's absurd," I said, giving Dale a hard look.

"I don't like you," he bit out.

I laughed. "Maybe I should text my friend who does venue licensing down at—"

"No, no," he said quickly, holding up his hands the same way he did with Salt earlier. He was a fucking coward, just like I'd guessed. "I don't want any trouble. Just want things to run smoothly."

"Do you own this place?" I asked bluntly.

"No, I'm the manager—"

"Who owns it?"

His cheeks turned ruddy. "I'm not telling you."

I rolled my eyes and faded the green light over the venue down, pushing blue up. "I'll find out anyway. No need to be so elusive."

"Bitch," he muttered under his breath.

Tara and Drew stiffened, but I ignored him. "Do you want to know how much I make per hour Dale? And do you want to pay me that? Or do you want to get back downstairs to check on your bar and all the other shit you need to tend to?"

Dale hovered for a moment, but then grumbled, "Fine."

Then he was gone. I snorted. It'd been awhile since I'd scared off someone so easily. I gave Tara a knowing look. "You need to get back down there, the show is going to start soon. Have fun."

Tara winked and headed for the door, Drew following after her. "Well, thank you again."

"You're welcome. Close the door on your way out, please."

"Yes, ma'am." The door shut softly, shutting me into the small room with a perfect view.

I frowned and focused on the lighting console, using my phone flashlight to look everything over. I played with the settings until I had a good sense of how this one worked, then looked up as the music playing through the venue stopped, followed by cheers and claps.

I stood up to look out the window.

This time, they opened the set with everyone on stage without Salt.

The moment Salt stepped on stage, there was a ripple that swept through the venue. I watched as people came closer, drawn in like moths to his flame.

For the first time in ages, everything in my life melted away and I became completely entranced by music.

It was like sliding into cool water on a roasting summer day. A comforting breeze whispering *'welcome back'* in my ear. Beckoning me into the arms of the very thing that had saved me, cursed me, helped me, ruined me.

I brought a mix of red and white light onto the stage, haloing Salt as he started to play his guitar. I gave the other three a dark red. A heavy base note reverberated through my bones as Salt stepped up the mic.

His voice.

It would probably be what destroyed me at the end of all of this. Subduing any forces of logic or reasons with a baritone croon that had my thighs squeezing tighter.

The lyrics were sexually charged. Obsessive. Possessive. Salt burned through my veins as I adjusted the lighting, finding the sweet spot. It would look good on camera, giving him a sort of ethereal god-like appearance.

Now I could sit and watch.

And listen.

My clit throbbed as I stared at Salt, my breath catching. I glanced at the door nervously, but then...

I just couldn't help myself.

My fingertips grazed my dress until I gripped the hem, hiking the skirt up. I looked at the doorway again. But lust twisted through me, turning me into *his* helpless plaything.

"This is too much."

My whisper was lost in the sound of him.

The chorus was charged with aggression, but only on the surface. Nerves rolled through me as I slid my fingers against my pussy, sucking in a breath.

I was so wet.

"Fuck," I groaned, needy. So fucking needy.

Why couldn't I just walk away from him? I was trapped. Caged in. There was no leaving, no escaping. *I want him.*

I continued to stare out the window at the stage. Beneath the harsh chorus was a deep longing, the kind I recognized immediately. The window became a mirror, and he was the beauty to my ugly, horrid reflection.

I just wanted him. Was that so fucking wrong? After years of not feeling wanted, was it so bad to be with someone who did?

Just the thought of having to inform the board of us being together terrified me. It could hurt my reputation. A CEO sleeping with an artist wasn't new, but I wasn't that type of CEO.

My head tipped back, my eyes slanting as I watched him, touching myself unapologetically. A shudder rolled through me as I fought against the sheer fabric of my hose.

It was getting in the way.

I bit my bottom lip hard, the pain only turning me on more. I looked down. Without a second thought, I grabbed the crotch of fabric and ripped. It split with ease, giving me the access I wanted to touch myself.

A whimper left me as he moved into the next song, but it was just as depraved and addicting. *Slower. Deeper.*

I curled my fingers inside myself, gasping at how wet I was. *Fuck.* My eyes closed as I pushed myself hard and fast, pumping them in and out to the beat of Salt's music. A needy fever burned through me, catching fire as I played with myself.

His music was what I'd been looking for. Rosethorn needed him, he needed us. Which meant I'd need to be his boss, I'd need to somehow put a stop to being with him.

And yet—every single one of those sane thoughts evaporated as my orgasm washed over me, reverberating through my entire body. I slapped my hand over my mouth as I came.

My moans harmonized with Salt's voice, muscles melting into the chair.

Holy shit, I just came from listening to him.

SIXTEEN
SALT

SWEAT SLICKED my body as I stepped off stage. I breathed out the moment I was out of view from the rest of the venue. *Where is Pepper?*

I'd seen her go off with Tara, but she'd never returned. I raked my guitar string smudged fingers through my hair, looking around the backroom wildly.

"Hey."

I looked up at Tara, startled by her. She raised a brow as she slid off an amp, rolling her shoulders.

"Watching you play is always something else," she said. "Got them warmed up for us."

"It'll be a great show," I said. "Where's Pepper?"

She offered a sly smile. "She's running lights. Told her she didn't have to, but she jumped right in. It was nice of her."

I clutched my guitar a little tighter. "That *was* nice of her."

I was a little surprised, although I shouldn't have been. Standing around and doing nothing seemed like it would be torture for her, so of course she'd found something to stay busy.

"The light booth is on the other side of the venue, up a set of stairs, and in a private room." Tara wiggled her brows.

"I don't know what you mean by that," I said lightly.

Before she could quip back, Jack came off stage with his bass, his body gleaming. "That was great," he said.

"It was," I agreed. "Does Tyler need help with the drum set?"

"Nah," Jack said. "That's what you pay us for. Um, can I talk to you for a minute, though?"

What the fuck could this possibly be about? "Sure," I said.

He put his arm around my shoulder as we moved out of the way of the steps. I almost shrugged him off, but felt like that would not be received well.

"So, why is the Rosethorn CEO here?" he asked.

"She just came to listen."

He made a face. "Okay. Listen, dude. Word of advice, okay? You're a good looking guy. She has a lot of power. Don't let her take advantage of you, you know?"

My breath whooshed out of me from his implication. "Jack. You're not saying you think she'd use that to try and fuck me? Surely not."

"I'm just saying, it happens all the time. That woman has no feelings. Plus, she's a lot older than you. You're too young to be fucking around with someone like *that*. It wouldn't be good for your career to get entangled with her."

Everything went dead cold, and I didn't just shrug him off, I shoved him back. And without skipping a moment, I did something bad. "You're fired."

Jack's expression scrunched up with laughter, but the longer I stared at him, the more it melted into shock. Then more shock. Then anger.

"*What?*"

"You're fired," I repeated. "One, you're not a fucking feminist. You were repeatedly a dipshit in the garage yesterday, and I just have zero interest in working with someone with so little respect for women. Two, what you just insinuated is beyond disrespectful to both me and Pepper."

"Pepper?" he scoffed. "So you're on a first name basis then? Already fucking her?"

"Jack," I warned, my temper scorching all reason. "Get the fuck out before I break your jaw."

"I'm not stupid. She's hot as fuck, Salt, but you should tread lightly given who she is. This is a stupid thing. I get that you're young, but—"

"She's just an acquaintance," I lied. "Get the fuck out. Now."

What she was, was *mine*. And I needed to touch her now, the way I'd been imagining since we got off the phone last night.

"Sure," Jack sneered. "Musicians talk, man. This was fucking stupid. You don't piss off the band."

I sighed and unclasped my mask, giving him a look that made him take a step back. "Do I need to tell you to leave again?"

"No. I'm out of here. Good fucking luck with that record deal. You're gonna need it if you become her little pet."

I stood still, clenching my fist as I watched him pack up and go. Tyler and Eric approached warily, but Tyler shook his head.

"I don't know what that was, but that fucker was off beat half of the time. I got a good bass player who would be down to fill his spot," Tyler said.

I breathed out slowly. "That would be great. Sorry."

"I'm glad he's gone," Eric said with a shrug. "Bad vibes."

"Agreed."

Tyler grimaced. "You're not dating the CEO, are you?"

"No," I said. "She's here to listen tonight. That's all."

Both of them accepted that. The three of us debriefed, and I glanced up as Tara waved from the stairs. "Put in a good word for us with your boss, please. A record deal would change our lives for the better."

Before I could say anything else, Tara darted up the steps onto the stage. The other band members shuffled up behind her. The crowd was super engaged tonight, and I felt the excitement in the air, magnetically charged. I looked through the doorway at the stage as the lights changed from red to a pearlescent blue that made the four of them pop.

"I'm out for the night," Tyler said. "See you Monday for practice?"

"Yeah, if that works."

"I'll be there," Eric said.

"Great. See you then." I took my guitar to its case in the corner and put it away carefully, tossing my mask into a black bag next to it. I pulled out a black hoodie and tugged it on, my stomach twisting at the thought of having to cross the bar right now. But, with any luck, everyone's focus would be on Tara's band. I grabbed my guitar case and bag, and left the room.

"Salt!"

Fuck. All I wanted was to get to Pepper. Why the fuck was everyone up my ass today? I turned as Dale approached me down the hall.

"Was I worth it?" I asked, not keeping the venom out of my tone. I was over his behavior and Jack's.

Was Jack wrong to give a warning? I knew Pepper wasn't using me in any way. But the fact that he'd guessed so easily that there was something between us made me wonder if I was being reckless.

Dale blanched. "You were. I'm sorry I was a dick earlier.

She just rubbed me the wrong way. If anything, I probably owe her now for running the lights..."

"You do. I'm going to go sit in the light booth with her."

Dale nodded, but clearly there was something else he wanted to say. I raised a brow as I waited, and he finally spilled. "I just want you to be careful. I know tonight didn't go as smoothly as usual, but your performance was great. And I just want to warn you about having someone like Pepper interested in you. Just be careful."

Ugh. Everyone was on me tonight. "She can't hurt me," I said.

"She can hurt anyone in this city, aside from a handful of CEOs of other companies. Rosethorn may be a small label, but it's the biggest independently owned one there is. The roster they have is damn good. Everyone wants to work for them, especially since they treat their artists and employees well."

"And all of that is because of Pepper," I said. "At least, that's what I've heard."

He winced. "I don't like her because of what happened to my sister. But I don't like any of the suits in this town, they're all a bunch of snooty assholes. I don't want to see you get trapped in something you can't get out of."

"I'll be careful." Frustration clawed up my spine. His warning was starting to get under my skin. So was Jack's.

They were wrong about her.

But I knew a different Pepper, didn't I?

The one he knew was the woman who told him his sister was a piece of shit to his face.

The one I knew was the woman who'd begged me to fuck her.

Needless to say, we weren't the same. But he didn't know that.

"I'll be in the booth," I said. "Can I leave my equipment back here? I'll grab it after the show."

"Of course. We'll pay out once the show ends and the bar closes. It'll be a late night."

"Thanks," I said. I set down my guitar case against the wall, but kept my bag in hand. "I'm going to go cool off." I needed to get the fuck out of here. Between firing Jack and dealing with everything else, I felt claustrophobic. Like walls were caging me in.

I wanted Pepper. It'd been days since I'd felt her skin against mine, and I was desperate. Crazed for her.

"Maybe pull your hood up if you don't want to be stopped," he suggested. "They're a little wild for you. We sold a lot at the bar and our social media girl told me the bar is getting tagged online a lot. It'll be a good payout."

If the comment section on my most recent video was any indication, he was right. But, I'd be a liar if I said I didn't enjoy it. I may or may not have been an attention whore sometimes.

But I needed Pepper's attention the most right now.

SEVENTEEN
SALT

I SAID goodnight to Dale and pulled my hood up before going out the door. I was quick, moving along the edge of the crowd, sticking to the wall, avoiding eye contact. I made it to the door on the other side, pushed it open, and darted up the staircase. The scent of smoke and stale beer followed.

The door to my right had to be the one to the lighting booth. I stepped through it quickly. A squeal followed.

My eyes widened as I shut the door slowly behind me.

It was dark in here, but that didn't keep me from seeing how flushed Pepper's skin was. She had her skirt tugged down, her eyes wide as she stared at me like I was a ghost.

Slowly, very slowly, I narrowed my eyes on her. "What did you do?"

"Nothing," she rasped.

I dropped my bag to the floor and reached behind me, twisting the lock on the door. "Spread your legs."

"No."

I laughed and stalked towards her like a beast going after

prey. I stopped when I was toe to toe, her heels shiny and perfect against my scuffed boots.

"Look at me," I whispered.

She wouldn't. She was embarrassed. *What did she do?* I grabbed hold of her chin and gently tipped it up, forcing her to look me in the eye. Using my knee, I wedged her knees apart. Her body was hot and wound up, her mascara smudged beneath her pretty hazel eyes.

Oh. The way she was looking at me right now made me pause. Her pupils were blown, her lips parted, waiting for a kiss.

"How was the show?" I purred.

"Good," she whispered. "You were phenomenal."

"Mm. What was your favorite song?"

Her lashes fluttered. "Um..."

I leaned down, using my free hand to feel her thigh, running my palm over her until it came to her core. Heat rolled off her in waves as I felt a hole in her pantyhose.

"You naughty little slut," I whispered. Excitement curled through me. "What happened here, Pepper? Tell me. Now."

She shivered from my touch. "I... got a little carried away..."

"Up here while running lights?"

"While listening to you."

"I see." I knelt down so that my face was level with her, her thighs still spread, pussy wet against my fingertips. "So let me get this right, Pepper. I just want to make sure I'm understanding. You ripped your pantyhose so you could masturbate out in the open while listening to me sing?"

"Yes," she said, staring at me. "That's exactly what I did."

She rolled her chair back from me, turning towards the lighting console as the band hit the chorus. I glowered as she moved a few of the switches, her focus on them.

I snorted and grabbed the back of the chair, yanking hard

enough that she squeaked. I pulled her out of it and kicked it back, pulling her ass against the bulge in my jeans.

She gasped, her hands planting on the edge of the console. "I'm working."

"I was working too, but that didn't stop you from getting off to me."

I hiked her dress up and reached around, sliding two fingers inside the hole she'd made, ripping the sheer fabric further.

Pepper gasped, her muscles trembling as I bared her sweet ass. "Was that good for you, baby girl? Touching yourself when you shouldn't have? Did you come?"

"Yes," she cried. "I came so fucking hard I saw stars."

"Well, make a fucking wish, because you're about to see them again."

This was going to be hard and fast. The ache inside me demanded penance for her pleasuring herself when she knew what I planned to do to her tonight. I needed to be inside her, gliding in and out of her wet pussy while she moaned my name.

Music thrummed loud enough that the walls trembled.

"Keep doing your job," I growled. "Running the lights like you wanted."

"But—"

I slapped her ass hard, enjoying her whimper.

"Do your fucking job, Pepper, and I'll do mine."

"*Yes, Sir.*"

A streak of satisfaction rushed through me. Every time she submitted to me, it pleased me.

Her gaze lifted to the window, her hand trembling as she reached for one of the light switches as I unclasped my belt. The metal clinked and I unbuttoned and unzipped quickly, pulling my cock free. I ripped her pantyhose further until the head of my cock brushed against her flesh.

In one swift motion, I thrusted into her, filling her with every inch. Her scream was lost in the music, her back arching as she took me with ease, still so fucking wet from touching herself.

I grabbed a fistful of her hair, tugging her head back as I pumped into her, my other hand slapping the top of her ass cheek. She braced herself against the console, her voice ringing as I fucked her the way I'd been needing to.

"Fuck," I growled.

It was almost painful how hard I was for her. A euphoric rush followed as I fucked her hard and deep, gripping her hair as I took her.

The band hit the chorus and she reached up, struggling to focus on the lights. I liked watching her struggle. I liked knowing how competent she was at everything she did, but couldn't think clearly enough to do her job while taking my cock like a good girl.

Pepper moaned as she changed the lights, her pussy clenching around me, milking me. I released her hair and gripped her hips, my fingertips digging into her soft skin as I drove in and out.

Obsession. Possession. The darkness I did my best to hide from everyone. All of it was dragged to the surface by her, salt on an open wound. I grunted, my hips jerking as she clenched around me hard, her body tensing as she suddenly came.

"Fuck," I gasped, going still. I wasn't ready to come yet, but feeling her orgasm on my cock made it almost impossible to withhold. I squeezed my eyes shut and waited until she finished, feeling her go limp against the console, followed by her soft moan.

And then I started to fuck her again. This time slower, every thrust deeper.

"Salt," she panted. "You feel so good. Oh god—"

"Tell me you want me to breed your pretty little cunt," I growled.

"Please," she said. "Please breed me. Please, I'm begging you. I was so bad earlier…"

My eyes widened. What was she doing to me? Turning me into a goddamn monster. "Tell me," I choked out.

"I touched myself while listening to your voice. I couldn't help it. But now you're here and I'm yours. *Fuck.*"

My pace picked up as she spoke, her words tumbling out.

"*Please, please, please.* Please fuck me. Please breed me."

"You're going to walk out of this bar tonight in front of god and everyone with my cum inside you. Every single person kisses the ground you walk on. If only they knew what we were doing right now…"

She tensed around me. "Fuck," she whimpered. "It's our secret."

"Is that all it is?"

She didn't answer me. I growled and pulled out of her without warning. Pepper immediately protested, but I cut her off, spinning her around to face me. I lifted her, her legs wrapping around my waist as I backed her to the door, slamming into her again.

Her lips caught mine in a hungry kiss, our tongues fighting. She melted against me as my cock filled her again, her nails digging into my shoulders. The pain only made me harder, and I bit her bottom lip in response. She jerked against me, a whimper following.

I was so close. So fucking close.

"Fill me," she rasped between kisses. "*Please,* Salt."

The door shook as I thrusted into her once more, unable to control myself anymore. I buried my face against her neck as I came, pleasure bursting through me as I pumped her full of my cum. I moaned in her ear, completely wrapped up in her, everything about her.

My breaths were rapid as we melted against each other, our bodies fused together. She kissed my throat, her limbs relaxing completely.

For a moment, it was just us in the world. No bar, no band, no anything.

Just Pepper.

Just me.

Just the feeling of our bodies intertwined together.

"Come home with me tonight," I whispered.

She breathed out slowly. "I can't. I have work in the morning."

Work. Fuck. I just wanted to wake up next to her. I wanted to *be* with her.

"We can't do this again. You have to tell me the club—"

"I'll take you a club. As your Dom," I said. "But I'm not letting go. I don't care about anything else."

She grabbed my face, giving me a stern expression. "You are going to go places. You can't be tied down to someone like me. You deserve better."

"You're wrong," I whispered.

I needed her to see that about herself. We could find ways to work around our careers, but whatever this spark was between us deserved a chance to ignite.

She shook her head. "I'm not. Your music belongs at Rosethorn, but *this?* This toxic attraction? *This* doesn't belong anywhere in our lives."

"It doesn't have to be toxic," I said. "You could tell your board. Just tell them that we're together—"

"We've known each other for *days*." She scowled and then wiggled against me. "Put me down."

"No."

"Put me *down*."

I held her a moment longer and then pulled out, slowly setting her down. Before she could spin away, I went to my knees in front of her, running my hands up her thighs. I looked up at her, bunching the skirt of her dress up to look at her pussy, my cum dripping from her.

"I'm not going to give up the meeting tomorrow," I said as I pushed it back inside her with two fingers.

Her breath hitched. "I would never ask you to do that."

"I know. It crossed my mind though. That we wouldn't need to resist each other if that was the case."

"You're not giving this up. I'm certain that by the end of Friday I'll have contracts on my desk to review. A proposal..." Her words trailed off as I pushed more of my cum back into her.

"You could tell them no. Tell them you don't want me."

"We both know that I want you."

I drew my fingers back and reached up, offering them to her. She parted her lips, sucking my cum off them.

"You aren't even giving us a chance," I murmured.

"You *know* why I can't. It's unprofessional. It's..."

I swallowed hard and stood, releasing her dress. "Okay," I said. I hated this, but I wouldn't keep fighting her. "You don't need to stay for the rest of the show. I'll run their lights."

Pepper froze. "But..."

"But what?" I bit out. "The sex club is called The Garden. I'll text you their info tomorrow. It'll be perfect for you. I doubt you'll have any trouble finding a good Dom that will treat you right."

"Salt..."

"Go," I said, stepping away. I grabbed the chair I'd kicked away earlier and righted it, settling into it in front of the board.

"I'm not playing chase with a rabbit choking on their own snare."

Pepper was silent. "I just don't want to hurt you."

"Pepper. Go home." My voice was far more stern this time.

I heard the click of the lock and turned my head slightly, watching as she opened the door slowly. She stood still for a moment, but then fled, running away from this.

From me.

She was right, wasn't she? It was for the best. It was easier to stop now before we became entangled and trapped, caged in by our careers and insecurities.

I stood up, looking out the window. I watched her weave through the crowd. Once she was out of sight, I sat back down, forcing myself to focus on the stage. On the lights.

The scent of sex clung to me.

She was a crimson rose with thorns that would cut me and bleed me.

But I yearned for that pain.

For the type of love that would strangle me.

That would set me free.

She'd come back.

I hoped.

EIGHTEEN

PEPPER

CRYING myself to sleep left me feeling hungover the next morning. Usually, I kept my office door open, but today wasn't normal. So, I closed my door and shut myself in with coffee while I read through emails and ignored everyone else.

Last night was too much. I'd gone out to a bar to listen to Salt without panties on. I still couldn't believe I'd done that. I also couldn't believe that I enjoyed it.

I loved being praised. Really, I did. But I was also starting to realize that I enjoyed degradation, too. That the slight edge of humiliation sparked something unexpected inside me. I wasn't sure what to do with any of that information now, though. Everything was over and Salt would move on. I'd made the right choice.

A knock came at my door, and then it cracked open. Tommy poked his head in, giving a wave. "Have a moment?" he asked.

"Of course," I replied.

He slipped inside and shut the door behind him, coming to

stand behind the sleek chair in front of my desk. He had a look on his face I didn't like.

"I heard a rumor," Tommy said hesitantly.

A rumor. Already, I felt myself shutting down any emotions, bracing for whatever else he had to say. "What kind of rumor?" I asked, my tone flat.

He winced as he sat down on the edge of the chair, leaning forward to study me. "Okay. I heard that Salt fired his bass player last night... because of you."

"*What?*" I asked. "That didn't happen."

"Well, *something* happened," Tommy said.

He drew in a sharp breath, his stress evident in the way he ran his fingers through his hair. He didn't like whatever this rumor was, which meant I wasn't going to like it either.

"And I also heard that..." He trailed off and then shifted uncomfortably. "Did you sleep with him?"

Everything stopped moving. All the years of keeping my emotions in check had never been more useful than they were now. "Someone insinuated that we slept together?" I asked lightly.

I knew someone was watching us. Fuck.

Tommy nodded. "Yeah. Did you?"

Tommy had always been direct. And he knew me too fucking well.

The only card I had was to play into what everyone thought about me.

"Do you really think someone like Salt, a twenty-five-year-old horny songwriter covered in tattoos, would sleep with someone like me?"

He blinked and sat back slightly. He blew out a breath. "I don't know, Pepper. The divorce was hard on you. It's been a tough time, and I wouldn't blame you for having fun with someone younger. But Salt is way too young for you. And I mean, someone like you shouldn't even want to be with some-thing like him."

"Something?" I asked. "You mean someone?"

He sighed, clearly uncomfortable. "Yeah, of course. My point is that you wouldn't be interested in doing the stuff I'm sure that guy is into. You didn't even know what a Prince Albert piercing was until last week."

A mix of humiliation, fear, and anger crept up. "It wouldn't be wrong for me to have desires."

"Of course not," he said smoothly. "Of *course* not. But like... maybe not those desires."

"Tommy," I said, taken aback. "I know about you and Dan's sex life. It's not like you're not into stuff. I don't understand what you're thinking about me."

His knee was bouncing up and down. "I don't know what you want me to say. You're kind of a prude. You always have been. I love you, Pepper, and I know you'd never do anything sexual with a client."

"Well, then there's your answer," I whispered with a smile. *But Salt isn't a client. Yet.*

Tommy nodded and then his smile melted. "Right. Of course."

"Salt isn't a client yet. So if I did sleep with him, it wouldn't be wrong," I said. "And if he were a client, and I did sleep with him, I'd inform the board per the morality clause in my contract. The same one that both you and Jeff have. And then what?"

Tommy just stared.

"Nothing," I said. "Right? Because you'd be informed."

"It would make things difficult..."

"Difficult? Like how Jeff was difficult when he was fucking the intern for months and everyone knew about it but me?"

His cheeks flushed. "Yeah. Maybe not that bad. But it wouldn't be good."

All I did was nod. My heart was beating too fast. "He's too young."

"Oh, definitely," Tommy snorted, still nervous.

"Too hot for me, too."

Tommy agreed initially, but then frowned. "Pepper, you're—"

"He's just not my type. You can go."

He went still, frowning. "I feel like I've upset you."

"You have," I said. "Tommy, I love you, but you're a dumbass. And Dan is my favorite."

"Jesus," he gasped, covering his heart like he'd been shot.

We stared at each other for a moment, and both cracked smiles And this time, my smile was a little bit more genuine. Even though my feelings were hurt, and this had just been a painful reminder that—*don't fucking go there now.*

"I'm sorry I hurt you," he said. "I care about you, Pepper. Deeply. Are you okay?"

"The death date is coming up." It'd be my excuse to anyone close to me for the next week. "Just not a good time to be accused of bad behavior by someone who's known me for so long."

"Fuck. I'm sorry. I just heard that rumor and was so shocked, but I'll get those fires put out. And fuck that bass player for starting such gossip. That fucker is on my list now."

"Thanks," I said. "So that's where it came from? And not Dale?"

"Who the fuck is Dale?" Tommy snorted.

"Nobody." I was made of plastic. "Do you mind shutting the door on your way out? I just have a headache today."

"Of course. Let me know if you need anything."

"Will do."

The moment the door closed, I pushed my chair back, and sat on the floor, leaning against my desk as I forced myself to breathe.

My eyes closed as I counted to ten, fighting through the hurricane of emotions.

Deep breath, deep breath...

My whole body trembled. In the darkness of my mind, I remembered hiding like this years ago. Hiding in my closet while my parents fought. They never screamed. They never hit. It was always done in hushed whispers and passive aggressive actions. In the closet, I could feel things like sadness and fear. Outside of the closet, I had to be perfect again.

I thought for so long that part of me was dead. But maybe I'd been wrong. Everyone still saw me as Perfect Pepper. Everyone still saw me as this intimidating figure, without sexual needs or desires. I couldn't have a personality outside of the company I'd built.

God forbid I ever wanted someone like Salt.

Last night came roaring back. Leaving the club, calling an Uber while squeezing my thighs together and worrying that people *knew* where I'd been and what we'd been doing. I knew people saw us. I knew they'd talk. I'd still made the choice to go out and see him play.

And I didn't regret it.

I didn't regret touching myself to his music.

I didn't regret climaxing to the sound of him. To the feeling of him.

I didn't regret having sex with him again.

What I regretted was walking away. I regretted waking up in a massive bed, in silken sheets that were the only thing wrapped around my body. I regretted not taking more time to be with him.

Why did it have to be like this? I wiped my eyes gently and

then opened them, readjusting the light of my office. I wished that I could stay here, hidden forever.

I'd done the right thing by cutting things off with Salt.

Why didn't it feel that way?

NINETEEN
SALT

THE ROSETHORN RECORDS offices were in an intimidating high-rise that made my skin crawl. I got home at two a.m. this morning, slept for three hours, then woke up restless and unsure about the decision to even come to this meeting.

The last few nights, I'd either been at a club or on stage. Both on one of the nights, but don't remember which. I was exhausted. I was trying to chase away the void closing in on me.

The lobby was pristine. Shiny, waxed floors with tall mirrored ceilings that reflected everything and everyone. Sweat clung to me, my heart thumping wildly as I approached the front desk.

I was nervous.

I shouldn't have been. I didn't need this to happen. I didn't need it the way I knew every other songwriter and singer in Nashville needed it. Tara's plea to put in a good word for her came to mind, and my mouth went dry.

The lady sitting at the desk looked up expectantly.

I cleared my throat. "Hi. I have a meeting with Rosethorn Records? Simon Salt. I was told to get a visitor's badge at the front desk."

"Give me one second," she said, clicking her mouse rapidly. "Ten a.m.?"

"Yes." My fingers drummed against my thigh.

"Can I see your ID?"

"Sure." I pulled out my wallet and handed it to her, glancing around. Fuck, why was I nervous? Why did I even care?

After everything that happened with Pepper earlier this week, I needed to move on. I needed to go after this opportunity with everything I had, and pretend that the woman I wanted most wouldn't be my fucking boss if I got it.

If I didn't take it, Pepper would have no reason to keep resisting the spark between us. But I'd meant what I told her. I loved a good primal chase, but I wasn't going to hunt her down and force her to be with me like some fucking caveman.

But if, for whatever reason, the meeting went well... If this was something I wanted...

I wouldn't be able to walk away. I owed myself that much, didn't I?

Maybe it was some sort of sign that my birthday was next week. It was my least favorite day of the year. Without fail, I always spiraled into a miserable pit of eternal despair that took a couple days to pull myself out of.

So maybe I'd get a deal.

And that would make me feel at least a little human next Sunday.

Or I wouldn't.

And I'd go piss on my father's grave.

"Sir? Sir..."

I blinked, coming back to the moment. "Sorry. I'm anxious."

She smiled. "I'm sure you'll be okay. Here's your ID and visitor badge. Take the elevator on the right, Rosethorn is on floor fifteen and sixteen. You'll go to fifteen."

"Thanks."

I took the ID and badge and moved out of the way for the person behind me. After I got myself situated, I headed for the elevators.

Everyone around me was dressed like a lawyer. I felt painfully out of place in a denim jacket, black jeans, my boots, and a shirt that usually went over well on stage. Now, I was second guessing all of those choices.

The doors slid open and I stepped in, others filing in. I jabbed fifteen and pressed my back against the wall as more people joined. My heart pounded as I wrestled with my anxiety.

"Good morning, Ms. Jones."

The energy in the elevator shifted, and so god help me, I knew without evening opening my eyes that she was here.

Can't fucking escape her.

I opened them, and was proven right. Pepper stepped into the elevator, her gaze moving over me, expression cool and unreadable. This was the Pepper everyone else knew.

"Good morning." Her voice was so cold. Stiff.

The doors slid shut, caging us together. I stared at the back of her head, watching as she shifted uncomfortably. The elevator lifted within a few seconds, the doors slid open and a few people got off. Then it repeated, until it was just Pepper, me, and a man I didn't know.

"So you're just giving me the cold shoulder now?" the stranger muttered.

Pepper's shoulders stiffened in a way that made every

alarm bell in my head go off. She turned, casting him a glare that would shrivel the balls on any other man. "What did you say, Jeff?"

"Cold shoulder?" he quipped. "You know—"

"Not in front of a potential client." Her eyes finally danced over to me, but she quickly looked away.

Fuck. I just want you to look at me.

The man, Jeff, looked over at me curiously. He held out his hand. "Oh. I'm Jeff, nice to meet you. Sorry for the awkwardness, used to be married—"

"*Jeff*, I swear to god," Pepper snarled, spinning around. Her gaze was electric. "Shut the fuck up. *Shut up.*"

Jeff. Jeff. *He* was her ex-husband. This was the man that had been married to Pepper for years and never made her orgasm. Who'd shamed her for her desires.

This was the guy that'd made her doubt herself so much?

He was a couple inches shorter than me with sandy brown hair, bright blue eyes, and broad shoulders. Just a regular looking guy. Nothing special. Not worth spending fifteen years with for nothing in return.

Imagining the two of them together sent a slithering, boiling, writhing bolt of jealousy through me that made me nauseous.

"Oh, is this the guy you went to see play last week with Tommy and Dan? I still can't believe you went out on a Friday night—"

The doors opened. Pepper was out before Jeff could say anything else, her heels clicking with rage as she left. I watched her go, wishing I could run after her.

We both stepped off the elevator and my hands clasped behind my back before I did something stupid, like punch him.

"Sorry about that," Jeff chuckled. "What did she say your name was? Salt?"

My jaw ticked. "Yes. Salt. Where do I go to meet Tommy?"

"I'll show you," he said lightly, beaming again.

I hated him. God, I really fucking hated him. I swallowed my anger down and followed him through the office space, trying to look around and take it all in.

Ignore the fucker. Ignore him, ignore him, ignore him.

After firing Jack and snapping at Dale, I'd realized that I'd be an asshole to anyone who said anything about Pepper. And knowing that her fucking ex-husband was standing right next to me...

I really wanted to punch him. I wanted to also tell him that I'd fucked Pepper better than he ever could. And that he should quit his job so Pepper no longer had to see him every day.

Jeff pointed at a meeting room. "Go have a seat. Tommy will be in shortly. Normally I'd be joining too, but I have something else to do. Just need to impress Tommy, really."

Did he do anything here? Because that sounded like bullshit.

"And hey, let's just keep that little elevator exchange to us, if you don't mind. Don't need anyone getting all up in arms over nothing."

"Over you upsetting her?" I bit out. *Fuck. Stop. Stop before you cause a fucking scene.*

Jeff sighed. "I shouldn't say anything to you of course, but well... Pepper has had a hard time since our divorce. So I just try to keep things lively, you know? But she's refusing to let me invite my wife to an awards show."

"How long have you been married?" I asked.

"About two years."

"How long have you been divorced?"

The vein in his forehead ticked and I saw *it*. I saw his slimy temper, the enraging entitlement on his ugly fucking face. It oozed through the cracks of his professional veneer. "About the same time."

"I see." I forced a smile, flexing my hands behind my back. "I'll go take a seat."

He didn't say anything else as I stepped into the meeting room. The walls were painted a deep teal, with framed records hung in rows. I walked slowly around the mahogany table at the center, studying each one.

Rosethorn had a lot of big artists. Many I hadn't even realized belonged to them.

Pepper had been busy over the last fifteen years.

Am I really going to do this? It was scary. And I'd be giving up some control, which I certainly didn't like either.

But the stage called to me. I couldn't resist the beckoning of the music, it was too ingrained into me. Melodies haunted me, lyrics sang in my blood, and ever since I could remember picking up the guitar—I knew my life belonged to music.

I was going to do this. *If* the offer was good.

There was relief in that. I didn't like going back and forth when making decisions, so even committing to the possibility made me relax.

My phone buzzed. I pulled it out quickly, half expecting it to be Pepper. It wasn't her though, it was Beth.

Good luck, darling, we're rooting for you.

Warmth spread through my chest.

Thank you. I'll let you know how it goes

A knock at the door had me putting my phone down. I turned and smiled as Tommy filled the doorway, his energy contagious.

"Hey," he said. "Jeff put you in here?"

"Yeah," I chuckled. "I don't think he liked me."

Tommy snorted and glanced behind him before making a face. "No one likes him, so it doesn't matter. Let's go to my office, it has an actual view."

One more deep breath. "Lead the way."

TWENTY
PEPPER

IT'D BEEN a week since I'd seen Salt.

Two weeks since we met.

Tommy left a proposal on my desk at the end of the day last Friday. Their meeting was perfect, or so I'd heard. Salt had everything Tommy wanted, and Tommy had a vision of how we could take his career to the next level.

For one week, I'd let that proposal sit on my desk.

And every single day, I thought about Salt.

Despite the fact that everyone else went home for the weekend over an hour ago, I was still here.

Still staring at the damn papers.

All of my sex toys arrived earlier in the week. They'd helped the ache that was gnawing at my heart and pussy.

A knock at the door startled me. My head whipped up, but then I relaxed as Ellen leaned against the frame, offering a grim smile. She was dressed in yoga pants and a jacket, a gleam of sweat on her forehead.

"I don't think I've ever seen you stay late on a Friday unless something big was happening," she said.

I slowly covered the contract with another piece of paper as I sighed. "There's just a lot to do. Did you go for a run already?"

"Yeah, I've been off for a while now. Since I left at my normal time, unlike you. Does *a lot* have anything to do with you going to Russo's last week?"

I stiffened. "How the fuck do you know about that?"

"The same way I knew you were still working. Remember, our locations are shared on our phones?" She held hers up, flashing the screen. "You know this is how I show my love. By checking on my Sims. And I've been giving you time to confess to whatever's been weighing on you the last week, but you've been locked down tighter than a damn vault."

Fuck. I'd forgotten about the phone locations. Normally, I would have laughed, but since I was keeping secrets, it made me feel bad. "I went to listen to a potential client that night. I wanted to hear him again before his meeting with Tommy last Friday."

"Is that why you blew me off? Couldn't just tell me you wanted to go listen to a potential client? Or, I don't know, take me with you?"

Double fuck. I winced. "Are you open for dinner tonight?"

She gave me a flat expression. "I am, but only if that means you're going to tell me what's going on."

Lying to my best friend made me a bad person. I knew that. But I just wasn't ready to tell her about Salt. I still wasn't even sure what the fuck happened over the last two weeks.

It's over now.

I'd almost texted him a thousand times. By now, I was sure he'd forgotten all about me.

"My mother's death date is this weekend," I said softly. "And I've been a little frazzled between Jeff being a thorn in my side and this new client."

"Does this *client* have a name?" Ellen asked.

"Salt." Saying his name aloud felt like sharing a secret. "His name is Salt."

Ellen snorted. "Wild. Is that his first name?"

"No," I said.

"Hmm." Her shoulders softened. "I know this weekend will be hard on you. Let's make dinner, have some wine, and celebrate everything we have going for us. Whatever you're working on can wait."

It really couldn't. "Give me five minutes and I'll meet you at the elevator."

"Fine," she sighed dramatically, flashing me a smile.

I smiled back as she left and then pulled the papers back out. Tommy had put together a full portfolio on Simon. Over five hundred thousand followers, the majority of which he accumulated from a few very viral videos online. He hadn't recorded anything professionally before, and plenty of his fans were foaming at the mouth to be able to listen to him for longer than the sixty-second snippets he shared.

There were two songs in particular I was interested in. The one who had made me orgasm last Tuesday night and the one he'd closed with. The others needed work, but had a lot of potential.

He wrote his own songs. He already had a stage presence. He still had a band even if he allegedly fired one of them that night.

I traced my fingertips over the pictures of him. Tommy defined his look as sexy, mysterious, and emo. He wasn't wrong. Between his tousled hair, dark eyes, and tendency to wear all black with his leather mask—he fit that base description.

I would have chosen different words though.

Young. Hot. A sadistic sex demon with a voice that will rob your soul of sanity.

A sharp pain startled me—I'd been biting my bottom lip. The sting brought the memory of our last encounter roaring back. The sound room. Wrapping my body around him as he fucked me relentlessly. The way he'd figured out what I'd done to myself and the power exchange that followed.

The weight of this decision sat heavy on my shoulders.

If nothing happened between us, I would have approved without hesitation.

I would own his music.

It was the closest I'd ever get to making him mine.

So that was the answer then.

I opened my laptop quickly and logged into my email. I opened up my chain with Tommy and sent a brief message.

Hey Tommy,

Proposal looks good. Let's move forward.

Pepper
she/her
CEO of Rosethorn Records

Send.

I snapped my laptop shut and stood quickly, pulling on my jacket. I grabbed my bag from the bottom drawer and checked my phone.

No messages. At least, none I cared about.

Nothing from Salt.

Of course nothing from him. We'd made it clear that our fling was over. It'd been a week since I'd seen him, and over a week since we'd touched each other. Given how many would readily throw themselves at his feet, I knew I was just a forgotten memory.

I'd spent a lot of time getting used to my new vibrator this week, and thinking a little too much about getting back on my knees for him. I'd even done more research on kinks and explored things I might like. There was a whole world of pleasure I'd been missing out on.

More than anything else, I wanted to continue to explore what we had. The idea of starting over with someone else—after my experience with Salt—didn't appeal to me in any way.

I could find someone older. Someone who fit the picture of who my friends imagined me with. A man who'd already gone through a divorce, too. Maybe with older kids. A career that was set in stone, steady and respectful.

Not a broke, horny songwriter over a decade younger than me.

But, now the contract was signed. If we pursued a relationship, I'd have to inform the board, or risk my position as CEO. And I wasn't going to risk over fifteen years of work for anyone. It meant too much to me.

And telling everyone...

Well, it would never happen.

I flipped off my office light and headed for the elevators. Ellen pressed the button as I approached and bumped me with her shoulder.

"Do you want to stay over this weekend? We could go to some workout classes. Or the spa. Get facials and deep-tissue massages."

Ellen's parents owned a chain of high-end spas through the country, which meant we could go any time. She didn't need to work as my assistant, which was exactly why she was the perfect fit. Well, and a thousand other reasons, too.

"You know I'll be miserable company this weekend," I sighed. "I need to think about my mother for the next forty-eight hours and all the trauma she gave me by being a woman of god."

I also needed to stew about all the times I'd been told I wasn't good enough. Tommy's blunt questions last week still haunted me, so I'd be thinking about that, too.

Either I wasn't good enough, or I was too good. There was no in-between.

Ellen snorted. "From what you've told me, she was not a good mother. I'm sorry, Pepper. You know my parents love you. You can always call my mother and get her off my back."

I relaxed as we stepped on the elevator and took it down to the lobby. I leaned against her for a moment, laying my head on her shoulder. She rested her head against mine.

"I don't know how you put up with me," I whispered.

"Well, we both have our moments," she said. "The last one was me. Or do you not remember the absolute disaster of me dating that couple from Memphis?"

"Oh god." I strangled a laugh. "Okay, yeah, that was pretty bad."

She made a face. "Still bitter about the amount of gas money I wasted. It's the principle of the thing. Anyway, my point is, you're having a moment right now. A lot going on while you're starting to explore your *sexual* side."

My brows shot up. "I should have never shown you my sex toy shopping cart."

Her laugh rang through the lobby as we made our way out to the street. Her apartment was a few blocks from mine, which made getting together easier if we needed each other.

"Does the wife ever reach out to you?" I asked.

The Memphis couple had been married for ten years when they decided to open up their marriage. The husband was all for Ellen and his wife being together, until he realized that it meant they'd also have a relationship outside of *his* participation. It had gotten so stupidly messy that eventually Ellen cut them both off last summer. As a result, we'd spent many evenings drinking way too much wine, eating too much ice cream, and watching way too many true crime shows.

"She's tried." Ellen shook her head. "Not interested in being a third like that."

"I don't know how you do it," I said. "Being polyamorous."

She shrugged her shoulders. "It works for me. I like being solo polyamorous, because it meets all my needs. I like having partners while still being independent. Certainly beats being married to the same dipshit for fifteen years."

"Okay, *harsh*."

"Sorry," she chuckled and then glanced at me. "Are we not at the joking stage yet?"

I linked my arm in hers as we crossed the street. "I guess I should be by now, right? I mean, the whole thing is a fucking joke at this point. And I'm the punchline."

"Wrong," she quipped. "You're not the punchline, honey, Jeff is. He's a fucking idiot. If he worked for any other company, he would have been out on his ass years ago. What does he even do? You and Tommy take care of all the high-level shit while Jeff sits on his ass and rakes in money. He's a straight white man who has all the privilege in the world, and everyone bends over fucking backwards to keep it that way."

"God damn," I whispered, my eyes widening. "You're right, but what brought that on?"

She sighed. "I just hear things. Around the office. And I've heard the way he speaks about you when you're not in the room, Pepper, and the only reason I haven't blown up on him is because I want to stay working for you. The most stress I have is making sure that you eat, and keeping Jeff off his high horse."

"I need to give you a raise," I muttered.

She smirked. "It can go toward our wine collection."

I laughed as we rounded the block. "What kind of wine are we having tonight?"

Ellen hummed. "If I pull out the 1990 red, you either have to Uber home or crash on the couch."

I shoved Salt to the furthest corner of my mind and smiled. "Deal."

TWENTY-ONE
SALT

I SPENT my last day being twenty-five in bed, in the dark, doomscrolling social media. Eventually, I put on a movie and drifted in and out of sleep, trying to avoid thinking about my birthday. And my father. And the fact that I was living in the house that had trapped me for most of my life.

Messages piled up. *What are you doing for your birthday? Want to go out? Want to go to a club? Want to—*

I ignored all of them. Nancy and Beth were the only two people I'd maybe respond to, but they knew I always struggled this time of the year, so they'd bake a cake and force me to blow out candles some time next weekend.

My stomach grumbled again and I sighed, rolling over and draping my arm and leg over the side of the bed. Shadows grew darker in my bedroom as the sun set, my muscles begging me to move.

I didn't want food, though. What I actually wanted, I couldn't have, and that was Pepper.

A hoarse groan left me and I slowly let my body melt off the bed, my limbs colliding with the cool hardwood floor. I took the blanket with me and rolled onto my back, sprawling out to stare at the ceiling.

Every fucking year.

Maybe it would get easier one day, I wasn't sure. But every fucking year, my birthday felt like this monumental hurdle that left me feeling isolated. I could be in a room full of people who loved me, but I wouldn't feel it. All I would feel was the weight of my father's hatred. The weight of my mother's death. And I knew it wasn't my fault, but I still carried that guilt.

I had a therapy appointment next week, at least. That was one of the things Nancy had encouraged me to do when I first came into her life, and I was still grateful for it. I'd been seeing the same therapist for years now, and while I wasn't perfect and still struggled, I was a better person for it.

The meeting went well last week. Or, that's how I'd perceived it. Tommy walked me through the contract process and what his vision was for me. Mostly, we talked about what I wanted.

What kind of music did I want to make? What song would I choose for a single?

The one that made me think about Pepper the most was my first choice. I'd written that song during a low point, while holding onto the idea that there was someone out there who could love me. Someone who I could love back.

It'd been a week though, and I hadn't heard shit from Rosethorn. So maybe that opportunity really was dead.

Another grumble interrupted my thoughts. My stomach was starting to fucking hurt. "Fucking *why?*" I growled and sat up, annoyed that I had to eat something.

I stood up slowly and stretched, every muscle protesting. A workout would be good right now. Well, really anything but bed rotting would be good. But it wasn't going to happen. The best I could do was eat a little something.

I looked at my phone lying on my bed, my fingertips itching.

The only company to my misery was the desire to text Pepper. I wondered what she was doing today. What were her weekends like? What did someone like her do to relax?

I snatched up a throw blanket and pulled it around my shoulders, wearing it like a cape around my naked chest as I finally emerged from my bedroom. I went down the hall, haunted by the past. Remembering times my father punched these walls, times I'd hidden in the small linen closet.

Tightening the blanket around me, I entered the kitchen and yanked open the fridge. I had left over pizza...

I didn't want to cook. I wrinkled my nose and snatched a cold piece from the box, a Gatorade, and kicked the door shut.

This was a better pre-birthday than last year, at least. I was eating something instead of wasting away into the night.

I shoved the pizza down my throat and drained the Gatorade, and stared at the living room from the kitchen.

I couldn't keep doing this.

Everything had to go. I needed to sell the house. That, or fucking burn it down. Living here was eating away at me, and it didn't matter how convenient it was, I needed to get out.

Almost all the furniture belonged to him. A layer of dust had settled over everything. The kitchen, the garage, my bedroom, and the bathroom were the only parts of the house I frequented, and I'd decorated those the way I preferred. I'd even created a corner of my bedroom for recording videos, but it was all temporary.

My hand tightened on the plastic bottle and I tossed it into the recycling bin. In a blink, I was throwing myself back on my bed again and glaring at the wall.

Pepper came to mind. *Uninvited.* I buried my face in a

pillow and sighed, trying to chase her away, but no. It was fucking impossible.

Maybe she'd vetoed the proposal Tommy sent her. I reached around for my phone until I felt it and picked it up, looking at the screen.

It was driving me crazy.

"Don't do it," I whispered to myself.

I set my phone down. I refused to text her, even though every single part of me wanted to. My eyes shuttered as I went over everything that happened.

The coffee shop. Beaumont's. Our phone call. Russo's.

A complete whirlwind. In just a couple of nights together, her essence had permeated my soul. It went beyond a simple connection or a fleeting desire.

I wasn't new to the kink community. Once I met Nancy and Beth, I threw myself into it wholeheartedly. I loved being a Dom, I loved exploring desires with others. Through the community, I was able to find a healthy outlet for my sadistic tendencies and discover what I enjoyed, too.

But even with all the experience I'd gained over the years, none of it came close to the way Pepper made me feel. She was a match and my entire body was drenched in gasoline. The lust inside me burned hot.

The desperation. The constant craving. Knowing that there were so many things she'd never experienced, and I could be the one to show her.

I could be the one to *corrupt* her.

My imagination went wild. The things I wanted to do to her...

In the darkness of my mind, she appeared again.

I imagined her on her knees, looking up at me with her pleading eyes, begging me to fuck her.

Begging me to use her.

I knew how difficult it was for her to share that part of herself, especially given that her last partner never cared about her—at least not in that way. I couldn't imagine being married to someone for so long and not being able to explore sex together. It sounded like hell.

She deserved better.

I wondered what secret desires she had—CNC was just one of them. We'd briefly touched on that kink, but there was so much more we could do.

She needed to get to a point where her mind turned off. She was smart and driven and making decisions twenty-four seven, and there was clearly mental fatigue around that. She'd put up a fight against fully relaxing until she was forced to, but then she'd beg for the release.

What was waiting for me just under the surface?

It felt like there was a fissure in my life. Before Pepper, and after Pepper.

My therapist was going to have a fucking field day with me when I saw her next. She'd tell me I was doing that *thing*—latching on to someone who *might* love me. Obsessing. Creating a fantasy world in my head that would never become reality.

She wouldn't be wrong. Maybe it was just who I was. All of that didn't matter, though.

What mattered was imagining exactly what I wanted to do to her.

I imagined putting a collar on her. Not just any collar.

Working with leather was a hobby I'd picked up alongside woodworking while building sex furniture. The mask I wore on stage was a custom one I'd made.

The collar I wanted Pepper to wear would be made by my hands.

Nice, buttery soft black leather with a silver heart ring at the center. One I could loop my finger through and tug. My name engraved along the inside so it would always press against her soft skin. And with the collar, matching cuffs to restrain her.

I wanted to tie her down to my bed, fasten a vibrator between her pretty thighs, and make her come until she couldn't remember her name. I wanted her pleasure to be the focus. To show her that she deserved every fucking orgasm possible.

My breath hitched as my cock hardened, all of my blood rushing *down*.

"Fuck," I rasped.

I lifted my hips, grinding my cock against my bed. Dreaming of her beneath me.

I loved watching her expression freeze someone like jeff. The waves of power rolling off her in the elevator on Wednesday morning, the way that everyone gravitated to her. They were used to bowing down, and rightfully so. She was brilliant, determined, powerful.

It was a fucking gift to have even touched her.

I pushed myself back onto my knees, sliding my briefs down. My cock came free. Veins bulged along the length of me, hard from just thinking about Pepper. I spat into my palm, grabbing myself as I thought about fucking her. About putting a collar on her and pulling her hair while I drove in and out of her, making her squirt again.

I needed her.

"Pepper," I moaned, stroking myself faster.

Pleasure rushed through me. I grunted as I felt my orgasm mounting, images of fucking her flashing through my mind. I thought about us in her shower, the way she'd begged for my cock.

The way she pleaded was so fucking pretty.

"Fuck," I rasped, throwing my head back as I got closer.

My hips thrusted into my grip and I gave one final grunt, coming hard into my palm, heat filling my hand. I wished every last drop was going inside her so I could push it back in after we were done.

I shivered, relaxing completely. I opened my eyes and got off my bed quickly to head for the bathroom.

I needed a shower. I needed to eat something aside from cold pizza. And I needed to start gutting the entire house.

Which was exactly how I was going to spend the rest of the day.

And maybe, just maybe, I'd hear from Pepper.

TWENTY-TWO
PEPPER

MY MOTHER'S headstone gleamed in rays of morning light, her name engraved into the marble. A weight sat on my chest as I knelt down, placing a bouquet of white lilies there, tears stinging my eyes.

It was always hard. Even knowing how much she hurt me, how much she tried to stop me from becoming who I was, I still loved her.

It'd been fifteen years since she died.

Because of her, I was raised in a world where women were only meant to serve. They only knelt for god or their husband.

A woman was of value so long as she was obedient, virginal, pure.

How could I love a god who thought I was worth so little?

Even as a child, I'd always questioned the narrative they taught me. It wasn't until I was much older that I was able to look back that I realized just how twisted my childhood was.

Raised in a small Tennessee town by a church that was grooming me to have children and share the gospel. While I didn't have the bright blue eyes and blonde hair they preferred, I was still good enough.

Good enough to be taught that sex was a sin. Every movement I made was to be considerate of the men around me. If they touched me, it was because I tempted them. If I was doing better than the boys, I was showing off. If I showed a shoulder, I was punished. If I did anything they didn't see as part of their god's plan, I was destined to burn in hell.

Education, science, and confidence were all weapons of satan.

I left the cult when I was nineteen.

Since then, I'd been fighting the demons they'd let in. The demon who told me sex was a sin, the demon who told me I wasn't worthy, the demon who told me I should have settled down and had Jeff's children. Paisleigh should have been *my* daughter, right? I should have tried harder to be a good wife.

I was a selfish, horrid woman who deserved to suffer for wanting *more*.

At least I had my music. Maybe that was something they did right. Singing and playing piano was what made me dream of leaving. Much like the artists I signed onto my label, it was that dream that spurred me to get away from the life I was living and try for something more.

I knew my mother was rolling in her grave. When I took off to Nashville with a shred of hope and no money, she'd tried to bring me back.

I'd never forget her showing up on my apartment doorstep. I lived in an apartment I shared with Tommy, after meeting him at a bus stop—a questionable choice we still laughed about, given that it worked out. When my mom found out I was living with a man, she screamed that I turned to a life of sin.

When I told her he was gay? That only made everything a thousand times worse.

And that was the last time I saw her alive.

There was no greater hate than her love.

I still brought flowers to her grave every year.

Maybe they were flowers for who she could have been, if she'd been given the chance to grow.

I always said today was her death date, but really it was the date she had come to my door.

Numbness and resentment sat in the hollow cavern of my chest, next to a heart that was barely beating.

They buried her outside of Nashville, near where my grandparents were buried. My father's choice. Her funeral was probably the last time I'd ever see him.

Drawing in a sharp breath, I tore my gaze from the headstone and looked up.

I froze. My brows knit together as I spotted a looming figure in the distance.

"*Salt?*" I whispered in disbelief.

I stood as still as the graves that surrounded me. Watching him. Salt stood facing a headstone, his expression colder than the icy morning.

I was intruding, wasn't I? I continued to watch him though, my attention drawn from my own emptiness to the pain that radiated from him.

The memory of last Tuesday came roaring back. Then the moment in the elevator, where Jeff had humiliated me.

There wasn't a force strong enough in the universe that could keep me from going to him now. My feet moved, carrying me across the frost-laden graveyard to where he stood alone.

Was he stalking me? That would be absurd, right?

I studied him as I got closer. No, he wasn't watching me. I didn't even think he was aware that I was here. My steps slowed as I approached, the ground crunching underfoot.

"Salt," I whispered.

He jumped, clearly startled. His dark gaze met mine. After a moment of surprise, I saw a flash of anger cross his face.

"What are you doing here?" he bit out.

"I was visiting my mother's grave and saw you," I said quickly, gesturing toward her headstone. "I'm not stalking you or anything. I was just surprised to see you here."

Without fail, he always made my heart feel like a bird attempting to escape a cage. My entire body was constantly under his spell. The roses around his neck danced in the sunlight, enchanting me with their inky darkness.

He stared at me with amber eyes, luminescent and unnerving, then turned his attention back to the headstone.

Did I stay? Did I go?

I decided to stay. Slowly stepping up beside him, I looked down at it, reading the engraved letters.

It was newer, I realized. At least not nearly as old as my mother's. A bottle of vodka sat beneath the name *John Salt*.

Solemn silence settled over us. I swallowed hard, wondering who this person was to him. Salt was his last name— so was this his parent? A grandparent? Someone else? I didn't ask. Instead, I just stood with him, my thoughts racing a million miles a minute.

Today, I didn't have the strength to be perfect.

Without saying a word, his fingertips brushed mine. Cold and hunting for warmth. Our hands slid together.

I gripped him.

He gripped me back. Squeezing.

"Tell me about your mother."

I blew out a breath, my entire body deflating. "It's not a good story. It's pretty typical."

He tsked softly. "Nothing about you or your life is typical. But I do want to know why she named you Pepper."

An abrupt laugh bubbled up, echoing through the cemetery

loud enough that I glanced around. No one else was here, only us and the dead.

It was such a stupid story, but I told him anyway. "Naming me after a condiment was a choice, but certainly not the worst she ever made. The story I was told was that she saw it on a cooking magazine, which was the first thing she'd ever been allowed to read outside of the Bible."

Another gentle squeeze. "She wasn't *allowed* to read anything else?"

"No. She wasn't supposed to, anyway. Her purpose wasn't to be intelligent, it was to serve her husband and the church."

"I see."

"She died when I was twenty-one," I whispered. "And I don't miss her most of the time."

"But you still bring her flowers."

I nodded and glanced back over my shoulder at the white lilies I'd left. "I do every year. Cut flowers make me sad, because they just die anyway. But, lilies were her favorites. On the few occasions she got flowers, that's what she got. So yes, I bring them to her grave."

I looked back at him. Salt swallowed hard, looking down at the dirt. "I understand."

I believed him. I didn't press for him to tell me anything. I didn't really need him to.

I just knew that he understood the pain of hating the one who was supposed to love you and support you, while still bringing fresh flowers to their grave.

A gentle breeze rustled the trees, sweeping my hair back.

"My father hated flowers." Salt's grip on my hand tightened until it almost hurt, his words full of bitterness. "So I bring him a bottle of vodka. It was the only thing he ever did like. It was also the thing that killed him."

"Oh." I remembered the night at Beaumont's, and how he'd

refused Tommy's offer for a round. "Is that why you don't drink?"

He nodded. "I hate what alcohol did to him. Part of me blames it for who he was. Abusive, mean, drunk all the fucking time. He used to hit me every single night when he got home from work. It was even worse on my birthday." He paused, his breath shaking. I realized he was trembling. I turned to face him, but he wouldn't look at me, his gaze locked on the grave. "The worst one was when I was sixteen. As I got older, the abuse became more intense, so I expected his attack. I stayed out all night. I slept on a park bench and it was snowing that year. Cold. It was really cold."

Fuck. The idea of him as a teenager sleeping in the snow, scared of his father—it broke me. Tears burned in my eyes as he continued.

"I went home the next morning to change for school. I'd been wearing the same clothes for a few days, so I had to. I shouldn't have, though. I walked through the front door and he hit me with a bat. He'd been waiting for me."

My breath whooshed out of my lungs.

"He beat the shit out of me. Over and over. He broke my ribs. He broke my arm. But, I got up. And I hit him back for the first time. It was like I'd kicked a puppy. He broke down crying, telling me that I was the reason my mother was dead. That I was a curse. That I should have died, not her. He hated me, he hated everything about me, and I shouldn't have been alive. I was bleeding and broken and wasn't supposed to be alive. The next year was easier, but he still tried to hurt me. But here I am now, still bringing him fucking vodka."

Tears rolled down my cheeks. I leaned my head against his shoulder, holding his hand.

"I hate my birthday," he whispered.

"Is today your birthday?" I asked softly.

He squeezed my hand. "Yeah. I'm twenty-six now. Maybe you can worry a little less about what people would think about us if we actually took a chance on each other."

My heart ached for him. We stood in silence for a few minutes, both staring at the bottle of vodka that sat alone in the dirt, the clear liquid gleaming.

"Happy birthday, Simon," I whispered.

I'd never said his first name before. It felt intimate and forbidden.

He exhaled slowly, tipping his head back. I looked up at him, watching the shadows his long lashes cast down his sculpted cheeks. Dark circles marred the skin under his eyes, his hair messy. I wasn't any better off.

"It's some sort of fate that alcohol killed him, right?" he asked.

"Maybe," I said. "Is it fate that not believing in modern medicine is what killed my mother? She thought god would save her. She had pneumonia and it made her sicker until sepsis got into her blood and she died."

"Well. Maybe she should have prayed harder."

An unwelcome laugh escaped me and I covered my mouth, my cheeks flaring. He covered his mouth too, both of us staring in shock.

"Pepper, that was wrong of me, I'm so sorry," he said quickly.

"No," I snorted, shaking my head. "I needed that. And you're right. Maybe she should have prayed harder. Maybe he should have drank more."

Salt barked out a laugh, some of the tension melting. "Maybe he should have."

Everything felt a little better now.

He cupped my cheek and pushed my chin up. "They tried to smother us, but they failed. And now they're gone."

I nodded as he thumbed away my tears. "They tried," I whispered. "I still love her. Why do I still love her?"

"I still love him." His eyes teared up and he closed them as one escaped. I reached up, wiping it away as gently as he'd wiped away mine. "I fucking hate him. But I still love him."

"I think we love what we wanted them to be," I whispered. "We love ghosts."

He pressed his forehead to mine. "I'm tired of loving ghosts."

"Me too."

I slid my arms around him and hugged him tight, laying my head against his chest. He rested his chin on top of my head, his heart thumping wildly. I didn't think about Rosethorn. I didn't think about how inappropriate this was given that I'd approved Tommy's proposal.

I existed where he existed, and that made the misery easier.

"What are the odds of you being here today, huh? I haven't been able to stop thinking about you," he murmured. "I nearly texted you a hundred times over the last week. Every morning I woke up thinking about you."

Surprise made me swallow hard. I'd done a really good job of convincing myself he'd forgotten all about me. "Why didn't you?"

"Pepper," he rasped. He gripped my hair, giving me a tug. "What are you doing? I thought I'd scared you off. Does this mean I'm not with Rosethorn?"

I shook my head. "I approved Tommy's proposal. I dragged my feet on it, and for that, I'm sorry."

"Then what..."

"I don't know," I said. "I saw you here. And when you're around, I can't resist you. No matter how hard I try. Maybe I'm just losing my mind. I'm never good around this time of the year. It's always a few days of hell. I'll be more normal later this week."

"It's okay," he murmured. He opened his mouth to say something, but then shut it.

"What?" I asked, raising a brow.

He studied me, but then continued. "The sex club is open tonight. It's a Sunday, so a... different kind of church, you know."

My eyes widened. "The place you told me about, right? The Garden?" I'd spent some time looking at their website earlier this week.

He nodded.

Don't do it. Don't.

"I'll take you, if you want."

"Really?" I asked.

"Yes. Do you want to?"

More than anything else. The temptation was too great, but I still tried to resist. For a second. "Do *you?*"

The corner of his mouth tugged. "Yes. It's a bad idea. But yes, I want to take you there."

I took a deep breath. I wanted to go. I wanted to experience something new. I was tired of fitting into the cage I'd built for myself. I wanted to be free.

I wanted to be with him.

"I want to forget about everything else," I whispered.

"Me too."

My cheeks flamed. "Are you sure? Last Tuesday was—"

"I still stand by what I said then," he quipped, his nostrils flaring. "I don't chase, Pepper."

"I'm not running. At least for tonight."

His hand slid behind my neck, massaging my tendons. "For tonight. And tomorrow..."

"Tomorrow, Tommy opens his email. He reaches out to you

to set up another meeting. It'll probably take place later next week, and it'll be with everyone important."

"So a meeting with you."

"Yes," I murmured.

"And your ex-husband, who I almost punched when you left us in the elevator."

"You *what?*" I hissed. "Did he say something—"

"He made some comments," Salt said. "I don't like him. At all. I don't think he likes me too much either."

"What did you say to him?"

Now, he smirked. "He mentioned you were trying to keep him from inviting his wife to an awards show."

I threw up my hands. "For fuck's sake."

Salt chuckled. "If it makes you feel any better, I asked him how long he'd been married. Then how long he'd been divorced. He didn't like that question."

"*Oh.* I bet he didn't like that."

"He didn't."

Perhaps it was a little petty, but the idea of Salt making him feel like shit brought me an immense amount of joy. "Thanks for that." But then, I frowned. "Salt... Did you fire your bass player?"

Salt shrugged his shoulders. "Yes. He wasn't a good fit."

"Did you do it because of me? Tommy heard a rumor and approached me about it."

"What did you tell him?"

"I lied to him," I said. "Well, I didn't exactly lie. I just didn't tell him the truth."

"And what is the truth, Pepper?"

"We're not right for each other. You're too young, I'm too old. If they knew about us, they would judge us. They would think I've lost my mind."

"They'd think you were taking advantage of me," he said.

"That's what Jack suggested. Which is why I fired him, because that's the furthest thing from the truth. And the thing is, people are always going to talk. They're always going to judge. I've been dealing with it my entire life." He tilted his head slightly as he held my gaze. "You can't let other people dictate how you live your life. You can't let fear stop you from having what you want. Otherwise, you're just killing yourself for them."

"I started this company years ago," I said. "It's all I have."

"Would us being open change that? You're the CEO. The company is yours."

I'd been thinking about this nonstop since Tommy and I talked. I looked away as I considered what would happen if we told the board we were together.

"It would be a lot of pressure," I said. "It would put us in a completely different position. And if things ended badly between us, it would hurt both of our careers. There's a lot at stake."

"We don't need to decide right now," he murmured gently. "But I want you to know that I want you. I want to be with you."

"I want you too."

My admission was soft. Vulnerable.

He tugged me close to him and kissed the top of my head. "That's all I needed to know. Everything else can wait."

I leaned into him fully and closed my eyes. All of my emotions were on the surface today, but his presence was calming them.

"I make bad decisions when I'm with you," I whispered.

"Well, I think there's room for worse."

I snorted and craned my head back. "When that meeting happens, you have to promise me you'll behave."

A dark chuckle followed. "Mmmm, we'll see. No promises."

"I'm the boss, remember?" I asked.

His smile broadened. "At some point, I want to set up a scene with you where you can be a little brat and I can punish you for it."

"I'd like that. A lot."

"We'll see what else you like tonight," he said. "How about I come home with you? If anyone asks, you can say you picked up a stray."

I rolled my eyes, but then leaned up on my tip-toes and kissed him quickly on the lips. His fingers knotted in my hair and before I could pull away, and he kissed me harder, our lips parting as it deepened. He swept me against him, the taste of him warm and sweet.

When he finally pulled back, we were both breathless.

"Did you drive here?" I asked.

He nodded. "How about I meet you at your apartment in two hours?"

My stomach did a slow flip. "That sounds good. What... what should I wear?"

He raised a brow. "Do you want me to tell you what to wear?"

Even though I'd gone home hating myself for it, I'd also realized I loved wearing exactly what he told me to wear. There was something about the obedience and slight humiliation of it that had left me wanting more.

"Yes," I said. "I want you to tell me what to wear."

"Wear one of your work outfits," he said. "A skirt. A modest blouse. Your favorite heels."

I frowned. "That's it. That's what you want?"

"That's exactly what I want."

TWENTY-THREE
PEPPER

THE GARDEN WAS a two-story club with an entrance down a set of dimly lit stairs. The door was painted scarlet with flowers trailing over it. A large menacing man stood in front of it. He was well over six feet tall, with countless scars and tattoos. He raised a brow as Salt pulled me close to him, leading me down the stairs.

"Salt, a very honored guest," the man said. "Are you here to teach? You're early. People are just starting to arrive."

Salt shook his head. "For play, Boy. This is my partner. I want her to have a red band for no-touching, and we need masks. I will also take a red band. This is her first time."

The man—*boy?*—nodded. "Of course, Sir."

"Is your Mistress here tonight?"

"She is. Queen Nancy is too, by the way."

Salt groaned. "Damn it. Okay. Thank you for telling me."

I frowned in confusion. "Who is that?" I asked.

"My mother," he sighed.

My mouth dropped. "*What?*"

"Don't worry, she's not actually my mother. We have an

agreement with Mistress and Boy that they inform us when the other is present. We'll avoid wherever she's playing."

"Playing?" I asked.

"Engaging in kinky things," he clarified. "Like a scene."

I didn't know what to say. All of this was so new to me. "We don't have to go in if that makes you uncomfortable."

His laugh warmed me, and he gave my hip a gentle squeeze. "No, we are going in. Boy will get our masks and bands."

The man nodded and opened the door for us. I hesitated for a moment, peering through the doorway. The entry looked dark, music echoing from within. Salt gave me a gentle push and I stepped through the threshold, immediately moving to the side.

"Is your name really Boy?" I asked the man curiously.

"It is right now," Salt said gently. "His name is Boy. He belongs to his Mistress."

"Oh," I said. "I'm sorry if I shouldn't have asked that."

The man smiled patiently. "No worries at all. Welcome to The Garden. Thank you for being our guest. You're in good hands." His gaze flickered to Salt as the door shut behind him, and I could have sworn it was a look of lust.

Of course, I could see why.

I looked up at Salt as Boy disappeared behind the dark curtain. He looked at peace here, beautiful and strong, at home amongst the shadows and undertones of lust. He smirked and looked down at me.

"You're nervous," he said.

My stomach fluttered in response. "I am. I've never been somewhere like this."

"You're safe," he promised.

"I know. I'm with you."

His smirk softened and he hummed, sliding his hand into

my hair and giving me a kiss. I melted against him, moaning as our kiss deepened.

A throat cleared, but he didn't pull away immediately. He kissed me deeper for a few seconds longer before drawing back.

"Fuck," I whispered, completely dazed.

That kiss left me breathless and aching for more.

"I see why you want the band," Boy chuckled.

"She's mine," Salt said simply, taking a red bracelet from him, along with two masks.

"I have some forms for you to fill out," Boy said. "They're waivers and rules. If you have any questions, I'm certain Salt can answer them."

He nodded. "Thank you for your service."

Boy dipped his head and went back out the front door, his voice carrying as he greeted whoever waited on the other side.

"Hold out your wrist," Salt said.

I did as he asked, my pulse racing as his fingers grazed my skin. He put the red band around my wrist, taking his time. Then, he held up a black, masquerade-style mask.

"There are rules in this place," he said. "No photos. No filming. No sharing people's information. If you see someone you know, do not use their real name if you approach them."

I winced. "I hope I don't see anyone I know."

"Well, you can always ignore them if you do. You'll be masked, so I don't think anyone will bother you. And you'll be with me." He reached up and placed the mask on me, tugging at my hair until he let out a hum of appreciation. "Beautiful, as always. And I can still see your cheeks when you blush."

I gave his chest a playful slap, but he caught my hands, bringing my knuckles to his lips.

"If you need to leave at any point, you will let me know," he said seriously. "If anything is too much or makes you uncomfortable, you will let me know. And if something turns you on, makes you wet, you will let me know. Understood?"

"Yes," I whispered.

"Good. Read through the papers, sign them, and we'll go in."

I took the papers over to a small table while Salt fit his mask over his face. More patrons flowed into the venue, and I couldn't help but steal glances at them. I felt very out of place in the blouse and skirt I'd picked, given that they were all wearing more revealing outfits.

But Salt had told me to wear this. I trusted that he had a reason for it.

I read through the papers. The rules felt common sense, but I knew not everyone had the gift of that. No touching without consent, don't interrupt scenes, zero tolerance for homophobia and racism. If you heard the word 'red,' notify one of the dungeon masters floating around. Each one wore a bright orange safety vest, so they couldn't be missed. No blood play and no bodily fluids.

The bands that people wore told you what they were open to. Red meant no touching under any circumstances, and you belonged to someone. Green meant you were open to playing with others, or were searching for someone to play with. Yellow meant open to free use.

"How does free use work here?" I asked Salt.

"I'll show you once we get inside," he said.

I nodded, my nerves settling a little. I was still apprehensive, but I wasn't the same Pepper of a couple weeks ago. I'd learned a lot about the BDSM community and I knew that consent was key. I knew that Salt was here with me, and that really, tonight was about being a fly on the wall.

The idea of being watched while Salt played with me turned me on.

Once I had everything signed, he plucked the papers from my fingers and slid behind the black curtain Boy had gone behind earlier. Within a moment, he returned.

"Do you work here?" I asked.

"Occasionally," he said. "When I first joined the community, it was through Nancy."

"Your *mother*..."

He chuckled, his hand clasping my elbow and gently steering me down a hallway. We followed other people as they flowed out into a massive room. The ceilings were high and the lighting a pattern of white, blue, and purple. It was already full of people milling around watching different scenes that were taking place. Along the walls and at the center there were different pieces of equipment such as St. Andrew's Crosses, benches, and what appeared to be a rig for suspension. I took it all in, my mind racing as I realized just how much someone could do here.

"Nancy and Beth are a couple who saved me. When I ran away from home, I didn't have any money or any sort of job."

"How old were you?" I asked, frowning. We were learning so much about each other today. I wanted to know everything I could about him, even though it was a bad idea. *All* of this was a bad idea, but I was struggling to care anymore.

"I was seventeen when I left. And eighteen when I met Nancy. I went to a sleazy place that has since been shut down due to consent violations and a lot of other issues. A man offered me a lot of money to fuck him. I was going to do it, I needed the money, but she intervened. And don't get me wrong, we all support sex work here. But that would not have been a good situation at all. I ended up going home with her and they fed me, clothed me, gave me a place to sleep where I didn't have to be scared." His expression glazed over as he guided me to a platform with a small table and chairs. He pulled one out for me. "Sit."

I slid into the chair and thought he would take the other, but instead he moved close, sliding one arm around me and taking my face with his hand. He turned my attention across the room to where a woman was being tied down to a red bench.

"She's wearing a yellow band," he said softly. "The man tying her down is there for her safety and probably her Dom. Who knows? I can't make assumptions."

People crowded around her as the man finished tying her down. She was laid face down on the bench, her ankles spread and bound to two points, her wrists tied to the other two points. The man rose up and reached for the hem of her dress, tugging it back until her ass and pussy were exposed to the entire club.

She was beautiful.

My breath caught as I watched, completely entranced. Salt traced circles over my spine with his finger as he watched *me*. Not her, not anyone else in the club. Not the gorgeous woman with her beautiful ass and pussy out for everyone to see.

Me.

His devoted attention stroked something inside of me, something hot and needy.

"Spread your legs, baby girl," he whispered.

I did as he asked, biting my lower lip. The brief pain awakened something deeper. His calloused hand gripping my jaw slid down my neck, down my chest, trailing all the way down to my skirt.

How many times had I worn this skirt to work?

It wasn't anything special. But the way his fingers grazed the tops of my thighs as he tugged the hem back made it feel like the sexiest thing I owned.

I watched as the woman's presumed Dom cut her panties

away with scissors. A couple of men waited patiently, but they were clearly ready for whatever was about to happen.

"Fuck," I rasped as Salt's fingertips brushed against my panties.

"What do you think?" he murmured against my ear.

I watched her Dom yank his belt free and unbutton his pants, pushing them down far enough that his cock sprang free. My mouth fell open in shock as he lined himself up with her, thrusting inside her pussy in one smooth motion. Her yell echoed through the entire club.

Like a siren crying out into the night, it broke whatever tension or hesitance there was in the crowd. I watched as other areas that were designated for play were slowly taken over by more people. My heart thumped as his fingers moved my panties to the side.

The same fingers that slid up and down his guitar effortlessly strummed my clit. My breath squeezed out of me, electric tingles bouncing through my body.

I knew how aroused I felt, but didn't realize how wet I already was until his fingers slid into me with ease. He let out a low growl, pushing them deeper.

"Oh baby," he purred. "You're soaked. Such a needy little cunt."

"Oh god," I whined. Panic whipped through me as more people walked past us. "Can you do this here? In front of people?"

"I can," he said. "Fuck, you're wet. Keep watching, baby girl."

I couldn't look away unless he forced me too. A soft moan parted my lips as his fingers worked my pussy, my gaze locked on the woman tied down to the bench. Her Dom finished inside her, but he was replaced with the next in line.

"Is that safe?" I rasped.

"They're all wearing condoms. It's part of the rules here," Salt said. "Everyone should be tested before an event like this too if playing with multiple people. Sexual health and safety are taken seriously in spaces like this."

I swallowed hard. I'd watched porn like this before. But seeing it in real life while Salt fucked me with his fingers was entirely different. I felt naughty. I felt a little crazed.

I felt *good*.

Salt gripped the back of my neck, the pressure firm. Commanding. My gaze slid to him, tracing his expression. His dark brows, amber eyes, the feral hunger that mirrored what raged inside me.

I was his to use and play with and it made me feel wanted. Desired.

The pleasure was almost too much. I rocked my hips, fighting to not make any sounds. People walked past us, occasionally looking, but it was dark so I knew they couldn't see that I was riding his hand.

Or maybe they could.

Maybe they could see how slutty I was. How desperate.

Salt's *older* woman.

I was doing the exact fucking thing I'd been saying I wouldn't do. I'd willingly come to a sex club with him and now I was wrapped around his hand. His to play with. His to fuck.

It was so bad. But it felt so good.

My pussy clenched around his thick fingers, whimpering.

"Which one is your favorite?" he asked.

"Um..."

I could barely think. I looked around the room, my eyes widening further. A man was strapped to a giant X and was being flogged. Then there was someone on a table with something that looked like a wand shooting out electricity. The violet wand? Right? I'd read about it...

My gaze continued to roam until I saw a wooden pillory. A person was locked inside of it, their expression contorted in pleasure as the person behind them fucked them relentlessly, their yells blending into the cacophony of pleasure and heavy club music. Smoke shimmered in the room, purple spotlights beacons of carnality.

A staircase at the very back seemed to lead to more.

"What's on the second floor?" I asked.

"That floor is for fucking," he said. "There are beds."

"Just... beds for anyone..." My words grew faint as his fingers curled against the perfect spot. I couldn't stifle my groan and forgot about everything else, my eyes closing as I rode his fingers, my orgasm just out of reach.

Salt pulled his hand free and my eyes flew open.

"What the fuck?" I moaned. "I was so close—"

The two fingers he'd nearly made me come with slid between my lips.

"Suck," he demanded.

The taste of myself was sweet. Despite the flash of irritation I felt from not being able to come, I sucked his fingers dutifully, cleaning them with my tongue. I held his gaze, scowling as best as I could.

Salt tugged them free and tipped my chin up. "Good. You never answered me, though. Who did you enjoy watching the most?"

"It's hard to pick," I said. "The pillory... and the violet wand..."

He nodded. "Let's go take a closer look."

He didn't let me get up myself. Instead, his hands slid beneath my armpits and he lifted me, setting my feet on the floor. My head fell back as I looked up at him, taking in the breadth of his shoulders.

Salt lingered for a moment and then slid his hand into

mine. His calluses were rough against my palm as he led me through the growing crowd.

Everywhere I looked, I found something interesting and arousing to see.

And no one was judging others.

Everyone here wanted to be fucked. They wanted to be needed.

Just like me.

I turned my attention back to Salt as he led me across the room. Just like on stage with a guitar in hand, people seemed to gravitate toward him wherever he went. They wanted to know him, and he paid them no mind. In fact, he seemed to ignore anyone who tried to get his attention.

The purple lights splashed over his pale skin, tattoos peeking out. I looked to my left and paused, catching a glimpse of two people on their knees, the snap of a leather flogger against skin drawing my attention. His hand tightened on mine, but he paused too.

"Want to watch them?" he asked.

"Yeah," I said, intrigued. "Please."

"Tell me what about it turns you on," he instructed.

I watched for a moment, trying to understand it. The couple on their knees were blindfolded and bound, moans and cries drawn forth with every strike of the flogger. A woman in a latex suit wielded it with a fluid ease that spoke of practice and knowledge, her attention on her submissives and nothing else.

It was the attention. It was knowing that the two people on their knees were having their desires fulfilled.

I looked up at Salt. "I like how... *devoted* it feels."

"I see. What else?"

"I like that they're being watched, but all of their attention is on what's happening. And well, they're all very attractive."

He beamed. "They are. Would you ever want to be with another person?"

"I don't think so," I said, casting the three another glance. "I like watching. I liked watching the woman with the free use band, too. But, I want to belong to one person. And I want them to belong to me. Is that bad?"

He shrugged his shoulders. "I don't think so. I feel the same way." He glanced up at the scene, watching for a few moments before looking back down at me. "I couldn't share you with someone else. I'm too possessive. Obsessive."

"Are you obsessed with me?" I teased.

Salt nodded. "You know I am."

It would pass, wouldn't it? Eventually he'd go out on the road. He'd see the world, meet people who would worship him and his music.

He frowned. "Are you okay?"

"Yes. I was just thinking... Maybe I'm a little obsessed with you too. For better or worse."

His gaze darkened, swallowing me whole.

I leaned up on my tiptoes and kissed him. He yanked me against him, his hands exploring my body. I felt a sense of freedom in that. In being able to give myself to him in front of everyone.

I wanted more. Maybe it was because we'd kept everything a secret up until now, because I was trying to protect my company and his career.

Being able to kiss him out in the open meant more than anything else did to me at the moment.

He drew back, breathless. Then, he gently grabbed my chin and turned my head.

"Watch them."

TWENTY-FOUR
SALT

I WAS LIVING for her reactions. The way her breath caught, her eyes widened, her muscles tensed in reaction to what she was seeing. The lust in the air was thick. Addicting.

But not as addicting as her.

We stood at the edge of a small crowd surrounding a couple who were being flogged by a woman in a latex suit. Pepper's cheeks were red, her eyes glazed over with need. Curious glances occasionally skated over us, especially as I wrapped my arm around her waist and dragged her closer. I recognized some of the patrons here and wanted to make it clear Pepper was with me.

Her ass fit perfectly against my cock, the fabric barrier of our clothes a form of torture. I strained against my zipper. *Control.* I was fighting for control. More than anything, I just wanted to bend her over right here. In the middle of a crowd. I wanted to show the whole fucking world that she was mine.

Would she like that?

I knew she liked watching. That much was evident given

how wet she was already. My fingers slid inside her with such ease while she'd been sitting for me.

I was trying to ease her into this place. But over the weekend, I'd slowly descended into madness. After jerking myself off to the thought of her begging for me, I'd showered and finally started packing my father's belongings.

Seeing her at the cemetery had been some sort of fucked up sign.

I wanted her. I needed her.

Fucking control yourself.

Pepper shivered against me, tipping her head back as I swept her dark waves to the side and kissed along the curve of her neck. Fuck, her skin was so soft. I'd missed the feeling of her against my mouth, and it'd only been a few days. The scent of her perfume heated my blood.

My gaze locked on the two subs who were now fucking, their Domme commanding them, using them like two fuck toys. I recognized the Domme as Madam Knives, who was especially known in the community for her, well, knife play.

It was a fitting name.

"Do you like watching them fuck like little whores?" I asked Pepper.

She nodded, her breath hitching. "Yes."

My hand snaked up to her breasts, to the buttons of her high-neck blouse. Her head rested against my shoulder, a moan leaving her as I popped the first four buttons.

I pressed my lips to her ear. "You have my permission to be a little slut. No one will judge you here. If anything, they'll admire you. They won't touch you, they won't do anything without our permission. They don't know who you are, or who I am, so you aren't in danger. We're masked. They'll just watch with the same hunger you're watching those three with right now."

"Can we—" she cut herself off, her voice faltering.

My brows raised. She wasn't going to ask what I thought she was? Was she?

"Can we what?" I asked.

"I want... Can we use one of the areas? To play?"

I was surprised, although I shouldn't have been. I knew beneath the cool exterior she presented to the rest of the world was a woman starved for fire. Her appetite matched mine.

I spun her around, my hand settling around her throat. I gave the sides a squeeze. Gentle but firm. Her mask glittered beneath the lights of the club, smoke curling between bodies. Moans and cries echoed around us with the beat of the music, people grinding against each other.

"Is that what you want?" I asked her. "Do you want me to fuck you in front of everyone?"

She swallowed hard. "Because we've had to keep everything hidden, I like being able to kiss you out in the open. And I like the idea of you making me yours in front of a crowd."

Just hearing her say that turned me on even more. I closed my eyes for a moment, thinking. Calculating. The thought of showing the world just how much she was mine lit something primal inside me.

"We need to talk about kinks more," I rasped.

"I know safe words. You taught me, remember? And we talked about kinks the first night we were together. I'm still learning what I like. What I don't like." She raised a brow, my hand still around her throat. I felt her swallow. "I trust you. I trust you with my body."

Will you ever trust me with your heart?

"What about you?" she asked. "We've spent so much time talking about what I like, Salt. What do you like? What do you want to do to me?"

Fuck. I gave a quick glance around us and then released her neck, tugging her close. She leaned into me completely.

I realized she wasn't resisting.

She wasn't running.

She wasn't fighting what she wanted.

And she certainly wasn't fighting me.

Finally.

"I want to breed you in front of the whole world," I whispered in her ear. "I want to make you a collar with my name on it. I want you to wear it while I tie you to my bed and fuck you. I want to put you in a rope harness and suspend you in the air and make you come so many times you forget your name. I want to corrupt you. It turns me on knowing that you're so new to everything. I like knowing that I'm teaching you something, especially knowing how fucking smart and powerful you are."

"Oh," she whimpered.

Her hand rested on my chest.

And then slid down.

And down.

Until she grazed my erection and her nails grazed my stomach as she unbuttoned my jeans. The zipper went down, and she pushed her hand into my pants, cupping me.

"*Salt.*" God, I loved the way she said my name. "Is... is this for me?"

"All for you," I groaned.

"What else do you want to do to me?" Her hand moved, wrapping around me.

It'd been a long time since I'd been so surprised by someone. I felt it rattle me to the core. Her fingers stroked my cock slowly.

Edging me the same way I'd edged her.

I grabbed a fistful of her hair and pulled her head back,

making her look up at me. She started to pull her hand back, but I growled. "Don't you dare fucking stop, Pepper."

She tensed, but then relaxed again.

"I want to play with all the sex toys you ordered."

"Would you teach me how to use them?" Her eyes fluttered.

Someone was testing the waters tonight. "Yes," I said. "I'll teach you everything you want to know."

"What do you get in exchange?"

The corner of my mouth tugged. "Making you cry. Making you come. Fucking you for hours and hours."

Her hand kept stroking me. I was so fucking hard, I was about to burst. Every muscle burned with pleasure.

"I want your submission," I growled.

"You have it," she whispered. "But only in the bedroom."

"I want you to see me again."

Her breath hitched. She swallowed hard. "I can't tell anyone about you, Salt. I can't. The whole world will eat me alive."

"I know. I'll be your secret," I said. "I won't tell anyone. I swear to you. I just need to be yours. I don't care if you're my boss. You can have my music."

Her hand paused, her eyes widening. "Salt—"

"You can." Fuck. I shivered against her, baring the deepest part of me to her. I was offering her my music. I was offering her everything that was me. "I want it to be yours," I whispered.

"I'll protect it," she whispered back. "I'll protect it forever. No matter what happens. I promise that your music will be safe. I swear to you."

"I swear that I'll protect you. No matter what happens."

She nodded. "Seal it with a kiss."

I smiled. "Deal."

I brushed my mouth against hers. Her hand began to move up and down my cock faster as our kiss grew more fevered, and I couldn't take it any more.

I tucked my cock back in my pants. In one swift motion, I picked Pepper up and threw her over my shoulder. She yelped as I carried her through the crowd, heading straight for the staircase.

I needed a bed. And there were at least a dozen upstairs.

I moved past people as I carried her up each step, keeping her draped over my shoulders as I hit the top. I recognized one of the DMs and he recognized me too, giving a nod.

"I'm taking the King Room," I said.

"Got it. For how long?"

"As long as I want. Tell Mistress Eden that Salt says thank you."

He nodded and then stepped aside, allowing me down another hall. The sounds of people fucking followed, moans and cries blending together. Pepper wiggled for a moment, but then went still again.

I could feel her watching people. Catching glimpses of their sex.

All of the beds were clean, with sheets that were changed out after each scene. Condoms, dental dams, lube, and everything else needed to have safe sex with a stranger was available. It was part of the membership price, and well worth it. The doors stayed open, people could watch you fuck or get fucked. And DMs monitored everything for safety.

The Garden was the safest place like this in Tennessee. Mistress Eden operated everything with care. It was why I came here, although my membership was free.

A lot of the furniture in the club was made by me.

The King Room was at the very end of the hall. It was large and extravagant with a massive bed at the center, a sex bench, a pillory, a cross, and padded flooring to kneel or wrestle on. I set Pepper down right beyond the threshold and turned, flipping a sign over that said Do Not Enter on the doorframe.

They could watch us, but I didn't want a single soul near me while I fucked her.

The tattoo on my wrist was there for a fucking reason.

I wanted her to be mine. All mine.

Pepper looked around. "This is amazing."

I stalked towards her. Her legs squeezed together as she turned to face me, her spine straightening.

"Stay still," I commanded.

She nodded. A shiver passed through her as I started to circle her. The flush in her cheeks had crept down her neck to her chest, peeking through the opened buttons of her blouse. I felt the presence of others watching us curiously, not interrupting but just voyeuring.

I stopped once I was behind her. I stepped closer, placing my hand over her throat and tugging her back against me.

"Look at them," I whispered, drawing her attention to the strangers watching. "They aren't here for me. They're here to watch you. How does that feel?"

"I'm so wet," she whispered. "I want to show them..."

"Show them what?"

"That I'm yours."

I smiled and popped the fifth button of her blouse. I reached around to her hip, tugging the hidden zipper of her skirt, pulling it down and letting the piece fall to the ground.

Her body tensed. I felt her voice vibrate in my palm as she moaned.

"Turn around."

She turned, looking up at me.

"Oh yes," I whispered. "I like that look. All you care about right now is being fucked. Isn't that right?"

Pepper nodded. "Yes. I need you. Please."

"Do you remember how you begged last time?" I asked.

Understanding brightened her gaze. She grabbed the edge of her blouse and tugged it off, tossing it to the floor as she stepped out of her skirt.

And then slowly knelt in front of me.

A flicker of doubt marred her blissful expression, but I shook my head.

"Don't listen to that voice, baby girl," I whispered. "You're doing so well for me. You're on your knees *wanting* to beg me, and you look so damn gorgeous doing it."

Her expression relaxed as that little demon went away.

"Good girl," I whispered. "Look up at me."

She did as I asked.

"Good, sweetheart. You know your safe words, don't you?"

She nodded.

"You will use them if we do too much or if you need to stop."

"Yes," she said. "I will use them."

"And if you can't talk?"

She held up her hand, making a symbol. "I'll make this sign."

I smiled. "Good. I'm so proud of you for remembering."

She soaked up the praise like a rose drinking in sunshine. "Thank you, Sir."

I hummed deeply in approval. "Good. Are you sure you want to?"

"I am," she said. "I'm more sure of this than anything. We made a deal, remember?"

My music for her desire.

"Enthusiastic consent is sexy," I said softly.

She smiled. "I *really, really* want to worship your cock right now in front of all these strangers, Salt. *Please.* I want you to make me beg. I want you to make me come. I want you to use me."

"I see..." I trailed off with a chuckle. "Let's see if you can make me come. I have a lot of control."

She licked her lips. "I like a challenge."

TWENTY-FIVE
PEPPER

GETTING competitive about cock sucking was something I never could have guessed would turn me on, but here I was. My clit throbbed as I felt the eyes on my back, my hands pulling Salt's jeans and briefs down, his cock coming free.

Fuck, he was hard. Everything else melted away as I cupped his balls, gripping the base of his shaft. Exploring him.

I brought the tip to my lips, opening them and sucking him gently. The taste of pre-cum was salty on my tongue. I drew back, licking my lips before taking him deeper, stroking the base of his cock as I did so.

Aside from reading about BDSM, I'd also started reading about things like this. How to suck a cock, how to do it well. What was most pleasurable. I wasn't sure if any of it was true, but I was sure going to try. I moaned as I worked him, giving it everything I could.

I wanted to be good for him.

Heat spread through me at that thought.

I wanted to be really, really good for him.

Salt's fingers knotted my hair as his hips jerked forward, thrusting deeper. "Fuck," he grunted. "You're doing so well."

Am I? What if he's lying? What if—

I shoved that little voice away. Every time it raised its ugly head, I buried it again, focusing on my task. Just like he'd told me.

I wasn't worrying about anything right now, except for trying to make him come. It was my life goal. My entire mission.

I always got what I wanted, didn't I?

My head bobbed more enthusiastically. His groans were music to my ears. His muscles tensed beneath my touch as I found a rhythm, one that was bringing out all sorts of sounds from him.

I loved this.

When I was with Jeff, he never made sounds like this. He'd come quickly and then be done, always leaving me wanting more.

I pulled back for a moment. Breaths huffed out and I dragged in more air. My head spun as I looked up at Salt, the lighting in the room haloing him. Taking in every muscle, his sharp jaw, the flowers that bloomed up his hard chest.

I drank him in like a hungry little whore.

Needing more.

His cock brushed my lips and I opened my mouth for him. I took him deeper until he hit the back of my throat.

My eyes watered. I choked around him and started to pull back, but his hand grabbed hold of my head, keeping me in place. The gentle force sent a shock of pleasure through me. I liked that he was forcing me to take his cock deeper. I liked being touched this way.

Spit dripped down my chin. Panic set in for a moment, but he gave the back of my head a gentle tap.

"Calm down. Breathe through your nose."

I felt like I was falling, falling, falling. But, I did what he told me to, making myself relax. Breathing through my nose.

I was a fucking mess. People were watching me do this.

He pulled back, releasing me.

"Good girl," he praised. "See? You're starting to get it."

I gasped for air, tears rolling down my cheeks. I wiped away the spit on my chin, panting as I met his gaze once more.

I imagined that he loved me.

How fucked up was that?

I couldn't tell anyone about us. I couldn't do that without risking my reputation and career. People would tear into me if they knew I was with a man so young.

And yet...

"I'm yours," I rasped.

He nodded. "Mine to use for the night, however I please."

"Yes—"

My words were clipped as he thrust back into my mouth. He was far more relentless this time, pumping in and out, hitting the back of my throat each time. My hands slid up his thighs and then around his hips, nails digging into his firm ass as he fucked me faster.

All of my resistance had fallen away. Like the wings melting off Icarus as he flew too close to the sun, plunging me into a hell that I wanted to burn in.

I loved being used.

I loved being fucked.

This was the exact type of connection I was told was bad. That it was sinful. Too much. Too twisted, too dark.

It was none of those things.

It was holy. It was pure. It was a basic human instinct, being fulfilled in a consensual way. There was nothing wrong with wanting someone so much that I was on the cusp of coming just from having my throat fucked in front of strangers.

My pussy pulsed. Need rolled through me as I reached down between my spread thighs, circling my clit through my panties as he kept fucking my mouth.

So close. So close.

"You're a natural," he rasped.

I wanted to ask him if I was a good slut. If I was his good slut. Instead, I kept taking his cock, thinking about the way his fingers felt inside me earlier. Thrusting them in and out while strangers walked by. Stroking his cock in the middle of a crowd while watching others fuck.

They had no shame. No hang-ups around not being good enough.

I wanted that. I wanted to be so drunk on lust that I could let go of everything holding me back.

God, I wanted to be selfish.

My fingers worked my clit faster, my body strung up like a bow. *So close, so close, so close—*

Salt suddenly yanked back, gripping my hair and pulling my head away. "Are you touching yourself?" he snarled.

"Yes," I whimpered.

The tip of his boot shoved my hand away. My eyes widened as it nudged against my pussy, the leather cool against my skin through the thin fabric.

"You can hump my boot," he said. "But you may not touch yourself until I give you permission to. Understood?"

"But I'm so close," I whined. "I'm so close. I need to come."

"I promise you'll get the orgasms you deserve. But you need to earn them."

"Let me make you come," I said, giving his cock a quick stroke.

He dragged me closer again, his boot now wedged between

my thighs. "Oh, you're going to make me come. But you're not going to make yourself come until I let you. You can hump my boot like a good girl or we can leave."

Frustration tightened my chest. His fingers gripped my hair with a fierceness that hurt, but the hurt felt so good.

I wondered if he was serious.

Would he actually make me leave if I made myself come without his permission?

I didn't want to find out.

Pleasing him outweighed that streak of defiance.

His eyes sparkled with amusement. "I promise, we're going to explore that bratty part of you soon. But not tonight."

"You promise?" I whispered.

"I promise."

I believed him.

So, I opened my mouth as wide as I could. I stuck out my tongue, waiting for him to take my throat again. His jaw stiffened, his nostrils flaring as he looked at me like I was the only other person in the world.

Obsessive. Possessive.

I didn't want him to ever look at someone else that way. It would fucking kill me.

His cock slid against my tongue, and he moved slowly, deliberately, holding my gaze until his hip snapped. I groaned as he started to fuck me hard again, moving in and out brutally.

I relished every second of it.

My hips moved involuntarily, my pussy rubbing against his boot.

Was I really doing this? Was I really going to rub against him like this in front of a bunch of strangers?

Those thoughts floated away as a bolt of pleasure rushed through me. Little shocks of electricity tingled through my entire body, my hips moving again.

I was so fucking wet. My pussy pounded with the beat of my heart as he fucked my throat. *Harder. Harder.* I was spinning and spinning until I was nothing but *his.*

I cupped his balls, gently rolling them as he kept fucking me. I knew that he was on the edge.

"Fucking hell," he grunted. "Fuck."

I really wanted him to come. I really wanted him to fill my throat with every single drop. I raked my nails down his thighs, and that made his entire body jerk.

A groan escaped him and he gave one last thrust before the heat unleashed. I swallowed hard, feeling the gush of his cum down my throat. *I want more. I want it all.* I kept moving my hips as he filled me, his body jerking until he finally pulled back.

I swallowed everything down, licking my lips as I looked up with him.

"Was that good enough, Sir?"

He panted hard. The flowers inking his pale skin rose and fell with each labored breath.

I was addicted to the delirium pumping through my veins.

"Kiss my boot." His words were short. Firm.

My eyes widened. "Kiss your *boot?*"

Salt took a step back and pointed at the floor. "Kiss my fucking boot. The same one you were just rubbing your pussy on."

I knew I could tell him no. I could say *yellow* and slow things down. Or I could say *red* and stop it all at any time.

But I didn't want to stop.

There was a bit of resistance inside me. The idea of bending over, my ass facing a bunch of strangers as I kissed the same boot my pussy was just rubbing on terrified me.

But it also turned me on.

I planted my hands on the floor, and slowly bent over. I

stared at his boot, realizing that the shine glistening was from me.

"Oh," I whispered, licking my lips.

I'd made a mess on his boot.

I pressed my lips against the tip.

I kissed his boot before everyone.

"Good," he said. "I'm proud of you, baby girl."

I preened under the compliment.

"Now lick up that little mess you made."

This time, I didn't hesitate. I lowered myself, dragging my tongue over the leather. My eyes closed at the taste, and I liked it. I liked it a lot. I licked faster, huffing as I swiped away the glistening essence my pussy had left, cleaning it up just like he asked.

I felt his hand on the back of my neck, pulling me up. I whimpered as he pulled me to standing, my head falling back as I looked up at him.

His lips brushed mine. Gentle. So gentle that I was scared the kiss would break. It was fragile like glass.

"There's a pillory," he whispered. "I want to lock you in it and fuck you. How does that sound?"

"Anything you want," I rasped.

He kissed me again, and this time instead of glass, it was steel. It was deep and strong and all-consuming. My entire world tilted as he swept me into his arms, not losing a beat in our kisses as he carried me across the room to a wooden stock with a hole for my head, and two holes for my wrists.

Salt put me down. "Stay."

"Yes, Sir."

I watched as he inspected the furniture. He walked around it, checking everything once, twice.

"Have you ever made something like this?" I asked.

The corner of his mouth tugged. "I made this one."

My eyes widened. "You made this?"

"I made a lot of the furniture here. That's why I have a membership to this club. I don't think I could afford it otherwise," he chuckled. "I still double-check everything before using it to make sure it's safe. I like hurting you, but would never want to harm you. Do you get the difference?"

"Yes," I said. "I like... the pain. I just don't know why I like it."

"Because you like being punished," he said. "It turns you on to feel like you've paid penance for pleasure."

My mouth opened to argue, but then snapped it shut.

He wasn't wrong.

Salt's face softened as he unlatched the pillory. He swung the top half open, holding it in place as he looked up at me.

"Are you ready?" he asked.

"Yes."

I stepped forward, my skin prickling. I glanced over my shoulder at the doorway to the room and froze, seeing how many people watched us. A man stood at the very front wearing a mask, staring right at us. Worry shot through me as he looked directly at me.

Does he know who I am?

He didn't, right? It was possible. My hair was distinctive and made me easy to recognize. It was possible that a lot of people in the club knew who I was—

"Baby," Salt said gently. "The rest of the world doesn't matter. You're mine right now."

I tore my gaze away and refocused on Salt. He tilted his head slightly and smiled.

He was right. Nothing else mattered. After the hellish weekend we'd both had, we deserved to escape. All my worries fell away as I stepped forward.

"Spread your legs apart and hinge at your hips," he

instructed. "Your head will go in the center, your wrists in the other two places."

I did as he instructed, parting my legs and steadying myself on the heels I wore. "Should I take these off?"

"No."

With a smile, I hinged forward slowly, putting my neck and wrists in the correct spots. Salt lowered the upper half, bringing it down over me, and latched it into place.

It wasn't comfortable, but I knew that was part of this. Discomfort settled over me, my muscles straining as I felt cool air on my pussy, along with the eyes of anyone watching.

Salt stepped in front of me and knelt slightly, his face hovering in front of mine. "You will tell me if we need to stop," he said. "You'll use your safe words if it's too much."

"Yes," I said. "I will."

"*Good.*"

TWENTY-SIX
SALT

PEPPER WAS PERFECT.

And she was mine.

I circled her, admiring her body trapped inside the pillory.

Legs spread, pussy bared for the entire world. They watched us, hungry eyes feasting on our bodies. I liked being watched and knowing they'd never have either of us.

My cock twitched as I smoothed her ass with my calloused palm. I held it there for a moment, staring at the eye of the flower on the top of my hand, the dark ink vivid in contrast against her pale skin.

"Are you going to spank me?"

I heard a wisp of hope in her voice. I smiled to myself as I looped a finger in the band of her panties and tugged them down until they fell to the floor. She lifted one heel and then the other, kicking them to the side as best as she could without being able to turn around.

She had a gorgeous ass. Of course I knew that, I'd thought so since the first time I laid eyes on her in the coffee shop. Spankable. Biteable.

Fucking perfect.

I moved to the side just enough to allow any onlookers to catch a glimpse of her. I patted one ass cheek with my palm, and then the other, going back and forth between each side and warming them up. Slapping each one, I started to bring blood to the surface, making sure her body would be warm enough to take the spankings I wanted to give her.

"You're not going to be able to sit tomorrow, baby girl," I said.

"That's okay," she moaned. "I'm off tomorrow."

"Oh?"

She wiggled in the stocks, but couldn't go anywhere. "Yes," she said. "You'll stay the night with me?"

A tinge of vulnerability.

"Of course," I said. "I'd be happy to. Especially since I don't think we're getting out of here until at least two in the morning."

That seemed to make her relax. I stood up, admiring the way her skin bloomed pink and red.

She was warmed up enough.

The first spanking made her yelp. Her voice echoed through the elaborate room, bouncing off the walls straight to my cock. You'd think I would need more time to recover, but Pepper had this way about her that always turned me on.

Also, I needed her dripping with my cum before the night was through.

I slapped her other ass cheek hard. She picked up one of her heels, moving her hips.

I growled and stood up, wrapping an arm around her lower back and stomach, keeping her in place as I started to spank her relentlessly.

"Fuck," she cried. "It's too much! Fuck. Ow, ow, ow—"

Her scream followed.

I slapped her ass hard. Hard enough that my eyes widened slightly and I paused, hearing what sounded like a soft sob from her.

I cupped her pussy and *fuck*. She was so wet.

"*Yes.*"

Her whimper was breathy and soft.

"Please, Sir. Please. I need to come. I need to come so badly. I want more spankings and to come."

Her pleas were sweeter than a melody. I plunged two fingers inside her, feeling her clench around me. Her moan echoed from the other side of the stocks, her ass pushing back to meet my hand. My fingers pushed deeper, sliding in and out rapidly as I arched over her, using my free hand to spank her at the same time.

She'd gathered a crowd at the door, everyone watching. Staring. Heat rolled off her body and waves, her skin glistening with a sheen of sweat.

"Oh god—oh god—*yesyesyes!*"

Her legs began to shake, her pussy gripping my fingers hard as she climaxed. God, it was fucking beautiful. I kept finger fucking her through it, standing up just enough so I could see over the top of the stocks and watch her dark hair toss as she came, her unashamed cries making my cock pulse.

Her body went slack, her knees softening as she recovered. I pulled my fingers free and brought them to my mouth, sucking the taste of her wet cunt off them.

I spanked her again. And again. And again. Giving each cheek my attention, enjoying the way her body writhed, her pleas ignored. Her skin darkened as a couple of bruises started to form.

Her sobs grew louder. I gave her a break and walked around to the front, grabbing a fistful of her hair and pulling her head up.

She looked pretty when she cried.

My cock was fully hard now. I started to ask her if she was okay, but then she opened her pretty mouth.

She opened it wide, looking up at me as tears stilled down her gorgeous face, sliding out from under the mask she wore. I wanted to yank it off so I could see all of her, but I resisted the urge.

"Thank you," she rasped. "Please use me. I love this."

Fuck. I kept her head up by holding her hair and lined up my cock with her pretty lips, thrusting forward. She whimpered around me as I started to pump in and out, using her poor throat the same way I had earlier. Mascara darkened under her glassy eyes, her body draped in the pillory in a way that was turning me feral.

I pulled back as she coughed, allowing her to breathe.

"What do you say?" I asked, keeping my voice so low only she could hear me.

"Thank you, Sir," she panted. "Thank you."

"Louder," I snarled.

"Thank you, Sir!"

Nothing had ever satisfied me like this before. I let go of her head and went around to the other side, smacking her ass again. Another sharp cry, her body tensing before melting.

I gripped her cheeks hard and parted them, staring at her pussy and asshole. A sweet little hole I wanted to claim as mine. I'd already fucked her pussy and mouth, why not her ass too?

"Salt," she whispered.

"These holes need to be filled," I announced.

"Holes?" she echoed.

I needed to go toy shopping for Pepper at some point. I wanted a plug with a gem on the end to gleam in her ass while I bred her pussy. I made a note to myself as I turned and went to a small table, picking up a bottle of lube and condom.

I put the condom on quickly and poured a generous amount of lube into my palms, taking the bottle with me as I returned to Pepper.

Her ass was still bright red.

"I hope you think about me the next time you sit down," I said, dripping some of the lube between her cheeks.

She stiffened as I put the bottle aside, lubing my cock before circling her hole.

"I've never done anything there," she whined.

"Never?" I asked in disbelief. "You've never played at all here?"

"No," she rasped.

Well, I wasn't going in there, at least not for tonight. I'd breed her little pussy and tease her ass instead, and we'd work up to taking my cock over time.

"We'll save this for when we're alone," I said.

Before she could say anything else, I lined up my cock with her dripping pussy and thrust forward. And fuck. She felt so fucking good. A guttural groan left me as I grabbed hold of her hips, going still, just feeling her pussy clench around me. Milking me, wrapping every inch in hot silk.

"Oh god," she cried.

Her voice was angelic as she screamed, moaned, and begged.

"More," she rasped. "Fuck me. Please fuck me, Sir."

I dragged my cock back slowly until I was almost completely out of her, and then drove forward. A rhythm set between us, my lungs dragging in hurried breaths as I fucked her.

"Thank you, Sir."

Fuck. She was learning fast. She gave thanks repeatedly

with each thrust like a good girl. I leaned over her, wrapping my arms around her body and cupping her breasts. Her little *thank yous* faltered as I twisted her nipples, her cunt spasming around me.

She was so fucking close again.

The pillory shook with each thrust, the metal rattling against the wood. I closed my eyes, inhaling the sweet scent of her. Intoxicating. I sank my teeth into her skin, listening for her sharp cry, feeling her tense as the pain registered. I licked my lips as I studied the indentions my bite left, kissing down her back as I straightened.

I slowed down the pace, making every thrust punch. I was so close to filling her with every drop I'd been saving for her.

"Please. Please."

I couldn't hold back anymore. I pumped deep inside her and then released, gasping sharply as I climaxed. Cum spurted from me, filling her with every drop.

My muscles slackened, my head tipping back. I stayed like that until my orgasm tapered off, and then I blinked, coming back to reality. I looked down at her body, soaking up the sight of her.

"Thank you, Sir."

Fuck. She was perfect. "You're welcome," I said, pulling out of her slowly.

I took the condom off and cleaned up quickly before unlatching her, pulling her into my arms. She was limp, her head collapsing against my chest as I held her to me.

"Hold onto me," I murmured.

Her arms slid around my neck as I carried her to a soft chaise and settled, still cradling her. I felt her tears against my skin and pressed kisses to her head, stroking her gently.

"How are you doing?" I asked softly.

All she did was nod. I didn't know if that was good or not. I swallowed hard, thinking about how I should have set up more symbols to communicate.

Pepper lifted her head slightly. "Green."

I breathed out, my tension loosening. Her head nestled against me and I closed my eyes, letting the aftermath of our scene together settle.

More than anything now, I wanted to get us home and in bed.

"Pepper," I said softly. "Do you want to come home with me tonight?"

"Come to my place," she said. "Sleep over. It's closer."

"Okay, baby," I said. "I'll get us home."

TWENTY-SEVEN

SALT

I CARRIED Pepper through her front door and kicked it shut behind us, locking it quickly. She'd fallen asleep in the Uber and I was doing my best not to wake her, but I felt like I'd have to. She needed water and some food, and we both needed a shower. It was already two in the morning, but I knew if we went to sleep now, we wouldn't feel good in the morning.

"Baby," I whispered as I flipped on the lights. "We're home. You need food and water."

She lifted her head and blinked a few times. "Oh. How long did I fall asleep for?"

"A bit," I said.

The sub drop hit her pretty hard. I also needed to take care of myself, but that would come after.

"I'm awake," she said. "You can put me down."

I let her feet hit the floor, and then chuckled as she stumbled against me, backing me against the wall. She leaned up and kissed me hard, surprising me.

"Thank you," she said. "Thank you for tonight. And for

getting me home. My whole body feels like it's been hit with a truck."

"Well," I said, kissing her forehead. "We did a lot."

She nodded, but then her hand settled over my heart. "Are you okay?"

My breath was soft but sharp. "I'm always worried after scenes that I did too much."

Her hand was warm on my chest. "I loved every single thing you did to me tonight. I wanted it all, Salt. Every single part of it."

I swallowed hard, holding her gaze. The shadows that danced over her beautiful face, the smudged mascara around her eyes from crying. I stroked her cheek with the back of my fingers.

"I can go home if you don't want me to stay," I whispered.

"I want you to stay," she said. "I want you to sleep with me. In my bed. I want to wake up next to you. I want to dream next to you."

Maybe that was what I needed to hear. All tension in my chest unraveled. I dragged her into another kiss. A soft one, a needy one. She knotted her fingers in my shirt, and pulled me forward, leading me to the kitchen.

Both of us were exhausted, but we were still going to take care of each other. It was filling something inside of me I hadn't realized was missing until now.

I had a hard time being cared for.

An even harder time truly being vulnerable.

"What do you want to eat?" Pepper asked. "I can make us grilled cheese."

My brows shot up. "Is that your choice of cuisine for aftercare?"

She grinned, her body language carefree and relaxed.

"Grilled cheese and ice cream sounds pretty good right now. I may regret it tomorrow."

"It sounds perfect to me," I said. "I can cook it—"

"I have a specific way I make them," she said, wrinkling her nose at me. "Just relax. Or something."

"I'm going to get us water, Ms. Boss."

Her soft laugh warmed me. I opened up her cabinets, searching for glasses. I found two, and poured us each a cup with ice and water.

Pepper pulled out a lot of different cheeses. I shook my head as I spotted the price tag on a couple. "You can't judge until you taste it," she said. "I make the best grilled cheese."

"Kraft Singles are known to do the trick," I teased.

"So is this gruyere I'd sell my firstborn for."

I barked out a laugh. "Okay, well, drink this before you start doing that. You need to hydrate."

"Yes, Sir."

Such a brat. She reached for the glass and took a tentative sip.

"All of it," I said.

"I'll drink it all," she said. "Tell me about aftercare."

"What about it?" I asked.

"Well, I've read about it. And I know we've done it?"

Damn, I needed to do a better job at Domming. Her hand settled on my chest, stopping the edge of the spiral I was nearing.

"That wasn't a critique of you. I'm still learning. I've felt taken care of after we've been together. Well..."

"For the most part," I said, thinking about the night at Russo's. "I should have checked in on you."

She shook her head. "We're learning. I should have messaged you. It's a two-way street. I just want to know what you like for aftercare."

I took a long sip of water, holding her gaze until she sighed dramatically and followed suit. We downed our iced water together. The glass clinked against the marble topped counter as she put it down.

She bent over to open a cabinet and groaned, reaching back to rub her asscheek. "That's gonna hurt."

"Yeah, it will."

She shot me a look over her shoulder. "I'll be thinking of you all week."

I chuckled. "That was the goal."

She pulled out a pan for grilling. I hovered for a minute and then she pointed at the barstool. "Sit. Or if you want to shower, you can. You can use anything here you want."

"Hmm..." A hot shower sounded nice. A hot shower with Pepper sounded nicer, but we could take one together in the morning. "I think I'll take a quick shower and rinse off."

Pepper nodded. "Do you remember where everything is?"

"Yes. The magic shower and all that."

She snorted as pulled a loaf of fresh sourdough out of a bread box. She sliced off a few pieces, seemingly full of more energy than I'd expected.

"Are you sure you want to cook this late? I'm shocked you aren't ready for bed," I said.

"I passed out in the car. I don't even remember us getting here. I think that gave me energy for a second wave. I didn't eat much over the weekend, and figure you didn't either."

"I didn't," I admitted. "You're cute when you snore, by the way."

"Well, you'd be the first to think so."

I winked at her and then left the kitchen, winding my way through her apartment to the bathroom. It was dripping with luxury, but I didn't feel as out of place as I had last time. I stripped out of my clothes and managed to get the hot water to turn on, stepping beneath the stream.

"Fuck," I breathed out.

I stood there for a couple minutes just soaking in the heat. It seeped into my muscles, rinsing all my worries away. The scene tonight would live with me for the rest of my life, seeing how turned on she was by being watched and taken in front of a crowd. Knowing that she was mine. Out in the open, all mine.

After my shower, I dried off and pulled the towel around my waist. The scent of bread and butter made my mouth water as I went back to the kitchen, finding that Pepper had set us out plates, each with a gooey grilled cheese.

"Oh yeah," I said. "Those do look amazing."

"They are," she said, pulling out her barstool. She winced as she slowly sat down, wiggling her butt as she adjusted to the pain from being spanked. Her gaze raked over me, dipping down to the towel.

I took the other stool and drained another glass of water. Pepper picked up her grilled cheese, the bread crunching as she took a bite. Her eyes fluttered and she moaned.

My stomach grumbled. I picked mine up and took a huge bite. And damn, it was great. She smirked as she chewed, all too satisfied by my expression.

"Okay," I said after swallowing. "This is pretty fucking good."

The two of us inhaled our grilled cheese sandwiches and drank more water. Once we'd polished our plates, I piled them together and took them to the sink.

"Just put them in the dishwasher," she said.

I looked around and then frowned. "What dishwasher?"

She pointed at a large cabinet that definitely did not look like the front of a dishwasher. I grabbed the handle and tugged it down. It was, in fact, a dishwasher.

"I'm going to rinse off real quick," she said. "Want to eat ice cream and watch me shower?"

"The answer will always be yes to that question."

Pepper rummaged through her freezer before pulling out a pint of chocolate ice cream. I loaded the dishes and then slid behind her, gently grabbing her hips. She leaned back against me as she held up the ice cream.

"I don't even know if you like chocolate," she said.

"Who doesn't like chocolate?"

She turned around in my arms, making a face.

"Oh my god," I said. "Don't tell me *Jeff* didn't like chocolate."

"Hated it," she chuckled. "It's far more common than you think."

"And a tragedy," I teased.

Armed with ice cream and a spoon, I followed her back to the bathroom. She pulled out a small chair in front of a vanity and settled down, my eyes glued to her as I opened the pint and dug the spoon in.

Pepper turned to face me and slowly stripped her dress off. I took a bite of ice cream and felt a wave of comfort roll through me.

Honestly, there probably wasn't a greater form of aftercare than eating chocolate ice cream while watching my girlfriend strip.

Girlfriend.

The word didn't quite fit. Not because we hadn't established that yet, but because Pepper felt like more than just a girlfriend.

"You never told me about aftercare," she said. "Talk."

I licked my lips. "I like it when you try to boss me around."

She turned, her ass facing me as she continued to strip.

Bruises already spotted her skin, my handprint very clearly sprawling over her ass.

Fuck.

That was hot.

"Aftercare is important," I said. "I always practice aftercare for my subs, but I never take any for myself. This is making me realize that maybe I've been doing myself a disservice all along."

"What is it like?" she asked.

"What is what like?"

"How do you feel after a scene? I feel like I'm floating on cloud nine. And I feel very vulnerable. But I also feel really good."

She flipped on the water, steam swirling around the bathroom. And thank god for the glass walls. I dragged my chair closer and took another bite of ice cream, appreciating every part of her.

"I worry after scenes," I said. "I worry I went too hard or did too much or that I shouldn't have done anything to begin with. Words or reassurance help."

"I really, really loved what you did to me tonight," Pepper said as she stepped under the water.

My cock perked up as it streamed down her body. Her nipples were soft, her hair darkening as it dampened. Her eyes closed and she let out a soft moan, rolling her neck.

"Are you hurting anywhere?" I asked.

She nodded. "Yes, but I like the hurt. It's a reminder of everything we did together. What was your favorite part?"

I breathed out. "It's hard to pick. There was a moment when I had you in the pillory and knew everyone was watching us that I'll remember forever. I loved knowing you belonged to me completely in that moment."

"I loved knowing I was only yours. I was scared someone

might recognize us, but then I let that go. It's hard to let everything go."

"I know," I whispered, drinking her in.

She was beautiful. Heat clung to me, contrasting with the chill of the ice cream. I took another bite.

"I think I like being humiliated," she said. "Just a little. I don't know. I like being praised too."

"It's okay to like both," I said. "We can explore doing more with both."

"I want to try being tied up. Do you know how to do that?"

"Yes." I breathed in deep, inhaling the scent of her soap as she washed herself off. "Shibari is one of my favorite things to do."

And I had a thousand ideas of all we could try while she was tied up, but I was too tired to formulate any of them.

Pepper flipped off the water and stepped out, wrapping herself in a fluffy towel. I sat back as she stepped up to me, straddling my thighs. I scooped out a bite of ice cream and held it to her lips. She ate it, and then licked any remnants from the spoon.

"Good girl," I whispered. "You're unbelievably hot, Pepper. I'm lucky to be with you."

"I feel lucky to be with you."

She covered her mouth and yawned, which in turn made me yawn. Which made both of us smile like idiots.

"I think it's time for sleep," I said. "I'm fading."

"Me too."

We each took a few minutes to finish bedtime routines, turn off lights, put away the ice cream, and get more water. Finally, I collapsed beneath the blankets next to her in the dark.

She snuggled against me.

When was the last time I'd slept in the same bed as someone?

I wasn't sure.

"Simon?" she whispered.

Simon. Hearing her say my first name made my heart skip a beat. "Yes, baby?"

"I..."

I swallowed hard. *I love you.* It was way too soon to say that, right?

But she didn't finish her sentence.

And I couldn't help but think she'd almost said it.

"Me too, Pepper," I whispered.

She completely relaxed against me, her breaths evening out as she fell asleep.

I love you too.

TWENTY-EIGHT
PEPPER

I SLEPT in for the first time in years. Sunlight filtered through the curtains, and based on how bright it was, I knew that it was well past ten a.m.

Thankfully, I'd planned to take an extra day off. The original reason was because of my mother's death date, but this felt like a much better reason to not show up to work.

Every muscle ached. There was no way I would've been able to go to work today. I wasn't exactly sure what time Salt and I got home, but my entire body was sore. My asscheeks, pussy, thighs.

I loved it.

I loved the pain.

There was something deeply satisfying about knowing I could still feel what Salt and I did last night.

I'd read about subspace. A headspace that could happen for the submissive in a scene, and was often described as pure bliss. I barely remembered how the two of us got back to the apartment last night, all I knew was that he'd taken care of me. He'd brought me home and then we'd eaten grilled cheese, showered, and snuggled.

I'd fallen asleep next to him so easily. I'd even dreamed about him, although I wasn't sure exactly what about. I just knew that his presence was so intertwined into my being, I could feel him in the cells of my blood. The marrow of my bones. And I didn't want to change a thing.

Salt's arm was draped over me, his body warm against mine. I stirred against him, blinking slowly, drifting in and out of sleep.

Last night came flooding back. I thought about all of the things I'd seen at the club. Seeing so many people who were able to be open sexually without shame had healed a part of me.

Being with Salt had healed a part of me too.

Being trapped in the pillory was something I wanted to try again. Really, there were so many things I wanted to try. But maybe when my muscles weren't so sore.

I didn't want to hide anymore. That was the thing that was changing inside of me. For years, I'd been hiding parts of myself, but now that they'd seen the light, they hungered to be in the open. I wasn't sure I could go back to how I was before discovering these parts of myself. And there was still so much to learn, too.

Last night was something I would never forget. All of the pain and anger and sadness I'd felt over the weekend about my mother dulled. And not that what we'd done together was a fix or anything—it surely wasn't—but it had helped me see that there was more out there for me.

I didn't have to be what Jeff told me I was. Or anyone else, for that matter.

Salt stirred next to me. He was warm and comforting. I wished this could be us every morning, and not just today.

At least I didn't have to return to reality until tomorrow.

Salt let out a soft hum, his arm tightening around me.

"Morning," I whispered.

"Morning, baby," he murmured. He pressed his face against the top of my head, peppering gentle kisses. "How are you feeling?"

"Sleepy. Lazy. Sore," I said. I turned, rolling my body so that I faced him. I pressed my face against his chest and wound my arms back around him. "What are we doing today? Do you have to go anywhere?"

"I'm all yours," he said. "Maybe I can cook breakfast for you."

He had a morning voice. God, I felt... stupid. I felt silly. But not in a way that made me feel ashamed. I couldn't stop smiling, enjoying the croak of his tone. His voice was so deep, sending a shiver through me. His hand settled behind my head, gently massaging the base of my neck as we relaxed against each other.

"A slow morning sounds nice," I said. "I don't remember the last time I slept in."

"Mm."

"You probably wake up next to a lot of people." *Where the fuck did that come from?* It was the pesky self-doubts. The insecurities. All raising their ugly heads to ruin everything.

Salt grabbed a fistful of my hair, forcing me to look up at him. "When are you going to get it into your head that I don't want someone other than you? Yes, I'm a whore. I like sex." He rocked his hips and my eyes widened as I felt his cock against me, hard already. "I've been in orgies. I've fucked and been fucked and I love it all, but none of it comes close to the way you make me feel. I can do all of that with you. I want to do all of that with you. But I need you to trust me when I tell you that I only want you."

Fuck. "I'm sorry. I'm having a hard time understanding why you want *me* out of all people. And it's not fair to you, but it's a hard mindset to break."

"Don't let that little voice put words in my mouth. Please," he said, his lips pressing against my forehead. "Sex and intimacy don't go hand in hand for me all of the time. I can spank someone and not think anything of it the next day. But one kiss with you and I feel like I'm losing my mind. The last week without you was torture."

It'd been for me too.

I'd *missed* him.

My hair fell forward as I sat up slightly and studied him. I felt a choice looming, and for once, I was going to choose myself.

Emboldened by what I knew to be true, I decided I was going to choose us.

"I'm going to tell them about us."

Salt's eyes widened. "Rosethorn?"

"Yes." A weight lifted off my chest and I flopped back down onto the pillow, looking up at the ceiling. It felt right. It felt scary, but right. "They're going to judge me. And I don't know what will happen. But, we'll get you signed, and then I'll tell them."

"You can keep me a secret—"

"I don't want to."

He propped himself up, his throat bobbing. "I don't want any of this to hurt you, Pepper. And you have more to lose than me."

"That's not true," I said. "You have a career ahead of you in music. I know that we will be able to help get you to where you want to be. And I want that. It's why I started Rosethorn to begin with. I can't sing or play guitar or do anything musically to save my life. But I can help artists live their dreams. I can give them the chance to make beautiful music. And that's what we're going to do with you."

He tucked a strand of hair behind my ear.

"I'm tired of being perfect," I whispered. "I'm tired of caring what other people think of me. And don't I deserve to be happy?"

"I think you do."

I'd been going back and forth a lot about everything, but just saying that I would tell everyone on the team lifted a weight off my shoulders. "Also, I don't think you're a whore..."

Salt snorted. "It's a badge I wear honorably. Although, if you tell everyone about us, it'll tarnish your reputation. Won't it?"

"Maybe..." I trailed off as I slid my hand down between us, sucking in a breath as I felt him. "I don't think I care what they think of me."

"It'll just make you more eccentric," he teased, thrusting his hips. His cock was hard and hot against my palm. "The beautiful rich woman with her pet. Meanwhile, we both know who you get on your knees for."

My lips tugged. "You have a good point."

"I always do," he said. "What should I cook for breakfast?"

My brain short circuited as I looked down at his cock. He was still hard. "I want *you*."

"You'll have me later."

"But you're..."

"I'm what?"

I knew he was teasing me. I blushed as I tore my gaze from the veins along his cock, taking in his tattoos and muscles and the way he looked at me like I was everything.

"You're hard," I whispered.

"And?"

I licked my lips. "Can I help you with it?"

"Not yet."

I pouted as he rolled off me and then the bed. He stretched with a slow groan. We'd both slept naked, which I became fully aware of as he looked me over appreciatively.

"I have robes," I said. "If we want to remain... accessible."

He arched a brow playfully and turned. There were two silk robes hung up. I usually alternated between them throughout the week. One of them was lilac and the other black.

Salt surprised me by choosing the lilac one. He winked as he pulled it around himself and then left the bedroom. I immediately sat up, shaking my head.

Bruises marred my skin. My ass ached. And I loved it all. Every single part of it. I traced one on my thigh and then kicked the blanket all the way to the foot of the bed, smiling to myself.

Stupid, stupid choices.

But I felt happy.

And that made it worth whatever trouble might come our way.

TWENTY-NINE
SALT

IT'D BEEN a long time since I cooked for someone else, and I didn't hold back. Even with the grilled cheese and ice cream last night, my stomach felt like an empty pit. "I can Venmo you," I said as I piled pancakes, eggs, bacon, and potatoes on the bar where Pepper sat sipping on fresh orange juice with rosy cheeks and dreamy eyes.

"Don't be silly," she chided. "I'm starving. I think that was the most cardio I've gotten in a *long* time."

I poured another cup of coffee and joined her at the bar. I leaned over, sliding my hand behind her neck and pulling her in for a kiss. She softened against me, lingering until I drew back to admire her.

The silver sections that framed her face were striking against the silky black robe that hugged her body. Like the self-professed slut I was, I was all too aware of the fact that she was naked underneath.

Once we were fed, I wanted to find out what kind of sex toys she'd bought.

"What do you like to do outside of work?" I asked.

Her brows arched as she put a couple of pancakes on her plate. She poured the syrup along the side. "Are we on a date?"

I wished. I wanted to take her on every date I could. "I'm not sure this counts. But I'd like to take you on a date soon. And if we don't have to hide things, we can go wherever we want."

"Very true." Her voice tightened. "It's going to be a lot. I don't know if you want that type of pressure. I think I've gotten used to it for the most part, but I'm used to people thinking I'm a bitch. And it still bothers me, but not as much as it did when I was younger."

"They don't know the real you, just like they don't know the real me," I said with a shrug. "The internet thinks I'm a guitar-playing harlot."

"I don't know if they're wrong about that."

A laugh bubbled up. "Okay, fair enough. But my point is, they'll think what they want."

Pepper smiled as she sipped her coffee.

Everything felt right in this moment. The way the sunlight filled her apartment with warmth. It was open concept and minimal, but there were small things here and there that told the story of Pepper. Like the awards hanging on the walls, or the framed photos that sat on side tables or hung on the fridge. Pepper posing with famous musicians, songwriters, and even actors.

I noticed Jeff wasn't in a single one of them.

I heard a text and we both reached for our phones, but it was from mine. Nancy's text nearly made me choke.

Who's the girlfriend? Saw you two last night.

I couldn't just say Pepper was no one, because that wasn't true at all. Over the years, I'd never introduced Nancy and Beth to someone I was dating, even if it was long term.

But maybe it was time for that to change.

Do you want to meet her?

Of course. We're making dinner Friday night if
you want to bring her over. Beth will be
thrilled

I snorted. Nancy used Beth a lot to express her own emotions, so by saying *Beth* was thrilled, I knew Nancy was too.

Pepper gave me an easy smile. "What?"

"How do you feel about a little trip on Friday?" I asked hesitantly.

"A trip to where?"

My heart raced. This was a first. "Nancy and Beth are making dinner Friday night and invited us to join," I said. "They're my... they're family. You can say no."

"I think a trip would be a good way to end the work week."

"Perfect," I said. "We have the rest of the day alone..."

"What about band practice?"

"I cancelled," I said. "I'm all yours today, baby."

"Oh no. Whatever will we do?"

I narrowed my eyes on her. "Finish your breakfast, and then you'll find out."

A bratty little smirk. That was the dynamic I wanted to test out.

After breakfast, I cleaned up the kitchen against Pepper's protests that she could help. I didn't want her lifting a finger. Caffeinated, fueled, and hydrated—I was ready to play with her.

Pepper's spine straightened as I stepped up behind her, my hand gathering her dark waves and gripping them. I gave her a gentle tug and pressed her against the counter, grazing my lips against the curve of her neck.

Her breath hitched. "What are you going to do to me?" she whispered.

"I have *so* many ideas," I murmured. "Tell me about all the toys you bought."

A soft moan escaped her as I slid my other hand around to gently cup her throat. "I got... I got a lot of vibrators. I'd never used one before so I wanted to try them out. I've tried two so far..."

"Did you like them?" I asked.

"Yes." I felt her swallow hard. "I also got a few other things that sounded interesting."

"Like what?"

"Handcuffs... spreader bars."

Fuck. There were a thousand things we could do with those. "How are you feeling this morning?"

She turned around and leaned up on her tiptoes, sliding her arms around me. "I want you to use me again. Maybe no spanking, because I'm sore."

"I like when you communicate like that," I praised. "It helps me know what to do to you."

She smiled. "I like it when you praise me for communicating, it makes me wet."

The corner of my mouth tugged. "I like it when you're a little bit bratty. And let yourself be open."

"I like it when you choke me."

"Pepper," I chuckled, brushing my mouth against hers. She tasted sweet and sassy and like someone who was about to be screaming my name.

"I also got some rope..."

I growled and my hands slid down to her waist, hoisting her over my shoulder like I had last night. She squeaked as I carried her to her bedroom, slapping her asscheek to make her stop squirming.

"Oh god," she laughed as I tossed her down to the center of the bed.

The sash around her robe unravelled, unwrapping her like a perfect present. Her legs parted, revealing her pussy, her breasts soft and begging for a bite.

A couple weeks ago, she would have immediately snapped her legs shut. But now, she just went still under my gaze, her chest rising and falling. A blush crept across her skin and she let out a soft whimper.

"Stay there." My voice was thick with lust. "Where are the toys?"

"In my dresser drawer," she said.

Perfect.

I went to her dresser and pulled the top drawer open.

The amount of sex toys that Pepper bought made me grin. She had an entire arsenal now.

"How familiar are you with the concept of malicious compliance?" I asked as I perused the toys. Vibrating wands, toys that would suck her clit, variations of both together...

"I'm very familiar," she said. "I think I excel at it."

"I bet."

"Why?" she asked.

I picked out a toy that would suck her clit while thrusting in and out of her.

The rope she'd picked out was rough hemp. I glanced back at her and decided against Shibari for now. We'd play with the spreader bars, but I didn't want her to be sore from yanking against more restraints.

I'd just pin her down myself.

We'd need some ground rules, though.

I picked up the spreader bars and inspected them. I gathered the toy, a bottle of lube, and the bars and returned to the bed. Pepper raised up slightly, tilting her head curiously.

Seeing her legs spread, her pussy gleaming, I realized I liked fucking her during the day more than at night. I liked getting a view of everything.

"So what about malicious compliance?" she asked.

"Have you read any about bratting?"

"A little bit. I think I understand the idea." Something sparked in her gaze. "Do you want me to be a brat?"

"I think it could be fun for both of us," I said. "But there are certain things about it I don't like. Sometimes bratting is borderline disrespectful, and that doesn't turn me on. So we'd need some guidelines and understanding. Sit up."

She huffed and sat up, readjusting herself in front of me. "Tell me."

"I like it when you're sarcastic or snarky in your responses. It makes me want to spank the sass out of you. I like it when you argue. Or maybe if you want to try to overpower me."

"I could do that," she said brazenly.

Yeah, she was going to catch onto this fast.

"And maybe if I drive you a little crazy, you'll want to teach me a lesson." She rose up on her knees, sliding her robe down to her mid back. My brain short circuited as she cupped her breasts. "Right? Am I getting it right?"

"Yeah," I said. "I think you're getting it right."

"I can tell." She winked and then her gaze dropped to my lap.

My cock throbbed in response, hardening.

"I like it when you force me into submission," she said. "CNC. I'd like to try more of that. I know my safe words. And I'm sore, but I don't think you gave me everything you could have."

"Oh, I see," I said carefully, my expression stilling with a dangerous smile. "You can't handle everything I could do to you."

"How would you know?"

A soft growl left me and I tossed the toys I'd brought to the side. I lunged for her, but she was fast. I snatched the edge of her robe, but it slid off her as she rolled off the bed.

"See," she said, backing away with a taunting grin. "You can't catch me."

"Kneel," I said, standing up.

She backed all the way up to the door. "Make me."

The tension between us overflowed, and I moved fast. Pepper squealed as I reached for her, and she took off running down the hall.

Oh, it's on.

SHE WAS FUCKING FAST.

"Pepper," I growled, chasing her through the apartment.

Her laughter was a taunt. She was quick, but I still could anticipate her next move. She went right for the living room, and I snagged her elbow, yanking her back towards me.

Her elbow hit my stomach and I grunted in pain, and she froze. "Fuck," she said quickly. "Are you okay? We didn't negotiate that."

"I'm fine," I said. "Keep trying to fight me. Fuck around and find out, Pepper."

She didn't hold back. I'd never asked her if she knew self-defense, but based on the way she swept her foot against my calf to throw my balance off, she knew the basics.

Pepper wriggled out of my grip and ducked out of the way, giggling as she freed herself. A mix of excitement, frustration, and lust rolled into a ball as I stalked after her.

I was going to enjoy catching her and fucking her.

We were in the living room now, both squaring off around

the coffee table. It was made of glass and the edges were sharp, and that genuinely concerned me.

We needed to pause.

"Yellow," I said.

She stopped in her place. "What's wrong? What happened?"

"I don't like there being a table between us," I explained, pointing to the open space behind her sofa. "The edges are sharp. I won't catch you here and I don't want us wrestling here. It's too dangerous."

"Okay," she said. "I'll go to where you're pointing."

Good girl.

The two of us moved to the other side of the couch, resetting. It was easy to fall back into the push and pull. My arms were longer than hers and I reached for her, grasping her arm. She spun fast, attempting to yank out of my grip with a scream.

"No!"

Fuck. Her shout went straight to my cock as she struggled against me. I grunted as the butt of her palm hit my chest hard enough that she nearly slipped away.

She shouted again as I wrapped my arms around her. Pepper fought back, using her body weight to throw my balance off, but I was more prepared this time.

"I'm going to fuck you until you're begging me to stop," I snarled against her ear.

"No," she begged. "Don't touch me. I hate you, you're awful."

I brought her down to the floor hard, my hand cupping the back of her head so it didn't slam against the wood. She gasped, her expression dazing as she still fought.

"You're a fucking brat," I huffed as her hands slapped against me.

I grabbed hold of her wrists with one hand and pinned

them above her. She didn't stop fighting, her hips jerking against mine.

"Stop," she cried. "Stop. Don't touch me. Don't fuck me."

Her pleas sounded real.

"You're a monster," she gasped. "Why are you touching me this way?"

Her muscles tensed, her cries growing louder as I forcibly turned her over, shoved her face against the floor, and brought my hand down on her ass hard.

She screamed. "*Oh god!*"

"Such a fucking brat," I growled, spanking her again. She cried out, her entire body reacting to the impact. Her bruises were already well-formed from last night, but I didn't care. "I don't care how much this fucking hurts, you deserve it."

Her yelp faltered as I spanked her again and again until she was a trembling mess. "Fuck," she sobbed. "Fuck. It's too much. It hurts so bad, Sir."

I paused for a second as I used my weight to keep her in place. "Pepper," I whispered.

She swallowed hard, her breaths rapid. We both took a second, but then she said, "Green."

Okay.

The reassurance helped. And gave me everything I needed to know. I tightened my hold on her and brought my hand down on her ass repeatedly until she was trembling.

I shoved her away and got to my feet, standing over her. She stared up at me, tears streaking down her cheeks, a smile flashing for a split second.

"Someone's hard," she whispered.

I leaned down and grabbed a fistful of her hair, dragging her up. She whimpered as I pulled her to her feet and led her back down the hall to the bedroom. Pepper's nails raked against my wrists as I took her to the bed. Pain flared and I grunted as I grabbed the spreader bars and shoved her down onto the blankets.

"You little bitch," I hissed.

"Fuck you," she growled. "*Fuck* you."

She rolled over onto her back, panting as I grabbed one of her ankles. It was a struggle. I was going to have bruises too, and that sent a thrill through me as I finally got the fucking spreader bars on.

Pepper tried to clamp her knees shut, but that was not going to happen with these. She pushed against me, but it was no use as I adjusted her to the center of the bed and snatched the vibrator and the lube.

She put her hands over her pussy.

And I fucking laughed.

"Baby, that pussy belongs to me right now. I hope you don't plan on doing much talking tomorrow, because your voice is going to be hoarse from screaming my name."

I lubed up the toy and pulled her hands away, lining up the thrusting part of it with her entrance. Pepper pushed at my hands, wriggling as I shoved it inside of her.

She gasped, her hips bucking. God, she was doing fucking kegels and trying to push the fucker out.

"I swear to god," I said.

"What? You can't handle me?"

She was driving me insane. I clamped my forearm over her chest and held her down, just as I held the toy against her clit and pressedthe button.

Pepper's eyes widened, a gasp escaping her as she tensed for entirely different reasons. I held the toy in place as it vibrated, thrusting mercilessly while sucking her clit.

"Fuck," she rasped. "Oh god."

"What was that again about me not being able to handle you?" I snapped.

"I take it back," she cried, her eyes fluttering as the toy drove her to the edge.

I wasn't going to let her come.

"Do you want to come, baby?" I crooned softly. "You've been working so hard for that orgasm, huh?"

"Yes," she gasped, her expression morphing with pleasure.

"Nope." I pulled it out, keeping her pinned down as her eyes flew open.

"I was so close," she gasped. "You said I earned it."

"You haven't fucking earned a god damn thing."

Pepper pouted, but she was smart. She fluttered her lashes. "Please," she rasped. "Please let me come, Sir. Please. I'm begging you. I'm begging."

"I don't care," I snorted. "Beg all you fucking want. I'll let you come when I'm feeling merciful."

"Please, please."

I pushed it back inside of her slowly, fitting the suctioning part over her clit. I eased some of my weight, just enough so that I could look down at her pussy and watch her. Her thigh muscles were actively tensing, fighting those spreader bars, but that wasn't going to do anything.

Her moans became louder, her hips bucking. She went limp beneath me, her head tipping back as she chased the euphoric high of pleasure. I leaned down and sucked on one of her hard nipples, teasing them both as she got closer and closer.

"Yes," she whimpered. "Yes, yes—*no!*"

Yeah, I was a sadistic bastard. I'd turned the vibrator off right before she could come, robbing her of another orgasm.

"Salt," she groaned. "Please. I'm sorry I was a brat. I submit to you. I'm yours."

"Better," I said, pressing the button.

It roared to life again. And this time, I was confident she wanted it to stay, so I let go and adjusted my position. I swung my leg over her, hovering over her, slapping my cock between her breasts.

"Open your mouth," I grunted.

Pepper parted her lips obediently, tears streaking her pretty cheeks. I pushed her breasts together around my cock, and thrusted, fucking her tits while the sex toy did its job. She started to close her mouth but I moved forward, slapping her cheek with my cock.

"Keep that mouth open," I commanded.

"Please don't take the toy out," she whimpered before opening her mouth wide.

I used her breasts, pumping between them. Seeing her like this was enough to pull me straight to the edge.

I wanted to come when she did.

"Tell me when you're about to," I said.

She nodded, her pink tongue sticking out as she kept her mouth wide and ready.

"Good girl," I panted. "See how you get rewarded when you obey?"

"Yes, Sir," she whimpered.

I pinched one of her nipples, enjoying her sharp little yelp.

"I'm close," she said. "I'm so fucking close, fuck, fuck—"

I filled her mouth in one swift motion as she started to come, feeling her jerk beneath me from the invasion. Her hands gripped my thighs as I came, sending hot spurts of cum down her throat as she orgasmed. I grunted as she swallowed every drop, sucking as she strained beneath me.

"Fuck." My head was spinning. I slowly pulled back and slid off to the side, collapsing into the blankets.

I couldn't think straight.

Pepper's hand slipped into mine. The vibrator was still buzzing, the only sound aside from our labored breaths. I reached down quickly and turned it off, and then spread back out, squeezing her hand.

"Thank you," she whispered. "That was everything I wanted."

I turned my head to look at her. "We were rough."

Her eyes were closed, but she nodded, still catching her breath. She licked her lips. "I loved it."

"Me too."

I brought her hand to my lips, kissing the top gently. Somewhere in the bedroom, I heard one of our phones chime. She sighed and raised her head.

"That could be work," she said.

I groaned. "I'll find it."

"And then maybe we can take a long bath together."

"Will we both fit?" I asked as I got up. I found our phones on the floor and really had no idea when they'd ended up there.

I checked mine as I handed hers over.

An email had come through from Tommy.

"You got that?" she asked.

"Yeah," I said as I opened it.

Hey Salt,

We'd like to move forward with signing you on to Rosethorn. We'd like to set up another meeting with you this Thursday at 2:00 p.m. with our full team. Please RSVP if you are able to make it. If you're unable, just reply and we'll find another time.

Talk soon,

Tommy
he/him

Vice President and Director of A & R of Rosethorn
Records

My heart was already racing from the sex we'd just had, but now I felt another flood of different emotions. I reached down and unclasped the spreader bars and crawled back into place next to Pepper as she read the email, too.

She tossed her phone aside and looked up at me with a smile. "It'll be good. But you have to behave."

"Will you be there too?" I asked.

"Yeah. It's a meeting with all of us."

"Your ex will be there too, huh?"

"Unfortunately. Salt, promise me you'll treat me like you don't even know me. I'm going to tell them about us, but after you're signed. I don't want to risk your career."

"I'll behave," I promised.

At least, I'd try to.

THIRTY-ONE
PEPPER

I WAS SWEATING.

It was Thursday. Over the last couple days, I'd been in a blissful routine with Salt. I'd completely ignored all my concerns about the meeting, and instead just tried to enjoy us.

I'd learned a lot about him. I'd also learned a lot about myself. Like how much I enjoyed being a brat, CNC, and aftercare. I loved cuddling and eating chocolate after an intense scene. The high of it all was addicting.

But today was the day. We were having a meeting with Salt in thirty minutes, and I'd be in the same room with the man I was falling for, in front of people who had known me forever.

My ex-husband. My friend of almost twenty years. Kendra, Lee, and Scott all knew me too well. And then Ellen. Ellen would see straight through my lies.

Hence the sweat dripping down my back. I stared at my reflection in the bathroom mirror and swallowed hard.

I looked good. I had this new glow about me that definitely came from being with Salt. Since Sunday night, I'd lost count of how many times we had sex. Our routine was the same every day—we each went to work, then he'd come over to my apartment, and we'd play and make love until falling asleep draped in each other's bodies.

I wanted it to be like that forever.

My eyes closed and I practiced deep breathing exercises. Filling my lungs, holding the breath, and then exhaling slowly as my stomach did somersaults. It was going to be fine. I didn't do anything wrong. And Salt knew he needed to be on his best behavior.

Basically, he needed to not look at me the way he always did.

And I needed to be calm. Collected. Cold.

Perfect Pepper.

"Okay," I whispered.

I fixed my makeup and hair, straightened my blouse, and headed back out into the office. My heels clicked over the floors as I passed by Ellen's desk.

"Hey," she said in a loud whisper.

I backtracked a couple steps. "What?"

"The guy is here early. Jeff took him to the meeting room. Do you need me to grab anything?"

"No," I said. "Just bring yourself to take notes."

Ellen always took meeting notes when we had new clients. Although I wished that wasn't the case today. Even now, she narrowed her eyes on me.

"You're acting weird," she muttered.

"I'm fine. I'll be in the meeting room in a few."

Deep breath. Deep breath. Fuck my life.

I measured each step back to my office. This was how I normally walked, right? Everything was fine.

I went to my desk and gathered up my papers and laptop, stacking them neatly. Unstacking them because the order bothered me. Stacking them again as perfectly as I could. Then, I forced myself to back away, going to one of my windows and staring out at the Nashville skyline. It was sunny, with beautiful blue skies and not a single cloud in sight.

My palms were clammy.

They were going to know.

How could they not know?

A rap on the doorframe made me look over my shoulder. Tommy smiled expectantly. "You ready?"

"Yeah," I said, plastering on a smile.

"It'll be great," he said.

"It will be. We will need to recommend a lawyer for him before anything is signed, though."

Tommy's smile faltered. "A lawyer? Why? We don't usually do that."

"It's business," I said. "He doesn't even have an agent."

"Hasn't stopped us before. It's not like we're preying on him."

But we were. It was a business, at the end of the day.

And here I was once again, going into business with someone I cared about.

A sticky feeling rose up inside me. Was I doing the right thing? I wasn't sure. I didn't have time to think about it though, so I bottled all of my emotions and put a cap on them. A familiar level of peace came over me.

I gave Tommy a nod. "Let's go."

The walk to the meeting room gave me enough time to truly steel myself. Everyone else was already inside, I could hear their voices. Kendra's chuckles as she talked to Salt, Lee and Scott chatting away. I could see Jeff's head through the doorway. Ellen was already seated next to my chair.

Tommy went in first.

When I walked in, everyone stood up.

And I felt *him*.

"Good afternoon, everyone," I said, keeping my tone pleasant.

I looked up at Salt, finally meeting his irresistible gaze. He was wearing a black button down with the first two popped open, showing off his tattoos, the sleeves pushed up his muscled forearms. Black pants and boots. His scent made my mouth water—a masculine woodsy scent with floral undertones.

He was stunning.

It felt impossible to see him as anything else.

He was beauty, and in this room, I was the beast.

I always shook hands with clients, so I approached him and held out my hand. He took it, his calloused palm sliding against mine. Without fail, I always felt the electric shock of him.

Talk. Fuck. Say something.

"Hi Pepper," he said, pulling his hand away. "It's good to see you again."

Like he hadn't woken me up by eating me out this morning.

I felt like I was bathing in fire. "Good to see you again." I moved around to my chair at the head of the table and took a seat. Everyone was watching me. "I've met Salt, and so has Jeff and Tommy. But I suppose we can go around and introduce ourselves."

There was a moment of silence. Ellen cleared her throat, looking at Scott.

"Sure," Scott said, taking the lead after her nudge.

Salt settled down in a chair, his gaze landing directly on me. *Stop looking at me like that. Damn it, Salt.*

Jeff glanced at Salt, then slowly turned his head, looking at me. I ignored him, though, focusing on Scott.

"I'm Scott," he said. "I'm the director of legal for Rosethorn. We'll be seeing a lot of each other at first, and then hopefully you'll never have to lay eyes on me again. Except for company parties."

Salt chuckled, finally tearing his gaze from me. "Nice to meet you, Scott."

Kendra smiled and leaned forward. "I'm Kendra. Director of marketing. I like your music."

Salt smiled and the entire room lit up. God, he had charisma. A dark, brooding kind that wrapped around you until you'd do anything for him.

And he's mine.

Lee held up a hand. "Lee. Director of promotions. I just want to say, my wife loves your music. I think I've seen too many of your videos at this point."

That made everyone chuckle. Except for Jeff.

"What kind of music do you play, again?" Jeff asked.

The offhanded degradation alone made everyone in the room tense. Salt leveled his gaze on Jeff, but I said something before he could.

"Jeff, did you not read the file?" I asked. "Tommy sent one out with everything we needed to know about Salt, his music, his following."

His face turned red, his head snapping up as he looked at me. "I mean, a file isn't music—"

"Okay," Tommy interjected. "So, Salt here is a singer-songwriter. His songs are sexually charged, and I've heard them acoustic, but also with a band. With the band, it falls under indie rock with R&B, blues, and synthwave undertones."

"Correct," I said. "Today, we're meeting to talk about Salt's future with Rosethorn. We're going to discuss timelines, planning, and hear what questions he has for us. If all goes well, he'll continue with Scott and Jeff."

"He could just come with me," Scott said quietly. "Since Jeff is busy..."

"Busy with what?" I snapped.

"Okay," Tommy breathed out, flashing me an irritated look. "I'm sorry, Salt. Do we need to take five and—"

"It's okay," Salt said. "It seems like everyone is picking up the slack."

Oh god.

Ellen snorted and then covered her mouth. I needed to get everything back under control because it was spinning out fast.

Salt continued to sit there with a soft smile and looking completely unbothered. But he was getting under everyone's skin.

And into my panties.

I squeezed my thighs together and cleared my throat. "Let's get back on—"

"I'm not signing him on," Jeff interrupted.

For fuck's sake. "Salt, can you give us five minutes? I'm sorry."

"Sure," he said, standing up. "I'll just wait outside the door."

Silence followed as he stepped out, the tension in the room thickening. As soon as the door closed, I stood up and leaned over the table.

"What the *fuck* is your problem?" I yelled at Jeff, stunning everyone into silence.

Jeff rolled back from the table slightly. "You're overreacting."

"No, she's not," Kendra said. "The way you're behaving is unprofessional. You just told a client we want to his face that you won't sign him—and why?"

"I don't like him," Jeff snarled, looking at me. "I don't like the way he talks to you. I don't like the way..."

"The way?" I echoed. "The way *what*, Jeff?"

My tempter was boiling over and yes, I was making a scene.

And it felt really fucking good.

"I don't like how he looks at you!" he growled.

"What the fuck are you talking about?" Was I gaslighting him? Yes. Did I feel bad about it? Nope. "You just humiliated all of us in front of a new client. You didn't do your research. You didn't do your job."

"And it's not the first time," Scott quipped.

Jeff's cheeks turned even more red. He looked at me and then around the table. "I founded this fucking company."

"You co-founded it," Tommy said. "With me and Pepper. And Pepper is the CEO. Not you. Not me. This is her record label."

"But I still own it," Jeff said. "The only reason it's here is because of my money."

"The money you invested almost two decades ago," Tommy said. "And Pepper not only outranks you now, but she also makes more than you."

Jeff threw up his hands. "All of you are ganging up on me. I'm the reason this label even exists."

"And I'm the one who made *Forty under 40* last year," I said. "I'm the one who picks out our artists. My vision is what made this company. Tommy works his ass off, just like everyone else at this table. Everyone except for *you*. So I'm going to bring in our client, and you're going to sit there and do your goddamn job, or you're going to leave. Do you understand me?"

Jeff's lip curled into a snarl. "Or what? What would you do?"

"Jeff," Lee interjected. "You're not gaining any friends right now by behaving like an asshole."

"We need to get this moving," Ellen said. "Everyone has other meetings to attend before the end of the day. And that *young man*"—she glanced at me as she said that—"is out there waiting."

"Jeff, get up and welcome him back inside," I commanded, sitting back down in my chair.

He shot me a dirty look, but did as I asked. He rolled his shoulders before opening the door. "Hey, Salt. Sorry about that. Come on in."

Salt entered the room and returned to his seat.

I sent up a silent prayer that we could hold it together this time.

"Okay," I said. "Let's get into it."

THE MOMENT I sat down in my chair after the meeting, my phone chimed on my desk. My entire world felt like it was falling apart as I picked it up.

Fuck.

> We're going to play a little game. You're going to take your panties off for the rest of the day while I'm in these meetings.

"What?" I rasped.

My head was spinning. He wanted to do this here? And now? After that disaster of a meeting?

We'd managed to make it through the rest of the meeting in a professional way. It helped that Kendra and Lee had a lot of ideas they wanted to pitch for cementing his image and marketing him to the broader public.

Before I could text him back, Ellen stormed into my office. She shut the door and spun around, planting her hands on her hips. "What the *fuck* was that?" Ellen asked.

"What was what?" I whispered.

"You know exactly what," she said, crossing the office to my desk. "What is going on? That kid looked like he wanted to *eat* you."

"He's not a kid," I protested.

Her brows shot up. "Oh. Okay, I see. So what, all rules are off the table now? Sleeping with a potential client is crazy."

"We—"

"Don't you try to lie to me," she hissed. "I know you, Pepper. *I know you.* Is this the stranger you told me fucked your brains out a couple weeks ago?"

I couldn't say anything. All I could think about was the fact that Salt had texted me a command, and I hadn't obeyed him yet. That would get me in trouble, right?

"I'm not talking about this here," I said.

"He's too young for you."

"He's an adult," I argued. "I'm an adult. We're doing adult things."

"He's a *client*," she growled. She closed her eyes for a moment before looking at me, pleading with me. "For fuck's sake, Pepper. What are you thinking?"

"I'm thinking this is the first time anyone has ever wanted me," I whispered.

Ellen paused, and then her shoulders deflated. "Honey, that's not true."

"It is true," I said. "We're doing things I've never done before. Things I've always wanted to try. And I didn't plan for any of this to happen, but it did."

"But you could be his boss now," she said gently. "You can't keep doing this with him. It jeopardizes you, your career, your company, and his career too."

"Jeff fucked an intern and got her pregnant," I seethed.

"But you're not Jeff." She sighed, her expression turning grim. "Clearly. Everyone is fed up with him. But that's a whole other problem that doesn't matter right now. The industry will eat you alive if it gets out that you signed a client you're sleeping with."

"Well, you're the only one that knows."

"But not that only one that suspects. Because everyone has *eyeballs*, Pep, and the way that beast was just looking at you? Like he wanted to devour you? That is not the kind of man that will fall in love. He's the kind that will corrode every single part of you away until there's nothing left but him."

"You don't know him," I said simply. "You don't."

"You're right. But I do know you," she said. "And I care about you. I'm always here for you. And what are you imagining will happen? That a twenty-five-year-old will put his entire career aside for a middle-aged woman he has kinky sex with? He's getting his dick wet, and you're losing your fucking mind over it like some fresh out of high school virgin."

"Stop," I snapped. "I'm done with this conversation. I can't do this right now. I can't, Ellen. Please don't tell anyone."

"I'd never tell anyone," she scoffed. She threw up her hands. "I knew something was going on the last few weeks, but you weren't telling me. Why didn't you?"

"Because I knew you'd judge me."

"I'm not judging you." She came closer to the desk and leaned down, making me look up at her. "I am not judging you. I am worried about you. I am worried about you being fooled by another dumbass man. I just want the best for you. I just want you to make good decisions."

"I'm tired of making good decisions."

Ellen pressed her lips together, clearly wanting to say more, but biting her tongue instead. "I'm here for you, no matter what. I just hope you know what you're getting into."

"I do," I muttered, looking away.

I was fuming. Mostly because she was probably right.

This could blow up in both of our faces. And because I was a woman, I was held to a different standard.

"He's not a *beast*, by the way," I whispered, looking out the window. "If anything, I am."

She hummed in disapproval. "I have a stack of papers for you to sign and emails I need responses to."

"Okay," I answered robotically.

Ellen put them down on my desk and then sighed. "I just want you to be careful. I love you a lot."

Despite our heated conversation, I swallowed hard and looked up at her. "I love you, too."

"I don't want to see some punk hurt you."

"I'm more worried about hurting him."

She shook her head. "I couldn't give two shits about him."

"I know that." I chewed on my bottom lip. "Is it so wrong for me to want to be happy?"

"No," she said. "It's not. And it's not wrong to have desires, even if the rest of the world will tell you otherwise. But you need to be smart. You can't wreck your career for someone like him."

"He's a good person."

She shook her head. "He's a man. When are you telling the board? Or are you two keeping this a secret?"

"I'll have to tell them after he's officially signed," I said. "And I intend to."

"Hmm, okay. Just be careful. Jeff looked like he was about to explode. Anyway, let me know what you want for lunch and I'll put in an order."

"Okay. Thank you."

"Mm-hmm." She left quickly, shutting the door on her way out.

My shoulders sagged as I exhaled. My phone buzzed in my pocket and I clenched my thighs.

It was probably him.

I pulled my phone out, and found that I was right.

> Pepper. Answer me.

Fuck. I stood up quickly, glancing up at my office door. I went around my desk and turned the lock on the handle, my pussy already throbbing.

Ellen was right. I was losing it. This was a nightmare.

My phone rattled again.

> Three…

My fingers tapped rapidly.

> Stop, I'm here. I have a real job, remember? And what the fuck was that in the meeting room?

> None of that matters right now. You know my expectations

I scoffed, tempted to tell him to fuck off.

Instead, I sat back down in my chair. My really expensive chair, at my even more expensive desk.

Then, I propped my heel on the edge, sliding my fingers over my silk panties. Fuck, I was wet. I grabbed the phone and opened my camera, hesitating.

> Two…

Was I really going to do this?

"Fuck," I whispered.

I pulled the thatch of lace to the side and took a picture of my pussy. I sent it to him and waited.

My skin was clammy. Everyone was right outside my office. I was supposed to be working.

Take them all the way off. Touch yourself. Film. Send. I want to see how wet you are.

"Damn it." My breath caught.

Aren't you still in the building?!

Yes. In your ex-husband's office.

I don't think he likes me very much. If only he knew the truth...

Fuck. My pussy throbbed in response. There was something so *wrong* about this. It turned me on in a way that made me want to call Salt to my office and ride his cock on my desk.

Take them off. Leave them off. Show me how wet you are. Now.

The threat went straight to my cunt. I called him every curse in the book as I carefully took my panties off. What was I supposed to do with them? I tapped the red recording button and showed him that I was balling them up and putting them in my bottom drawer. Then I turned the camera around.

A soft moan escaped as I pushed a finger inside myself, showing him everything.

"Oh god," I whimpered.

I added a second finger, sliding them in and out. Imagining him watching me. Commanding me. He was forcing me to do this in my office in the middle of the work day, making me into his slut.

I shivered as I stopped the recording and sent it to him. My blood roared in my ears as I waited for his response.

A knock at the door nearly gave me a heart attack. I threw

my phone in my desk drawer and jumped up, adjusting my skirt and self. Fuck. My face was so red.

The doorknob twisted, Jeff's voice echoing from the other side. "Pepper? I need to grab the contracts for him to look over. Did you print them off?"

I wanted to scream. I marched to the door, unlocked it, and yanked it open. "Jeff, Scott has them," I snapped. "He's the fucking lawyer, remember?"

His eyes bugged out of his head. "Jesus, what's with the—"

"Do I look like the person that prints off contracts for this company?"

"Well, no, but—"

"Then go to the person who does." I slammed the door and locked it again.

His shadow lingered beneath the door, but eventually he walked off. I raked my fingers through my hair and closed my eyes, trying not to think about the fact that I could have been caught just now. I could have been caught sending a video of me fingering myself for the twenty-five-year-old songwriter sitting in my ex-husband's office.

That only turned me on more. *Why?*

I stared at my desk with my hands on my hips. I could hear my phone buzzing in the drawer.

"I should ignore him," I whispered to myself.

It wasn't going to work, though.

My body chose for me. I rushed back to the desk and pulled open the drawer, staring down at my phone. The screen flashed, his name beaming, a sign to stop all of this before it spun out of control.

It's too late.

I picked up my phone and sucked in a sharp breath, tears blurring my vision.

You're beautiful.

That was all he said.

Not another command, not another ask for more. Nothing like that.

They're going over contracts with me and all that stuff. I'll come see you around five

A pang of disappointment followed, and I realized it was because I wanted to keep playing.

Please behave.

I will. Don't touch yourself again for the rest of the day. Drink a lot of water. I want you hydrated before I see you in a bit

Fuck.

THIRTY-THREE
SALT

HER EX-HUSBAND REALLY HATED ME, and unfortunately, I got off on that.

Especially since now he couldn't get rid of me.

I sat in his office with him and Scott. He didn't know that Pepper sent me pictures of her pussy, or that I'd fucked her nonstop over the last few days. We'd been in some sort of feral frenzy, and I was starting to think that Pepper's sexual appetite outpaced my own.

We were the perfect match.

Jeff leaned forward to adjust a picture frame on his desk of him with a woman and a little girl. They looked happy, which I didn't think was a bad thing.

Scott handed me a water bottle as he sat down, glancing at Jeff. "Sure you want to be here? I can walk him through everything."

"Yep," Jeff said tightly. "Just going to listen while I work on plans for the LA awards. Pepper still won't let me bring Ally next week."

Next week? I made a mental note to ask Pepper about that. Not that she had to tell me when she was going out of town. We were still so new. But also... I did want to know if she was leaving.

"Jeff," Scott sighed. "You gotta stop, man."

Jeff was a lot different when Pepper wasn't in the room, I realized. Meaner? More two-faced.

I looked directly at him. "Why don't you like Pepper?"

Jeff glowered. "Who says I don't like Pepper?"

"Okay," Scott interjected. "This is not professional—"

"It's pretty clear you don't like her. Or me, for that matter." I was pushing it. I knew that, and yet I couldn't stop myself from continuing. "I haven't done anything wrong."

"You sure about that?"

I cocked my head, holding his unwavering gaze.

Did he know?

Did he know about Pepper and I?

"Salt," Scott cut in. "Let's go to my office."

"Sounds good to me."

Jeff didn't say another word as we got up and left. Scott sighed once we were out of earshot. "Beefing with him isn't a good idea," Scott warned under his breath.

We went into his office and he shut the door.

"Can I ask you something?" Scott said, gesturing to a chair.

I took it. "Sure."

"Is this what *you* want?"

My brows shot up. "Do you mean... what do you mean exactly?"

"Everything."

He was being vague. I knew that, but there was no way to discern what he was insinuating. His poker face was too good.

"It's everything I want," I said. "I love music."

"And you want Rosethorn? You don't have an agent or a lawyer. It's good practice to have both of those before signing contracts."

"I can get a lawyer," I said. "Although, you are a lawyer."

Scott chuckled. "I'm Rosethorn's lawyer."

"Are you trying to take advantage of me?" I asked.

"No, not intentionally. And this company is good."

"How long have you worked here?" I asked.

"Four years," he said. "Pepper hired me after the company acquired some big names. She's the best."

"And Jeff?"

Scott gave me a flat look. "I'm not at liberty to say. Let's get into everything, but like I said, a lawyer isn't a bad idea. Don't rush into any of this, kid. It's big stuff, and I'm nice enough to tell you that."

"Thanks," I muttered.

We spent the next hour going over contracts. Scott was fine. He was straight forward. He answered all of my questions about insurance, advances, and expectations. Pepper had prepared me well over the last couple days, and while I trusted her, she'd been clear not to trust everyone in the company. To ask questions, even though it was her label.

I could see why she hired Scott, though. He was patient and even gave me a couple of lawyer recommendations once I admitted I didn't really know anyone. Nancy probably would have, but it was easier to go through Scott.

The hour flew by, and I was handed over to Lee and Kendra, who I liked a lot more. The two of them were way more relaxed and I liked the ideas they had. We spent an hour going over marketing plans and where I could grow, what I wanted my image to be like.

All of it was a whirlwind.

It was exciting. It was exactly what I wanted. And while I was very focused on the tasks at hand, I couldn't help but think about Pepper.

Everyone but Jeff respected her. The way they spoke about her when she wasn't in the room was entirely different from the way he did, and it made me wonder just how long he'd been talking about her that way.

It infuriated me.

By the time the last meeting ended, everyone was packing up to leave for the day. Lee walked me to the elevators and I got on, but slid back out the doors without him noticing.

Pepper's office was across the floor. I sent her a quick text message that I was coming towards her, and slowed as I approached the doorway, hearing Jeff's voice.

"I don't want to sign him. I don't like him, Pepper."

"Jeff," she sighed. "What is going on with you?"

"With me? What about you? You're letting yourself go and we have a huge awards ceremony next week. What happened to you getting Botox? And—"

"Stop," she snapped. *Are you fucking kidding me?* My fury bubbled to the surface, but she continued. "You do not speak to me that way anymore. We are not married. You have got to stop behaving this way."

"I'm just being honest with you," he said. "Everyone thinks he's not a good fit for Rosethorn."

"I don't think so. In fact, I think he's the perfect fit. For years, my decisions are what have guided this company to success. Or have you forgotten that?"

"I'm the one who gave you the money for it."

"Yes, and you've paid yourself back for the investment tenfold. If you ever speak to me again the way you did earlier in front of a client or in front of our employees, I will eject you from your position."

"You bitch—"

I immediately filled the doorway and knocked the frame. Jeff spun around, his eyes widening slightly.

"Didn't you leave?" he snapped.

"Not yet," I said cooly. "But you're on your way out, aren't you?"

Jeff straightened his spine and scoffed, looking from me to Pepper and back again. She wouldn't look at me, her expression unreadable.

He shook his head, but pushed past me, pausing. "You're making a mistake, Pepper. A big fucking mistake."

I watched him go, and then stepped into the office.

"Shut the door," she whispered.

I pulled it closed, turning the lock silently.

She was stressed, and I felt guilty. I pressed my lips together as I rounded her desk and reached for her.

"Not here," she said, moving out of my grip.

"Pepper," I said softly. "The door is locked. They're leaving for the day. Let me hold you."

Her hands were planted on the desk. She turned to face me, tears swimming in her eyes. "Why me?" she asked. "Out of everyone you could have, why me?"

"Are we really back on that?" I asked. "After everything we've done together this week?"

"Yes, because this is *insane!*" she exclaimed. "This is crazy, Salt. We're crazy. Am I just a quick fuck? Because—"

"Stop," I interjected, reaching for her. I caught her wrists, but she looked away, her eyes glassy. "Pepper," I whispered. "I want *you.*"

"I'm a mess," she said, her tone going cold. "I'm so much older than you. Didn't you hear him? About needing facial work. And I have silver—"

"No," I said. "He's wrong. I think you're beautiful. If you

wanted to change things about your body, I'd support you, but I love everything about you the way you are. He's wrong, Pepper."

"I'm the CEO of this company, and everyone expects me to be perfect."

"You don't have to be perfect with me," I said. "I don't want you to be perfect."

She shook her head, barely hearing me. "He's not wrong. He's not—"

"Did he always used to talk to you like that?" I asked.

"Yes," she whispered.

Fuck. I hated him even more.

"He's stupid," I said simply. "He's jealous. When you're not in the room, everyone else speaks of you so highly. They respect you. They think you're great, despite what he says"

"But he knows the real me."

"No," I said sternly. "No, he doesn't. And he never deserved to be with you. And he no longer has any control over you, Pepper. You don't belong to him anymore. You never did."

"You shouldn't want me," she said. "You could be doing all of this with anyone else—"

"I don't want anyone else," I growled. "Pepper, I want *you*. How many times do I have to tell you that?"

"I don't need words."

My mouth felt dry. She finally looked up at me.

"You need me to show you," I said softly.

"Yes."

"Here?"

"Yes."

"Now?"

"Now," she whispered.

"You need to be reminded."

"Yes," she murmured. "Please. Because I feel like I'm losing my mind."

If that's what it took, I'd do anything.

I'd spend the rest of my life touching her, worshiping her, and reminding her that she was mine.

THIRTY-FOUR
PEPPER

I WAS SPIRALING. Just a little bit. And the only thing that was helping was his touch.

The way Jeff humiliated me today made me feel like a broken doll. I'd put so much from our marriage out of my mind, so many hurtful things that he used to say to me that I'd just let roll off. The comments about getting facial work, about graying early. He hated the silver streaks I now openly wore. Hated the fact that I was comfortable in my skin.

He hated that I looked happy.

Salt cupped his hand behind my neck. "Kneel for me."

I knelt down, looking up at him.

"Do you really think that's all you are to me, Pepper?" he asked. "Just a quick fuck?"

"Yes." The tears finally spilled over. "How could you possibly want me?"

All my doubts and fears were compounding together. I knew that, but I still couldn't stop it. I couldn't keep up the unfeeling facade I'd built up so carefully.

Not with him.

His fingers moved in jerky motions as he yanked open his jeans, his erection straining against the fabric. His tattoos danced across his skin, enchanting me like some sort of magic spell. *Mine* practically glowed neon on his wrist, flashing a warning sign that we were so incredibly fucked.

But I couldn't stop. He couldn't stop. There was something wrong with us, and maybe that was part of why this worked so fucking well.

Tears slid down my cheeks as I looked up at him.

"You're more than sex," he said as his cock slapped my cheek.

It made a heavy thud, my eyes fluttering as I took in the sight of him. The veins that bulged, the length and girth of him, the bead of pre-cum dripping from the head.

All for me.

I was selfish, wasn't I? After all the years of not being looked at the way he looked at me, his hard cock was a gift. One I wanted to lick and suck and give myself to.

He was turning me into a selfish slut.

That's what they'll all say about me. That I'm selfish and keeping him for myself and—

"I've never wanted someone the way I want you, Pepper. I've never *needed* someone this way. I don't care what they say about us. I don't care what your ex-husband thinks. Stand back up."

He grabbed a fistful of my hair and pulled me to my feet. I squeaked as our lips met, all of my worries melting away. Pleasure froze every muscle, my body bowing against his, his cock pressing against my stomach.

"*Mine*," he whispered. "You're mine. Not his. Not anyone else's. You don't even belong to yourself right now, you belong to me. Do you understand what I'm saying?"

"But what about me?" I rasped. "Are you mine too? Are you—"

He raked up my skirt and spun me around, bending me over my desk. The city skyline danced in my vision, the swollen sunset dripping gold over every building. I gasped as his fingertips met my soaked pussy.

He stiffened in surprise as he realized I wasn't wearing any panties.

Just like he'd asked.

"Fuck," he growled. "You want this. I know that you want this. Otherwise you wouldn't be working in your office without panties on. Have you been walking around like this since our texts earlier? Thinking about me fucking you? Thinking about calling me in here and having my cock inside you as you take your meetings? Fucking answer me."

"Yes," I groaned. "Yes. All day, Salt. All fucking day."

He leaned over me, his weight pinning me down as he whispered harshly, "How could you ever doubt that I am yours? How could you ever think that I go one fucking second of my day without dreaming about breeding your cunt, and fucking you until all you know is *my* name. Who the fuck do you think I am?"

"Mine," I whimpered.

He paused, lining up his cock with my entrance. I needed him now more than ever. I needed to know that I was his.

"*Salt*," I moaned.

I heard fabric rip and gasped, looking back over my shoulder just in time for him to stuff part of my skirt in my mouth.

"If you need me to stop, make your hand signal."

Yes, Sir. I couldn't say the words but I still tried to. They came out jumbled, quickly turning into moans as he forced his cock inside me.

Pleasure quaked through me as I was stretched by his cock. But I was greedy, and my cunt was greedy for every ridged inch. I wanted him to fuck me, own me, breed me, mark me, destroy me, and stain my soul with his cum. The lust raging between us was infectious and dangerous, but I just didn't care. I didn't care if he ruined me.

I *wanted* him to ruin me.

"Fuck," he grunted. "You're never leaving me. I'll never let you go. They'll never stop me from having you. I don't care that you're older than me. I don't care that we're from different worlds. I just—" *thrust* "—don't—" *thrust* "—care.*"

Every thrust was him staking his claim. My voice was muffled by the fabric in my mouth, my hands dragging over the desk top. Papers scattered to the floor, the wood creaked as he fucked me mercilessly. There was nothing gentle about him right now, nothing soft. Just raw lust, a live wire electrifying us both, robbing us of any sort of freedom from its shock.

They'd talk about us. They'd keep hating me. Not only was I a powerful woman, I was a rich woman. And not only was I a rich woman, I was a woman who had desires. I was a woman who was having sex, and being fucked in the way that they could only dream about.

I was a woman who had it all. And I knew that after this moment, I would spend the rest of my life fighting to keep it.

My ex-husband didn't want to be with a woman who was both sexual and smart. You could only be one or the other. If you were both, you were too powerful.

Salt wanted me to be both. He made me feel sexy. He made me feel wanted. It didn't matter that he was more than a decade younger than me, it didn't matter that he'd enraged my ex-husband, it didn't matter that what we were doing may be wrong in the eyes of so many.

He wanted me to be sexy and smart.

He wasn't threatened by my strength.

It only made my submission sweeter.

The phone on my desk started to ring. I gasped, freezing even as Salt kept fucking me. He reached around and yanked the fabric from my mouth.

"Answer it," he demanded.

"But—"

"*Now.*"

Fuck, fuck, fuck. I whimpered as I reached across the desk and picked up the phone, my eyes rolling back as he hit the right spot. My voice shook as I forced myself to answer. "He-Hello?"

"Pepper, it's Ellen. Are you staying late tonight? I was about to head home, but I can hang around if you want—"

"No," I rasped. "Go home, Ellen. Okay?"

"Are you okay? I'm worried about you."

Salt fucked me harder.

"I just need to get some things done." God, I could barely think.

"Need anything?"

"No," I huffed. "No. I'm fine. Thanks, Ellen. I'll text you later when I get home."

Salt leaned over and hung up the phone. My squeak was muffled right as he shoved the fabric back into my mouth, his finger hooking the inside of my cheek as he slammed into me. The desk creaked as he shoved me flat, my breasts pressing against the hardwood.

"I'm going to breed this cunt," he whispered. "I'm going to fill you so you know that you belong to me every time you stand, sit, walk, fucking breathe. I want it dripping down your fucking thighs."

"*Yes, yes, yes,*" I chanted through the fabric, tears blurring my vision.

He grabbed a fistful of my hair, yanking hard enough that the tears fell down my cheeks. I was so fucking wet, the sound of our skin slapping together reverberated through the office.

"I'm going to come," I attempted to whimper.

When I climaxed, it was a full body experience. All my fears and worries loosened in my chest, replaced by a blissful space I wished I could live in forever.

"Fuck," he grunted, finally losing control.

His cock slid in and out of me until he gave one last jerky thrust, his grip tightening on me as he came inside me. My entire body melted against the desk beneath us.

"You've awakened something in me," he whispered against my ear.

I clenched my pussy around his cock in response, and his fingers in my hair tightened.

"Fuck," he rasped.

I did it again, still feeling that he was hard. He'd just filled me, and yet...

He pulled the fabric from my mouth and kissed me hard. His tongue met mine, stroking it before biting my bottom lip. He released me, his cock still inside me.

"Am I keeping you warm?" I teased him.

He pinched a bruise on my ass hard enough I had to swallow my squeal. "Tonight," he said. "We're going on a date tonight. We're going to go out and have dinner."

"We can't," I whined. "We can't yet. Not until I tell them."

Salt sighed. "As soon as they know, I'm showing you off to the entire world."

Excitement shot through me.

"Get on your knees," he said as he pulled out.

I slid back, my knees hitting the floor. His cum dripped out, pooling on the polished hardwood. I turned to face him, his slick cock looming before my lips.

"Clean our cum off. I want the taste of me to be with you until we get home."

Home.

His voice was harsh, his dark eyes drowning me with lust. I parted my lips slowly, pushing my tongue out, darting to the head of his cock. I batted my eyes, completely gone for him. I didn't care who walked in right now, I wouldn't stop. I wouldn't stop sucking his cock for anyone.

He jerked my head forward, filling my throat in one swift thrust.

I sucked him, tasting us together. The tang of our orgasms was an erotic potion. The sounds I made filled my office, the last of the sunlight spilling over us.

He gently pulled my mouth away. I leaned forward, resting my head against his hip, closing my eyes.

"Pepper," he murmured. "You can't keep doubting that I want you."

He was right. Even though I wasn't sure I'd ever truly understand. He held out his hand and I took it, allowing him to help me to my feet.

Salt tipped my chin up. "Tomorrow, we're going to dinner with my family. And tonight we're going to rest. We're going to watch a movie and order food. And we're going to forget about everyone that works in this building."

"Okay," I said softly. "I'm sorry, I didn't even ask you how your meeting went."

"They were good," he said. "Scott gave me some lawyer recommendations. I'm going to reach out to have the contracts reviewed before I sign anything."

"Good," I murmured. "I take it the time with Jeff didn't go well."

"I didn't meet with him," he said. "Well, I did briefly. We butted heads and then Scott took me to his office."

"He suspects something," I said. "Ellen knew immediately. You were..."

"I can't stand by and let Jeff treat you that way. Even if I didn't know you, I wouldn't be okay with it. That's not who I am," Salt said. "I'm sorry. But it's not. And I held myself back, Pepper. That was me behaving."

"The way you looked at me..."

"Is the way I'll always look at you. And I'm not sorry for that." He kissed my forehead gently. "Let's go home."

"Yeah," I said. "Let's go home."

THIRTY-FIVE
PEPPER

FOR ONCE IN MY LIFE, I left work early on a Friday so I could ride with Salt to Nancy and Beth's for dinner. He picked me up and the moment I got into his car, I felt a weight lift.

"Sorry, it's not the nicest car," he said, wincing as his ancient Honda hit a pothole on the road.

"I don't care," I said. "I don't even have a car. I never drive anywhere."

"*How?*" he snorted. "You're the ultimate passenger princess."

I smiled as I looked out the window. "I'll wear that badge with honor. One, I hate driving. It makes me anxious. Two, after my divorce, I moved into my apartment and it's just a few blocks from work. And Ellen lives just a couple blocks away, too. Everything I need is within walking distance."

"So you just walk around?"

"Yeah."

He shook his head. "What about when it rains?"

"Have you heard of umbrellas?"

Salt chuckled. The scenery changed from concrete and steel to trees and land, the sky turning a hazy purple as the sun dipped down. He reached over, his hand settling on my knee for a moment, giving me a gentle squeeze.

"Are you nervous?" I asked him.

"A little. Nancy and Beth mean the world to me. I think you'll like them."

"I'm more worried about them liking me," I said.

Another squeeze. "They'll like you. Nancy is a little intimidating at times, but I don't think I have any worries about that with you."

"No, I like powerful women," I said.

"Me too."

This weekend was going to be a change of pace for the two of us. Instead of staying at my apartment, we were going to stay at his house tonight and tomorrow. He didn't have any shows planned either, so it would be quiet.

It would be a nice break before the chaos of next week. My eyes widened as I dawned on me that I hadn't told him about my trip. I'd almost forgotten about it between everything that'd been happening.

"I forgot to tell you," I said. "I'm going on a trip next week. It's for The Guild of Music Supervisors Awards show in LA."

"Oh yeah," he said. "That asshole mentioned it. I meant to ask you about it, too. When do you leave?"

"Friday," I sighed. "I still need to pick out a dress. And it's too late to make any appointments, although maybe I can squeeze in a facial on Monday..."

"You look beautiful as you are," Salt said. "They'll worship the ground you walk on."

I laughed. "Baby, you've been to LA. Everyone is beautiful there. I'll look like a frog."

He brought my hand to his lips and kissed my knuckles

before adjusting in his seat, his eyes on the road. "I think that's the first time you've called me baby."

My cheeks warmed. "Do you like being called baby?"

"Yeah, coming from you."

Part of me wanted to ask him to come to LA with me. But I knew if I did that, it would cause problems. Especially since I told Jeff he couldn't bring Ally. And because our relationship was still a secret.

Hopefully, by the end of next week, the contracts would be signed. Salt had sent them over to a lawyer earlier today, and I hoped they would move fast.

I just wanted ink on paper so I could finally tell everyone about the two of us.

Maybe it was a little shady. Maybe I was making bad decisions, but I was long past backpedaling at this point. I was committed to being with him.

Regardless of what happened, I wanted to be his.

It was crazy how fast things could change. But, I knew deep down in my bones that what we had was right for me.

"Maybe you can help me pick out my dress," I said.

"I'd like that."

He slowed the car and turned off onto a narrow road. I drank up the last of the sunshine, studying the trees that lined the street. "I bet it's beautiful out here in the fall."

"It is. Would you ever want to live somewhere like this?"

"Maybe," I said. "It would be a pain to go into the office. But I've also thought about changing my hours and splitting them so I could work from home. Being so close to the office, I just felt like it made sense to go in every day. But if I lived further away, I'd want to change that."

"I mean, you *are* the boss."

I was. And I also was always flexible with everyone else's schedules, so why can't others be with mine?

Salt turned onto a driveway and pulled past a gate, easing down the gravel until we came to a roundabout with a tree at the center. A beautiful house was in front of us, and to the right I could see a large garage and a small red barn.

The front door opened and a woman with a bright pink mohawk stepped out and waved.

I wasn't sure what to expect, but the friendly welcome alleviated some of the tension I felt.

"That's Beth," he laughed, turning off the car. "Okay. I'm very anxious. I've never done this before. If you want to leave at any point—"

"Simon," I said gently, leaning over to kiss his cheek. "We're both nervous. But, it'll be good." *I hoped.*

My phone beeped. I picked it up and stared.

Jeff had texted me.

> Are you fucking that guy? The new client? I heard rumors about the two of you, Pepper. Is there something going on???

> We need to talk

> Seriously. If this is happening then it's a problem. I know it's the weekend but this is urgent

> HELLO???

Fuck. I'd be a liar if I said my heart wasn't beating out of my damn chest. I felt like I couldn't breathe.

I turned my phone off before he could say anything else.

Salt pressed his lips together in concern. "You okay? You look pale."

"Yeah." I put my phone away. Rumors were just rumors, I reminded myself. Jeff didn't have proof, and he wasn't going to ruin my night. "We've got this."

He stole one more soothing kiss, and we both got out of his car.

Beth came down the front steps to meet us with open arms. Salt bent down to give her a hug, and she patted his back, but then turned her full attention on me.

"I'm Beth," she said. "Are you a hugger?"

"Sure," I said. "I'm Pepper—"

She gave me a big hug that had Salt sighing. "She's always like this. At least she asked for consent—"

"Oh shush," Beth said, pulling back. Her cheeks were rosy and I felt a wave of comfort from her, one that brought my heart rate down just a bit. "You are gorgeous, Pepper. Come on inside. We don't bite hard."

Salt sighed dramatically again, but he was smiling. I followed Beth up the front stairs and looked around her front porch. There was an abundance of potted plants, a porch swing, and a myriad of kitschy things that made me smile. A clay fairy tucked away beneath the leaves of a pothos, pride flags wavering in random places. The welcome mat had a rainbow and said *homo sweet homo*.

"I love your house," I said.

"Thank you, Nancy lets me do whatever the hell I want. And I like to have fun."

"Where is Nancy?" Salt asked as we stepped into the foyer.

"She is in the wine cellar being extremely picky about which bottle she wants us to have tonight," Beth said. "Oop. There she is."

A tall, gracefully beautiful woman emerged from a set of stairs at the end of the hall and held up two bottles of wine like a man holding a fish in his dating profile. "I got them," she announced, smiling as she approached. "Hi, Pepper, it's nice to meet you."

"It's nice to meet you too," I said.

Nancy gave Salt a hard look. "You look like you're sweating through your boxers."

"Nancy," he groaned. "I'm not."

She wiggled her brows, but then gave him a loving smile. It was clear they both loved him, and that warmed my heart. Maybe it was because I'd gone without parental figures in my life for years, but just knowing he had them made my chest feel light.

"I have to give him a little bit of a hard time. Been our kiddo for years and has never brought someone home, so it's my obligation to make him a little anxious," Nancy said.

I laughed, my hand finding his. I was pretty sure both of our palms were drenched. "We're both a little nervous."

"I told her we don't bite hard," Beth said with a smirk.

"Well come on in and get settled. I'll pour us wine, assuming you drink. Simon, there's soda in the fridge."

"Thanks," he mumbled.

Beth and Nancy headed towards the kitchen.

"Is it okay if I drink?" I asked Salt under my breath.

"Of course," he said. "Passenger princess. Remember?"

"Yeah." I smiled to myself as we followed them.

The kitchen was just as gorgeous as the rest of the house, and like the front porch, was a mixture of country-styled decor, queer, and kinky things. Salt followed my gaze as my eyes widened on some of the pictures on the fridge.

"Oh," he said. "I maybe should have warned you. Beth and Nancy are very openly kinky."

"Yes, we are," Beth chimed. "Have a seat at the bar. Dinner will be ready soon."

Salt pulled out a stool for me and I perched on top of it, the nerves returning full blast for just a few seconds. He sat down next to me, his hand sliding beneath the bar and settling on my leg. "What are we having?" he asked.

"Baked lasagna with Beth's homemade sauce," Nancy said. "Garlic bread, a strawberry poppyseed salad, and fresh rolls."

"That sounds wonderful," I said.

"So," Nancy said as she uncorked a bottle. "We're having a nice Blaufränkisch with dark cherry notes."

"She's showing off," Beth snickered.

"Just a little. He's told us nothing about you."

"*Nancy*," Salt hissed.

I laughed. I could handle bluntness any day of the week. "We haven't told a lot of people about our relationship quite yet."

"It's still new," Salt said.

"So what do you do?" Beth asked. "I build furniture."

"Sex furniture," Nancy clarified.

"I think that's fun," I said. "I've never been good at building things."

"That's not true at all," Salt quipped. "You built a whole company."

Beth and Nancy both raised their brows.

His hand gave me a reassuring squeeze. "I'm the CEO of Rosethorn Records," I said.

"That's amazing," Beth said.

Nancy studied me a little closer before pouring three glasses of wine. "Is that how you met Simon?"

"We technically met in a coffee shop first," I said,

There was a warm timbre to his chuckle. "Coffee shop. Then one of my shows."

"Isn't Rosethorn who you're signing with?" Beth asked.

"Yes," we both said.

Nancy slid the wineglass toward me. "Sounds like you need this."

I picked it up by the stem, swirling the wine in the glass. I took a sip and hummed in delight. It was delicious.

The timer on the oven went off. Beth started to turn for it, but Nancy held up her hand. "Go set the table with the good plates and napkins. Simon, give her a hand. Pepper can help me."

Salt lingered for a moment, but I waved my hand at him. "I'll help Nancy," I said. "You help Beth. It won't take long."

He pressed his lips together, glancing at her and then me. "Okay."

Salt slid off the stool, and he followed Beth to the dining room, where I could see a china cabinet just inside the space.

The moment he was out of ear shot, I looked at Nancy.

She was studying me. Scrutinizing.

I wasn't going to beat around the bush, "You probably think I'm too old for him—"

Nancy barked out a laugh, one that startled me. "No. I was thinking that you're the first person he's ever brought home, and you must be something pretty damn special." She grabbed an oven mitt and pulled the lasagna out of the oven. "You feel that way though, huh?"

"I worry about how we'll be perceived when we tell more people. The two of us tried to fight what we were feeling, but that didn't work out. I realize that I'm in a position of power, but I've done everything I can to ensure that he's protected in case our relationship doesn't work out the way we'd like."

"I don't think you're taking advantage of him, if that's what you're worried about."

I frowned. "He's not taking advantage of me either."

"I know he's not. There is a power dynamic here, but you are both adults. What are you worried about?"

I barely knew this woman, but I still decided to be forthright. "I worry that things are going too fast. And that everyone will judge us. But I don't think hiding our relationship is working. I want to be out in the open with our relationship. I just worry about the rumors and the consequences. Do you know what I mean?"

She put her hand on her hip and gave me a withering look. "Darling, you're talking to a woman who's not only a lesbian, but a professional Domme. You want to know something? People are always going to judge." She shrugged. "Does it matter if you're happy and not hurting anyone?"

My reputation and career were everything to me. It was the only thing I had to show the world—proof I'd been existing and contributing in some small way.

But was I happy? That was the question I'd been asking myself for years. When Jeff told me he'd been seeing someone and wanted a divorce, I'd been so cordial, because deep down it was a relief. It was a relief to know I didn't have to keep being unhappy with him.

The longer I sat with my decision to tell the board about our relationship, the more right it felt, even though I still had a thousand concerns.

"He is really talented," I said softly. "My record label will be perfect for his music. He'll go places."

"I know," she said. "And I also know nothing's stopping you from going along with him. Just like nothing stopped me from coming to live here with Beth."

We were both silent, and then she shrugged her shoulders again.

"Alternatively, he could just be a fling for you."

I bristled. "I..."

"I wouldn't judge you if that were the case. But I know Salt thinks of you as more than that, if he brought you here. So if you don't want to hurt him, you should break things off sooner than later. Don't string him along. He doesn't deserve that, after everything he's gone through."

Don't string him along.

That was the last thing I wanted to do.

"As far as your age gap goes, I'm not the right person to ask. Beth is almost twenty years younger than me and a Mom of two grown kids who are out living their lives. We've been together for a few years now. She's the absolute love of my life. If you're both able to communicate and create a healthy relationship, then really, age is just a number. Right?"

"Yeah," I said, relaxing a fraction. "I'm glad that he has you and Beth. I'm glad we met like this instead of..." I trailed off, my face warming.

Nancy grinned. "I caught a glimpse of the two of you that night and went on my merry way."

"Oh god." I hid my face in my hands, but Nancy didn't seem to care. She just winked and gestured at the food.

"Let's take everything to the table. I think we've let Simon sweat enough. He's never brought someone to meet us before, and he's probably thinking I'm either embarrassing him or trying to scare you off. Have I scared you off?"

"No," I laughed. "No you haven't scared me off."

"Good. Let's eat and celebrate the weekend."

THIRTY-SIX
SALT

DINNER WASN'T A DISASTER. In fact, by the time it was time for us to go, I had to practically cart Pepper out the front door. I knew Beth would love her, but even Nancy was a goner.

It wasn't a surprise, though.

"Drive safe," Nancy said as she walked me to the car. Pepper was already in the front seat of my Honda, being cute and tipsy. "Text us when you get home."

"I will," I said. "Thank you for dinner."

"Of course. Come over again soon," she said. She lingered for a moment and then drew in a deep breath. "You're both diving in headfirst."

"We are," I agreed.

"Just make sure you take care of yourself. It's easy to make a lot of stupid decisions when you love someone."

"We're being careful," I murmured, glancing back at the car.

"She's risking a lot. So are you."

"It'll be worth it."

Nancy nodded, and I knew there was more she wanted to say. But she didn't. Instead, she gave me a quick hug and started toward the front door where Beth waited. "Night," she called.

"Good night."

I waved at Beth and then got into the front seat, starting up my car. I glanced over at Pepper and beamed.

"I love them," she sighed happily. "They're so sweet. Dinner was amazing. Thank you."

"Thank you for coming with me," I said. "Ready to sleep?"

"Mmm, maybe." There was a hint of mischief in her voice. "You mentioned you have a surprise for me tomorrow."

"I do," I said.

I'd been planning a scene over the last few days. And since we'd be at my house, we would be using the garage. I'd set everything up already.

"What's the surprise?"

"Surprises are surprises," I said as I pulled out of the driveway and onto the road. "We'll get some good rest tonight. And you'll find out tomorrow."

The drive back to my house went by fast. Pepper dozed off, which wasn't a surprise. The longer I knew her, the more I wondered how she didn't nap all the time. Her brain was always going.

Not that mine was much different.

The neighborhood was quiet for a Friday night. It was nicer now than it was a few years ago. I parked in the drive and got out quietly, going around to the passenger side. I opened the door and leaned in, unbuckling her.

Pepper's eyes slowly opened and she gave me an easy smile in the dark. "Hey," she whispered.

"Hey."

I kissed her softly. Her arms wound around my neck, and I scooped her against me, lifting her and kicking the door shut behind me. She giggled as I carried her up the sidewalk and to the front door, letting us inside.

Bringing her here felt like taking her into my past. But in all the darkness, she was a beacon, and instead of worrying—I felt comforted by her presence.

"It's not as nice as your place," I said, setting her down.

She wobbled for a second, but then regained her balance, looking around the living room.

"This is where you grew up?"

"Yeah," I said.

Pepper took a few steps away as she took it all in. I felt like I was going to jump out of my skin, like she was seeing a part of me that I kept private.

"I want to sell it soon," I said. "It reminds me too much of him. The only reason I've been here is because it has a garage and that's good for band practice, plus it is paid for. I've just had to pay utilities and taxes."

She nodded. "I know someone who could help you get it on the market, if you want."

I thought about it. I'd been dragging my feet about it all. But maybe it was time to move on.

In my life, there were a few moments of big change. In the past, I could distinctly pick out those instances as they were happening, and I could feel it now. Like I was standing on the edge of a cliff with invisible wings, not entirely sure of myself or if I'd make it.

Maybe Pepper was my wings.

"I'm curious to see what surprise you have for me..."

"Well, there *are* perks of having a garage."

"I can buy a house with a garage."

I raised a brow, she looked up at me with a smile.

Was she asking what I thought she was asking? Or insinuating that?

Pepper winced. "Sorry. I'm probably moving too fast. I'm probably also making assumptions."

"I mean, all you said was that you could buy a house with a garage."

"Right." She made a face, her cheeks rosy.

My smile pulled into a laugh. "We'll revisit whatever idea you have brewing after I sell the house. Good?"

"Yes."

I kissed her forehead gently. Her hands slid into mine and she stepped back, leading me into the living room. When I redecorated the place, it'd really just become a space to hold all of the vinyl records I'd collected over the last few years. A record player sat on top of a thrifted hutch with six shelves, all full of albums. My taste in music varied greatly, so it was a collection that bounced between Frank Sinatra, AC/DC, Marina and the Diamonds, various folk artists, and god knew what else.

"You've collected so much." Her hands fell away as she turned to read the names on the sleeves.

"I have," I said. "I like the way record players sound."

She nodded eagerly. "The superior listening method. What do you want to listen to?"

"You pick."

Pepper hummed to herself as she perused the shelves. Eventually, she plucked one out and held up the album. Miles Davis, *Kind of Blue*. She carefully slid it out of the sleeve and lifted the transparent top on the player, pressing the lever that lifted the needle. She lowered it to the outer edge and pressed play. Soulful jazz filled the living room and chased away all the nightmares that lingered.

She shut the lid, then turned to face me, holding out her hand. "Dance with me?"

"Of course," I said.

Our palms slid against each other, fingers intertwining as I tugged her close. It felt natural to have her in my arms and to start swaying. My chin rested on top of her head, eyes drifting shut as her presence enveloped me. This was far more nerve-wracking than being in a room full of music industry reps. Dancing with Pepper had butterflies fluttering in my chest, completely bewitched by her.

As the song ended, I pressed a kiss to the top of her head before murmuring, "I like thinking about the future. What do you want your future to look like?"

"After my fumble, I think you go first," she chuckled nervously.

I snorted. "That wasn't a fumble."

But, I thought about it. What I wanted for myself. For us. I closed my eyes again as we gently moved, soaking in the gentle sound of the crooning trumpet.

"I want it to look just like this," I whispered. "But not in a house of bones. Somewhere new, somewhere I can build the life I want."

"A home."

I nodded as her ear pressed against my chest.

"I want a place for music. A place to play my guitar and sing. A nice kitchen to make meals in for someone I love." I squeezed her hand lightly. "I want a place to come home to between shows around the world."

"Mmm. Yes. I want a place where I can escape everything else. I miss listening to music the way I used to."

"I still want to write you a song."

She shook her head with a soft laugh. "You don't need to do that."

I *did* need to do that. The idea of writing a song for her had possessed me. Eventually, the lyrics and music would come tumbling out. "Where do you see your future, Pepper? What do you want?"

"Well, I also want a home. I want to sell my apartment and get a place that's a little further from work. I want to be a better friend to Ellen. I want Jeff to be fired so I don't have to keep... dealing with him."

I frowned, worried he'd done something more. "Did something else happen?"

"No," she said quickly. "No. Nothing to worry about. But, I want to stop making Rosethorn in my entire life. And I want you. I want you in it. However you end up fitting, I just know I want you there."

"I want you in mine too."

With that confession between us, we continued dancing, moving together slowly around the room. Where our words were silent, the feel of our bodies and the music binding us together echoed.

When we did tell everyone, I knew it might initially make things tougher. But whatever came our way, I was ready. It was hard to see past what was in front of us, but dreaming about it helped. "I want to win Ellen over outside of the meeting room," I said. "Since she's your best friend."

Pepper made a noise. "She may not like you at first."

"That's fine," I said. "I'll win her over. Who else do I have to win over?"

"Dan. Tommy's husband."

"I can do that," I said. "Easy. I know Tommy likes me."

"He likes you for the company—it may take a little longer to win him over otherwise. He's known me for a really long time, and he still thinks of me as prudish and perfect," she said.

"Well, if he's known you for a long time, he should know that you're full of surprises."

She smiled against my chest. "You're right. I plan to talk to him soon, but things have been a little tense. And unfortunately, I just don't think you and I are good at hiding things."

We certainly weren't. "It'll be worth it."

I believed it would be. But then again, maybe I was being selfish. I knew that our personal relationship wasn't necessarily influencing our business relationship, but I didn't want either one of us to feel obligated to work together in that way.

"Are you sure you want me?" I asked.

Pepper's head snapped up, her gaze meeting mine. "Of course I want you. Have I made you doubt that?"

"I just worry that you feel like you have to give me a chance with your record label because you... like me."

She shook her head. "I believe in your music. I think that you are talented, and that you're exactly what we're looking for. And none of that has anything to do with how much I like you. I would've taken you on even if there wasn't anything between us."

I could hear the difference when she slipped into business mode. And maybe that helped me believe her.

Her gaze melted from cold to dreamy. "I promise you that whatever happens between us, Rosethorn will still be good for you."

I believed her.

I just hoped that I could always be good for her, too.

THIRTY-SEVEN
SALT

"ARE YOU READY?"

"Yes," she whispered.

I held my hand over Pepper's eyes as I guided her through the door to the garage. Cushioned tiles interlocked across the floor, which would keep both of us from hurting ourselves on the concrete. Above it was a rig for suspension. I'd picked out ropes and had a bag full of toys to surprise her with.

I knew *exactly* what I wanted to do to her.

Pepper's breath caught as I revealed it all to her. Her body nearly vibrated with excitement and anticipation. After a good night's sleep and an even better breakfast, we were ready for a different kind of activity.

"Is that for tying me up?" she asked.

"Yes," I said. "I want to tie you up and suspend you in the air and fuck you. I have other plans too, but I want them to be a surprise. If you want me to tell you—I will, of course."

"No," she said. "I want to be surprised. I like that."

I guessed she would say that. "I'm not so sure you'll like me after," I chuckled.

"We'll see about that. I want to go as far as I can without truly breaking."

A soft growl left me as I pushed her to the center of the garage. Pepper was dressed in black silk pajamas, her nipples hard beneath the fabric. I slowly circled until I came to a stop in front of her, tipping her chin up with a finger.

"Who am I?" I asked.

"Mine," she whispered.

"And who are you?"

"Yours," she said, her lashes fluttering as she started to fall into a submissive headspace. Over the last week, a ritual had started to form between us, and I loved it. We'd also tried out a few new things, such as rope play. "Yours to touch. Yours to use. Yours to fuck."

"Good girl," I praised. "You know your safe words."

"I do. I trust you."

"And I trust you." I leaned down, brushing my lips against hers. "Strip until you're naked."

"Yes, Sir."

She shivered, which reminded me I needed to run the space heaters for the garage. She started to strip as I turned one on, keeping my eyes on her.

Once she was naked, I went to the black bag I'd prepared and pulled out my rope and safety shears. The rope I'd picked out was bright pink, and I couldn't wait to see Pepper bound up.

I walked up behind her, and she stiffened as I approached. I swept her hair behind her neck, kissing the curve gently.

Her breath hitched. "I want you," she murmured.

"I know."

The ropes slid over her skin, neon pink cupping her breasts in a diamond pattern as I tied her into a harness. She whimpered, her eyelashes batting as I moved her like a doll wherever I needed her, raising her limbs. The sound of the hemp sliding over flesh, her raspy breaths and occasional stifled whimpers—it created its own erotic rhythm, a song written by two of us.

Melody and lyrics.

"Don't be afraid to moan," I told her as I created a pattern down her stomach, knuckles grazing her. "Spread your legs."

She parted them as she pushed her fingers through my hair. "I love the way you touch me."

I smiled. She didn't know what I had planned for her yet, and that comment brought me an immense amount of excitement.

Especially knowing what I was going to do to her.

I finished the body harness, and then took a step back to look over her. Her legs remained parted for me.

"Good," I said. "Turn around."

She turned around slowly, giving me a perfect view of her ass. Bruises were still healing from last Sunday, although most of them had faded into a mottled yellow and pink.

"Do you remember your safe word?" I asked.

"Of course," she said. "Always."

"Good girl."

I left her standing there, going into the bag I brought with me. I rummaged through to find the blindfold. The moment my fingers brushed silk, I pulled it out, and then crept slowly behind her, every step measured. The tension in the room thickened, the calm before the storm. I knew she was fighting the urge to turn around to look at me.

"You're so obedient," I teased.

"I like being a good girl for you."

"I know you do. You do such a good job at it."

I lifted the blindfold and fit it around her eyes, pulling the silk back behind her head. I knotted it quickly, giving it a firm tug to ensure that it was in place. Her body went very still, adjusting to her vision being taken.

"What are you going to do to me?" she whispered.

"You'll know soon enough."

It was an ominous answer, but the part of kink I enjoyed most was the psychological aspect. I wanted her to be on edge. I wanted her to be wondering what I was going to do to her next.

Would it be pleasurable? Or would it be painful?

Guessing was part of the fun.

I'd spent hours planning the scene. Deciding exactly what I wanted to do to her in these moments—these precious fucking moments that I got to dominate one of the most powerful women I'd ever met in my entire life.

Her trust was a gift.

I left her standing there as I did one more check of the suspension rig. The cushioned tiles were down in case something went wrong and she fell, but that wouldn't happen. I double-checked my safety shears again, all of the carabiners, and then grabbed another fifty feet of rope.

Pepper tensed as I crept up behind her, reaching around and grabbing her wrists. I lifted them above her head, leaving them there.

"You will stay like this."

"Yes, Sir."

"I want you to talk to me while I tie you up," I said. "I want to know how everything is making you feel as I do it to you."

"I can do that."

She swallowed hard, her breath hitching as I attached the double-column tie around her wrist to a carabiner, suspending them in the air. It was just high enough to keep her on her tiptoes.

"Talk to me, baby girl."

"I feel... I feel powerless, but I also feel powerful. I know you're in control, but I trust you. I know you're going to do things to me that may hurt, but I want your pain. I want your marks. I want everything. I'm excited. I'm nervous. A little scared. And I'm *really* turned on."

Her words were a waterfall while I continued to work. I smiled to myself. I could listen to Pepper talk about anything all day forever.

"You make me feel special," she continued. "You make me feel cared for. And you make me feel heard."

"You make me happy." I pinched one of the bruises, drawing a squeal from her.

She yanked against the ropes, but she wasn't going anywhere. Not for a long, long time.

"Remember everything you've just said when you're sobbing my name."

I reached for her thigh, slowly lifting her right leg to a ninety-degree angle. Using the rope, I created column ties, bringing the ends up to her wrist. I took my time, making sure every knot was secure, that none of it was applying pressure to a spot on her body that could actually create damage. As much as I loved Shibari, I always worried about something going wrong. That worry wouldn't go away, which was also why I needed her to continue to communicate.

"Is anything pinching?" I asked. "Is anything feeling numb?"

"There's an intense pressure where the rope is, but no numbness. No pinching. The rope makes me feel safe."

"Thank you for telling me, sweet girl," I praised, giving her hair a gentle tug. I kissed the side of her neck before kneeling down behind her.

More rope. Always more rope. I used it to make a tie around her thigh and then reached for her calf. She struggled just a bit, not wanting to fully lean her weight into the ropes. I gave her ass a slap, looking up at her. Even though she couldn't see me.

"Let go," I growled. "Trust the ropes. They've got you and they're not going anywhere."

She sucked in a breath. I knew how hard trust like this was for her. It was hard for me too. But I also knew that once she let go, she would more than likely enjoy it.

I was patient. I waited, rubbing her body gently until she slowly gave her weight over to the ropes.

"Good," I murmured, kissing her thigh.

Her leg was suspended in the air, her arms suspended, her weight held by those points. I gently moved her leg back, bending it so that her foot pointed up as if she were doing a runner's stretch.

Pepper released a soft hiss.

I paused. "Too much?" I asked.

"I can feel it in my front thigh. The stretch. It's a little too intense for me."

I adjusted the angle so that it was a gentler pull. "Here?"

"Yes. I think I could stay like that."

"Good." I did another column tie around her ankle and attached it to the one around her upper thigh, keeping that leg bent.

And now, she was officially suspended in the air.

She couldn't run from me.

She was completely at my mercy.

That realization seemed to dawn on her too. A little rabbit slowly realizing it was caught by the predator sharpening its teeth.

"Salt," she rasped.

I pressed my body against her, kissing the middle of her back as I ran my palms over her body, the ropes framing her perfectly. She whimpered as I slid my hand lower, cupping her pussy.

"My, my, my," I whispered. "You're so wet, baby. Does giving up control turn you on? Do you *like* submitting to me?"

"Yes," she whimpered, her breaths quickening as I slowly, so painfully slowly, circled her clit with my fingers. Just enough to make her moan before releasing her, leaving her suspended in the air. "Salt," she groaned.

Her head tilted as she listened to me walk away. My cock throbbed against my jeans as I went to my bag, pulling out a wireless Hitachi wand vibrator.

Oh yes, I was evil. But it was a good sort of evil. It was a sort of evil that would make Pepper come over and over and over again until she was nothing but a little, stupid, brainless mess.

Which was exactly what she needed.

With the vibrator in one hand and a bundle of rope in the other, I made a tie right below the head of the toy and then took it back to Pepper.

"What are you doing?" she whispered.

"So many questions. So very curious."

"Salt," she groaned. "Tell me."

"No."

She cursed under her breath, pulling against the ropes and swinging just slightly.

I slapped her ass. Hard. She yelped, her body going still. "You're nothing but my fuck toy right now," I snapped. "You are at my mercy. Accept it. Give up the control. Stop fucking resisting. Your pussy is mine, your orgasms are mine. *Mine.*"

"Yes," she cried. "I understand."

I couldn't help but stare at her for a few moments. The way the ropes showcased her turned me on. I was looking forward to fucking her and filling her.

I did another check over the suspension points. Everything

looked good. Then, I positioned the vibrator against her pussy, fighting a devious chuckle as she started to put together what was happening. I took my time getting the rope nice and secured, making sure this fucker wasn't going anywhere.

I stood up to admire my work.

But there were two more pieces to our puzzle. One of them may be too much.

She'd asked me to push her as far as she could go without truly breaking.

"I'm scared," she whispered.

"You should be."

In reality, she had nothing to fear. We both knew that. But her body didn't. Right now, her body was screaming about being tied up.

She couldn't see anything because of the blindfold. And she couldn't escape me because of the ropes.

I grabbed the set of noise canceling headphones and took them to her. I leaned up to kiss the side of her neck, then whispered in her ear.

"You want me to push you," I murmured. "Remember, you are safe. You deserve pleasure. Your one purpose from here until the end of our scene is to orgasm. Over and over. Yes?"

"Yes." Her voice trembled.

"Good girl."

I put the headphones on her. She stiffened again, a moan following. "I can't hear anything. I can't see anything."

I circled her, trailing my fingertips around her body in a loop. A shark, a demon, a beast prowling round and round.

"Salt. *Salt.*" Her breaths turned ragged as she adjusted to the sensory deprivation. "What are you doing to me?"

I stopped once I was in front of her.

And pressed the button on the vibrator.

Her scream echoed through the room, nearly overpowering

the buzz of the toy. The rope jerked as she tensed, her head tossing back as she moaned, shaking as the vibrator teased her clit.

"Oh god, oh god, oh god."

She was beautiful. Fuck, she was so goddamn beautiful. I stalked around her as her cries grew louder, and then deeper as she struggled against the vibrator. Pleasure battered her relentlessly, sweat creating a sheen over her soft skin as her first orgasm hit.

My cock was begging to be touched. I sucked in a breath as she came, her body tensing against the ropes before fully collapsing, panting hard.

But the vibrator didn't stop.

"Oh god," she whimpered. "Make it stop. Make it stop. It's too much. Oh god. *Fuck, fuck, fuck. Fuckkk.*"

I stopped in front of her and reached up, sliding two fingers between her lips. She moaned around them and then sucked, wetting them for me. I pulled them free and then brushed my knuckles over her nipples, watching them pebble as the vibrator hummed.

Her words melted into incoherent whimpers. I watched her expression as I lowered my mouth to one of her breasts, taking her nipple into my mouth and sucking as her face contorted, body writhing as her pleasure started to build again.

"I hate you," she whimpered.

I laughed and then bit down hard, causing a shocked cry to escape her lips. I immediately soothed the bite with gentle swipes of my tongue, massaging her. I reached down between her spread thighs and pushed the vibrator hard against her clit.

"Fuck!" she shouted. "No, no, no, no—"

Her head tipped back as I held the vibrator there, sucking her breasts, alternating between biting and pleasing, until her hoarse scream followed. Her second orgasm came, every muscle trembling as the waves crashed over her, pulling her down beneath a tide of euphoria, and I was swept along with it.

I was addicted to the high of watching her come undone for me.

And I was selfish.

Greedy.

I'd keep taking her orgasms until she couldn't give anymore.

THIRTY-EIGHT
PEPPER

THE VIBRATOR WAS RELENTLESS.

My voice crescendoed beneath the merciless pleasure being forced on me. It was too much. I'd never experienced anything like this before, didn't even think it was possible. I was constantly on the edge of coming, unable to turn away from it, unable to escape.

I was exactly where he wanted me to be.

Oh god, oh god. There was no rest. Even after two orgasms, the wand kept me on the cliff, all of my muscles tensing as the build up started again.

I was a slave to the pleasure, completely submitting to Salt.

The ropes squeezed my body. A never-ending pressure that made me feel like I was being held. I was grounded in the safety of them.

Salt's tongue swept over my nipples, drawing another moan for me.

I couldn't hear him. I couldn't see him. I desperately wanted to.

But in the darkness, I could only feel myself and him. It

was scary, but I knew I wasn't alone. I knew he was here with me. He would never let me go, would never leave.

Falling, falling, falling. Deeper down into the pleasurable darkness,every part of me consumed by flames.

My breaths shortened into pants. His calloused palms were rough over my hips, sliding over my skin and sending shock-waves of need through me.

Finally, he released the vibrator, allowing a few moments of relief. It still vibrated against my pussy, but wasn't as intense as before with his added pressure.

"I want to see you. Please. I want to see you so bad," I begged.

All I received was a pinch. The pain bolted through me, dragging out a whimper.

But then his touch left me. I sucked in a breath, listening even though I couldn't hear anything. "Salt," I cried. "Where are you going? Don't leave me."

For a moment, full panic set in. The realization that he *could* leave me if he wanted to. He could leave me tied up like this all night, long, with a vibrator against my pussy until it was completely raw.

Until every last drop of pleasure was squeezed out of my body.

I blinked, opening my eyes only to see nothing but the black silk he'd put around my head.

"Salt!" I yelled. "Please. Please don't leave me. Please. Fuck, I need you."

My nerve endings sizzled. Every wave of pleasure was growing more and more intense.

Begging became too easy. I whimpered again, torn between fear and lust.

"Please, please, please," I whispered.

My orgasms belong to him. *Everything* belonged to him. He owned my body, my pussy, my mind, my heart.

I wasn't sure how many times I said please. I lost count. I kept saying it until my voice became ragged. The panic continued to grow, my entire body searching for his presence. I just needed him. I just needed to know he was here.

Please, please, please, please.

Fingertips brushed my hip and I gasped in relief. Strong arms wrapped around me, pulling me against him as his hand came to rest around my throat.

The relief that flooded me was so intense, a third as orgasm engulfed me. He squeezed the sides of my throat, taking my breath as I came again, my back arching as much as it possibly could while being tied this way.

The headphones lifted slowly, and I let out a soft sob. "I didn't know where you went. You left me. You fucking left me."

"I never left you." His voice was deep and delicious, wrapping me in a blanket of warm comfort. He kissed the side of my neck, his hold turning gentle. He was hugging me, I realized. "I will never leave you, Pepper. I told you that you're safe with me. Don't you remember that?"

Tears spilled over as he pulled my blindfold free. I blinked a few times as my eyes adjusted to the light. Everything was much brighter now, I felt as if I were coming up from under the surface of a raging river.

He gripped my hips and then he slowly lowered to the floor behind me.

What is he going to do to me? I bit my tongue, a thrill rolling through me. My eyes fluttered as pleasure continued to batter me, the vibrator turning my pussy into a live wire.

"Fuck," I gasped.

Every muscle froze as I felt his tongue against my asshole.

"Salt," I gasped. "Not there."

"Why not?" he asked. "Your body belongs to me. It's time I use every hole properly."

My mouth dropped. I'd never been fucked there. His tongue rimmed me, gently probing as the vibrator continued.

He slapped my ass cheek. "Stop resisting. You're here until I let you go, so you might as well give in."

He had a point. I wasn't going anywhere.

I relaxed, forcing myself to melt into the ropes that cradled me. I let my head fall forward, looking down at myself. I could see the bite marks on my breasts, the bruising on my thighs, the vibrator tied against my pussy. The ropes were going to leave marks too, and I couldn't wait to see what I looked like in a mirror when he was done with me tonight.

"That's right," he rasped between licks. "You're finally getting it, aren't you? What are you right now?"

"Yours." Any coherent thoughts were drifting away. "Your... toy."

"Yes. My fuck toy. Mine."

My throat was dry. My eyes shut as everything drifted away. This time, my mind wrapped around the sensations flowing through me. I loved the way he gripped my ass cheeks, how the rough rope dug into my flesh, the constant thrum of the vibrator, and the stretch of my muscles from being suspended in the air.

I wasn't me. I wasn't anything, just his.

A flash of pain interrupted the pleasure. I realized after a second that he'd bit my asscheek. He sunk his teeth in harder, until I was writhing and jerking, begging him to stop. But I didn't actually want him to stop. I didn't want him to make it end. In fact, I wanted to tell him to take everything he wanted. I wanted to be used.

His tongue circled over the bite, soothing the pain.

My breath hitched as I heard a cap and then the coolness of

lube being applied to me. I wasn't sure when he'd grabbed more things to tease me with, it could have been at any moment. My head was swimming, on cloud nine as I sank further and further into blissful subspace.

Something cool pressed against my ass. "What is that?" I rasped.

"It's a plug. A small one," he said. "It has a jewel on the end. I want to put it into you and then fuck you."

"Oh," I rasped.

He took everything slow. My eyes slowly shut as I focused on the sensations, the slight discomfort of being used there. The ring of muscles slowly accepted the plug, my mind actively reminding my body to relax and trust.

"Good girl," he murmured. "Fuck. You look so beautiful like this, Pepper. We're almost there."

He kept talking me through it in soft tones, his voice hypnotizing. Finally, I realized I'd taken all of it. The jeweled plug filled my ass in a way I'd never felt before.

Then, I felt his fingers against my pussy, dipping inside me.

"Oh fuck," I moaned.

I took him with ease, his fingers brushing against my G-spot. The spot he always found with confidence and knew how to tease so well. I was so incredibly wet.

"I feel so full," I whimpered.

"Do you like it?"

"Yes."

With the vibrator, everything was a thousand times more intense. My nerves popped and snapped, every part of me drowning in the sensations.

The mounting pressure was different this time. Every time his finger circled my G-spot, the pressure grew and grew. I recognized the same feeling I'd had the first night he and I were together.

"Salt," I gasped. "I might squirt. Stop before I squirt."

"We're not stopping," he said. "Not stopping for anything. Let your body do what it needs to do."

"Salt," I cried. My cheeks flamed. "I don't want everything to get ruined."

His palm slapped my ass. "*Come*," he demanded.

There was no possible way I could come a fourth time. Right? There was no way, and yet every muscle started to tremble as the pressure grew again.

He maintained the rhythm, never faltering, never stopping.

A sob left me. I was shattering, my mind overwhelmed.

I loved it.

My voice cracked as I cried his name, begging him to stop. I knew he wouldn't. I didn't want him to.

This time when I came, my entire body seemed to go with it. This was the closest I'd ever get to heaven. Liquid gushed from me, dripping to the floor, squirting everywhere. Salt thrust his fingers into me faster, sending my body into a frenzy. *Am I screaming?* I wasn't sure of anything except my hellish climax.

This was the type of pleasure I'd been missing out on my entire life.

My body went limp, everything floating... *drifting...* My pussy was raw, my throat parched, every muscle spent. The vibrations stopped as tears rolled down my cheeks.

"Good girl," Salt purred. "You did so well for me. You're so pretty when you're my little mess, baby. I love seeing you like this."

I heard his words and smiled, but that was all I could do.

"Let's get you out of these ropes."

I whined as I felt the tug of them. My eyes drifted open and then closed, catching glimpses of him as he untied me—glimpses of the dark roses that inked his neck and the thorns that trailed down his chest.

This was my church. This was where I'd kneel. His eyes were stained glass windows, his body a temple, and he was a god I wanted to worship. A kinder god than the one I'd been raised to love.

His arms cradled me as I was lowered to the floor. I smiled up at him, watching as his brows knit together.

He always did that when he was worried. Always broody. Always thinking.

I wondered what that scowl would look like in twenty years. What would he be like? What would *we* be like?

"Baby," he murmured, his lips brushing my forehead. "Talk to me. You're being quiet right now."

"I feel so good," I croaked. "I feel drunk."

"It's the endorphins."

The last of the ropes fell from my body and I raised my head, looking down at myself. Red marks wrapped around me, just like the thorns that wrapped around him.

He brushed his fingertips over them, tracing as he hummed. "You're going to have marks."

"I love them."

His scowl deepened. "Maybe we should have talked more about leaving marks because you have that awards show—"

"I don't care about anything else right now. I just want you. I'm yours." I reached up, placing my hand against his cheek. "I'm all yours."

"They'll talk," he whispered.

"Then let them fucking talk."

Salt paused, but then flashed me a dark look. "I like it when you're like this. When you don't care what they think or say."

He scooped me into his arms, his muscles hard as he held me against his bare chest. I tucked my face against his neck as he carried me through the house to his bedroom. The sheets felt warm against my skin as he laid me down in the center, his hands holding my face.

"Mmm, look at you," he chuckled. "You have this stupid look on your face right now. I love it."

I leaned up and kissed him. It was a soft kiss. A butterfly kiss. But then, it deepened, exploding to a corrosive, needy devouring.

This is where I belong.

This is where I always want to be.

THIRTY-NINE
SALT

THE AIRPORT LOOMED in front of us, the line of cars at departures winding up slowly to drop off travelers. It was Friday morning, and Pepper was leaving for LA.

I glanced over, giving her an easy smile.

Her hand slid into mine. "I'll send you pictures," she said. "It'll be great. And maybe you can tell me what to wear..."

"You'll be beautiful and powerful and get all the awards," I said.

I actually had no idea what awards were even being handed out. Pepper laughed as I eased the gas pedal, getting closer to where I'd drop her off.

"What are you going to do in the next few days?" She asked.

"I have a show at Eros on Friday night," I said. "Otherwise, I'll be in the workshop making furniture."

I'd actually be making a surprise for her. I'd ordered some nice black leather and had everything I needed to start on her collar. It was going to be beautiful.

"If Jeff acts up, call me," I said. "I can fake an emergency. I can pretend to be your long-lost friend or something."

She laughed. "It'll be okay. I mean, I'll have to deal with his shit, but I've gotten pretty good at avoiding him. And I don't think he'll want to talk to me very much anyway, since Ally isn't coming along."

"Just don't let him get to you," I said. "He's a pathetic man."

"I won't let him," she said confidently. "Here we go."

I pulled into a spot between two cars and hopped out, opening the trunk. Pepper joined me, waiting patiently as I pulled her bags out for her.

She reached for the handle, and I circled her wrist gently, tugging her close. A light breeze tousled her hair as her head tipped back, her eyes shining in the early morning light.

Pepper curled her fingers in the lapel of my jacket. "I'll be home Monday."

"I'll be picking you up," I said. "If your flight info changes, just let me know."

"Of course. And... I'll send you photos."

I raised a brow. "What kind of photos?"

"Oh, you know. The fun kind."

She leaned up on her tiptoes and brushed her lips against mine. I kissed her hard and fast and didn't draw back until we were both breathless.

"Okay," I said. "Be safe. Text me when you land."

"I will. One more kiss."

I kissed her once more and then stepped back, smiling as I shut the trunk. She pulled up the handle on her suitcase and waved as she headed towards the doors.

I hated watching her go. I'd be counting down the days until she was home.

Pepper disappeared into the airport. A honk broke my

reverie and I sighed, getting into the driver's seat and pulling out into traffic.

A new normal was starting to set in, and I loved it. I loved everything about it.

I loved *her*.

She was smart and driven and funny and loved music the same way I did. And the longer I knew her, the more certain I was that everything would work out for the better. I was hopeful.

Maybe the curse was finally lifting.

The drive out to Nancy and Beth's went by fast. I pulled into the driveway and got out, stretching with a groan. I doubted Beth would be up this early to work, but I was ready to get a start on the day. It'd keep me distracted from thinking about Pepper too much.

I drew in a breath of fresh air and darted to the garage. I unlocked the door, stepped inside, and flipped on the lights. Some of the pieces we'd been working on were close to being finished, but today I was making Pepper's collar.

Turning on the space heaters, I headed to my work table and rolled my shoulders. The leather was sitting on my table already, thanks to Beth or Nancy.

Working with leather was completely different than working with wood. But like working with wood, every single thing I did was with intention. With Pepper centered in my mind, I dove into the process fully, the creativity of it consuming me.

It was like when I played guitar. I got lost in the moment, the entire world slipping away. Time didn't have any meaning. It was just me and the process of creating something new.

All I felt was happiness in making something for her.

I'd picked out a heart ring that would sit at the center

against her throat. It was a little typical maybe, but I didn't care. It meant something to me.

Over the last few weeks, I'd learned a lot about myself. I'd learned a lot about what I wanted. As I prepared for my life to change with the record deal, I found myself savoring the quiet moments I had now.

If everything went well with Rosethorn, then I wasn't sure what to expect in the coming months.

But I knew Pepper would be in it.

And that was enough to soothe my nerves about big changes.

"Someone is up early."

I was pulled out of my thoughts as Beth approached, putting a cup of coffee down next to me.

"You're a saint," I said.

"I know," she chuckled, her gaze moving to the collar. "Mmm. Someone is lucky. I take it that's for Pepper?"

"Yes," I said, glancing down at the strips of leather I was debossing with a floral pattern.

"Things are pretty serious then."

"They are," I said. I took a sip of coffee and then looked up at Beth. "You seemed to like her a lot."

"I did," Beth said. "I thought she was wonderful. I think the two of you look good together."

"*But?*"

Her expression softened, a hint of worry. "You're moving fast."

"I know."

"And you're so young," she sighed.

"I know what I'm doing, though," I said. "And I know the way I feel about her is different than anything I've felt before."

"I can see it," she said. "Nancy and I both can. I'm still worried about what might happen if it doesn't work out."

My throat burned. I looked down at the collar and took another sip of coffee. "I don't think that will happen. It's different this time."

Beth nodded. "I believe you. And as always, your craftsmanship is beautiful. I think she'll love it."

"Thank you," I said.

"I'm headed back to the house to make some breakfast, but afterward I'll be out to finish sanding down the new spanking bench. Come in if you want something to eat."

"I'll emerge in a bit," I said. "I'm going to focus on this."

"Okay. Just make sure you take care of yourself, Simon."

I wasn't sure if her warning in regards to breakfast, or to Pepper.

FORTY
PEPPER

THE AWARDS SHOW was the exact kind of place that always made me feel less than.

Of course, I didn't show it. To the entire industry, I was perfect. I was the CEO of Rosethorn, and many of our artists were snatching up awards left and right. I was proud of them and the work we'd done, and excited for what was to come.

The only thorn in my side was Jeff.

I'd managed to avoid him completely until tonight. Throughout the week, his texts had grown more erratic, and I was hoping that by ignoring him, they'd slowly fizzle out.

I checked my phone and smiled at Salt's message.

> Have fun tonight, baby. You deserve everything good in the world.

A deep breath in, another out. I smoothed my hands down the emerald velvet suit he'd helped me pick and turned, studying myself in the bathroom mirror. I needed to get back out there and keep socializing. The table I'd be seated at would be with Jeff and other music industry big names I'd know.

Fingers crossed they were people I liked, so I could keep ignoring Jeff.

"Everything will be fine," I whispered to myself.

As silly as it may have been, I was already missing Salt. I wished I was at home in his arms, being deliciously tortured instead of being here.

Never in my life had I been so certain of something, aside from when I'd left the cult. There'd been a deep knowing that had driven me to make that decision, and that choice had changed my life for the better.

The knowing I felt with Salt... it was like that.

There was clarity in my heart for the first time in ages. It was crystal clear that we were meant to be together.

Even more, I was in love with him.

With my thoughts unburdened, I rolled my shoulders back and put on my face. The Rosethorn Records CEO face, with the gleaming smile of a woman who knew exactly what she wanted.

A woman who not only knew, but got *exactly* what she wanted.

I stepped out of the bathroom and proceeded down the hall, headset-wearing people darting by me. The venue was massive, with the awards taking place in a large auditorium that had a floor space for tables. I flashed my badge to one of the men in a tuxedo that guarded the doors, then entered the space.

As always, everything was dripping with money. Beautiful people mingled, their chatter a deafening roar above the hum of music from the most recent Top 40 artists. The stage stretched across the entirety of the back wall, a podium waiting for whomever would be presenting and accepting awards tonight.

Awards like this never went to me, and I was glad for that. I liked being in the background of the industry, and would dread ever having to stand up and make a speech.

"Ms. Jones," a woman greeted with a smile. It took a minute to remember who she was, but I recognized her as a producer who was quickly becoming one of the best in the industry.

"Ms. Austen," I said, holding out my hand. "It's a pleasure to meet you."

"You as well."

I did that at least another fifty times. Chatting with people who'd probably whisper about me if they knew who I loved.

And I wouldn't care.

The concerns for my reputation and what the world would think of me paled in comparison to the passion I had for Salt. I felt lighter with each step, making the rounds, until a grating voice interrupted me.

"Well, look who it is. I wasn't sure you'd actually be here."

I took a deep breath and turned around, forcing a smile as Jeff approached me. He was wearing an expensive tuxedo, his eyes narrowing on me in annoyance. My spine stiffened, but I reminded myself he didn't have any control over me.

"You've been avoiding me," he said under his breath, smiling at a couple of people who passed by us.

"I don't know what you're talking about." I wasn't playing games with him. I wasn't going to give him fuel for the fire either.

"You know exactly what I'm talking about," he said. "Is it because of your new boyfriend?"

My heart skipped a beat. Luckily, a man I knew well approached us. Richard Jaxon was the CEO of a record label we competed with heavily, but I liked him. We hated each other professionally, but I'd rather talk to him than stand next to Jeff.

"Richard," I greeted, pitching my voice louder to drown out whatever bullshit Jeff was about to spout.

"Oh, hello Pepper," he said, leaning in to give a kiss on the cheek.

I gave his arm a squeeze. "You're looking well."

"Thanks, it's directly related to me topping you on the charts last quarter."

My laugh was undeniably wicked. "Call me at the end of next quarter, darling. I'm sure you'll be licking your wounds."

He laughed. "That's why I like you, Pepper." His shark eyes glistened with amusement, but then flattened slightly as he saw Jeff. "Jeff," he greeted less enthusiastically. "How's it going?"

"Oh, you know," Jeff quipped. "Just being ignored by my ex-wife."

Richard's brows shot up and my nostrils flared. "Heavy emphasis on the *ex* part," I said. "Where are you seated, Richard? I haven't looked at the charts yet."

"I think I'll actually be at your table," he said. "Should be us and a couple of music producers."

"Wonderful," I said. I looped my arm into his, shooting Jeff a dirty look. "Do you mind walking me to the table?"

"Of course," he said.

Richard guided me across the room, the two of us making our way through the crowd. Everyone was dressed to the nines —silk and diamonds, velvet and suits—all with price tags that would make even me feel faint.

"Between you and me, I don't like your label president. Didn't the two of you get a divorce?" Richard asked under his breath.

"Yes, we did," I said. "Thank god for that."

An easy laugh left him. "Why have we been enemies for so long, again?"

"Because you're a bastard," I said. "But I'd still rather talk to you than Jeff."

We slowed as we approached the table we were assigned to. He pulled out my chair, and I gave a nod in thanks, taking a seat. There were four other chairs around the table dressed in black and gold linens. I glanced over my shoulder, spotting an open bar in the back corner that I wanted to take advantage of.

Richard sat down to my right. The chair to my left screeched over the floor and my gaze snapped to Jeff as he plopped down.

"Can't keep ignoring me," he muttered.

"For fuck's sake," I sighed.

"I just don't understand why you won't even text me back," he said. "Actually, I do. I bet it's because you're being controlled by someone, huh? He doesn't want you talking to me."

"You're delusional," I said. "And you're acting poorly. This is a work event."

"I mean, we work together, and yet you keep ignoring me. Which is kind of unprofessional. What's also unprofessional is the fact that you wouldn't let me bring Ally here—"

"Are you really going to bring that up now?" I asked.

Richard glanced between the two of us, and then cleared his throat. "How about we talk about something else? Do you have any interesting artists coming up or projects down the line I should be worried about?"

"Of course," I said, offering him a smirk.

"Oh yeah," Jeff said. "*Pepper* has decided to sign on this boy who is covered in tattoos and wears a mask. And—"

"That is a gross understatement of who he is," I corrected. "Salt is a singer-songwriter, and I'm sure you will be seeing more of him soon. I don't know how much you are on social media, but he's been doing well. His music is great. It'll be a good launch, and that's all I'll say."

"Yes, keep your cards to your chest," Richard chuckled. "Salt, you said? I think I've heard of him. Janet probably sent me some of his videos. I swear my wife is the reason why we end up signing on all the good artists. Handsome fellow, right? Rose tattoos?"

Jeff's face was beet red.

"Yes," I said. "What about you? What secrets are you holding on to?"

"We're getting ready to sign on someone who I think will make some waves. She has a large presence, unique sound. Excellent songwriter. We'll see what happens—you know how the business is. Sometimes you can sign on the best and they flop, other times you sign on a nobody, and they skyrocket in the charts."

"So true," I said. "Looking forward to hearing her."

He smiled. "We should get dinner sometime, outside of all of this. Janet would love to meet you at some point."

"I'd love to meet her," I said. "Next time you're in Nashville, just let me know."

"I could join you," Jeff interjected.

"You're not invited," I said pleasantly.

"Bitch," Jeff muttered under his breath.

I stared at him and wondered how the fuck I'd ever loved him. Thinking back to all those years ago, I realized that I'd been so caught up in believing him when he said I was his world, I never took the time to make sure his actions matched his words.

Now, I knew better.

"I'm going to get a glass of champagne," I said, flashing Jeff another dirty look.

"Fine," he muttered.

I got up and crossed the ballroom, weaving between people. I felt eyes on me, but ignored them this time. I slid my hand into the pocket of my pants, and cursed. I must have left my phone at the table.

"Damn it," I said, glancing back at the table.

I was already at the bar, though. I'd sneak a text to Salt once I got back.

"What can I get you?" the man at the bar asked.

I needed something stronger than champagne at this point. "Moscow mule?"

He nodded. "I got you."

I smiled and smoothed my hands down my pantsuit. I felt way better in this suit than the dress I'd packed, and I was glad to be wearing it. It made me feel powerful, and that power was keeping me from losing it on my ex-husband.

Just another day of this. Tomorrow there was a breakfast with more industry professionals, I'd relax in the evening, and then fly home on Monday.

We were so close to the finish line. Salt's lawyers were fast returning everything to him, so we'd officially sign next week.

I couldn't wait. Kendra and Lee were already coming up with plans for how to move forward with promotion, and Tommy was putting together a selection of producers for Salt to work with in the recording studio.

The bartender came back with my drink quickly. "Thanks," I said.

"Of course."

I smiled and lifted my glass, taking a sip. The lights started to dim in the room—my sign to head back to the table. I steeled myself as I approached it again.

"Have you seen my phone?" I asked Jeff as I sat down.

"Yeah." Jeff pushed it across the table. "Here it is. You left it."

I frowned as I took it and slid it into my purse. I almost texted Salt, but with Jeff's hawk eyes on me, I decided to do so later.

Applause filled the room as a performer emerged on stage. I fully ignored Jeff and forced myself to focus.

Just a little longer, and I'd be able to go home to him.

FORTY-ONE
SALT

I WAS FUCKING CURSED. I knew I was cursed. *I don't know why I thought anything would ever be any different.*

Everyone always left. It didn't matter what I tried to do differently. It didn't matter that I'd gone to therapy and worked on myself and made sure I was a good person, because *fuck.*

I *was* good.

Just not good enough.

I slammed back a shot of vodka, the burn of it rushing down my throat. I felt sick. The alcohol couldn't chase her away, no matter how many shots I did.

My vision swam as I read Pepper's text message again.

> Simon, we're done. When I return to
> Nashville, you'll be nothing more than a client.
> You aren't good enough for me. I deserve
> someone better.

My breaths shortened again. The pain radiating through my entire body was breaking me. I tried calling her for the fifteenth time, but it went straight to voicemail.

"Fuck this," I rasped.

I grabbed my phone and threw it across the house as hard as I could. It hit the mirror above the couch, shattering the glass and sending shards flying everywhere.

I wanted to break everything.

Fuck.

I was just like my father, wasn't I? Panic rushed through me. What the fuck was I doing? I grabbed the bottle and tipped it down the sink, gripping the edge of the counter.

Fuck. My thoughts continued to spiral. I closed my eyes for a moment, trying to understand what I'd missed. What had I missed? Where did I go wrong?

I loved her. I loved her so much, and it wasn't supposed to be this way. It didn't matter that our lives had crashed together, they were meant to be intertwined.

I'd missed something. We'd fallen into everything so fast, but it'd felt so right that I never stopped to second-guess it. Did something go wrong in one of our kink scenes?

Did I hurt her?

The fear of hurting her made it hard to breathe.

I looked back up at the mirror and cursed. Some of the shards had stayed in the frame, and I could see myself.

I needed help.

My head tipped back as tears started to fall. I needed to call Nancy. Because this was too much, and I couldn't handle this alone.

Finally, I left the kitchen and went into the living room. I was wearing my shoes, at least. The glass crunched underfoot until I found my phone, my hands shaking as I texted Nancy.

I need help please. I'm sorry.

Are you at home?

Yes

I'll be there ASAP

Don't bring Beth

I couldn't let Beth see me like this. Fuck, she'd been right to warn me, hadn't she? I'd burned too hot and fast and now everything was on fire.

I tried calling Pepper again, but it went to voicemail. "Pepper," I rasped. "Please fucking call me back. I don't understand what's going on."

Ending the message, I wiped my eyes and stepped away from the majority of the glass covering the floor, until I found a spot that seemed clear enough and sat down.

And I cried.

I hated crying. All the years of abuse from my father growing up, and I'd learned how to hold the tears in. But I wasn't strong enough to do that anymore, so I just let them fall.

A soft knock eventually sounded, but I barely noticed it. The sound of the front door opening had my head lifting.

"Simon?" Nancy's voice followed. "There you are."

I looked up at her and didn't say anything. She looked around the living room for a moment, but she didn't look horrified. Instead, she refocused on me. "What happened?"

"She broke it off."

Nancy shut her eyes for a moment, her expression flickering with a wince, but then she opened them and came over to me. "Christ, did you have a drink?"

"Yeah. Why the fuck am I so cursed?"

She knelt down slowly and pressed her lips together. "You're not cursed, Simon."

"I feel like I am," I whispered. "Everyone always leaves. Everyone—"

"Beth and I will never leave you."

"You will one day, I'm sure."

Her brows drew together. "We won't."

"How can you possibly know?"

"Because we love you." She shrugged her shoulders. "It's that easy. You want to know a secret?"

"Not really."

"Well, that's too damn bad." She turned her head, glancing at the living room. Embarrassment crept in at the sight of the broken mirror.

"I didn't mean for that to happen," I whispered. "I tossed my phone too hard and it broke."

Nancy nodded slowly and then looked back at me. "The secret is that we're all cursed, Simon. Every single one of us. We all carry the weight of those who have harmed us. The feeling that we aren't good enough. That we don't deserve to be here. That we don't deserve love."

Fuck. My vision blurred with more tears.

"We all carry curses. But you know what else? We also carry the ability to break them."

"How?" I bit out. "How am I supposed to? I don't want to be anything like him. And I feel like... I don't know. I don't know, Nancy. I'm sorry. I shouldn't have called, I shouldn't have—"

"You did the right thing by calling," she said. "And the way you break a curse is by doing exactly what you've been doing. You found your music. You created a future for yourself that is nothing like your father. You are *nothing* like him."

"I'm more like him than not," I whispered back. "You just don't know what I'm really like. You don't know who I really am. I don't understand why the two of you are so kind to me. I've never done anything for you. All I've done is eat your food and be a pain in the ass. Why did you even bother stopping me all those years ago?"

"Because once I broke my curse, I wanted to help other people break theirs," she said. "I know exactly what it feels like to carry the burden of a parent who didn't love you the way they should have. I know exactly what it feels like to fall apart and think everyone hates you. I've lived through it, kid. The Nancy you know now is not the same woman I was years ago. Before Beth."

I shook my head. "Did Beth change you? Did she fix you?"

"No," she said. "Of course not. I fixed myself. Did loving Beth make me a better person? Yes. But I had to do the work myself. I had to be the one to grow."

"I tried," I said, my voice breaking. "I tried. I tried so hard this time. I love her. I don't know what I did wrong. I don't know what happened."

"I can't tell you. I'm surprised, because I know what love looks like, and I think she loved you back. I think you should give everything some time. I'm sure she'll come around."

"She told me she was done."

"And she may be for now," Nancy said patiently. "And I know it hurts, but if that's the case, you have to be done for now, too."

"I don't want to be, though. We talked about our future together. We talked about what it would be like. It doesn't make any sense."

She released a slow sigh. "I don't have the answer for that. But I do know we need to get some food in you. And maybe be prepared for you to throw up. Plus, you cut yourself on some of the glass, so you need bandaids too."

I looked down at my hands. I hadn't even noticed.

Nancy stood up and held out her hand. When I didn't immediately take it, she nudged me with her boot. "Get up."

"I don't want to," I muttered. "I wish I could just stop feeling this way."

"Wishing isn't going to get you anywhere. No one else can do this for you. You have to love yourself enough to break the curse first. And then she can love you enough to remind you that you were never cursed to begin with. Now, *get up*."

AFTER THE DINNER, I booked an Uber to my hotel and waited. And of course, Jeff being Jeff, I spotted him walking towards me.

I held up my hand as he approached. "I'm not interested in talking."

"Well, that's too bad," he snapped. "You've been avoiding me for days."

"Because I don't want to talk to you," I said firmly. "I want nothing to do with you outside of work."

He threw up his hands. "You've changed, Pepper. Is he manipulating you? Forcing you to act like this?"

My ears started to ring. "What are you talking about?"

Jeff rolled his eyes. "You know exactly who I'm talking about. The fucking punk tattooed kid."

What the fuck?

"I reached out to that bass player he fired," Jeff said. "And he told me how the two of you were together. And then seeing how he treated you last week, I knew it was true. What the hell is going on? What are you thinking?"

"I don't know what you're talking about," I said. I was going to keep playing ignorant. "My ride is almost here."

I started to turn away from him, but his hand shot out and gripped my arm, yanking me back to face him.

"I know the two of you are together because I saw your fucking text messages," he snarled. "I saw what he's been saying to you. Telling you to get on your knees and shit? What the fuck is wrong with you?"

"You *read* my text messages?" I asked, jerking my body away. "What the fuck is wrong with *you?*"

"You're the one that's in trouble," he said. "You've been fucking a client, Pepper—"

"You fucked an intern!" I yelled.

"This is different—"

"It's not different," I said. "Actually, it is different, because Salt isn't signed yet. He is not a client yet. And the moment he is, I will follow through on my part and notify everyone of our relationship, but until then, I am not violating any of the contracts we have in place. But you know what did violate those contracts? Fucking an intern while married to the goddamn CEO."

"That was forever ago," he growled. "This is different. This isn't like you."

"You don't know me, Jeff," I spat. "You never did. And you've lost out on your chance to ever get to know me."

"He has you under his thumb," he said. "He's manipulating you."

"No, he's not," I argued. "I love him, Jeff. I love him and there's nothing you can do about it."

He scoffed. "Well, I already did."

Ice filled my veins. "What do you mean?"

"I doubt he'll take you back," he sneered. "I know I never would."

"*Jeff*," I rasped. "What the fuck did you do?"

The car pulled up and he took a step back, holding up his hands. "I'm done here."

"What the fuck did you do?!" I yelled, but he was already walking away.

Fuck. What the fuck happened? I yanked open the passenger door and slid in. My heart hammered as I looked down at my phone. When I'd pulled up the app to call an Uber, I hadn't seen any notifications. Had I missed something?

Something was wrong.

"What did he do?" I whispered to myself.

The car lurched forward as I pulled up my texts.

Salt's messages were gone.

I closed my eyes, forcing myself to breathe. Jeff had gotten into my phone when I left it at the table tonight. My cheeks burned as I pulled up my phone book, scrolling to look for his name.

It was gone.

Fuck. *Fuck.*

Panic settled in and I called the only person who could get me the info ASAP.

Tommy picked up. "Pepper? Everything okay?"

"No," I said. "No. I need you to text Salt right now."

"What? Why—"

"Tommy," I growled. "I'm asking you as a friend to do this for me without any questions asked. Do you understand me? Please. If you can't, then hand the phone to Dan."

Dan's voice was a soft grumble in the background. "I heard my name."

"It's Pepper," Tommy said. "Okay. What do I need to text him?"

"Text him that Pepper called you. Jeff got into my phone

and deleted his information. I don't know what else he sent, but it was something bad."

"What?" Tommy hissed. "What the fuck? Why would he do that?"

"Because Salt and I are together." I was met with silence. "You can be mad at me later," I said.

"I asked you. I *asked* you if you were, Pepper," Tommy hissed. "I knew it. Damn it—"

"You do not have the right to lecture me right now," I snapped. "Put Dan on the phone."

Dan must have snatched the phone away. "What's going on?"

"I need you to text Salt and tell him that whatever I said to him wasn't from me, it was from Jeff. Jeff got my phone. Also, I'm not as vanilla as both of you assholes think, and I'm in love with him. So please do this for me."

"God damn," Dan mumbled. "Okay, hold on."

A sense of relief washed over me as I heard his thumbs going.

"Message sent. Darling, you have some explaining to do. I think Tommy is having a heart attack or something."

"Well, he needs to put his business hat on, because I need to fire Jeff. I'm done with this. For too long, I've let him get away with his bullshit. I'm flying home early tomorrow and will be on your doorstep as soon as I figure out what Jeff said to Salt."

"Finally," Dan breathed out. "Okay. Have you checked your blocked phone contacts?"

"No," I said. "Walk me through how to do it."

Dan's voice was calm and soothing. I could hear Tommy ranting in the background, but chose to ignore him as he walked me through how to unblock a number.

The moment the car pulled up to the hotel, I hopped out, paid the driver quickly and rushed into the building.

"We're getting rid of the son of a bitch," I told Dan as I stepped onto the elevator. "I'm not playing nice anymore."

"Love to hear it," he said. "It's going to be good. And Pepper?"

"Yeah?"

"I know we give you a hard time, but we care about you. I'm sorry if I've ever said something that hurt your feelings in regards to being naive or innocent."

I exhaled slowly, my eyes stinging. "Thank you. I'm sorry I haven't been a good friend."

"Well, we have time to make up for that. Get home, see your boy, and come over as soon as you can. Once Tommy finishes having his breakdown, he'll jump into action."

"Thank you." My phone started to ring and I saw Salt's name as I stepped out of the elevator. "I've got to go."

"Okay. Be safe."

We hung up, and I immediately answered Salt's phone call.

"Simon," I rasped. I stepped into my hotel room and locked the door behind me. "It wasn't me. It wasn't me. Whatever he said, whatever it was, it wasn't me."

He released a shaky breath. "Okay. One, are you okay?"

"Yes," I said. "Are you?"

"No," he said. "But I will be."

"What did he say?"

He let out a gentle hum. "I don't need to repeat it to you."

"I need to know," I whispered.

"The text said '*Simon, we're done. When I return to Nashville, you'll be nothing more than a client. You aren't good enough for me. I deserve someone who isn't like you.*'"

I leaned against the wall, my heart still racing. "He was

wrong. He couldn't be more wrong. I'm not leaving you, Simon."

"I—" His voice faltered. "I didn't react well to the text message. I'm at Nancy and Beth's."

"I'm so sorry," I whispered.

"It's not your fault at all," he said.

"We're going to fire him. I'm leaving tomorrow instead of Monday, and I'm going to meet up with Tommy. And Ellen. I need to text Ellen. And Scott, for that matter. We're going to get rid of him. The fact that he sent you this message is crazy."

Salt let out a soft hum. I closed my eyes and let out a slow breath.

"Did you believe him?" I asked.

"Yes."

"And then you couldn't get a hold of me because he blocked the number."

"Yeah," he murmured. "I don't know if I'm right for you, Pepper. That's the thing about that message. Maybe he wasn't wrong. Maybe we are moving too fast. Maybe..."

"No. Jeff is too good at saying things that can unravel you," I said. "He reached out to that bass player and confirmed his suspicions about us. And then he read our texts. But, he's wrong. You are good enough for me. And I do deserve someone like you. I don't care what the world says, we love on our own timeline and in our own way."

"*Love*."

"Yes," I whispered. "Can we switch to video?"

"I'm a mess right now, Pepper. I don't want you to see me like this."

"Please?"

He hesitated for a moment, but then pressed the video call button, turning on his camera. I did the same, sucking in a breath as I looked at him. He was in bed, his eyes dark and stormy and full of so much sadness.

What Jeff sent had pierced through both of us like a sharpened arrow. My chest ached because I knew how Jeff was. He always knew how to rip open a wound and pour vinegar on it.

"I wish I was there," I choked out.

"No, you don't," he whispered. "I don't smell good. And I cried like a baby. And accidentally broke a mirror and cut my hands."

"*Salt*. Your hands?"

"I'm okay," he said. "I'll be okay."

"I'm coming home to you tomorrow."

"I'll pick you up from the airport."

"Yes," I said. "Please. And please don't listen to what Jeff said. He's wrong, Salt. He's so wrong about everything."

"I will," he said. "I promise."

I could feel my heart finally starting to calm. I kicked off my shoes and flopped down at the end of the bed.

"Take off your clothes and makeup. Get ready for bed. Fall asleep with me," he murmured.

"I think I'll do just that."

FORTY-THREE
SALT

MY HEART RACED as I sat in the line for the airport. I'd already circled around three times, counting down the minutes until I saw her.

I pulled into an empty spot and looked up at the doors.

There she is.

Pepper walked out and ran straight for me.

I got out of the car quickly and met her in three long strides, lifting her up as her arms wound around my neck. I inhaled the scent of her, holding her tight.

"I'm sorry," she breathed out.

"I am too," I said.

"For what?" she asked as she leaned back.

"Well, for one, I ruined your trip. I promise that next time you leave for a few days, I won't completely lose it." I was still recovering from the whiplash of that fucking text message, the aftermath, and then the phone call.

The relief I'd felt had been immeasurable, but then I made a choice.

I put her down, but still kept her close, tipping her head up. Her eyes were red and I knew she was exhausted. We'd both fallen asleep on the phone last night, but I was certain we'd only slept three hours or so. Her flight back home was insanely early, but I was thankful she was standing here in front of me now.

I needed to tell her what I was feeling. Nancy and Beth had stitched me back together last night, but it made me realize just how much more work I still had to do.

I drew in a deep breath and then squared my shoulders. "Because of you, I've realized that I have been living with this feeling of being cursed for too long. And because of you, I want to be better. I want to do better."

"Salt, you're already more than good enough," she said, her eyes searching mine.

"I still don't feel it though. And I'm making the promise here and now that I'm going to change that," I said. "I want my future to be with you. I want to wake up next to you, believing that even if you do leave my side, you'll come back."

"I will," she said. "They can say whatever they want about us. I don't care if they say that I'm too old, or we're too different, or we're wrong for each other. I don't care if they say I'm cold, or I shouldn't have desires, or I should be professional. None of it matters when I'm with you, and I want that forever. I'm choosing you."

"I choose you too," I whispered.

Our lips brushed against each other as we kissed, and that kiss spun out of control, consuming us in its flames. I'd never get enough of her.

"Take me home," she rasped. "I need you. I need to feel you. *Please.* We'll figure everything else out afterward, but right now I just need *you.*"

I needed her too. "Your place or mine?"

"Mine," she said. "I have to go to Tommy's later. We're firing Jeff, but need to make a plan. I'm going to have Ellen meet us, too. You should come with us."

"Would that be okay?" I asked.

"I don't know," she said. "I don't care. I'm pulling the CEO card, because I *am* the CEO. I'm going to do whatever the fuck I want, especially after this weekend."

"I support that," I chuckled, stealing one more kiss. I glanced back at the car and wrinkled my nose. "We better go before people start honking."

I picked up her suitcase and carried it to my car, opening the door for her. She slid into the passenger seat, and I stowed her bag in the back. Less than thirty minutes later, I parked in the garage beneath her apartment building.

I was counting down the seconds until I was able to hold her. She drummed her fingers on her thighs as we took the elevator up, and the moment her front door clicked shut behind us, I backed her against the wall, her lips meeting mine.

"Fuck," she gasped. "You have no idea how much I've missed you."

"I've missed you too. I was losing my mind. I think Saturday night may have broken me."

"I still can't believe he sent that message," she said. "I'm so sorry. I didn't realize what happened, he deleted everything."

It'd been a nightmare. I hated that bastard more than I thought possible. "I know, baby. You don't need to explain, we've already talked through it. None of that matters right now. All that matters is that we're together."

"I'm yours," she said, kissing me harder.

My cock throbbed in response, and I knew I needed her. I needed to feel her wrapped around me, buried in her silken heat. It'd been too long since I touched her. If I didn't have her now, I was going to go insane.

The sense of urgency drove both of us. She tugged my shirt overhead. Her hands ran down my chest, tracing my tattoos as her dark eyes swept up to mine, pleading for more.

Fuck. "I need you now, or I'm going to die," I said.

"*Yes.*"

We stripped as we made our way to the bedroom, tossing our clothes to the floor, our mouths fused together.

"I'm yours," she whimpered.

A growl left me as I pushed her back onto the bed. The mattress bounced, her legs spreading for me, giving me a perfect view of her pussy. I reached down, stroking myself as I knelt between her thighs.

"Say it again," I demanded.

"I'm yours," she said, stretching out as I crawled on top of her. "Please fuck me. I need you *now*. I need to be with you. I need to come after everything has happened."

I needed her just as badly. All of the fear and desperation that I'd felt, all of the thoughts that had circulated through my head and turned into a hurricane that ripped me apart—all of them came together and disappeared beneath her touch.

I leaned down, kissing up her body, her skin soft to my lips. She sucked on her breath, her hips moving impatiently.

"Please," she begged.

I trailed more kisses up to her breasts, pausing to suck and play with each of them, and then lined my cock up with her pussy. I reached down between us, rubbing the head over her clit, and then lower, feeling how wet she was.

"Fuck," I gasped.

"I told you," she said. "I *need* you."

"I know, baby."

In one swift thrust, I filled her all the way to the hilt. Her cry echoed through the room, blending with my grunt as pleasure rocked through both of us. Her pussy gripped my cock, pulsing around me, slick and hot.

It wasn't just a physical connection though. It was a connection of our hearts, finally being together again, and knowing that everything was going to be okay.

Knowing that we chose each other.

Her lips parted on a gasp as I pulled my hips back, dragging my cock out of her before thrusting back in. Every movement was measured, even with the desperation that burned in my veins.

I wanted to savor every second with her. The way her dark hair splayed out over the blankets, the sounds she made, the way her eyes never left me as I pumped in and out, claiming every inch of her.

I wrapped my arms around her and surprised us both by rolling over onto my back, seating her on top of me. Her hands planted on my chest, her eyes widening slightly.

And then she began to rock, taking me at her own pace. The hunger in her expression mirrored the same hunger I felt, our bodies melding with every cherished movement.

"I'm so close," she whimpered, her hips moving faster.

"Come for me," I moaned, cupping her breasts and teasing her nipples.

"Choke me," she gasped. "Please."

Fuck. I slid my hand around her throat, gently squeezing the sides. Her pussy was pulling me closer and closer to the edge, and right as she started to come, my own orgasm stormed through me. We cried out together, our voices creating a melody as I filled her with every last drop.

"I love you," she said as she fell forward.

I sucked in a breath, grabbing a fistful of her hair and

making her look up at me. Her eyes widened, her cheeks turning more red as I searched her expression.

"I love you too," I whispered. "I love you, Pepper."

Tears filled her eyes and she nodded, kissing me hard. I wrapped my arms around her, holding her tight as we sank into each other.

She was the melody of my heart.

And I'd have the chance to sing that song forever.

FORTY-FOUR
PEPPER

MONDAY MORNING ARRIVED bright and early. I stood in the main meeting room with Ellen, Scott, and Tommy, who were seated and ready for what would take place in the next hour.

Despite jet lag and yesterday's whirlwind of emotions, we'd managed to pull together a plan. After hearing everyone speak, I'd come to realize the situation with Jeff was far worse than I'd ever realized.

Not only had he been completely slacking on his work, I'd learned just how often Kendra, Lee, and Tommy had been doing his tasks over the last few years. The fact that I'd never realized the depth of his ineptitude told me I needed to be a better leader, but that would be my focus after this.

We had to get through step one first.

Ellen sat next to me with a smug smile on her face. After making love, Salt and I had picked up Ellen, and the three of us had shown up on Tommy's doorstep. The tension ran high until they eventually crumbled, and just like I'd expected—everyone loved Salt.

And they finally understood that what was between us went beyond physical attraction.

Jeff's voice echoed through the office. My entire body tensed, but Tommy offered me a comforting smile.

"It's for the best," he said. "Just remember that. You aren't alone in this decision, we all voted for him to leave."

We'd taken a vote early this morning, before the office was even officially open. Everyone had agreed to fire him, and Scott had acted fast with the paperwork.

He'd been preparing for this day for a long time, apparently.

"His severance pay is good, too," Scott said. "We're being kind. He should leave without any issue if he's professional about it."

Ellen made a face as she tapped her pen on her notepad. "That's a big *if*. I've got security on standby."

I reached under the table, giving her hand a squeeze. She squeezed it back, offering me the sort of comfort only we could give to each other.

"Thank you for being here," I whispered to her.

"I wouldn't miss this for the world," she said.

I spotted Jeff through the doorway and steeled myself.

It's going to be okay. This is for the best.

Here we go.

Jeff's eyes widened slightly as he stepped through the doorway. "Is this *emergency* meeting about what I think it is?" he asked as he shut the door behind him. "I flew home early for this."

"Take a seat, Jeff," I said.

He ranked his fingers through his hair and then pulled out a chair across from us, sitting down. He looked at Tommy immediately. "Did she finally fess up to her little attachment to the new client?"

"We are here to talk about you," Tommy said.

"Me?"

"Yes," I said. "You. Not only was your behavior over the weekend a complete violation of my privacy and a direct sign that you have zero respect for me, it has been brought to my attention that you have not been completing your assigned duties for a very long time. Longer than acceptable. Your severance—"

"Severance?" Jeff scoffed. "You're kidding? Right?"

"No," I said. "No one is joking here."

Jeff's expression contorted from anger to laughter. His head tipped back. "This isn't happening. You can't fire me."

"Rosethorn can fire you," I said. "It was voted on."

"Everyone would have had to vote for me to be fired then," he said in disbelief.

The silence in the room told him the truth. And it was taking every ounce of professionalism not to grin like a damn idiot.

His head snapped to the side as he looked at Tommy and Scott. "*You* voted against me? After everything I've done for you? For all of you?"

Scott cleared his throat and silently slid a stack of papers across the table. "This is your severance package."

Jeff's expression went blank. He stared at it for a moment and then shook his head, shoving back from his seat. "This is insane. She's just doing this because she's been caught fucking a client—"

"That language is unacceptable," Tommy interjected. "You do not speak about her that way."

"She's my wife, she's—"

"I am not your wife," I said, raising my voice just enough to interrupt him. "I haven't been your wife for a long time, and I'll never be your wife again. You do not know me, Jeff."

"I know that this is crazy," he growled. "Is that bastard making you do this? Is he—"

"Jeff," Scott interrupted. "The entire board of directors voted against you. Because you have been behaving poorly for years. You've taken advantage of your position repeatedly, you have been a poor leader. You've disrupted relationships with other clients by being an asshole. You haven't been doing your job."

"I founded this fucking place—"

"I founded this place," I corrected.

"I own—"

"The share that you own will still exist," I said. "You'll still continue to make money from Rosethorn, although Tommy and I would like to buy you out at a significant amount that would leave you set for a while. We're being generous."

He sneered, jamming his finger down on the table. "What is it about him, huh? Is he fucking you—"

"Alright," Ellen said, bristling as she stood up. "Jeff, you're the dumbest motherfucker I've ever worked with in my entire life. Everyone here *hates* you. You're nothing more than an unlikable idiot tripping on the power you think you have. Get the fuck out of the office or else we're calling security."

"You can't speak to me that way—"

"Jeff, you're fired," I said calmly. "Leave. Any further questions can be emailed to our lawyer—" he tried to speak over me but I continued, "—and you are to turn in your badge to security. You are free to pack your belongings, but we are finished here."

"You're such a bitch!" he shouted. "You've had it out for me ever since our divorce. You can't do this."

"It's already done," I said.

Tommy stood up and went around the table. He opened

the door to the meeting room and gestured like Jeff was a dog. "Out."

The rage in the room had a metallic taste to it. The four of us waited as Jeff snatched up the papers and turned to leave. He stormed out, and I sucked in a breath as I spotted Salt standing with Kendra and Lee.

Jeff spotted him too.

"You son of a bitch," Jeff snarled, rushing towards him.

"*Jeff!*" I shouted, following after him.

Salt's gaze darted past Jeff to me right as he attempted to punch him. It wasn't a very good attempt, and in one swift motion, Salt grabbed his arm, twisted, and put him in a headlock.

"Call security," Tommy growled, pushing past me. "Pepper, let me handle this."

"Get the fuck off me!" Jeff shouted, shoving against Salt.

He released him, but Jeff turned around and tried to punch him again. This time, Lee and Tommy pulled him back, dragging him away.

"My fucking god," Ellen said next to me. "He's insane. Good riddance."

"He is." I shook my head as Salt slid his arm around my waist and tugged me close, as we watched Jeff get into it with Tommy and Lee, and then the security guards. My mouth dropped as Tommy punched Jeff hard enough that his head snapped back.

"Damn," Kendra said. "I think he'd been holding that back for a while."

"Me too," I said.

Scott rushed past me. "Y'all owe me a goddamn bonus for the legal shit I'm doing this week."

I snorted. Kendra crossed her arms. Ellen started to pull out her phone to take a picture, and I hissed.

"*Ellen.*"

"*What?* You're telling me you don't want a record of the trash being taken out?"

Salt laughed. "I do."

She smirked and snapped a picture. "You're winning me over pretty fast."

"I'm trying," he chuckled.

Kendra looked at the two of us and let out a hum. "We gotta at least make it *seem* like the man is single when it comes to marketing."

"I'm not worried about any of that right now," I said. "We need to sign him first."

"I'm ready to sign when you are," Salt said. "I talked to my lawyer on Friday. Everything is good."

Jeff's voice faded as he was finally removed from the office. I raised a brow as Tommy, Scott, and Lee returned to us.

"He's ready," I said.

"Thank fucking god," Tommy said. "Let's go get you signed."

"I think we could all use a treat, so I'm going to book the restaurant down the street for lunch," Ellen said.

"Yes, please," I chimed. "That would be perfect."

She gave my arm a squeeze and slid past us. I let my breath out slowly, feeling a weight lift.

Everything was going to work out. Jeff was gone, Salt was here, and the future looked bright.

"I'm going to take a moment with Salt," I said. "Scott, can you get everything together?"

"Yes," he said. "We'll meet in your office in twenty."

"Great."

I looked up at Salt and smiled. He followed me to my office and slowly shut the door behind him. The click of the lock being turned echoed through my office. I turned to face him, and he pulled me into a hug, squeezing me tight.

All of the worries I'd felt over the last few weeks finally completely melted away.

We'd made it.

"Are you okay?" he asked.

"Yes. I feel free," I said. "Are you ready for this? Are you sure this is what you want?"

"Yes," he whispered. "I'm more sure of this than anything else, Pepper. My music is yours."

"And my heart is yours."

He swallowed hard, brushing his knuckles along my cheek. "I'll take good care of it."

"I know you will," I murmured, leaning up to kiss him.

Music brought us together. Music would keep us together. I knew now more than ever that I made the right choice by choosing myself, by choosing happiness. I knew that whatever lay ahead, Salt would be next to me, and we'd take each step together.

Our kiss deepened into something hungry and ferocious. I drew back breathless, my lashes fluttering. "We *do* have twenty minutes..."

"Not long enough to get into too much trouble," he sighed. "But long enough to make you come."

"Salt," I whimpered as he pulled me back into a hard kiss.

I wound my arms around his neck, feeling the spark as he backed me up to my desk and lifted me with ease, sitting me on top.

"Can't wait to sign my life away to you in this room after fucking you in it," he said.

"Does this mean you get to call me your boss now?" I asked as he kissed down my neck.

Salt smirked as he lowered down onto his knees and shoved my legs apart. "Absolutely not."

"What are you going to do to me?" I asked, gasping as his fingers brushed against my bare pussy.

He let out a low groan. "God damn it, Pepper. No panties? On today of all days?"

I stifled a moan as his tongue caressed my clit. Pleasure shot through me, my hand clasping over my mouth as I fought the sounds I wanted to make. Two fingers slid inside me with ease, caressing me as he worked his magic on me.

"Fuck," I squeaked.

"Keep your voice down," he said between licks. "I'd hate for them to think I'm doing something terrible to you."

I strangled a laugh. His fingertips curled against the spot he knew so well, and my legs trembled as he drove me to the edge without mercy. I gripped his hair, shaking as my climax came hard and fast, just like Salt had come into my life.

He got up, looming over me as I unraveled from my orgasm. I gripped his shirt and dragged him into another kiss, tasting myself on his lips.

"I have a gift for you," he said softly. "Now may not be the right time to give it. But..."

"What is it?" I asked.

He reached into his pocket and withdrew a long slender box. I pushed my skirt down, closing my legs as I took it from him, sliding the top off.

Oh. A buttery black leather collar sat inside with a heart at the center, etched with a gorgeous floral design that matched his tattoos. I slowly lifted it out of the box, my vision blurring with tears.

"Did you make this?"

"Yes," he said. "I can make a new one if you don't like it—"

"I love it," I said, running my fingertips over it. "I absolutely love it."

I turned it over, my eyes widening.

Words were etched on the inside.

"I wanted those words to be against your skin," he murmured. "I never wanted either of us to forget."

"I never will."

Forever mine.

ALSO BY CLIO EVANS

Contemporary/Small Town Romance:

CITRUS COVE SERIES

Broken Beginnings (Citrus Cove 1)

Stolen Chances (Citrus Cove 2)

Hidden Roots (Citrus Cove 3)

WHYNOT SERIES

Cactus Heart (Whynot 1)

STANDALONES

The Perfect Gift (Christmas Cuckold Novella)

The Perfect Escape (Summer Spanking Novella)

The Perfect Hunt (A Primal Fall Hunting Novella)

Mine: A Reverse Age Gap Romance

Monster Romance:

CREATURE CAFE SERIES

Little Slice of Hell

Little Sip of Sin

Little Lick of Lust

Little Shock of Hate

Little Piece of Sass

Little Song of Pain

Little Taste of Need

Little Risk of Fall

Little Wings of Fate

Little Souls of Fire

Little Kiss of Snow: A Creature Cafe Christmas Anthology

Little Drop of Blood

Little Heart of Stone

Little Spark of Flame

Warts & Claws Inc. Series

Not So Kind Regards

Not So Best Wishes

Not So Thanks in Advance

Not So Yours Truly

Not So Much Appreciated

Freaks of Nature Duet

Doves & Demons

Demons & Doves

Three Fates Mafia Series

Thieves & Monsters

Killers & Monsters

Queens & Monsters

Kings & Monsters

Galactic Gems Series

Cosmic Kiss

Cosmic Crush

Cosmic Heat

ABOUT CLIO EVANS

A lover of myths, legends, BDSM, and queer joy in media–Clio Evans is the author of the Citrus Cove Series, Creature Cafe Series, Warts & Claws Series, and more.

From Austin but now living in Chicago, they can always be found drinking coffee or thinking about the perfect kinky happy ending for their books.

Join them on Instagram, Facebook, TikTok, or their newsletter for new releases, updates, and more!

www.clioevansauthor.com